Limerick County

30012 004017

D1433713

Leabharlann Chontae Luimni

THE FEAST OF THE GOAT

BY THE SAME AUTHOR

The Cubs and Other Stories

The Time of the Hero

The Green House

Captain Pantoja and the Special Service

Conversation in the Cathedral

Aunt Julia and the Scriptwriter

The War of the End of the World

The Real Life of Alejandro Mayta

The Perpetual Orgy

Who Killed Palomino Molero?

The Storyteller

In Praise of the Stepmother

A Fish in the Water

Death in the Andes

Making Waves

The Notebooks of Don Rigoberto

MARIO VARGAS LLOSA

■ THE FEAST ■
OF THE GOAT

**TRANSLATED FROM THE SPANISH
■ BY EDITH GROSSMAN ■**

LIMERICK COUNTY LIBRARY
00401795

WITHDRAWN FROM STOCK

faber and faber

First published in the USA in 2001
by Farrar, Straus and Giroux
First published in Great Britain in 2002
by Faber and Faber Limited
3 Queen Square, London WC1N 3AU

Printed in England by Clays Ltd, St Ives plc

All rights reserved
© Mario Vargas Llosa, 2001

The right of Mario Vargas Llosa to be identified as author of this work has been asserted
in accordance with Section 77 of the Copyright, Designs and Patents Act 1988

A CIP record for this book
is available from the British Library

ISBN 0–571–20771–5 (cased)
ISBN 0–571–21555–6 (pbk)

2 4 6 8 10 9 7 5 3 1

To Lourdes and José Israel Cuello,
and so many other Dominican friends

The people celebrate
and go all the way
for the Feast of the Goat
the Thirtieth of May.

—"They Killed the Goat"
A Dominican merengue

THE FEAST OF THE GOAT

1 Urania. Her parents had done her no favor; her name suggested a planet, a mineral, anything but the slender, fine-featured woman with burnished skin and large, dark, rather sad eyes who looked back at her from the mirror. Urania! What an idea for a name. Fortunately nobody called her that anymore; now it was Uri, Miss Cabral, Ms. Cabral, Dr. Cabral. As far as she could remember, after she left Santo Domingo (or Ciudad Trujillo—when she left they had not yet restored the old name to the capital city), no one in Adrian, or Boston, or Washington, D.C., or New York had called her Urania as they did at home and at the Santo Domingo Academy, where the sisters and her classmates pronounced with absolute correctness the ridiculous name inflicted on her at birth. Was it his idea or hers? Too late to find out, my girl; your mother was in heaven and your father condemned to a living death. You'll never know. Urania! As absurd as insulting old Santo Domingo de Guzmán by calling it Ciudad Trujillo. Could that have been her father's idea too?

She waits for the sea to become visible through the window of her room on the ninth floor of the Hotel Jaragua, and at last she sees it. The darkness fades in a few seconds and the brilliant blue of the horizon quickly intensifies, beginning the spectacle she has been anticipating since she woke at four in spite of the pill she had taken, breaking her rule against sedatives. The dark blue surface of the ocean, marked by streaks of foam, extends to a leaden sky at the remote line of the horizon, while here, at the shore, it breaks in resounding, whitecapped waves against the Sea Walk, the Malecón, where she can make out sections of the broad road through the palms and almond trees that line it. Back then, the Hotel Jaragua faced the Malecón directly. Now it's to the side. Her memory brings back the image—was that the day?—of the little girl holding her father's hand as they entered the hotel restaurant so the two of them could have lunch together. They were given a table next to the window, and through the sheer lace curtains Uranita could see the spacious garden and the pool with its diving boards and swimmers. In the Patio Español, surrounded by glazed tiles and flowerpots filled with carnations, an orchestra was playing merengues. Was that the day? "No," she says aloud. The Jaragua of those days had been torn down and replaced by this massive shocking-pink structure that had surprised her so much when she arrived in Santo Domingo three days ago.

Were you right to come back? You'll be sorry, Urania. Wasting a week's vacation, when you never had time to visit all the cities, regions, countries you would have liked to see—the mountain ranges and snow-covered lakes of Alaska, for instance—returning to the island you swore you'd never set foot on again. A symptom of decline? The sentimentality of age? Curiosity, nothing more. To prove to yourself you can walk along the streets of this city that is no longer yours, travel through this foreign country and not have it provoke sadness, nostalgia, hatred, bitterness, rage in you. Or have you come to confront the ruin of your father? To learn what effect seeing him has on you, after so many years. A shudder runs the length of her body. Urania, Urania! What if after all these years you discover that behind your determined, disciplined mind, impervious to discouragement, behind the fortress admired and envied by others, you have a tender, timid, wounded, sentimental heart?

She bursts into laughter. Enough foolishness, my girl.

She puts on sneakers, slacks, a tailored blouse, and pulls back her hair. She drinks a glass of cold water and is about to turn on the television to watch CNN but changes her mind. She remains at the window, looking at the ocean, the Malecón, and then, turning her head, at the city's forest of roofs, towers, domes, belfries, and treetops. It's grown so much! When you left, in 1961, it sheltered three hundred thousand souls. More than a million now. It has filled up with neighborhoods, avenues, parks, hotels. The night before, she felt like a foreigner as she drove a rented car past the condominiums in Bella Vista, and the immense El Mirador Park, where there were as many joggers as in

Central Park. When she was a girl, the city ended at the Hotel El Embajador; beyond that point, it was all farms and fields. The Country Club, where her father took her on Sundays to swim in the pool, was surrounded by open countryside, not the asphalt, houses, and streetlights that are there now.

But the colonial city has not been modernized, and neither has Gazcue, her neighborhood. And she is absolutely certain her house has hardly changed at all. It must be the same, with its small garden, old mango tree, and the flamboyán with red flowers bending over the terrace where they used to have lunch outdoors on weekends; the sloping roof and the little balcony outside her bedroom, where she would go to wait for her cousins Lucinda and Manolita, and, during that last year, 1961, spy on the boy who rode past on his bicycle, watching her out of the corner of his eye and not daring to speak. Would it be the same inside? The Austrian clock that sounded the hours had Gothic numerals and a hunting scene. Would her father be the same? No. You've seen him failing in the photos sent to you every few months or years by Aunt Adelina and other relatives who continued to write even though you never answered their letters.

She drops into an armchair. The rising sun penetrates to the center of the city; the dome of the National Palace and its pale ocher walls sparkle gently under a curve of blue. Go now, soon the heat will be unbearable. She closes her eyes, overcome by a rare inertia, for she is accustomed to always being active and not wasting time in what, since her return to Dominican soil, has occupied her day and night: remembering. "This daughter of mine is always working, she even repeats her lessons when she's asleep." That's what Senator Agustín Cabral, Minister Cabral, Egghead Cabral used to say about you when he boasted to his friends about the girl who won all the prizes, the student the sisters always held up as an example. Did he boast to the Chief about Uranita's scholarly achievements? "I'd like so much for you to know her, she has won the Prize for Excellence every year since she enrolled at Santo Domingo. It would make her so happy to meet you and shake your hand. Uranita prays every night for God to protect that iron health of yours. And for Doña Julia and Doña María as well. Do us this honor. The most loyal of your dogs asks, begs, implores you. You can't refuse: receive her. Excellency! Chief!"

Do you despise him? Do you hate him? Still? "Not anymore," she says aloud. You wouldn't have come back if the rancor were still sizzling, the wound still bleeding, the deception still crushing her, poisoning her, the way it did in your youth, when studying and working became an obsessive defense against remembering. Back then you did hate him. With every atom of your being, with all the thought and feeling your body could hold. You wanted him to suffer misfortunes, diseases, accidents. God granted your wish, Urania. Or rather, the devil did. Isn't it enough that the cerebral hemorrhage brought him a living death? A sweet revenge that he has spent the last ten years in a wheelchair, not walking or talking, depending on a nurse to eat, lie down, dress, undress, trim his nails, shave, urinate, defecate? Do you feel avenged? "No."

She drinks a second glass of water and goes out. It's seven in the morning. On the ground floor of the Jaragua she is assaulted by the noise, that atmosphere, familiar by now, of voices, motors, radios blaring at full volume, merengues, salsas, danzones, boleros, rock, rap, all jumbled together, assailing one another and assailing her with their shrill clamor. Animated chaos, the profound need in what was once your people, Urania, to stupefy themselves into not thinking and, perhaps, not even feeling. An explosion of savage life, immune to the tide of modernization. Something in Dominicans clings to this prerational, magical form: this appetite for noise. ("For noise, not music.")

She doesn't remember a commotion like this in the street when she was a girl and Santo Domingo was called Ciudad Trujillo. Perhaps it didn't exist back then: perhaps, thirty-five years ago, when the city was three or four times smaller, provincial, isolated, made wary by fear and servility, its soul shrinking in terrified reverence for the Chief, the Generalissimo, the Benefactor, the Father of the New Nation, His Excellency Dr. Rafael Leonidas Trujillo Molina, it was quieter and less frenetic. Today, all the clamor of life—car engines, cassettes, records, radios, horns, barks, growls, human voices—seems to resound at top volume, producing vocal, mechanical, digital, or animal noise at maximum capacity (dogs bark louder, birds chirp with more enthusiasm). And New York is famous for being noisy! Never, in the ten years she has spent in Manhattan, have her ears been subjected to anything like the brutal, cacophonous symphony in which she has been immersed for the past three days.

The sun burns the silvery tops of towering palms, the broken sidewalk with so many holes it looks bombed, the mountains of trash that some women with scarves tied around their heads sweep up and collect in inadequate bags. "Haitians." They're silent now, but yesterday they were whispering among themselves in Creole. A little farther on, she sees two barefoot, half-naked Haitian men sitting on boxes under dozens of vividly colored paintings displayed on the wall of a building. It's true, the city, perhaps the country, has filled with Haitians. Back then, it didn't happen. Isn't that what Senator Agustín Cabral said? "You can say what you like about the Chief. History, at least, will recognize that he has created a modern country and put the Haitians in their place. Great ills demand great remedies!" The Chief found a small country barbarized by wars among the caudillos, a country without law and order, impoverished, losing its identity, invaded by its starving, ferocious neighbors. They waded across the Masacre River and came to steal goods, animals, houses, they took the jobs of our agricultural workers, perverted our Catholic religion with their diabolical witchcraft, violated our women, ruined our Western, Hispanic culture, language, and customs, imposed their African savagery on us. The Chief cut the Gordian knot: "Enough!" Great ills demand great remedies! He not only justified the massacre of Haitians in 1937; he considered it a great accomplishment of the regime. Didn't he save the Republic from being prostituted a second time by that marauding neighbor? What do five, ten, twenty thousand Haitians matter when it's a question of saving an entire people?

She walks quickly, recognizing landmarks: the Casino de Güibia, converted into a nightclub, and the bathing beach that reeks now of sewage; soon she'll reach the corner of the Malecón and Avenida Máximo Gómez, the itinerary followed by the Chief on his evening walks. After the doctors told him it was good for his heart, he would walk from Radhamés Manor to Máximo Gómez, with a stop at the house of Doña Julia, the Sublime Matriarch, where Uranita once gave a speech and almost couldn't get the words out, and come down the George Washington Malecón, turn this corner, and continue on to the obelisk that imitated the one in Washington, moving at a brisk pace, surrounded by ministers, advisers, generals, aides, courtiers, all at a respectful distance, their eyes alert, their hearts expectant, waiting for a gesture, an expression that would allow them to approach the Chief, listen to him, be worthy of his conversation even if it was a reprimand.

Anything except being kept at a distance, in the hell of the forgotten. "How many times did you walk with them, Papa? How many times were you worthy of having him talk to you? And how many times did you come home saddened because he did not call to you, fearful you were no longer in the circle of the elect, that you had fallen among the censured? You always lived in terror that the story of Anselmo Paulino would be repeated in you. And it was repeated, Papa."

Urania laughs and a couple in Bermuda shorts walking past in the opposite direction think she is smiling at them: "Good morning." She isn't smiling at them but at the image of Senator Agustín Cabral trotting along this Malecón every evening, among the deluxe servants, attentive not to the warm breeze, the sound of the sea, the acrobatics of the gulls, the brilliant stars of the Caribbean, but to the Chief's hands, eyes, gestures that perhaps would call to him, prefer him over all the rest. She has reached the Agrarian Bank. Then comes Ramfis Manor, where the Ministry of Foreign Affairs is still located, and the Hotel Hispaniola. Then a half-turn.

"Calle César Nicolás Penson, corner of Galván," she thinks. Would she go or would she return to New York without even looking at her house? You'll go in and ask the nurse for the invalid and go up to the bedroom and the terrace where they take him for his siesta, the terrace that turned red with the blossoms from the flamboyán. "Hello, Papa. How are you, Papa? Don't you recognize me? It's Urania. Of course, how could you recognize me? The last time you saw me I was fourteen and now I'm forty-nine. A lot of years, Papa. Wasn't that your age the day I left for Adrian? That's right, you were forty-eight or forty-nine. A man in his prime. Now you're almost eighty-four. You're an old man, Papa." If he's in any condition to think, he's had a lot of time over the years to draw up a balance sheet of his long life. You must have thought about your ungrateful daughter, who in thirty-five years never answered a letter, never sent a photo or a birthday card or a Christmas card or a New Year's greeting, not even when you had the hemorrhage and aunts, uncles, and cousins thought you would die, not even then did she come or ask about your health. What a wicked daughter, Papa.

The little house on César Nicolás Penson, corner of Galván, probably no longer receives visitors in the entrance foyer, where it was the custom to place an image of the Virgin of Altagracia and the bronze plaque that boasted: "In this house Trujillo is the Chief." Have you kept it as proof of your loyalty? No, you must have thrown it in the ocean, like the thousands of Dominicans who bought one and hung it in the most conspicuous place in the house so that no one would doubt their fidelity to the Chief, and, when the spell was broken, tried to wipe away the traces, ashamed of what it represented: their cowardice. I'll bet you made yours disappear too, Papa.

She has reached the Hispaniola. She is sweating, her heart racing. A double river of cars, vans, and trucks moves along Avenida George Washington, and it seems to her that they all have their radios on and the noise will shatter her eardrums. Occasionally a man's head will look out of some vehicle and for an instant her eyes meet a pair of male eyes that look at her breasts, her legs, her behind. Those looks. She is waiting for a break in traffic that will let her cross, and again she tells herself, as she did yesterday and the day before yesterday, that she is on Dominican soil. In New York nobody looks at a woman with that arrogance anymore. Measuring her, weighing her, calculating how much flesh there is in each one of her breasts and thighs, how much hair on her pubis, the exact curve of her buttocks. She closes her eyes, feeling slightly dizzy. In New York not even Latins—Dominicans, Colombians, Guatemalans—give such looks. They've learned to repress them, realized they mustn't look at women the way male dogs look at female dogs, stallions look at mares, boars look at sows.

In a pause between cars she races across the road. Instead of making a half-turn and returning to the Jaragua, her steps, not her will, lead her around the Hispaniola and back along Independencia, an avenue that, if memory serves, starts here, with a double line of leafy laurels whose tops meet over the road, cooling it, until it divides in two and disappears in the middle of the colonial city. How many times did you stroll, holding your father's hand, in the murmuring shade of the laurels along Independencia? The two of you would come down to the avenue from César Nicolás Penson and walk to Independencia Park. In the Italian ice-cream parlor, on the right, at the beginning of El Conde, you would eat coconut, mango, or guava ice cream. How proud you felt holding that gentleman's hand—Senator Agustín Cabral, Minister Cabral. Everybody knew who he was. They would approach him, hold out their hands, doff their hats, bow, and police and soldiers would click their heels when they saw him pass by. How you must have missed those years of importance, Papa, when you became just another poor devil in the crowd. They were satisfied with insulting you in "The Public Forum," but they didn't put you in jail, like Anselmo Paulino. It was what you feared most, wasn't it? That one day the Chief would give the order: Egghead goes to jail! You were lucky, Papa.

After three-quarters of an hour she still has a long way to go to reach the hotel. If she had taken money, she would go into a cafeteria to have breakfast and rest. She constantly has to wipe perspiration from her face. The years, Urania. At forty-nine one is no longer young. No matter what shape you're in compared with other women. But you're not ready yet to be tossed out with the trash, judging by the looks that come from right and left and rest on her face and body, the insinuating, greedy, brazen, insolent looks of males accustomed to undressing all the females on the street with their eyes and thoughts. "Forty-nine years that really become you, Uri," said Dick Litney, her colleague and friend from the office, in New York, on her birthday, a bold statement that no man in the firm would have allowed himself to make unless he, like Dick that night, had two or three whiskeys under his belt. Poor Dick. He blushed and became confused when Urania froze him with one of those slow looks she had used for thirty-five years to confront the gallantries, sudden off-color jokes, witticisms, allusions, or unwelcome moves from men, and sometimes women.

She stops to catch her breath. She feels her heart beating wildly, her chest rising and falling. She is at the corner of Independencia and Máximo Gómez, in a crowd of men and women waiting to cross. Her nose registers a range of odors as great as the endless variety of noises hammering at her ears: the oil burned by the motors of the buses and escaping through their exhausts, tongues of smoke that dissipate or remain floating over the pedestrians; smells of grease and frying from a stand where two pans sputter and food and drinks are for sale; and that dense, indefinable, tropical aroma of decomposing resins and underbrush, of perspiring bodies, an air saturated with animal, vegetable, and human essences protected by a sun that delays their dissolution and passing. A hot odor that touches some intimate fiber of memory and returns her to childhood, to multicolored heartsease hanging from roofs and balconies, to this same Avenida Máximo Gómez. Mother's Day! Of course. May with its brilliant sun, its torrential downpours, its heat. The girls from Santo Domingo Academy selected to bring flowers to Mama Julia, the Sublime Matriarch, progenitor of the Benefactor and the example and symbol of Dominican mother-hood. They came from school in a bus, wearing their immaculate white uniforms and accompanied by Mother Superior and Sister Mary. You burned with curiosity, pride, affection, respect. You were going to represent the school in the house of Mama Julia. You were going to re-cite for her the poem "Mother and Teacher, Sublime Matriarch," which you had written, memorized, and recited dozens of times in front of the mirror, in front of your classmates, in front of Lucinda and Mano-lita, in front of Papa, in front of the sisters, and which you had silently repeated to yourself to be sure you would not forget a single syllable. When the glorious moment arrived in Mama Julia's large pink house, you were disconcerted by the military men, ladies, aides, delegations crowded into gardens, rooms, corridors, overwhelmed by emotion and tenderness, and when you stepped forward to within a meter of the old lady smiling benevolently from her rocking chair and holding the bouquet of roses Mother Superior had just presented to her, your throat constricted and your mind went blank. You burst into tears. You heard laughter, encouraging words from the ladies and gentlemen who surrounded Mama Julia. The Sublime Matriarch smiled and beckoned to you. Then Uranita composed herself, dried her tears, stood up straight, and firmly, rapidly, but without the proper intonation, recited "Mother and Teacher, Sublime Matriarch," in an unbroken rush. They applauded. Mama Julia stroked Uranita's hair, and her mouth, puck-ered into a thousand wrinkles, kissed her.

At last the light changes. Urania continues on her way, protected from the sun by the shade of the trees along Máximo Gómez. She has been walking for an hour. It is pleasant to move under the laurels, to see the shrubs with the little red flowers and golden pistils, either cayenne or Christ's blood, to be lost in her own thoughts, lulled by the anarchy of voices and music, yet alert to the uneven places, potholes, depressions, irregularities in the sidewalk, where she is constantly on the verge of stumbling or stepping on garbage that stray dogs root through. Were you happy back then? You were, when you went with a group of students from Santo Domingo Academy to bring flowers to the Sublime Matriarch on Mother's Day and recite the poem for her. Though when the protective, beautiful figure of her own childhood vanished from the small house on César Nicolás Penson, perhaps the very notion of happiness also disappeared from Urania's life. But your father and aunts and uncles—especially Aunt Adelina and Uncle Aníbal, and your cousins Lucindita and Manolita—and old friends did everything possible to fill your mother's absence with pampering and special treats so you wouldn't feel lonely or deprived. Your father was both father and mother during those years. That's why you loved him so much. That's why it hurt you so much, Urania.

When she reaches the rear entrance of the Jaragua, a wide, barred gate for cars, stewards, cooks, chambermaids, porters, she doesn't stop. Where are you going? She hasn't made any decision. Her mind, concentrating on her girlhood, her school, the Sundays when she would go with her Aunt Adelina and her cousins to the children's matinee at the Cine Elite, hasn't even considered the possibility of not going into the hotel to shower and have breakfast. Her feet have decided to continue. She walks unhesitatingly, certain of the route, among pedestrians and cars impatient for the light to change. Are you sure you want to go where you're going, Urania? Now you know that you'll go, even though you may regret it.

She turns left onto Cervantes and walks toward Bolívar, recognizing as if in a dream the one- and two-story chalets with fences and gardens, open terraces and garages, which awaken in her a familiar feeling, these deteriorating images that have been preserved, somewhat faded, chipped along the edges, made ugly with additions and patchwork, small rooms built on flat roofs or assembled at the sides, in the middle of the gardens, to house offspring who marry and cannot live on their own and come home to add to the families, demanding more space. She passes laundries, pharmacies, florist shops, cafeterias, plaques for dentists, doctors, accountants, and lawyers. On Avenida Bolívar she walks as if she were trying to overtake someone, as if she were about to break into a run. Her heart is in her mouth. You'll collapse at any moment. When she reaches Rosa Duarte she veers left and begins to run. But the effort is too much and she walks again, more slowly now, very close to the off-white wall of a house in case she becomes dizzy again and has to lean on something until she catches her breath. Except for a ridiculously narrow four-story building where the house with the spiked fence used to be, the house that belonged to Dr. Estanislas, who took out her tonsils, nothing has changed; she would even swear that the maids sweeping the gardens and the fronts of the houses are going to greet her: "Hello, Uranita. How are you, honey? Girl, how you've grown. Mother of God, where are you off to in such a hurry?"

The house hasn't changed too much either, though she recalled the gray of its walls as intense and now it's dull, stained, peeling. The garden is a thicket of weeds, dead leaves, withered grass. Nobody has watered or pruned it in years. There's the mango. Was that the flamboyán? It must have been, when it had leaves and flowers; now, it's a trunk with bare, rachitic branches.

She leans against the wrought-iron gate that opens to the garden. The flagstone path has weeds growing through the cracks and is stained by mildew, and at the entrance to the terrace there is a defeated chair with a broken leg. The yellow cretonne-covered furniture is gone. And the little polished glass lamp in the corner that lit the terrace and attracted butterflies during the day and buzzing insects at night. The little balcony off her bedroom no longer is covered by mauve heartsease: it is a cement projection stained with rust.

At the back of the terrace, a door opens with a long groan. A woman in a white uniform stares at her curiously.

"Are you looking for someone?"

Urania cannot speak; she is too agitated, too shaken, too frightened. She remains mute, looking at the stranger.

"Can I help you?" the woman asks.

"I'm Urania," she says at last. "Agustín Cabral's daughter."

2 He woke, paralyzed by a sense of catastrophe. He blinked in the dark, immobilized, imprisoned in a web, about to be devoured by a hairy insect covered with eyes. At last he managed to stretch his hand toward the bedside table where he kept the revolver and the loaded submachine gun. But instead of a weapon he grasped the alarm clock: ten to four. He exhaled. Now, at last, he was fully awake. Nightmares again? He still had a few minutes: he was obsessive about punctuality and did not get out of bed before four o'clock. Not a minute before, not a minute after.

"I owe everything I am to discipline," he thought. And discipline, the polestar of his life, he owed to the Marines. He closed his eyes. The entrance tests at San Pedro de Macorís for the Dominican National Police, a force the Yankees decided to create in the third year of the occupation, were very hard. He passed with no difficulty. During training, half of the candidates were eliminated. He relished every exercise demanding agility, boldness, audacity, or stamina, even the brutal ones that tested your will, your obedience to a superior, plunging into mudholes with a full field pack or surviving in the wild, drinking your own urine and chewing on stalks, weeds, grasshoppers. Sergeant Gittleman gave him the highest rating: "You'll go far, Trujillo." And he had, thanks to the merciless discipline of heroes and mystics taught to him by the Marines. He thought with gratitude of Sergeant Simon Gittleman. A loyal, disinterested gringo in a country of hagglers, bloodsuckers, and assholes. Had the United States had a more sincere friend than Trujillo in the past thirty-one years? What government had given them greater support in the UN? Which was the first to declare war on Germany and Japan? Who gave the biggest bribes to representatives, senators, governors, mayors, lawyers, and reporters in the United States? His reward: economic sanctions by the OAS to make that nigger Rómulo Betancourt happy, to keep sucking at the tit of Venezuelan oil. If Johnny Abbes had handled things better and the bomb had blown off the head of that faggot Rómulo, there wouldn't be any sanctions and the asshole gringos wouldn't be handing him bullshit about sovereignty, democracy, and human rights. But then he wouldn't have discovered that in a country of two hundred million assholes, he had a friend like Simon Gittleman. Capable of initiating a personal campaign in defense of the Dominican Republic from Phoenix, Arizona, where he had been in business since his retirement from the Marines. And not asking for a cent! There still were men like that in the Marines. Not asking, not charging for anything! What a lesson for those leeches in the Senate and the House of Representatives he'd been feeding for years; they always wanted more checks, more concessions, more decrees, more tax exemptions, and now, when he needed them, they pretended they didn't know him.

He looked at the clock: four minutes to go. A magnificent gringo, that Simon Gittleman! A real Marine. Indignant at the offensive against Trujillo by the White House, Venezuela, and the OAS, he gave up his business in Arizona and bombarded the American press with letters, reminding everyone that during all of the Trujillo Era the Dominican Republic had been a bulwark of anti-Communism, the best ally of the United States in the Western Hemisphere. Not satisfied with that, he funded—out of his own damn pocket!—support committees, paid for publications, organized conferences. And to set an example, he came to Ciudad Trujillo with his family and rented a house on the Malecón. This afternoon Simon and Dorothy would have lunch with him in the Palace, and the ex-Marine would receive the Juan Pablo Duarte Order of Merit, the highest decoration the Dominican Republic could bestow. A real Marine, yes sir!

Four sharp, now it was time. He turned on the lamp on the night table, put on his slippers, and got up, without the old agility. His bones ached and he felt pains in his leg and back muscles, the way he had a few days ago at Mahogany House, on that damn night with that anemic little bitch. He ground his teeth in annoyance. He was walking to the chair where Sinforoso had laid out his sweat suit and gym shoes when a suspicion stopped him cold. Anxiously he inspected the sheets: the ugly grayish stain befouled the whiteness of the linen. It had leaked out, again. Indignation erased the unpleasant memory of Mahogany House. Damn it! Damn it! This wasn't an enemy he could defeat like the hundreds, the thousands he had confronted and conquered over the years, buying them, intimidating them, killing them. This lived inside him, flesh of his flesh, blood of his blood. It was destroying him at precisely the time he needed to be stronger and healthier than ever. That skinny little cunt had brought him bad luck.

He found his jockstrap, shorts, and undershirt, immaculately washed and ironed, along with his exercise shoes. He dressed with great effort. He never had needed much sleep: when he was a young man in San Cristóbal, when he was the head of the rural guards on the Boca Chica sugar plantation, four or five hours had been enough, even if he had been drinking and fucking till dawn. His ability to recover physically with a minimum of sleep contributed to his aura of superiority. Not anymore. He woke exhausted and couldn't sleep for even four hours; two or three at the most, and those plagued by nightmares.

The night before, he lay sleepless, in the dark. Through the window he could see the tops of trees and a piece of sky studded with stars. From time to time, in the clear night, he heard the chatter of those old biddies, night owls declaiming poems by Juan de Dios Peza, Amado Nervo, Rubén Darío (which made him suspect that among them was the Walking Turd, who knew Darío by heart), Pablo Neruda's *Twenty Poems of Love*, and the risqué stanzas of Juan Antonio Alix. And, of course, the verses of Doña María, the Dominican writer and moralist. He laughed aloud as he climbed on the stationary bike and began to pedal. His wife had ended up taking herself seriously, and periodically would organize literary evenings in the skating rink at Radhamés Manor and bring in actresses to recite dumb-ass poems. Senator Henry Chirinos, who passed himself off as a poet, would participate in these soirees, feeding his cirrhosis at public expense. To ingratiate themselves with María Martínez, those bitches, just like Chirinos himself, had memorized entire pages of her *Moral Meditations* or speeches from her theater piece, *False Amity*. They recited them, and then the biddies applauded. And his wife—for that fat, stupid old woman, the Bountiful First Lady, was his wife—had taken the business about being a writer and moralist seriously. And why not? Didn't the newspapers, the radio, the television say so? Wasn't *Moral Meditations*, with a prologue by the Mexican José Vasconcelos, required reading in the schools, and wasn't it reprinted every two months? Hadn't *False Amity* been the greatest stage hit in the thirty-one years of the Trujillo Era? Hadn't the critics and reporters, the university professors, priests, and intellectuals, praised her to the skies? Didn't they devote a seminar to her at the Trujillonian Institute? Hadn't her concepts been acclaimed by the bishops, those traitorous crows, those Judases, who after living out of his wallet were talking now, just like the Yankees, about human rights? The Bountiful First Lady was a writer and a moralist. No thanks to her, but to him, like everything else that had happened in this country for the past three decades. Trujillo could turn water into wine and multiply loaves of bread if he fucking well felt like it. He reminded María of this during their last argument: "You forget you didn't write that shit, you can't even write your name without making grammatical mistakes, it was that Galician traitor José Almoina, paid by me. Don't you know what people say? That the first letters of *False Amity*, F and A, stand for Find Almoina." He laughed again, open, joyful laughter. His bitterness had vanished. María burst into tears—"How you humiliate me!"—and threatened to complain to Mama Julia. As if his poor ninety-six-year-old mother was in any shape for family arguments. Like his own brothers and sisters, his wife was always running to the Sublime Matriarch to cry on her shoulder. To make peace, he'd had to cross her palm again. What Dominicans whispered was true: the writer and moralist was a grasping, avaricious soul. And had been from the time they were lovers. When she was still a girl she'd thought of setting up a special laundry for the uniforms of the Dominican National Police, and made her first money.

Pedaling warmed his body. He felt in shape. Fifteen minutes: enough. Another fifteen of rowing before he began the day's battle.

The rowing machine was in a small adjoining room filled with exercise equipment. He had begun rowing, and then a horse's whinny vibrated in the silence of dawn, long and musical, like a joyful paean to life. How long since he'd ridden? Months. He had never tired of it, after fifty years it still excited him, like his first sip of Carlos I Spanish brandy or his first sight of the naked, white, voluptuous body of a woman he desired. But this thought was poisoned by the memory of the skinny little thing that son of a bitch had managed to get into his bed. Did he do it knowing he would be shamed? No, he didn't have the balls for that. She probably told him about it and gave him a good laugh. It must be making the rounds now of all the gossipmongers in the coffee shops along El Conde. He trembled with mortification and rage as he rowed in a steady rhythm. He was sweating now. If they could see him! Another myth they repeated about him was: "Trujillo never sweats. In the worst heat of summer he puts on those woolen uniforms, with a velvet three-cornered hat and gloves, and you never see a drop of sweat on his forehead." He didn't sweat if he didn't want to. But when he was alone, when he was doing his exercises, he gave permission to his body to perspire. Recently, during this difficult time, with so many problems, he had denied himself his horses. Maybe this week he'd go to San Cristóbal. He'd ride alone, under the trees, along the river, like in the old days, and feel rejuvenated. "Not even a woman's arms are as affectionate as the back of a chestnut."

He stopped rowing when he felt a cramp in his left arm. He wiped his face and looked down at his pants, at his fly. Nothing. It was still dark outside. The trees and shrubs in the gardens of Radhamés Manor were inky stains under a clear sky crowded with twinkling lights. What was that line of Neruda's that the moralist's babbling friends liked so much? "And stars tremble blue in the distance." Those old women trembled when they dreamed that some poet would scratch their itch. And all they had near at hand was Chirinos, that Frankenstein. Again he laughed out loud, something that did not happen very often these days.

He undressed and, wearing slippers and a robe, went to the bathroom to shave. He turned on the radio. They read the newspapers on the Dominican Voice and Caribbean Radio. Until a few years ago the news bulletins had begun at five. But when his brother Petán, the owner of the Dominican Voice, found out that he woke at four, he moved the newscasts up an hour. The other stations followed suit. They knew he listened to the radio while he shaved, bathed, and dressed, and they were painstakingly careful.

The Dominican Voice, after a jingle for El Conde Hotel Restaurant announcing a night of dancing to Los Colosos del Ritmo under the direction of Maestro Gatón and featuring the singer Johnny Ventura, highlighted the Julia Molina Widow of Trujillo Prize to the Most Prolific Mother. The winner, Doña Alejandrina Francisco, who had twenty-one living children, declared when she received the medal with the portrait of the Sublime Matriarch: "My twenty-one children will give their lives for the Benefactor if they are asked to."

"I don't believe you, bitch."

He had brushed his teeth and now he was shaving as meticulously as he always had, ever since he was a kid in a shantytown in San Cristóbal. Back when he didn't even know if his poor mother, to whom the entire country now paid homage on Mother's Day ("A well-spring of loving-kindness and mother of the preeminent man who governs us," said the announcer), would have beans and rice that night to feed the eight mouths in her family. Cleanliness, caring for his body and his clothing, had been, for him, the only religion he practiced faithfully.

After another long list of visitors to the home of Mama Julia, to whom they would pay their respects on Mother's Day (poor old woman, serenely receiving a caravan of schools, associations, institutes, unions, and thanking them in her faint little voice for their flowers and courtesy), the attacks began on Bishops Reilly and Panal, "who neither were born under our sun nor suffered under our moon" ("Nice," he thought), "and who meddle in our civil and political life, overstepping the bounds into the terrain of the criminal." Johnny Abbes wanted to go into Santo Domingo Academy and drag the Yankee bishop out of his refuge. "What can happen, Chief? The gringos will protest, natu-rally. Haven't they protested everything for a long time now? Galíndez, Murphy the pilot, the Mirabal sisters, the attempt on Betancourt, and a thousand other things. It doesn't matter if the dogs bark in Caracas, Puerto Rico, Washington, New York, Havana. What happens here is what matters. The crows in their cassocks won't stop conspiring until they've been scared out of it." No. It wasn't time yet to settle the score with Reilly or that other son of a bitch, that shitty little Spaniard Bishop Panal. The time would come, they would pay. His instincts never deceived him. For now he wouldn't touch a hair on their heads, even if they kept fucking with him, like they'd been doing since Sun-day, January 24, 1960—a year and a half already!—when the Bishops' Pastoral Letter was read at every Mass, inaugurating the campaign of the Catholic Church against the regime. Backbiters! Crows! Eunuchs! Doing that to him, a man who had been decorated in the Vatican by Pius XII with the Great Cross of the Papal Order of St. Gregory. On the Dominican Voice, Paíno Pichardo, in a speech delivered the night before in his capacity as Minister of the Interior and Religious Practice, recalled that the state had spent sixty million pesos on the Church, whose "bishops and priests are now doing so much harm to the Catholic faithful of the Dominican Republic." He turned the dial. On Caribbean Radio they were reading a letter of protest from hundreds of workers because their signatures had not been included on the Great National Manifesto "against the disturbing machinations of Bishop Thomas Reilly, a traitor to God, Trujillo, and his own manhood, who, instead of remaining in his diocese of San Juan de la Maguana, ran like a scared rat to hide in Ciudad Trujillo behind the skirts of American nuns at Santo Domingo Academy, a vipers' nest of terrorism and conspiracy." When he heard that the Ministry of Education had deprived Santo Domingo Academy of its accreditation because "the foreign nuns were in collusion with the terrorist plotting of the Bishops of San Juan de la Maguana and La Vega against the State," he turned back to the Dominican Voice in time to hear the announcer report another victory for the Dominican polo team in Paris, where, "on the beautiful field of Bagatelle, after defeating the Leopards five to four and dazzling the assembled connoisseurs, it was awarded the Aperture Cup." Ramfis and Radhamés, the most applauded players. A lie, to beguile Dominicans. And him. In the pit of his stomach he felt the rush of acid that attacked every time he thought about his sons, those successful failures, those disappointments. Playing polo in Paris and fucking French girls while their father was fighting the battle of his life!

He dried his face. His blood turned to vinegar whenever he thought of his sons. By God, it wasn't his fault. His line was healthy, he was a sire of thoroughbreds. The proof was there, in the children his seed had created in other wombs, in the belly of Lina Lovatón, for instance: robust, energetic men, a thousand times more deserving of the place occupied by those two drones, a pair of nonentities named after characters in an opera. Why had he allowed the Bountiful First Lady to give his sons names out of *Aida*, that damn opera she saw in New York? Those names had brought them bad luck, turned them into operetta buffoons instead of real men. Bums, idlers without character or ambition, all they were good for was getting drunk. They took after his brothers, not him; they were as useless as Blacky, Petán, Peepee, Aníbal, that collection of crooks, parasites, derelicts, and losers. None of them had a millionth of his energy, his will, his vision. What would happen to this country when he died? He was sure Ramfis wasn't even as good in bed as all the asslickers said he was. So he fucked Kim Novak! He fucked Zsa Zsa Gabor! He stuck it to Debra Paget and half the actresses in Hollywood! Big deal. If he gave them Mercedes-Benzes, Cadillacs, mink coats, even Crazy Valeriano would be fucking Miss Universe and Elizabeth Taylor. Poor Ramfis. He suspected that his son didn't even like women very much. He liked the appearance, he liked people to say he was the best lover in the country, better even than Porfirio Rubirosa, the Dominican known all over the world for the size of his prick and his prowess as an international cocksman. Was the Great Fucking Machine playing polo with his sons on the field of Bagatelle? The fondness he had felt for Porfirio ever since he'd joined his corps of military adjutants, a feeling he still had despite the failed marriage to his oldest daughter, Flor de Oro, improved his mood. Porfirio had ambition and he had fucked great cunts, from the Frenchwoman Danielle Darrieux to the multimillionaire Barbara Hutton, without giving them so much as a bouquet of flowers; instead he squeezed them and became rich at their expense.

He filled the tub with bath salts and bubbles and sank into the water with the same intense satisfaction he felt every dawn. Porfirio always led the good life. His marriage to Barbara Hutton lasted a month, the indispensable time for getting a million dollars from her in cash and another million in property. If Ramfis or Radhamés were at least like Porfirio! That walking cock spurted ambition. And, like every conquering hero, he had enemies. They were always coming to him with gossip, advising him to get Rubirosa out of the diplomatic service because the scandals were a stain on the national image. They were jealous. What better propaganda for the Dominican Republic than a cocksman like him? From the time of his marriage to Flor de Oro, they had wanted him to tear off the head of the mulatto fuck who'd seduced his daughter and won his admiration. He wouldn't do it. He knew who the traitors were, he could smell them out before they even knew they were going to betray him. That's why he was still alive and so many Judases were rotting in La Cuarenta, La Victoria, on Beata Island, in the bellies of sharks, or fattening Dominican earthworms. Poor Ramfis, poor Radhamés. Just as well that Angelita had some character and stayed with him.

He got out of the tub and took a fast shower. The contrast between hot and cold water revitalized him. Now he was full of energy. As he applied deodorant and talc, he listened to Caribbean Radio, which ex-

LIMERICK COUNTY LIBRARY 0040179

pressed the ideas and slogans of the "malevolent brain," his name for Johnny Abbes when he was in a good mood.

There was a ranting attack on "the rat of Miraflores, that Venezuelan scum," and the announcer, assuming the proper voice for talking about a faggot, stated that in addition to starving the Venezuelan people, President Rómulo Betancourt had brought misfortune to Venezuela, for hadn't another plane of Venezuelan Airlines just crashed, at a cost of sixty-two fatalities? The fucking queer wouldn't get his way. He had convinced the OAS to impose sanctions, but he who laughs last laughs best. None of them worried him—the rat of Miraflores Palace, the Puerto Rican junkie Muñoz Marín, the Costa Rican bandit Figueres. But the Church did. Perón had warned him, when he left Ciudad Trujillo on his way to Spain: "Watch out for the priests, Generalissimo. It wasn't the fat-bellied oligarchs or the military who brought me down; it was the crows. Make a deal with them or get rid of them once and for all." They weren't going to bring him down. What they did was fuck with him. Starting on that black January 24 in 1960, exactly sixteen months ago, they fucked with him every day. Letters, memorials, Masses, novenas, sermons. Everything those shits in cassocks said and did against him resonated overseas, where the newspapers, radios, and televisions talked of Trujillo's imminent fall now that "the Church had turned its back on him."

He put on his shorts, undershirt, and socks, which Sinforoso had folded the night before and placed next to the closet, beside the hanger with the gray suit, white shirt, and blue tie with white flecks that he would wear this morning. How did Bishop Reilly spend his days and nights inside Santo Domingo Academy? Fucking the nuns? They were hideous, some had hair on their faces. He remembered Angelita studying at that school, the one for decent people. His granddaughters too. The nuns had worshiped him until the Pastoral Letter. Maybe Johnny Abbes was right and it was time to act. Since the manifestos, articles, and protests on radio and television, in various institutions, and in the Congress hadn't taught them a lesson, strike the blow. The people did it! Overran the guards placed there to protect the foreign bishops, broke into Santo Domingo Academy and the bishop's palace in La Vega, dragged the gringo Reilly and the Spaniard Panal out by the hair, and lynched them. Avenged the insult to the nation. Regrets and excuses would be sent to the Vatican, to the Holy Father John Asshole— Balaguer was a master at writing them—and the punishment of a handful of those responsible, chosen from among common criminals, would be exemplary. Would the other crows learn their lesson when they saw the bishops' bodies drawn and quartered by popular wrath? No, it wasn't the right time. He wouldn't give Kennedy an excuse for making Betancourt, Muñoz Marín, and Figueres happy by ordering an invasion. Keep a cool head and proceed with caution, like a Marine.

But the dictates of reason did not convince his glands. He had to stop dressing, blinded by a rage that flooded his entire body, a river of lava rising to his brain, which seemed to be on fire. He closed his eyes and counted to ten. Rage was bad for the government and bad for his heart, it would give him a coronary. The other night, in Mahogany House, it had brought him to the verge of an attack. He began to regain his composure. He always knew how to control his anger, when he had to: dissimulate, pretend to be cordial and affectionate with the worst human trash, the widows, children, brothers and sisters of traitors, if necessary. That's why he had been carrying the weight of a country on his shoulders for almost thirty-two years.

He was involved in the complicated task of securing his socks with garters so there would be no wrinkles. Now, how pleasant it was to give free rein to his rage when there was no risk to the State, when he could give rats, toads, hyenas, snakes what they deserved. The bellies of sharks bore witness to the fact that he had not denied himself the pleasure. Wasn't the Galician traitor José Almoina a corpse in Mexico? And the Basque Jesús de Galíndez, another serpent who bit the hand that fed him? And Ramón Marrero Aristy, who thought that because he was a famous author he could write articles in *The New York Times* against the government that paid for his drunken binges, his books, his whores? And the three Mirabal sisters who played at being Communist heroines, weren't they there too, proof that when he let loose the flood of his rage no dam could contain it? Even Valeriano and Barajita, the crazy couple on El Conde, could testify to that.

He sat holding his shoe, remembering the celebrated pair. A real institution in the colonial city. They lived under the laurels in Colón Park, between the arches of the cathedral, and when they were most affluent they would appear in the doorways of the elegant shoe shops and jewelry stores on El Conde, doing their crazy act so that people would toss them a coin or something to eat. He had often seen Valeriano and Barajita, in their rags and absurd adornments. When Valeriano thought he was Christ, he would drag a cross; when he was Napoleon, he would brandish his broomstick, bellow orders, and charge the enemy. One of Johnny Abbes's *caliés* reported that Crazy Valeriano had started to make fun of the Chief, calling him the Cop. He was curious. He went to spy on them from a car with tinted windows. The old man, his chest covered with little mirrors and beer bottle caps, strutted around with the air of a clown, displaying his medals to a horrified crowd that did not know whether to laugh or run away. "Applaud the Cop, you assholes," screamed Barajita, pointing to the gleaming chest of the madman. Then he felt the heat run through his body, blinding him, urging him to punish their audacity. He gave the order on the spot. But the next morning, thinking that crazy people don't really know what they're saying and that instead of punishing Valeriano he ought to catch the comedians who had told the couple what to say, on a dark dawn like this one he told Johnny Abbes: "Crazy people are just crazy. Let them go." The head of the Military Intelligence Service, the SIM, grimaced: "Too late, Excellency. We threw them to the sharks yesterday. Alive, just as you ordered."

He stood, his shoes on his feet. A statesman does not repent his decisions. He had never repented anything. He would throw those two bishops to the sharks, alive. He began the stage of his morning ritual that he performed with real delight, recalling a novel he read when he was young, the only one he ever thought about: *Quo Vadis?* A tale of Romans and Christians. He never forgot the image of the refined and wealthy Petronius, Arbiter of elegance, who revived each morning thanks to massages and ablutions, ointments, essences, perfumes, and his slave girls' caresses. If he had the time, he would do what the Arbiter did: spend the entire morning in the hands of masseuses, pedicurists, manicurists, barbers, bathers, after the exercises for stimulating his muscles and activating his heart. He had a short massage at midday, after lunch, and a more leisurely one on Sundays, when he could spare two or three hours from his pressing obligations. But the times weren't right for relaxing with the sensual delights of the great Petronius. He had to be content with the ten minutes he spent applying the perfumed Yardley deodorant that Manuel Alfonso sent to him from New York—poor Manuel, how could he go on, after his operation?—and the gentle French moisturizing cream Bienfait du Matin, and the cologne, also Yardley, with the light meadow scent, that he rubbed on his chest. When his hair was combed and he had touched up the ends of the thin brush mustache he had worn for twenty years, he powdered his face generously until he had hidden under a delicate whitish cloud the dark tinge of the Haitian blacks who were his maternal ancestors, something he had always despised on other people's skin, and on his own.

He was dressed, with jacket and tie, at six minutes to five. He checked this with satisfaction: he never went past the hour. It was one of his superstitions; if he did not walk into his office at five sharp, something bad would happen that day.

He went over to the window. It was still dark, as if it were midnight. But he saw fewer stars than he had an hour earlier. They were shining less bravely. Day was about to break and soon they'd run away. He picked up a walking stick and went to the door. As soon as he opened it, he heard the heels of the two military adjutants.

"Good morning, Excellency."

"Good morning, Excellency."

He responded with a nod. At a glance he could tell that they were dressed correctly. He did not allow slovenliness or disorder in any officer or man in the Armed Forces, but among the adjutants, the unit responsible for guarding him, a missing button, a spot or wrinkle on trousers or tunic, a carelessly placed visored cap were grave faults punishable by several days of rigorous discipline and, at times, expulsion and a return to the regular battalions.

A light breeze stirred the trees of Radhamés Manor as he passed, and he heard the whisper of the leaves and, from the stable, another whinnying horse. Johnny Abbes, a report on the progress of the campaign, a visit to San Isidro Air Base, a report from Chirinos, lunch with the Marine, three or four audiences, a meeting with the Minister of the Interior and Religious Practice, a meeting with Balaguer, a meeting with Cucho Álvarez Pina, president of the Dominican Party, and a walk along the Malecón after he had visited Mama Julia. Would he sleep in San Cristóbal to take away the bad taste of the other night?

He walked into his office, in the National Palace, when his watch said five. Breakfast was on his desk—fruit juice, buttered toast, fresh-brewed coffee—with two cups. And, getting to his feet, the flabby silhouette of the director of the Intelligence Service, Colonel Johnny Abbes García:

"Good morning, Excellency."

3 "He isn't coming," Salvador exclaimed suddenly. "Another night wasted, you'll see."

"He'll come," Amadito immediately replied, with some impatience. "He put on his olive-green uniform. The adjutants were ordered to have the blue Chevrolet ready for him. Why won't you believe me? He'll come."

Salvador and Amadito were in the back of the car parked across from the Malecón, and they'd had the same exchange several times during the half hour they had spent there. Antonio Imbert, at the wheel, and Antonio de la Maza, who sat beside him with his elbow out the window, made no comment this time either. The four men were tense as they watched the handful of vehicles driving from Ciudad Trujillo, their yellow headlights piercing the darkness, on the way to San Cristóbal. None of the cars was the 1957 sky-blue Chevrolet with curtained windows that they were waiting for.

They were a few hundred meters from the Livestock Fairgrounds, where there were several restaurants—the Pony, the most popular, was probably full of people eating grilled meat—and some bars that had music, but the wind blew to the east and the sounds did not reach them, though they could see the distant lights through the palm trees. Yet the crash of waves breaking against the rocks and the clamor of the undertow were so loud, they had to raise their voices to be heard. The car, doors closed and lights off, was ready to pull away.

"Do you remember when we first started coming to the Malecón to enjoy the breeze and nobody worried about the *caliés*?" Antonio Imbert put his head out the window and filled his lungs with the night air. "Here's where we began talking seriously about this."

None of his friends answered right away, as if they were consulting their memories or had not paid attention to what he was saying.

"Yes, here on the Malecón, about six months ago," Salvador Estrella Sadhalá replied after a while.

"Earlier than that," Antonio de la Maza murmured without turning around. "In November, when they killed the Mirabal sisters, we talked about it here. I'm sure of that. And we'd already been coming to the Malecón at night for a while."

"It seemed like a dream," Imbert mused. "Difficult, and a long way off. Like when you're a kid and imagine you'll be a hero, an explorer, a movie star. Damn, I still can't believe it'll be tonight."

"If he comes," Salvador grumbled.

"I'll bet anything you want, Turk," Amadito repeated, full of conviction.

"The thing that makes me wonder is that today's Tuesday," Antonio de la Maza complained. "He always goes to San Cristóbal on Wednesday. You're one of the adjutants, Amadito, and you know that better than anybody. Why did he change the day?"

"I don't know why," insisted the lieutenant. "But he'll go. He put on his olive-green uniform. He ordered the blue Chevrolet. He'll go."

"He must have a nice piece of ass waiting for him at Mahogany House," said Antonio Imbert. "A brand-new one that's never been opened."

"If you don't mind, let's talk about something else." Salvador cut him off.

"I always forget we can't talk about asses in front of a saint like you," the man at the wheel apologized. "Let's just say he has something nice planned in San Cristóbal. Can I say it like that, Turk? Or does that offend your apostolic ears too?"

But nobody was in the mood for jokes. Not even Imbert; he talked only to fill the waiting time somehow.

"Heads up!" exclaimed De la Maza, craning his neck forward.

"It's a truck," replied Salvador, with a simple glance at the approaching yellow headlights. "I'm not a saint or a fanatic, Antonio. I practice my faith, that's all. And ever since the bishops sent their Pastoral Letter on January 24 last year, I'm proud to be a Catholic."

In fact, it was a truck that roared past, its swaying load of cartons tied down with ropes; its roar grew fainter and finally disappeared.

"And a Catholic can't talk about cunts but he can kill, is that right,

Turk?" Imbert tried to provoke him. He did it often: he and Salvador Estrella Sadhalá were the closest friends in the group; they were always trading jokes, at times so pointed that others thought they would come to blows. But they had never fought, their friendship was unbreakable. Tonight, however, Turk did not show a trace of humor:

"Killing just anybody, no. Doing away with a tyrant, yes. Have you ever heard the word 'tyrannicide'? In extreme cases, the Church allows it. St. Thomas Aquinas wrote that. Do you want to know how I know? When I began to help the people in June 14 and realized I'd have to pull the trigger someday, I consulted with our spiritual adviser, Father Fortín. A Canadian priest, in Santiago. He arranged an audience for me with Monsignor Lino Zanini, the papal nuncio. 'Would it be a sin for a believer to kill Trujillo, Monsignor?' He closed his eyes and thought. I could repeat his exact words, with his Italian accent. He showed me the passage from St. Thomas, in the *Summa Theologica*. If I hadn't read it, I wouldn't be here tonight with all of you."

Antonio de la Maza had turned around to look at him:

"You talked about this with your spiritual adviser?"

His voice was angry. Lieutenant Amado García Guerrero was afraid he would explode into one of those rages he had been prone to ever since Trujillo had his brother Octavio killed, years before. Outbursts like the one that was about to destroy the friendship that united De la Maza to Salvador Estrella Sadhalá. But Salvador calmed him down:

"It was a long time ago, Antonio. When I began to help June 14. You think I'm such an asshole that I'd confess something like this to a poor priest?"

"Turk, explain to me why you can say asshole and not ass, cunt, or fuck," Imbert joked, trying once again to ease the tension. "Don't all dirty words offend God?"

"Words don't offend God, only obscene thoughts," Turk replied in resignation. "Assholes who ask asshole questions may not offend Him. But they must bore Him to death."

"Did you take communion this morning so you'd come to the great event with a pure soul?" Imbert continued the teasing.

"I've taken communion every day for the past ten years," Salvador acknowledged. "I don't know if my soul is the way a Christian's soul should be. Only God knows that."

"It is," thought Amadito. Of all the people he had known in his thirty-one years, Turk was the one he admired most. Salvador was married to his aunt, Urania Mieses, whom Amadito loved dearly. From the time he had been a cadet at Batalla de Las Carreras Military Academy, whose director was Colonel José León (Pechito) Estévez, Angelita Trujillo's husband, he had spent his days off at the house of the Estrella Sadhalás. Salvador had become extremely important in his life; he confided in him about his problems, troubles, dreams, and doubts, and asked his advice before making any decision. The Estrella Sadhalás gave the party to celebrate Amadito's graduation, carrying the sword of honor—first in a class of thirty-five officers!—attended by his eleven maternal aunts, and, years later, for what the young lieutenant thought would be the best news he'd ever receive, his acceptance into the most prestigious unit in the Armed Forces: the military adjutants responsible for the personal safety of the Generalissimo.

Amadito closed his eyes and inhaled the salt-laden breeze blowing in the four open windows. Imbert, Turk, and Antonio de la Maza were quiet. He had met Imbert and De la Maza at the house on Mahatma Gandhi, and that meant he had witnessed the fight between Turk and Antonio, so violent he expected them to start shooting, and, months later, he also witnessed the reconciliation of Antonio and Salvador for the sake of a single goal: killing the Goat. No one could have told Amadito on that day in 1959, when Urania and Salvador gave him a party and countless bottles of rum were consumed, that in less than two years, on a mild, starry night, on this Tuesday, May 30, 1961, he would be waiting for Trujillo in order to kill him. So many things had happened since the day when, shortly after he arrived at 21 Mahatma Gandhi, Salvador took him by the arm and gravely led him to the most private corner of the garden.

"I must say something to you, Amadito. Because of the fondness I have for you. That all of us in this house have for you."

He spoke so quietly that the young man leaned his head forward to hear him.

"What's this about, Salvador?"

"It's about my not wanting to do anything to hurt your career. You may have problems if you keep coming here."

"What kind of problems?"

Turk's expression, which was usually serene, contorted with emotion. Alarm flashed in his eyes.

"I'm collaborating with the people in June 14. If anyone finds out, it would be very dangerous for you. An officer in Trujillo's corps of military adjutants. Just think about it!"

The lieutenant never could have imagined Salvador as a clandestine conspirator, helping the people who had organized to fight against Trujillo following Castro's June 14 invasion at Constanza, Maimón, and Estero Hondo, which had cost so many lives. He knew that Turk despised the regime; Salvador and his wife were careful in front of him, but sometimes they let slip antigovernment remarks. Then they immediately fell silent, for they knew that Amadito, though he had no interest in politics, professed, like any other officer in the Army, a blind, visceral loyalty to the Maximum Leader, the Benefactor and Father of the New Nation, who for three decades had controlled the destiny of the Republic and the lives and deaths of all Dominicans.

"Not another word, Salvador. You've told me. I heard it. I've forgotten what I heard. I'm going to keep coming here, like always. This is my home."

Salvador looked at him with the clear-eyed sincerity that communicated a joyful sensation of life to Amadito.

"Let's go have a beer, then. Let's not be sad."

And, of course, when he fell in love and began to think about marriage, the first people he introduced to his girlfriend, after his Aunt Meca—his favorite among his mother's eleven sisters—were Salvador and Urania. Luisita Gil! Whenever he thought of her, regret twisted his gut and anger boiled up inside him. He took out a cigarette and placed it in his mouth. Salvador lit it for him with his lighter. The good-looking brunette, the charming, flirtatious Luisita Gil. After some maneuvers, he had gone with two friends for a sail at La Romana. On the dock, two girls were buying fresh fish. They struck up a conversation and went with them to the municipal band concert. The girls invited them to a wedding. Only Amadito could go; he had a day off, but his two friends had to return to barracks. He fell madly in love with the slender, witty little brunette with flashing eyes, who danced the merengue like a star on the Dominican Voice. And she with him. The second time they went out, to a movie and a nightclub, he could kiss and hold her. She was the woman of his life, he could never be with anybody else. The handsome Amadito had said these things to many women since his days as a cadet, but this time he meant it. Luisa took him to meet her family in La Romana, and he invited her to lunch at Aunt Meca's house in Ciudad Trujillo, and then, one Sunday, at the Estrella Sadhalás': they were delighted with Luisa. When he told them he was planning to ask her to marry him, they were enthusiastic: she was a lovely woman. Amadito formally asked her parents for her hand. In accordance with regulations, he requested authorization to marry from the commanding officers of the military adjutants.

It was his first clash with a reality that, despite his twenty-nine years, splendid grades, magnificent record as a cadet and an officer, he had known nothing about. ("Like most Dominicans," he thought.) The reply to his request was delayed. He was told that the corps of adjutants had passed it along to the SIM, so that they could investigate the person in question. In a week or ten days he would have his approval. But the reply did not come in ten, or fifteen, or twenty days. On the twenty-first day the Chief summoned him to his office. It was the only time he had exchanged words with the Benefactor even though he had been close to him so often at public functions, the first time this man whom he saw every day at Radhamés Manor had directed his gaze at him.

From the time he was a child Lieutenant García Guerrero had heard, from his family—especially his grandfather, General Hermógenes García—at school, and later as a cadet and an officer, about Trujillo's gaze. A gaze that no one could endure without lowering his own eyes, intimidated and annihilated by the force radiating from those piercing eyes that seemed to read one's most secret thoughts and most hidden desires and appetites, and made people feel naked. Amadito laughed at the stories. The Chief might be a great statesman whose vision, will, and capacity for work had made the Dominican Republic a great country. But he wasn't God. His gaze could only be the gaze of a mortal man.

It was enough for him to walk into the office, click his heels, and announce himself in the most martial voice his throat could produce— "Second Lieutenant García Guerrero, at your service, Excellency!"—to feel electrified. "Come in," said the sharp voice of the man who sat at the other end of the room behind a desk covered in red leather, writing and not looking up. The young man took a few steps and stood at attention, not moving a muscle or thinking, looking at the meticulously groomed gray hair and impeccable attire—blue jacket and vest, white shirt with immaculate collar and starched cuffs, silvery tie secured with a pearl—and at his hands, one resting on a sheet of paper that the other covered with rapid strokes of blue ink. On his left hand he saw the ring with the precious iridescent stone, which, according to the superstitious, was an amulet given to him when he was a young man, a member of the Constabulary Guard pursuing the "bandits" who rebelled against the United States' military occupation, by a Haitian wizard who assured him that as long as he kept it on he would be invulnerable to enemies.

"A good service record, Lieutenant," he heard him say.

"Thank you very much, Excellency."

The silver-colored head moved and those large staring eyes, without brightness and without humor, met his. "I've never been afraid in my life," the boy later confessed to Salvador. "Until that gaze fell on me, Turk. It's true. As if he were digging up my conscience." There was a long silence while those eyes examined his uniform, his belt, his buttons, his tie, his visored hat. Amadito began to perspire. He knew that the slightest carelessness in dress provoked such disgust in the Chief that he could erupt into violent recriminations.

"A service record this good cannot be stained by marriage to the sister of a Communist. In my government, friends and enemies don't mix."

He spoke quietly, not releasing him from his penetrating gaze. Amadito thought that at any moment the thin, high-pitched voice would crack.

"Luisa Gil's brother is one of the June 14 subversives. Did you know that?"

"No, Excellency."

"Now you know." He cleared his throat and added, without changing his tone: "There are a lot of women in this country. Find another one."

"Yes, Excellency."

He saw him make a gesture of assent, ending the interview.

"Permission to withdraw, Excellency."

He clicked his heels and saluted. He left with a martial step, hiding the anguish that paralyzed him. A soldier obeyed orders, especially if they came from the Benefactor and Father of the New Nation, who had taken a few minutes of his time to speak to him in person. If he had given that order to him, a privileged officer, it was for his own good. He had to obey. He did, clenching his teeth. His letter to Luisa did not contain a single word that was not true: "With a heavy heart, and though I suffer because of it, I must renounce my love for you and tell you, sadly, that we cannot marry. My superiors forbid it because of your brother's anti-Trujillista activities, something you hid from me. I understand why you did. But by the same token I hope you also understand the difficult decision I find myself obliged to make, against my will. I will always think of you with love, but we will not see each other again. I wish you good luck. Don't be angry with me."

Had the beautiful, happy, slender girl from La Romana forgiven him? Though he hadn't seen her again, he hadn't replaced her in his heart. Luisa had married a prosperous farmer from Puerto Plata. But if she eventually forgave him for breaking off their engagement, she never could have forgiven him for the other thing, if she ever found out about it. He would never forgive himself. And even if, in a few moments, the bullet-ridden body of the Goat were lying at his feet—he wanted to empty his pistol into those cold iguana eyes—he would not forgive him either. "At least Luisa will never know." Not her, not anybody except those who planned the ambush.

And, of course, Salvador Estrella Sadhalá; devastated by hatred, alcohol, and despair, Lieutenant García Guerrero had come directly to his house at 21 Mahatma Gandhi, in the small hours of that morning, from the brothel of Pucha Vittini, alias Pucha Brazobán, at the top of Calle Juana Saltitopa, where he had been taken, afterward, by Colonel Johnny Abbes and Major Roberto Figueroa Carrión, so that with a few drinks and a good piece of ass he could forget the unpleasantness. "Unpleasantness," "sacrifice for the Fatherland," "test of will," "blood offering to the Chief": those were the things they had said to him. Then they congratulated him for having earned a promotion. Amadito took a drag of his cigarette and tossed it onto the road: a tiny explosion of fireworks when it hit the asphalt. "If you don't think about something else, you're going to cry," he told himself, mortified at the thought that Imbert, Antonio, and Salvador might see him burst into sobs. They would think he was afraid. He clenched his teeth so hard it hurt. He had never been as sure about anything as he was about this. While the Goat lived, he would not, he'd be nothing but the ambulatory despair he had been since that January night in 1961 when the world collapsed around him, and he had run to 21 Mahatma Gandhi and taken refuge in Salvador's friendship so he wouldn't put a gun in his mouth and pull the trigger. He told him everything. Not right away. Because when Turk opened the door, surprised at dawn by the pounding that roused him, his wife, and his children from bed and from sleep, and found on the threshold Amadito's broken silhouette reeking of alcohol, the young man could not say a word. He opened his arms and threw them around Salvador. "What is it, Amadito? Who died?" They took him to his bedroom, put him to bed, let him give vent to his feelings, babbling incoherently. Urania Mieses prepared mint tea that she fed to him by the spoonful, as if he were a little boy.

"Don't tell us anything you'll be sorry for," Turk interrupted.

Over his pajamas he wore a kimono with ideograms. He sat at a corner of the bed, looking at Amadito with affection.

"I'll leave you alone with Salvador." His Aunt Urania kissed him on the forehead and stood up. "So you can talk more freely, so you can tell him what it would make you sad to tell me."

Amadito thanked her. Turk turned off the overhead light. The shade on the bedside lamp had a design that the light of the bulb turned red. Clouds? Animals? The lieutenant thought that if a fire broke out, he wouldn't move.

"Go to sleep, Amadito. Things will seem less tragic in the light of day."

"It won't make any difference, Turk. Day or night I'll still make myself sick. It'll be worse when I sober up."

It began that afternoon, in the headquarters of the military adjutants, next to Radhamés Manor. He had just returned from Boca Chica, where Major Roberto Figueroa Carrión, liaison between the Head of the Joint Chiefs of Staff and Generalissimo Trujillo, had sent him to deliver a sealed envelope to General Ramfis Trujillo at the Dominican Air Force Base. The lieutenant entered the major's office to report on his mission, and Figueroa Carrión received him with a mischievous expression. He showed him the red file folder on his desk.

"Can you guess what I have here?"

"A week's leave for me at the beach, Major, sir?"

"Your promotion to first lieutenant, boy!" His superior happily handed him the folder.

"I stood there with my mouth open, because it wasn't my turn." Salvador didn't move. "I still have eight months before I can apply for a promotion. I thought it was a consolation prize because I was denied permission to get married."

Salvador, at the foot of the bed, was ill at ease and made a face.

"Didn't you know, Amadito? Your friends, your superiors, didn't they tell you about the test of loyalty?"

"I thought they were just stories," Amadito said with conviction, with fury. "I swear. People don't bring that up, they don't brag about that. I didn't know. It took me by surprise."

Was that true, Amadito? One more lie, one more pious lie in the string of lies that had been his life since he enrolled at the Military Academy. Since his birth, for he had been born almost at the same time as the Era. Of course you had to know, had to suspect; of course, in the Fortress at San Pedro de Macorís, and then, among the military adjutants, you had heard, intuited, discovered, in the jokes and boasts, in the excited moments, the bravado, that the privileged, the elect, the officers entrusted with positions of greatest responsibility were subjected to a test of loyalty to Trujillo before they were promoted. You knew very well it existed. But now Second Lieutenant García Guerrero also knew that he never had wanted to know in detail what the test involved. Major Figueroa Carrión shook his hand and repeated something he had heard so often he had begun to believe it:

"You'll have a great career, boy."

He ordered him to pick him up at his house at eight that night: they would go for a drink to celebrate his promotion, and take care of a little business.

"Bring the jeep." The major dismissed him.

At eight o'clock, Amadito was at his superior's house. The major did not invite him in. He must have been watching at the window, because before Amadito could get out of the jeep, he appeared at the door. He jumped into the jeep, and without responding to the lieutenant's salute, he ordered, in a falsely casual voice:

"To La Cuarenta, Amadito."

"To the prison, Major, sir?"

"Yes, to La Cuarenta," the lieutenant repeated. "You know who was waiting for us there, Turk."

"Johnny Abbes," murmured Salvador.

"Colonel Abbes García," Amadito corrected him with quiet irony. "The head of the SIM, yes."

"Are you sure you want to tell me this, Amadito?" The young man felt Salvador's hand on his knee. "Won't you hate me afterward because you know that I know too?"

Amadito knew him by sight. He had seen him slipping like a shadow along the corridors of the National Palace, getting out of his black bulletproof Cadillac or climbing into it in the gardens of Radhamés Manor, entering or leaving the Chief's office, something that Johnny Abbes and probably nobody else in the entire country could do—appear at any hour of the day or night at the National Palace or the private residence of the Benefactor and be received immediately—and always, like many of his comrades in the Army, Navy, or Air Force, he had felt a secret shudder of revulsion at that flabby figure stuffed into a colonel's uniform, the personified negation of the bearing, agility, martial air, virility, strength, and elegance that military men had to display—the Chief said it every time he spoke to his soldiers on the National Holiday and on Armed Forces Day—that fat-cheeked, funereal face with the little mustache trimmed in the style of Arturo de Córdoba or Carlos López Moctezuma, the most popular Mexican actors, and a capon's dewlaps hanging down over his short neck. Though they said so only among their closest friends and after a good many glasses of rum, the officers despised Colonel Johnny Abbes García because he wasn't a real soldier. He hadn't earned his stripes the way they had, by studying, going through the academy, living in barracks, sweating to rise through the ranks. He had his as payment for the undoubtedly dirty services he had rendered to justify his appointment as the all-powerful head of the Military Intelligence Service. And they distrusted him for the grim acts that were attributed to him, the disappearances, the executions, the sudden falls into disgrace of powerful people—like the recent plunge of Senator Agustín Cabral—and for the terrible accusations, denunciations, and calumnies in the newspaper column "The Public Forum" that appeared every morning in *El Caribe* and kept people in a state of anxiety because their fate depended on whatever was said about them there, and for the intrigues and the operations directed against sometimes apolitical and decent people, peaceable citizens who had fallen somehow into the infinite nets of espionage that Johnny Abbes García and his vast army of *caliés* spread into every corner of Dominican society. Many officers—Lieutenant García Guerrero among them—felt authorized in their heart of hearts to despise this individual in spite of the confidence the Generalissimo had in him, because they thought, as did many men in the government, including, apparently, Ramfis Trujillo himself, that Colonel Abbes García's undisguised cruelty brought the regime into disrepute and justified its critics. And yet, Amadito recalled a discussion after a dinner well watered by beer, among a group of military adjutants, when his immediate superior, Major Figueroa Carrión, came to Abbes's defense: "The colonel may be a devil, but he's useful to the Chief: everything bad is attributed to him and only the good to Trujillo. What better service is there? For a government to last thirty years, it needs a Johnny Abbes who'll stick his hands in shit. And his body and head, if he has to. He takes the heat. Our enemies, and sometimes our friends, concentrate their hatred on him. The Chief knows this, that's why he keeps him close. If the colonel didn't watch the Chief's back, maybe the same thing would have happened to him that happened to Pérez Jiménez in Venezuela, Batista in Cuba, Perón in Argentina."

"Good evening, Lieutenant."

"Good evening, Colonel, sir."

Amadito raised his hand to his visor and saluted, but Abbes García extended his hand—a hand as soft as a sponge, wet with perspiration—and patted him on the back.

"Come this way."

Near the sentry box crowded with half a dozen guards, past the iron grillwork at the entrance, was a small room that must have been used as an administrative office, with a table and a couple of chairs. It was dimly lit by a single bulb dangling from a long cord covered with flies; a cloud of insects buzzed around it. The colonel closed the door, pointed them to the chairs. A guard came in with a bottle of Johnnie Walker Red ("The brand I prefer because Juanito Caminante's my namesake," the colonel joked), glasses, an ice bucket, and several bottles of mineral water. While he served the drinks, the colonel talked to the lieutenant as if Major Figueroa Carrión weren't there.

"Congratulations on your new stripe. And that service record. I'm very familiar with it. The SIM recommended your promotion. For distinguished military and civic service. I'll tell you a secret. You're one of the few officers denied permission to marry who obeyed without requesting a review. That's why the Chief is rewarding you, moving your promotion ahead by a year. A toast with Juanito Caminante!"

Amadito took a long drink. Colonel Abbes García had almost filled the glass with whiskey, with only a splash of water, and the liquid was like an explosion in his brain.

"At that point, in that place, with Johnny Abbes pouring you a drink, didn't you guess what was coming?" murmured Salvador. The young man detected the grief flooding through his friend's words.

"That it would be hard and ugly, yes, Turk," he replied, trembling. "But never what was going to happen."

The colonel poured another round. The three men had begun to smoke, and the head of the SIM spoke of how important it was not to allow the enemy within to raise his head, to crush him every time he attempted to act.

"Because as long as the enemy within is weak and disunited, it doesn't matter what the foreign enemy does. Let the United States holler, let the OAS kick, let Venezuela and Costa Rica howl, they can't do us any harm. In fact, they unite Dominicans like a fist around the Chief."

He had a thin drawling voice, and he avoided the eyes of the person he was talking to. His eyes were small, dark, rapid, evasive, moving constantly as if seeing things hidden from other people. From time to time he wiped away sweat with a large red handkerchief.

"Especially the military." He paused to flick the ash from his cigarette onto the floor. "And especially the military elite, Lieutenant García Guerrero. To which you now belong. The Chief wanted you to hear this."

He paused again, drew deeply on his cigarette, took a drink of whiskey. Only then did he seem to discover that Major Figueroa Carrión existed:

"Does the lieutenant know what the Chief expects of him?"

"He doesn't need anybody to tell him, he has more brains than any officer in his class." The major had the face of a toad, and alcohol had accentuated and reddened his swollen features. Amadito had the impression that their conversation was a rehearsed play. "I imagine he knows; if not, he doesn't deserve his new stripe."

There was another pause while the colonel filled their glasses a third time. He put in the ice cubes with his hands. "*Salud*" and he drank and they drank. Amadito told himself he liked rum and Coca-Cola a thousand times more than whiskey, it was so bitter. And not until that moment did he understand the joke about Juanito Caminante. "How dumb not to get it," he thought. The colonel's red handkerchief was so strange! He had seen white, blue, gray handkerchiefs. But red ones! What an idea.

"You're going to have greater and greater responsibilities," said the colonel, with a solemn air. "The Chief wants to be sure you're up to the job."

"What am I supposed to do, Colonel, sir?" All this preamble irritated Amadito. "I've always obeyed the orders of my superiors. I'll never disappoint the Chief. This is a test of loyalty, right?"

The colonel, his head lowered, was staring at the table. When he looked up, the lieutenant noticed a gleam of satisfaction in those furtive eyes.

"It's true, for officers with balls, Trujillistas down to the marrow of their bones, you don't have to sweeten the pill." He stood up. "You're right, Lieutenant. We'll finish our little piece of business and celebrate your new stripe at Puchita Brazobán's place."

"What did you have to do?" It was a struggle for Salvador to speak; his throat was raw, his expression morose.

"Kill a traitor with my own hands. That's how he said it: 'And without your hands trembling, Lieutenant.' "

When they went out to the courtyard of La Cuarenta, Amadito felt his temples throbbing. Beside a large bamboo tree, next to the chalet that had been converted into a prison and torture center for the SIM, near the jeep they had come in, was another, almost identical jeep, its headlights turned off. In the back seat, two guards with rifles flanked a man whose hands were tied and whose mouth was covered by a towel.

"Come with me, Lieutenant," said Johnny Abbes, getting behind the wheel of the jeep where the guards were sitting. "Follow us, Roberto."

As the two vehicles left the prison and took the coastal highway, a storm broke, filling the night with thunder and lightning. The violent downpour kept them from speaking.

"Just as well it's raining, even if we get wet," the colonel remarked. "It'll break the heat. The campesinos were praying for a little rain."

He didn't remember how long they drove, but it couldn't have been very long, because he did remember that when he went into Pucha Vittini's brothel after parking the jeep on Calle Juana Saltitopa, the clock on the wall of the foyer was striking ten. Everything, from the time he picked up Major Figueroa Carrión at his house, had taken less than two hours. Abbes García drove off the highway, and the jeep bucked and shook as if it were going to fall apart as they crossed a field of tall weeds and stones, followed closely by the major's jeep, whose headlights lit the way. It was dark, but the lieutenant knew they were moving parallel to the ocean: the sound of the waves had grown so loud that it filled his ears. He thought they were near the small port of La Caleta. As soon as the jeep stopped, so did the rain. The colonel jumped down, followed by Amadito. The two guards were well trained: without waiting for orders they pushed out the prisoner. In a flash of lightning the lieutenant saw that the gagged man wore no shoes. During the drive he had been absolutely docile, but as soon as he touched the ground, as if finally aware of what was going to happen, he began to twist, to roar, trying to loosen the ropes and gag. Amadito, who until then had avoided looking at him, observed the convulsive movements of his head as he attempted to free his mouth, say something, perhaps plead for mercy, perhaps curse them. "Suppose I take out my revolver and shoot the colonel, the major, the two guards, and let him run away?" he thought.

"Instead of one dead man on the rocks, there'd be two," said Salvador.

"Good thing it stopped raining," Major Figueroa Carrión complained as he climbed out. "I'm soaked, damn it."

"Do you have your weapon?" asked Colonel Abbes García. "Don't make the poor bastard suffer any more."

Amadito nodded, not saying a word. He took a few steps until he stood next to the prisoner. The soldiers released him and moved away. The man did not start to run, as Amadito thought he would. His legs would not obey him, fear kept him nailed to the weeds and mud in the field, where a strong wind blew. But though he did not attempt to escape, he continued moving his head, desperately, right and left, up and down, in a useless effort to get rid of the gag. He continued his choked roaring. Lieutenant García Guerrero put the barrel of his pistol to the man's temple and fired. The shot deafened him and made him close his eyes for a second.

"Again," said Abbes García. "You never know."

Amadito, bending over, touched the head of the man sprawled on the ground—he was still and silent—and shot again at point-blank range.

"That's it," said the colonel, taking his arm and pushing him toward the jeep of Major Figueroa Carrión. "The guards know what they have to do. Let's go to Puchita's and warm things up."

In the jeep, driven by Roberto, Lieutenant García Guerrero was silent, half listening to the conversation between the colonel and the major. He remembered something they said:

"They'll bury him there?"

"They'll throw him in the ocean," explained the head of the SIM. "It's the advantage of these rocks. On top, they're sharp as knives. Down below, there's an entrance to the sea, very deep, like a well. Full of sharks, waiting. They eat them in seconds. It's really something to see. They leave no trace. Sure, rapid, and clean, too."

"Would you recognize the rocks?" Salvador asked.

No. All he remembered is that before they got there, they had passed that small bay, La Caleta. But he could not reconstruct the entire route from La Cuarenta.

"I'll give you a sleeping pill." Salvador put his hand back on his knee. "You'll sleep six, eight hours."

"I haven't finished yet, Turk. Be patient a little longer. So you can spit in my face and throw me out of your house."

They had gone to the brothel of Pucha Vittini, nicknamed Puchita Brazobán, an old house with balconies and a dry garden, a place frequented by *caliés*, people connected to the government and the SIM, for whom, it was rumored, Pucha, a foulmouthed, good-natured old woman, also worked, having risen through the hierarchy of her trade to the rank of administrator and director of whores, after having been one herself in the brothels on Calle Dos, starting very young and achieving great success. She received them at the door and greeted Johnny Abbes and Major Figueroa Carrión like old friends. She grabbed Amadito's chin: "What a sweetie pie!" She led them to the second floor and sat them at a table near the bar. Johnny Abbes asked her to bring Juanito Caminante.

"It took me a while to realize it was the whiskey, Colonel, sir," Amadito confessed. "Johnnie Walker. Juanito Caminante. Easy, and I didn't get it."

"It's better than any psychiatrist," said the colonel. "Without

Juanito Caminante I couldn't keep my mental equilibrium, the most important thing in my work. To do it well, you need serenity, cold blood, icy balls. Never mix emotions with reason."

There were no clients yet except for a little bald man with eyeglasses who sat at the bar, drinking a beer. A bolero played on the jukebox, and Amadito recognized the dense voice of Toña la Negra. Major Figueroa Carrión stood up and went to dance with one of the women whispering in a corner under a large poster for a Mexican movie with Libertad Lamarque and Tito Guizar.

"You have steady nerves," Colonel Abbes García said approvingly. "Not all the officers are like you. I've seen lots of tough men fall apart at the critical moment. I've seen them shit themselves in fear. Because even if nobody believes it, it takes more balls to kill than to die."

He poured the drinks and said, "*Salud.*" Amadito drank greedily. How many drinks? Three, five, he soon lost all notion of time and place. Besides drinking he danced with an Indian girl whom he caressed and took into a little room lit by a bulb covered in red cellophane swaying over a bed that had a brightly colored quilt. He couldn't fuck her. "I'm too drunk, baby," he apologized. The real reason was the knot in his stomach, the memory of what he had just done. Finally he found the courage to tell the colonel and the major he was leaving because he'd had too much to drink and felt sick.

The three of them walked to the door. There it was, waiting for Johnny Abbes, his black bulletproof Cadillac and his chauffeur, and a jeep with an escort of armed bodyguards. The colonel gave him his hand.

"Aren't you curious to know who he was?"

"I prefer not to know, Colonel, sir."

Abbes García's flabby face stretched into an ironic smile as he wiped it with his fiery red handkerchief:

"How easy it would be if you could do these things without knowing who was involved. Don't fuck with me, Lieutenant. If you jump in the water you have to get wet. He was in June 14, the younger brother of your ex-girlfriend, I believe. Luisa Gil, wasn't it? Well, see you soon, we'll do some more things together. If you need me you know where to find me."

The lieutenant felt Turk's hand on his knee again.

"It's a lie, Amadito." Salvador tried to comfort him. "It could have been anybody. He lied. To destroy you, to make you feel more involved, more of a slave. Forget what he told you. Forget what you did."

Amadito nodded. Very slowly, he pointed at the revolver on his belt.

"The next time I fire that, it will be to kill Trujillo, Turk," he said. "You and Tony Imbert can count on me for anything. You don't have to change the subject anymore when I come to the house."

"Heads up, heads up, this one's coming straight toward us," said Antonio de la Maza, raising the sawed-off barrel to the window, ready to fire.

Amadito and Estrella Sadhalá gripped their weapons too. Antonio Imbert started the engine. But the car coming down the Malecón toward them, moving slowly, on the lookout, wasn't the Chevrolet but a small Volkswagen. Using its brakes, until the driver saw them. Then it made a U-turn and drove to where they were parked. It stopped beside them, its headlights off.

4 "Aren't you going up to see him?" the nurse says at last.

Urania knows the question has been struggling to pass the woman's lips ever since she came into the little house on César Nicolás Penson, but instead of asking the nurse to take her to Señor Cabral's room, she went to the kitchen and fixed herself some coffee. She has been sipping it for the past ten minutes.

"First I'll finish my breakfast," she answers, not smiling, and the nurse lowers her eyes in confusion. "I need strength to climb those stairs."

"I know there was trouble between you and him, I heard something about it," the woman apologizes, not knowing what to do with her hands. "I was just asking. I already gave him his breakfast and shaved him. He always wakes up very early."

Urania nods. She feels calm and confident now. Again she examines the decay around her. The paint on the walls has deteriorated, and the tabletop, the sink, the cupboard, everything looks smaller and misaligned. Was it the same furniture? She didn't recognize anything.

"Does anyone come to visit him? Anybody in the family, I mean."

"Señora Adelina's daughters, Señora Lucindita and Señora Manolita, always come about noon." The woman—tall, no longer young, wearing slacks under her white uniform—stands in the kitchen doorway and does not hide her discomfort. "Your aunt used to come every day. But since she broke her hip, she doesn't go out anymore."

Aunt Adelina was a good deal younger than her father, she couldn't be more than seventy-five. So she broke her hip. Was she still so devout? She took communion every day, back then.

"Is he in his bedroom?" Urania drinks the last of her coffee. "Well, where else would he be? No, don't come up with me."

She climbs the staircase with the discolored railing where, she remembers, pots filled with flowers used to hang, and she can't shake the feeling that the house has shrunk. When she reaches the upper floor, she notices the chipped tiles, some of them loose. This had been a modern house, comfortable, furnished with taste; it has fallen on hard times, it's a hovel compared to the houses and condominiums she saw the night before in Bella Vista. She stops at the first door—this used to be his room—and before she goes in, she knocks a couple of times.

She is greeted by intense light that pours through the wide-open window. The glare blinds her for a few seconds; then she begins to make out the bed covered by a gray spread, the old bureau with its oval mirror, the photographs on the walls—how did he get hold of her graduation picture from Harvard?—and, finally, in the old leather chair with its broad back and arms, an old man in blue pajamas and slippers. He looks dwarfed by the chair. He has grown wrinkled and smaller, just like the house. She is distracted by a white object at her father's feet, a small chamber pot, half filled with urine.

Back then his hair was black except for some distinguished gray at his temples; now the sparse hairs on his bald head are yellowish, dirty. His eyes were large, sure of themselves, masters of the world (when he wasn't near the Chief); but these two slits staring at her are tiny, beady, frightened. He had teeth and now he doesn't; he can't be wearing his dentures (she paid the bill for them a few years ago), because his lips have collapsed and his cheeks are so sunken they almost touch. He has shriveled, his feet barely touch the floor. To look at him she used to have to raise her head, stretch her neck; now, if he were to stand up, he would reach her shoulder.

"It's Urania," she murmurs, approaching him. She sits on the bed, a meter from her father. "Do you remember that you have a daughter?"

There is internal agitation in the old man, movements of the pale bony hands with tapered fingers that rest on his legs. But the narrow little eyes, although they don't move away from Urania, remain unexpressive.

"I don't recognize you either," Urania whispers. "I don't know why I came or what I'm doing here."

The old man has begun to move his head, up and down, down and up. His throat emits a long, harsh, strangled moan, like a lugubrious song. But in a few moments he is calm again, his eyes still fixed on her.

"The house used to be full of books." Urania glances at the bare walls. "What happened to them? Of course, you can't read anymore. Did you have time to read back then? I don't remember ever seeing you read. You were a busy man. I'm busy too now, maybe even more than you in those days. Ten, twelve hours in the office or visiting clients. But I make time to read a little every day. Early in the morning, watching the sun come up behind the Manhattan skyscrapers, or late at night, looking at the lights in those glass beehives. I really like it. On Sundays I read for three or four hours, after *Meet the Press*. The advantage of being single, Papa. You knew that, didn't you? Your little girl was left behind to dress the saints. That's what you used to say about unmarried women: 'What a failure! She never caught a husband!' Neither did I, Papa. Or rather, I didn't want to. I had offers. At the university. At the World Bank. At the office. Just think, a boyfriend may still turn up. At the age of forty-nine! It isn't so terrible being an old maid. For one thing, I have time to read instead of taking care of a husband and children."

He seems to understand, to be so interested he doesn't dare move a muscle in case he interrupts her. He sits very still, his narrow chest rising and falling rhythmically, his tiny eyes focused on her lips. Outside an occasional car passes, and footsteps, voices, snatches of conversation approach, rise, fall, and are lost in the distance.

"My apartment in Manhattan is full of books," Urania continues. "Like this house when I was a girl. Law, economy, history. But in my bedroom, only Dominican books. Testimonies, essays, memoirs, lots of histories. Can you guess the period? The Trujillo Era, what else? The most important thing that happened to us in five hundred years. You used to say that with so much conviction. It's true, Papa. During those thirty-one years, all the evil we had carried with us since the Conquest became crystallized. You're in some of those books, an important figure. Minister of Foreign Affairs, senator, president of the Dominican Party. Is there anything you weren't, Papa? I've become an expert on Trujillo. Instead of playing bridge or golf, or riding horses, or going to the opera, my hobby has been finding out what happened during those years. It's a shame we can't have a conversation. You could clarify so many things for me, you lived them arm in arm with your beloved

Chief, who repaid your loyalty so shabbily. For instance, I would have liked for you to tell me if His Excellency also took my mother to bed."

She sees that the old man is shaken. His fragile, shrunken body has given a start in the chair. Urania moves her head closer and observes him. Is it a false impression? He seems to be listening, making an effort to understand what she is saying.

"Did you allow it? Resign yourself to it? Use it to further your career?"

Urania takes a deep breath. She examines the room. There are two photographs in silver frames on the night table. Her first communion, the year her mother died. Perhaps she left this world with a vision of her little girl enveloped in the tulle of that beautiful dress, with that angelic look. The other photo is of her mother: young, black hair parted in the middle, eyebrows tweezed, eyes melancholy and dreamy. It's an old, yellowing photograph, slightly creased. She goes to the night table, raises the photograph to her lips, and kisses it.

She hears a car braking at the front door. Her heart skips a beat; without moving from her place, she can see, through the curtains, the sparkling chrome, the gleaming body, the flashing brilliance of the luxurious automobile. She hears footsteps, the doorbell chimes two or three times, and—hypnotized, petrified, not moving—she hears the maid opening the door. She hears but doesn't understand the brief conversation at the foot of the stairs. Her madly beating heart is about to explode. Taps on the door. An Indian girl, wearing a maid's uniform, her expression terrified, looks in the half-opened door:

"The President has come to visit you, señora. The Generalissimo, señora!"

"Tell him I'm sorry but I can't receive him. Tell him Señora de Cabral does not receive visitors when Agustín is not at home. Go on, tell him."

The girl's footsteps move away, timid, indecisive, going down the staircase with the railing where flowerpots hang, ablaze with geraniums. Urania replaces her mother's photograph on the nightstand and returns to the corner of the bed. Trapped in the chair, her father looks at her in alarm.

"That's what the Chief did to his Minister of Education, early in his government, and you know all about it, Papa. What he did to the young scholar, Don Pedro Henríquez Ureña, a refined, genial man. He came to see his wife while Don Pedro was at work. She was brave enough to tell him she didn't receive visitors when her husband wasn't home. At the beginning of the Era it was still possible for a woman to refuse to receive the Chief. When she told him what had happened, Don Pedro resigned, left the country, and never set foot on this island again. Which is why he became so famous as a teacher, a historian, a critic, a philologist, in Mexico, Argentina, and Spain. Lucky for him the Chief wanted to go to bed with his wife. In those early days, a minister could resign and not have an accident, or fall off a cliff, or be stabbed by a madman, or eaten by sharks. He did the right thing, don't you agree? His action saved him from becoming what you became, Papa. Would you have done the same thing or looked away? Like your hated good friend, your despised dear colleague, our neighbor Don Froilán. Do you remember, Papa?"

The old man begins to tremble and moan that macabre song. Urania waits until he settles down. Don Froilán! He would whisper in the living room, on the terrace or in the garden with her father, whom he came to see several times a day during the periods when they were allies in the internecine struggles among the Trujillista factions, battles the Benefactor encouraged in order to neutralize his collaborators by keeping them busy protecting their backs from the knives of enemies who were, in public, their friends, brothers, and fellow believers. Don Froilán lived in the house across the way; on its tiled roof there are, at this very moment, a row of half a dozen pigeons standing at attention. Urania goes to the window. It hasn't changed much either, the house of that powerful man who was also a minister, senator, intendant, chancellor, ambassador, everything one could be during those years. Even Minister of Foreign Affairs, in May 1961, when the great events took place.

The house is still painted gray and white, but it too has grown smaller. An extension of four or five meters has been built on, out of harmony with the projecting pointed arch at the entrance in the style of a Gothic castle, where she often saw, on her way home from school in the afternoons, the elegant figure of Don Froilán's wife. As soon as the woman saw her she would call: "Urania, Uranita! Come here, let me look at you, darling. What eyes, my girl! You're as pretty as your mother, Uranita." She would stroke her hair with carefully manicured hands, the long nails painted a deep red. Urania would feel so dreamy when those fingers moved through her hair and caressed her scalp. Eugenia? Laura? Did she have a flower name? Magnolia? She's forgotten. But not her face, her snowy skin, silken eyes, regal figure. She always seemed to be dressed for a party. Urania loved her because she was so affectionate, because she gave her gifts and took her to the Country Club to swim in the pool, and, above all, because she had been her mother's friend. She imagined that if she hadn't gone to heaven, her mother would be as beautiful and aristocratic as Don Froilán's wife. There was nothing attractive about him, however. Short, bald, fat: no woman would have looked at him twice. Was it the need to find a husband or self-interest that made her marry him?

This is what she asks herself in bewilderment as she opens the box of chocolates, wrapped in metallic paper, that the lady has given her, with a kiss on the cheek, when she came to the door of her house and called her—"Uranita! Come, I have a surprise for you, darling!"—after the girl climbed down from the school bus. Urania goes into her house, kisses the lady—she's wearing a blue tulle dress, high-heeled shoes, enough makeup to go to a dance, a pearl necklace, jewels on her hands—opens the box wrapped in gift paper and tied with a pink ribbon. She looks at the luxurious chocolates, impatient to try them but not daring to—wouldn't that be bad manners?—when the car stops on the street, very near the house. The lady gives a start, the strange kind of movement horses make suddenly, as if hearing a mysterious order. She has turned pale and her voice is urgent: "You have to go." The hand resting on her shoulder twitches, clutches at her, pushes her toward the entrance. When she obediently picks up her book bag and is about to leave, the door opens wide: the overwhelming figure of the gentleman in a dark suit, starched white cuffs and gold cuff links projecting from the sleeves of his jacket, blocks her way. A gentleman who wears dark glasses and is everywhere, including her memory. She stands paralyzed, openmouthed, looking, looking. His Excellency gives her a reassuring smile.

"And who is this?"

"Uranita, Agustín Cabral's daughter," replies the lady of the house. "She's just leaving."

And, in fact, Urania leaves without even saying goodbye because she is struck dumb. She crosses the street, goes into her house, climbs the stairs, and from her bedroom she peers through the curtains, waiting, waiting for the President to come out of the house across the way.

"And your daughter was so naive she didn't even wonder what the

Father of the Nation was doing there when Don Froilán wasn't home."
Her father, calm now, listens, or seems to listen, not taking his eyes off
her. "So naive that when you came home from Congress, I ran to tell
you about it. I saw the President, Papa! He came to visit Don Froilán's
wife, Papa! What a look you had on your face!"

As if they had just informed him of the death of someone he loved.
As if he had just been diagnosed with cancer. He turned red, turned
pale, turned red again. And his eyes, looking into the girl's face again
and again. How could he explain it to her? How could he warn her of
the danger the family was in?

The narrow little eyes of the invalid want to open wide, want to be
round.

"My dear, there are things you can't know, can't understand yet. I'm
here to know them for you, to protect you. I love you more than anything in the world. Don't ask me why, but you have to forget about
this. You weren't at Froilán's house. You didn't see his wife. And certainly, certainly not the person you dreamed you saw. For your own
good, sweetheart. And mine. Don't repeat it, don't tell anybody about
it. You promise? Never? Not anybody? You swear?"

"I swore," says Urania. "But not even that was enough to make me
suspect anything. Not even when you threatened the servants that if
they repeated the girl's fairy tale they would lose their jobs. That's how
innocent I was. By the time I discovered why the Generalissimo paid
visits to their wives, ministers could no longer do what Henríquez
Ureña did. Like Don Froilán, they had to resign themselves to wearing
horns. And gain something from it since they had no alternative. Did
you? Did the Chief visit my mother? Before I was born? When I was
too little to remember? He visited them when the wives were beautiful. My mother was beautiful, wasn't she? I don't remember him coming here, but he might have before I was born. What did my mother
do? Did she accept it? Did she feel happy, proud of the honor? That
was the norm, wasn't it? Good Dominican women were grateful when
the Chief deigned to fuck them. You think that's vulgar? But that was
the verb your beloved Chief used."

Yes, that one. Urania knows, she has read it in her extensive library
on the Era. At night, after a few glasses of Carlos I Spanish brandy,
Trujillo, so careful, refined, elegant in his speech—a snake charmer
when he set his mind to it—would suddenly come out with the filthi-

est words, talk the way they talk on a sugar plantation, in the bateys, among the stevedores on the Ozama, in the stadiums or brothels, talk the way men talk when they need to feel more macho than they really are. At times the Chief could be savagely vulgar, repeating the harsh curses of his youth, when he was a plantation overseer in San Cristóbal or a guard in the constabulary. His courtiers celebrated them as enthusiastically as the speeches written for him by Senator Cabral or the Constitutional Sot. He even boasted of the "cunts he had fucked," something his courtiers also celebrated even when that could make them potential enemies of Doña María Martínez, the Bountiful First Lady, and even when those cunts were their wives, sisters, mothers, or daughters. It wasn't an exaggeration of an overheated Dominican imagination, uncontrollably heightening virtues and vices and embellishing real anecdotes until they became fantasies. Some stories were invented, enhanced, colored by this fierce vocation of her compatriots. But the story of Barahona had to be true. Urania hadn't read it, she had heard it (feeling nauseated), told by someone who was always close, very close, to the Benefactor.

"The Constitutional Sot, Papa. Yes, Senator Henry Chirinos, the Judas who betrayed you. I heard it from his own filthy mouth. Are you surprised I was with him? As an official of the World Bank I couldn't avoid it. The director asked me to represent him at the reception given by our ambassador. I mean, the ambassador of President Balaguer. Of the democratic civilian government of President Balaguer. Chirinos made out better than you did, Papa. He got you out of the way, he never fell into disfavor with Trujillo, and in the end he changed direction and adjusted to democracy even though he had been as much of a Trujillista as you. There he was, in Washington, uglier than ever, puffed up like a toad, tending to his guests and drinking like a sponge. Allowing himself the luxury of entertaining his companions with anecdotes about the Trujillo Era. He of all people!"

The invalid has closed his eyes. Has he fallen asleep? His head rests against the back of the chair and his wrinkled, empty mouth hangs open. He looks thinner and more vulnerable this way; through his bathrobe, she catches a glimpse of his hairless chest, the white skin and prominent bones. His breathing is regular. She notices only now that her father wears no socks; his insteps and ankles are those of a child.

He hasn't recognized her. How could he have imagined that this official of the World Bank, who has given him the director's greetings in English, is the daughter of Egghead Cabral, his former colleague and crony? Urania manages to keep her distance from the ambassador after the greeting demanded by protocol, exchanging banalities with people who are obliged to be there, as she is, because of their positions. After a time, she prepares to leave. She approaches the circle listening to the ambassador of the democratic country, but what he is saying stops her cold. Ashen, spotted skin, the maw of an apoplectic beast, a triple chin, his elephantine belly about to burst out of the tight blue suit with its fancy vest and red tie, Ambassador Chirinos says it happened in Barahona, toward the end, when Trujillo, in one of those acts of bravado he was so fond of, announced that in order to set an example and activate Dominican democracy, he, who was retired from government (he had set up his brother Héctor Bienvenido, nicknamed Blacky, as puppet president) would declare his candidacy not for the presidency but for an obscure provincial governorship. And as an opposition candidate!

The ambassador of the democratic country snorts, takes a breath, observes the effect of his words with tiny eyes that are too close together. "Think of it, ladies and gentlemen," he says ironically: "Trujillo, a candidate opposed to his own regime!" He smiles and continues, explaining that in the election campaign, Don Froilán Arala, one of the Generalissimo's right-hand men, delivered a speech urging the Chief to declare not for the governorship but for what he still was in the hearts of the Dominican people: President of the Republic. Everyone thought Don Froilán was following the Chief's instructions. Not so. Or, at least—Ambassador Chirinos empties his glass of whiskey with a malicious glint in his eyes—not so that night, for it might also be true that Don Froilán had done as the Chief ordered and the Chief changed his mind and decided to go on with the farce for a few more days. He would do that sometimes, even if it made his most talented collaborators look ridiculous. Don Froilán Arala's head might display a pair of baroque horns, but it also boasted exceptional brains. The Chief penalized him for his hagiographic speech as he usually did: by humiliating him where it hurt most, in his honor as a man.

All of the local elite were at the reception given for the Chief by the leaders of the Dominican Party of Barahona. They danced and drank. Suddenly, when it was very late, the Chief, feeling very good, before a huge audience composed exclusively of men—military from the local garrison, ministers, senators, and deputies who were accompanying him on the campaign tour, governors, political leaders—whom he had been regaling with recollections of his first campaign tour three decades earlier, and adopting that sentimental, nostalgic look he put on suddenly at the end of parties, as if succumbing to an attack of weakness, exclaimed:

"I have been a well-loved man. A man who has held in his arms the most beautiful women in this country. They have given me the energy to go on. Without them, I never could have done what I did." (He raised his glass to the light, examined the liquid, confirmed its transparency, the sharpness of its color.) "Do you know which was the best of all the cunts I fucked?" ("Forgive me, my friends, for the vulgarity," the diplomat apologized, "I'm quoting Trujillo exactly.") (He paused again, inhaled the bouquet of his glass of brandy. The silvery head looked for and found, in the circle of gentlemen listening to him, the fat, livid face of the minister. And he concluded:) "Froilán's wife!"

Urania grimaces in disgust, as she had on the night when she heard Ambassador Chirinos add that Don Froilán had smiled heroically, laughed, celebrated with the others the Chief's witticism. "White as a sheet, not fainting, not falling down with a heart attack," declared the diplomat.

"How was it possible, Papa? How could a man like Froilán Arala, cultured, educated, intelligent, accept that? What did he do to all of you? What did he give you that turned Don Froilán, Chirinos, Manuel Alfonso, you, all his right- and left-hand men, into filthy rags?"

You don't understand, Urania, though there are many things about the Era that you've come to understand; at first, some of them seemed impenetrable, but after reading, listening, investigating, thinking, you've come to understand how so many millions of people, crushed by propaganda and lack of information, brutalized by indoctrination and isolation, deprived of free will and even curiosity by fear and the habit of servility and obsequiousness, could worship Trujillo. Not merely fear him but love him, as children eventually love authoritarian parents, convincing themselves that the whippings and beatings are for their own good. But what you've never understood is how the best-educated Dominicans, the intellectuals of the country, the lawyers, doctors, engineers, often graduates of very good universities in the

United States or Europe, sensitive, cultivated men of experience, wide reading, ideas, presumably possessing a highly developed sense of the ridiculous, men of feeling and scruples, could allow themselves to be as savagely abused (they all were, at one time or another) as Don Froilán Arala was that night in Barahona.

"Too bad you can't speak," she repeats, returning to the present. "We'd try to understand it, together. What made Don Froilán maintain a slavish loyalty to Trujillo? He was loyal to the end, like you. He didn't take part in the conspiracy, and neither did you. He went on licking the hand of the Chief who boasted in Barahona that he had fucked his wife. The Chief who kept him traveling through South America as Chancellor of the Republic, visiting governments from Buenos Aires to Caracas, from Caracas to Rio or Brasília, from Brasília to Montevideo, from Montevideo to Caracas, just so he could go on fucking our beautiful neighbor in peace."

It is an image that has pursued Urania for a long time, one that makes her laugh and makes her indignant. The image of the Era's Minister of Foreign Affairs getting in and out of planes, traveling to South American capitals, obeying the peremptory orders that waited for him at every airport so he would continue his hysterical journey, pestering governments for inane reasons. Just to keep him from returning to Ciudad Trujillo while the Chief was screwing his wife. Crassweller himself, the best-known biographer of Trujillo, mentioned it. So everybody knew, including Don Froilán.

"Was it worth it, Papa? Was it for the illusion that you were wielding power? Sometimes I think it wasn't, that success was secondary. That you, Arala, Pichardo, Chirinos, Álvarez Pina, Manuel Alfonso, really liked getting dirty. That Trujillo pulled a vocation for masochism up from the bottom of your souls, that you were people who needed to be spat on and mistreated and debased in order to be fulfilled."

The invalid looks at her without blinking, without moving his lips or the small hands resting on his knees. Like a mummy, a small embalmed man, a wax doll. His robe is faded, threadbare in places. It must be very old, bought ten or fifteen years ago. There's a knock on the door. She says "Come in," and the nurse appears, carrying a plate with pieces of mango cut into half-moon shapes and some mashed apple or banana.

"At midmorning I always give him some fruit," she explains from the door. "The doctor says his stomach shouldn't be empty for too long. Since he barely eats, I have to feed him three or four times a day. At night, just some broth. May I?"

"Yes, come in."

Urania looks at her father and his eyes remain on her; they don't move to look at the nurse even when she sits in front of him and begins to give him little spoonfuls of food.

"Where are his dentures?"

"We had to take them out. He's gotten so thin they made his gums bleed. For what he eats, broth, cut-up fruit, purees, things from the blender, he doesn't need them."

For a long while they are silent. When the invalid finishes swallowing, the nurse brings the spoon up to his lips and waits patiently for the old man to open his mouth. Then, delicately, she gives him the next mouthful. Does she always do this? Or is her delicacy due to the presence of his daughter? No question. When she's alone with him she must scold him and pinch him, like nannies with babies who don't talk yet, when their mothers can't see them.

"Give him a few mouthfuls," says the nurse. "He wants you to. Isn't that right, Don Agustín? You want your daughter to give you this nice food, don't you? Yes, yes, he'd like that. Give him a few mouthfuls while I go downstairs for his glass of water. I forgot it."

She places the half-empty plate in Urania's hands, who accepts it mechanically, and she goes out, leaving the door open. After hesitating a few moments, Urania brings the spoon that holds a slice of mango up to his mouth. The invalid, who has still not taken his eyes off her, closes his mouth, clenching his lips like a difficult child.

5 "Good morning," he replied.

Colonel Johnny Abbes had placed on his desk the daily morning report on the previous night's events, along with warnings and suggestions. He liked reading them; the colonel didn't waste time on stupid shit, like the former head of the SIM, General Arturo R. Espaillat (Razor), a graduate of West Point who'd bored him with his lunatic strategies. Had Razor worked for the CIA? They assured him he had. But Johnny Abbes couldn't confirm it. If there was anybody not working for the CIA it was the colonel: he hated the Yankees.

"Coffee, Excellency?"

Johnny Abbes was in uniform. Though he made an effort to wear it with the correctness Trujillo demanded, he could not do more than his flaccid, misshapen physique allowed. Fairly short, with a protruding belly that complemented his dewlaps, and a prominent chin divided by a deep cleft. His cheeks were flabby too. Only his cruel, shifting eyes revealed the intelligence behind the physical calamity. He was thirty-five or thirty-six years old but looked like an old man. He hadn't gone to West Point or to any military academy; he wouldn't have been admitted, for he lacked a soldier's physique and a military vocation. He was what Gittleman, the Benefactor's instructor when he was a Marine, would have called "a toad in body and soul": no muscles, too much fat, and an excessive fondness for intrigue. Trujillo made him a colonel overnight when, in one of those inspirations that marked his political career, he decided to name him head of the SIM to replace Razor. Why did he do it? Not because Abbes was cruel but because he was cold: the iciest individual Trujillo had ever known in this country of hot bodies and souls. Was it a fortunate decision? Recently the colonel had made errors. The failed attempt on the life of President Betancourt was not the only one; he had also been wrong about the supposed uprising against Fidel Castro by Commanders Eloy Gutiérrez Menoyo and William Morgan, which had turned out to be a trick by the Beard to draw Cuban exiles to the island and capture them. The Benefactor was thoughtful as he turned the pages of the report and sipped his coffee.

"You insist on pulling Bishop Reilly out of Santo Domingo Academy," he murmured. "Sit down, have some coffee."

"If you'll permit me, Excellency?"

The colonel's melodious voice dated from his youth, when he had been a radio announcer commenting on baseball, basketball, and horse races. From that period, he had kept only his fondness for esoteric reading—he admitted he was a Rosicrucian—the handkerchiefs he dyed red because, he said, it was a lucky color for an Aries, and his ability to see each person's aura (all of it bullshit that made the Generalissimo laugh). He settled himself in front of the Chief's desk, holding a cup of coffee in his hand. It was still dark outside, and the office was half in shadow, barely lit by a small lamp that enclosed Trujillo's hands in a golden circle.

"That abscess must be lanced, Excellency. Our biggest problem isn't Kennedy, he's too busy with the failure of his Cuban invasion. It's the Church. If we don't put an end to the fifth columnists here, we'll have problems. Reilly serves the purposes of those who demand an invasion. Every day they make him more important, while they pressure the White House to send in the Marines to help the poor, persecuted bishop. Don't forget, Kennedy's a Catholic."

"We're all Catholics," Trujillo said with a sigh. And demolished the colonel's argument: "That's a reason not to touch him. It would give the gringos the excuse they're looking for."

Though there were times when the colonel's frankness displeased Trujillo, he tolerated it. The head of the SIM had orders to speak to him with absolute sincerity even when it might offend his ears. Razor didn't dare use that prerogative in the way Johnny Abbes did.

"I don't think we can go back to our old relationship with the Church, that thirty-year idyll is over," Abbes said slowly, his eyes like quicksilver in their sockets, as if searching the area for ambushes. "They declared war on us on January 24, 1960, with their Bishops' Pastoral Letter, and their goal is to destroy the regime. A few concessions won't satisfy the priests. They won't support you again, Excellency. The Church wants war, just like the Yankees. And in war there are only two options: surrender to the enemy or defeat him. Bishops Panal and Reilly are in open rebellion."

Colonel Abbes had two plans. One, to use the *paleros*—thugs armed with clubs and knives led by Balá, an ex-convict in his service—as a shield while the *caliés* rioted, pretending to be recalcitrant groups that had broken away from large protest demonstrations against the terrorist bishops in La Vega and at Santo Domingo Academy, and killed the prelates before the police could rescue them. This formula was risky; it might provoke an invasion. The advantage was that the death of the two bishops would paralyze the rest of the clergy for a long time to come. In the other plan, the police rescued Panal and Reilly before they could be lynched by a mob, and the government deported them to Spain and the United States, arguing that this was the only way to guarantee their safety. Congress would pass a law establishing that all priests who exercised their ministry in the country had to be Dominicans by birth. Foreigners or naturalized citizens would be returned to their own countries. In this way—the colonel consulted a notebook—the Catholic clergy would be reduced by a third. The minority of native-born priests would be manageable.

He stopped speaking when the Benefactor, whose head had been lowered, looked up.

"That's what Fidel Castro did in Cuba."

Johnny Abbes nodded:

"There the Church started out with protests too, and ended up conspiring to prepare the way for the Yankees. Castro threw out the foreign priests and took drastic measures against the ones who were left. What happened to him? Nothing."

"*So far*," the Benefactor corrected him. "Kennedy will send the Marines to Cuba any day now. And this time it won't be the kind of mess they made last month at the Bay of Pigs."

"In that case, the Beard will die fighting," Johnny Abbes agreed. "And it isn't impossible that the Marines will land here. And you've decided that we'll die fighting too."

Trujillo gave a mocking little laugh. If they had to die fighting the Marines, how many Dominicans would sacrifice themselves with him? The soldiers would, no doubt about that. They proved it during the invasion sent by Fidel on June 14, 1959. They fought well, they wiped out the invaders in just a few days, in the mountains of Costanza, on the beaches of Maimón and Estero Hondo. But the Marines . . .

"I won't have many with me, I'm afraid. The rats running away will raise a dust storm. But you won't have a choice, you'll have to die with me. Wherever you go you'll face jail, or assassination by the enemies you have all over the world."

"I've made them defending the regime, Excellency."

"Of all the men around me, the only one who couldn't betray me, even if he wanted to, is you," an amused Trujillo insisted. "I'm the only person you can get close to, the only one who doesn't hate you or dream about killing you. We're married till death do us part."

He laughed again, in a good humor, examining the colonel the way an entomologist examines an insect difficult to classify. They said a lot of things about Abbes, especially about his cruelty. It was an advantage for somebody in his position. They said, for example, that his father, an American of German descent, found little Johnny, still in short pants, sticking pins into the eyes of chicks in the henhouse. That as a young man he sold medical students cadavers he had robbed from graves in Independencia Cemetery. That though he was married to Lupita, a hideous Mexican, hard as nails, who carried a pistol in her handbag, he was a faggot. Even that he had gone to bed with Kid Trujillo, the Generalissimo's half brother.

"You've heard what they say about you," he said, looking him in the eye and laughing. "Some of it must be true. Did you like poking out chickens' eyes when you were a kid? Did you rob the graves at Independencia Cemetery and sell the corpses?"

The colonel barely smiled.

"The first probably isn't true, I don't remember doing it. The second is only half true. They weren't cadavers, Excellency. Bones and skulls washed up to the surface by the rain. To earn a few pesos. Now they say that as head of the SIM, I'm returning the bones."

"And what about you being a faggot?"

The colonel didn't become upset this time either. His voice maintained a clinical indifference.

"I've never gone in for that, Excellency. I've never gone to bed with a man."

"Okay, enough bullshit," he cut him off, becoming serious. "Don't touch the bishops, for now. We'll see how things develop. If they can be punished, we'll do it. For the moment, just keep an eye on them. Go on with the war of nerves. Don't let them sleep or eat in peace. Maybe they'll decide to leave on their own."

Would the two bishops get their way and be as smug as that black bastard Betancourt? Again he felt his anger rise. That rat in Caracas had gotten the OAS to sanction the Dominican Republic and pressured the member countries to break off relations and apply economic pressures that were strangling the nation. Each day, each hour, they were damaging what had been a brilliant economy. And Betancourt was still alive, the standard-bearer of freedom, displaying his burned hands on television, proud of having survived a stupid attempt that never should have been left to those assholes in the Venezuelan military. Next time the SIM would run everything. In his technical, impersonal way, Abbes explained the new operation that would culminate in the powerful explosion, set off by remote control, of a device purchased for a king's ransom in Czechoslovakia and stored now at the Dominican consulate in Haiti. It would be easy to take it from there to Caracas at the opportune moment.

Ever since 1958, when he decided to promote him to the position he now held, the Benefactor had met every day with the colonel, in this office, at Mahogany House, wherever he might be, and always at this time of day. Like the Generalissimo, Johnny Abbes never took a vacation. Trujillo first heard about him from General Espaillat. The former head of the Intelligence Service had surprised him with a precise, detailed report on Dominican exiles in Mexico City: what they were doing, what they were plotting, where they lived, where they met, who was helping them, which diplomats they visited.

"How many people do you have in Mexico to be so well informed about those bastards?"

"All the information comes from one person, Excellency." Razor gestured with professional satisfaction. "He's very young. Johnny Abbes García. Perhaps you've met his father, a half-German gringo who came here to work for the electric company and married a Dominican. The boy was a sports reporter and something of a poet. I began to use him as an informant on people in radio and the press, and at the Gómez Pharmacy gatherings that the intellectuals attend. He did so well I sent him to Mexico City on a phony scholarship. And now, as you can see, he's gained the confidence of the entire exile community. He gets on well with everybody. I don't know how he does it, Excellency, but in Mexico he even got close to Lombardo Toledano, the leftist union leader. Imagine, the ugly broad he married was secretary to that Red."

Poor Razor! By talking so enthusiastically, he began to lose the directorship of the Intelligence Service that he had trained for at West Point.

"Bring him here, give him a job where I can watch him," Trujillo ordered.

That was how the awkward, unprepossessing figure with the perpetually darting eyes had appeared in the corridors of the National Palace. He occupied a low-level position in the Office of Information. Trujillo studied him at a distance. From the time he had been very young, in San Cristóbal, he had followed those intuitions which, after a simple glance, a brief chat, a mere allusion, made him certain a person could be useful to him. That was how he chose many of his collaborators, and he hadn't done too badly. For several weeks Johnny Abbes García worked in an obscure office, under the direction of the poet Ramón Emilio Jiménez, along with Dipp Velarde Font, Querol, and Grimaldi, writing supposed letters from readers to "The Public Forum" in the paper *El Caribe*. Before putting him to the test, he waited for a sign, not knowing exactly what form it would take. It came in the most unexpected way, on the day he saw Johnny Abbes in a Palace corridor conversing with one of his ministers. What did the meticulous, pious, austere Joaquín Balaguer have to talk about with Razor's informant?

"Nothing in particular, Excellency," Balaguer explained when it was time for his ministerial meeting. "I did not know the young man. When I saw him so absorbed in his reading, for he was reading as he walked, my curiosity was piqued. You know how much I love books. I could not have been more astonished. He cannot be in his right mind. Do you know what he was enjoying so much? A book about Chinese tortures, with photographs of those who had been decapitated and skinned alive."

That night he sent for him. Abbes seemed so overwhelmed—with joy, fear, or both—by the unexpected honor that he could hardly get the words out when he greeted the Benefactor.

"You did good work in Mexico," he said in the sharp, high-pitched voice that, like his gaze, had a paralyzing effect on his interlocutors. "Espaillat told me about it. I think you can take on more serious tasks. Are you interested?"

"Anything Your Excellency desires." He stood motionless, his feet together, like a student in front of his teacher.

"Did you know José Almoina in Mexico? A Galician who came here with the Republican exiles from Spain."

"Yes, Excellency. I mean, only by sight. But I did know many people in the group he meets with in the Café Comercio. They call themselves 'Dominican Spaniards.' "

"This individual published a book attacking me, *A Satrapy in the Caribbean,* that was paid for by the Guatemalan government. He used an alias, Gregorio Bustamante. Then, to throw us off the track, he had the gall to publish another book in Argentina, *I Was Trujillo's Secretary,* and this time he used his own name and praised me to the skies. That was several years ago, and he feels safe there in Mexico. He thinks I've forgotten that he defamed my family and the regime that fed him. There's no statute of limitations on crimes like that. Do you want to take care of it?"

"It would be a great honor, Excellency," Abbes García responded immediately, with a confidence he had not shown until that moment.

Some time later, the Generalissimo's former secretary, private tutor to Ramfis, and hack writer for Doña María Martínez, the Bountiful First Lady, died in the Mexican capital in a rain of bullets. There was the obligatory outcry from the exiles and the press, but no one could prove, as they claimed, that the assassination had been the work of "the long arm of Trujillo." A fast, impeccable operation that cost less than fifteen hundred dollars, according to the bill submitted by Johnny Abbes García on his return from Mexico. The Benefactor inducted him into the Army with the rank of colonel.

The elimination of José Almoina was just one in the long series of brilliant operations carried out by the colonel, killing or maiming or severely wounding dozens of the most outspoken exiles in Cuba, Mexico, Guatemala, New York, Costa Rica, and Venezuela. Lightning-quick, clean pieces of work that impressed the Benefactor. Each one a small masterpiece in its skill and secrecy, the work of a watchmaker. Most of the time, in addition to killing off enemies, Abbes García arranged to ruin their reputations. The unionist Roberto Lamada, a refugee in Havana, died of a beating he received in a brothel in the Barrio Chino at the hands of hoodlums who filed a complaint against him with the police, charging him with attempting to stab a prostitute who refused to submit to the sadomasochistic perversions the exile had demanded; the woman, a tearful mulatta with dyed red hair, appeared in *Carteles* and *Bohemia*, displaying the wounds the degenerate had inflicted on her. The lawyer Bayardo Cipriota perished in Caracas in a homosexual dispute: he was found stabbed to death in a cheap hotel, wearing panties and a bra, with lipstick on his mouth. The forensic examination determined that he had sperm in his rectum. How did Colonel Abbes manage to establish contact so rapidly, in cities he barely knew, with denizens of the underworld, the gangsters, killers, traffickers, thugs, prostitutes, pimps, and pickpockets, who were always involved in the scandals, the delight of the sensationalist press, in which the regime's enemies found themselves embroiled? How did he set up so efficient a network of informants and thugs throughout most of Latin America and the United States and spend so little money? Trujillo's time was too valuable to be wasted checking into details. But from a distance he admired, like a connoisseur with a precious jewel, the subtlety and originality with which Johnny Abbes García rid the regime of its enemies. Exile groups and hostile governments could never establish any link between these horrendous acts and the Generalissimo. One of his most perfect achievements had to do with Ramón Marrero Aristy, the author of *Over*, a novel, known all over Latin America, about sugarcane cutters in La Romana. The former editor of *La Nación*, a frantically Trujillista newspaper, Marrero had been Minister of Labor in 1956, and again in 1959, when he began to send reports to Tad Szulc, a journalist, so that he could defame the regime in his articles for *The New York Times*. When he was found out, Marrero sent retractions to the gringo paper. And came with his tail between his legs to Trujillo's office to crawl, cry, beg forgiveness, and swear he had never betrayed him and never would betray him. The Benefactor listened without saying a word and then, coldly, he slapped him. Marrero, who was sweating, reached for his handkerchief, and Colonel

Guarionex Estrella Sadhalá, head of the military adjutants, shot him dead right there in the office. Abbes García was charged with finishing the operation, and less than an hour later a car skidded—in front of witnesses—over a precipice in the Cordillera Central on the road to Constanza; in the crash Marrero Aristy and his driver were burned beyond recognition. Wasn't it obvious that Colonel Johnny Abbes García ought to replace Razor as the head of the Intelligence Service? If he had been running the agency when Galíndez was kidnapped in New York, an operation directed by Espaillat, the scandal that did so much harm to the regime's international image probably would never have come to light.

Trujillo pointed at the report on his desk with a contemptuous air:

"Another conspiracy to kill me led by Juan Tomás Díaz? And organized by Consul Henry Dearborn, the asshole from the CIA?"

Colonel Abbes García abandoned his immobility long enough to shift his buttocks in the chair.

"That's what it looks like, Excellency." He nodded, not attributing too much importance to the matter.

"It's funny," Trujillo interrupted him. "They broke off relations with us, obeying the OAS resolution. And called home their diplomats but left us Henry Dearborn and his agents so they could keep on cooking up plots. Are you sure Juan Tomás is part of it?"

"No, Excellency, just some vague hints. But ever since you dismissed him, General Díaz has been seething with resentment and that's why I keep a close eye on him. There are these meetings at his house in Gazcue. You should always expect the worst from a resentful man."

"It wasn't the dismissal," Trujillo said aloud as if talking to himself. "It was because I called him a coward. To remind him he had dishonored the uniform."

"I was at that luncheon, Excellency. I thought General Díaz would get up and leave. But he stayed, turned pale, broke into a sweat. When he left he was staggering, like a drunk."

"Juan Tomás was always very proud, and he needed a lesson," said Trujillo. "He conducted himself like a weakling in Constanza. I don't allow weak generals in the Dominican Armed Forces."

The incident had occurred a few months after the defeat of the landings at Constanza, Maimón, and Estero Hondo, when all the members of the expeditionary force—including Cubans, North Americans, and Venezuelans, in addition to Dominicans—were either dead or in prison, and the regime discovered, in January 1960, a vast network of clandestine opposition called June 14, in honor of the invasion. Its members were students and young professionals of the middle and upper classes, many from families that were part of the regime. At the height of a cleanup operation against the subversive organization, in which the three Mirabal sisters and their husbands were very active—the mere thought of them made the Generalissimo's blood boil—Trujillo held a luncheon in the National Palace for some fifty military and civilian figures prominent in the regime, in order to punish his boyhood friend and comrade in arms, who had held the highest positions in the Armed Forces during the Era and whom he had dismissed as commander of the Military Region of La Vega, which included Constanza, because he had not exterminated the last concentrations of invaders scattered across the mountains. General Juan Tomás Díaz had been asking in vain for an audience with the Generalissimo ever since. He must have been surprised to receive an invitation to the luncheon, after his brother Gracita sought asylum in the Brazilian embassy. The Chief did not greet him or say a word to him during the meal, and did not even glance at the corner where General Díaz was seated, far from the head of the long table, a symbolic indication of his fall from grace.

Suddenly, as they were serving the coffee, over the conversations buzzing around the long table, over the marble of the walls and the crystal of the blazing chandelier—the only woman present was Isabel Mayer, the Trujillista caudilla in the northeast—the thin, sharp voice known to all Dominicans rose, taking on the steel-barbed tone that foretold a storm:

"Aren't you surprised, gentlemen, by the presence at this table, surrounded by the most outstanding military and civilian figures in the regime, of an officer stripped of his command because he was not equal to the task on the field of battle?"

Silence fell. The fifty heads flanking the huge quadrangle of embroidered tablecloths all froze. The Benefactor did not look toward General Díaz's corner. He inspected the other diners one by one, a surprised expression on his face, his eyes very wide and his lips parted, asking his guests to help him solve the mystery.

"Do you know who I mean?" he continued, after a dramatic pause.

"General Juan Tomás Díaz, Commander of the Military Region of La Vega at the time of the Cuban-Venezuelan invasion, was dismissed in the middle of the war for conduct unbecoming an officer in the face of the enemy. Anywhere else, such behavior is punished with a summary court-martial and a firing squad. Under the dictatorship of Rafael Leonidas Trujillo Molina, the cowardly general is invited to lunch at the Palace with the nation's elite."

He said the last sentence very slowly, syllable by syllable, to emphasize his sarcasm.

"If you'll permit me, Excellency," stammered General Juan Tomás Díaz, making a superhuman effort, "I'd like to recall that at the time of my dismissal, the invaders had been defeated. I did my duty."

He was a strong, robust man, but he had shrunk in his seat. He was very pale and his mouth kept filling with saliva. He looked at the Benefactor, but he, as if he had not seen or heard him, glanced around for a second time at his guests and spoke again:

"And not only is he invited to the Palace. He goes into retirement with full salary and all the prerogatives of a three-star general, so that he can rest knowing he did his duty. And enjoy a well-deserved leisure on his cattle ranches, in the company of Chana Díaz, his fifth wife, who is also his niece, his brother's daughter. What greater proof of the magnanimity of this bloodthirsty dictatorship?"

When he finished speaking, the Benefactor's head had looked all around the table. And now it stopped at the corner where General Juan Tomás Díaz was sitting. The Chief's face was no longer the ironic, melodramatic one it had been a moment before. It was frozen in deadly seriousness. His eyes had taken on the solemn fixity, piercing and merciless, with which he reminded people who it was who ruled this country and the lives of Dominicans. Juan Tomás Díaz looked down.

"General Díaz refused to follow an order of mine and permitted himself to reprimand an officer who was carrying it out," he said slowly, scornfully. "At the height of the invasion. When our enemies, armed by Fidel Castro, by Muñoz Marín, Betancourt and Figueres, that envious mob, had ruthlessly landed and murdered Dominican soldiers, determined to have the heads of every one of us sitting at this table. That was when the military commander of La Vega discovered he was a compassionate man. A delicate man, an enemy of violent passions, who could not bear to watch the shedding of blood. And he permitted himself to disregard my order to shoot in the field every invader captured with a gun in his hand. And to insult an officer who, respectful of the chain of command, gave their just deserts to those who came here to install a Communist dictatorship. The general permitted himself, in that time of danger for the Fatherland, to sow confusion and weaken the morale of our soldiers. That is why he is no longer part of the Army, even though he still puts on the uniform."

He stopped speaking in order to take a drink of water. But as soon as he had, instead of continuing, he stood abruptly and took his leave, bringing the luncheon to an end: "Good afternoon, gentlemen."

"Juan Tomás didn't try to leave, because he knew he wouldn't have reached the door alive," said Trujillo. "Well, what conspiracy is he involved in?"

Nothing very concrete, really. For some time, at his house in Gazcue, General Díaz and his wife, Chana, had been receiving many visitors. The pretext was seeing movies, shown outdoors in the courtyard, with a projector run by the general's son-in-law. Those attending were a strange mixture. From well-known men in the regime, like the host's father-in-law and brother, Modesto Díaz Quesada, to former officials who were distant from the government, like Amiama Tió and Antonio de la Maza. Colonel Abbes García had made one of the servants a *calié* a few months ago. But the only thing he found out was that the gentlemen talked constantly while they watched the films, as if they were interested in the movies only because they could muffle their conversations. In short, these weren't the kinds of meetings where bad things were said about the regime between drinks of rum or whiskey, the kind worth keeping in mind. Except that yesterday, General Díaz had a secret meeting with an emissary of Henry Dearborn, the supposed Yankee diplomat who, as Your Excellency knows, is the head of the CIA in Ciudad Trujillo.

"He probably asked a million dollars for my head," Trujillo remarked. "The gringo must be dizzy with so many shiteaters asking for financial aid to finish me off. Where did they meet?"

"In the Hotel El Embajador, Excellency."

The Benefactor thought for a moment. Would Juan Tomás be capable of organizing something serious? Twenty years ago, maybe. He was a man of action back then. But he had become a pleasure seeker. He liked drinking and cockfights too much, and eating, having a good time with his friends, getting married and unmarried—he wouldn't risk it all trying to overthrow him. The gringos were leaning on a weak branch. Bah, there was nothing to worry about.

"I agree, Excellency, for the moment I think General Díaz presents no danger. I'm following his every move. We know who visits him and who he visits. His telephone is tapped."

Was there anything else? The Benefactor glanced at the window: it was still dark, even though it would soon be six o'clock. But it was no longer silent. In the distance, along the periphery of the National Palace, separated from the street by a vast expanse of lawn and trees and surrounded by a high spiked fence, an occasional car passed, blowing its horn, and inside the building he could hear the cleaning staff, mopping, sweeping, waxing, shaking out the dust. He would find offices and corridors clean and shining when he had to cross them. This idea produced a sense of well-being.

"Excuse me for insisting, Excellency, but I'd like to reestablish security arrangements. On Máximo Gómez and the Malecón, when you take your walk. And on the highway, when you go to Mahogany House."

A couple of months earlier he had abruptly ordered a halt to security operations. Why? Perhaps because during one of his excursions at dusk, as he was coming down Máximo Gómez on the way to the ocean, he saw police barricades at every intersection blocking pedestrian and car access to the Avenida and the Malecón while he was on his walk. And he imagined the flood of Volkswagens with *caliés* that Johnny Abbes had unleashed on the area all around his route. He felt stifled, claustrophobic. It had also happened at night, on his way to the Fundación Ranch, when all along the highway he saw the Beetles and the military barricades guarding his passage. Or was it the fascination that danger had always held for him—the indomitable spirit of a Marine—that led him to defy fate at the moment of greatest danger for the regime? In any case, it was a decision he would not revoke.

"The order stands," he repeated in a tone that allowed no discussion.

"As you wish, Excellency."

He looked into the colonel's eyes—Abbes immediately lowered them—and he skewered him, with a humorous barb:

"Do you think the Fidel Castro you admire so much walks the streets like me, without protection?"

The colonel shook his head.

"I don't believe Fidel Castro is as romantic as you are, Excellency."

Romantic? Him? Maybe with some of the women he had loved, maybe with Lina Lovatón. But, outside the sentimental arena, in politics, he had always felt classical. Rational, serene, pragmatic, with a cool head and a long view.

"When I met him, in Mexico, he was preparing the expedition of the *Granma*. They thought he was a crazed Cuban, an adventurer not worth taking seriously. From the very first, what struck me was his total lack of emotion. Even though in his speeches he seems tropical, exuberant, passionate. That's for his audience. He's just the opposite. An icy intelligence. I always knew he'd take power. But allow me to clarify something, Excellency. I admire Castro's personality, the way he's been able to play the gringos for fools, allying himself with the Russians and the Communist countries and using them against Washington, like the bumpers on a car. But I don't admire his ideas, I'm not a Communist."

"You're a capitalist through and through," Trujillo said mockingly, with a sardonic laugh. "Ultramar did very well, importing products from Germany, Austria, and the socialist countries. Exclusive distributorships never lose money."

"Something else to thank you for, Excellency," the colonel admitted. "The truth is, I never would have thought of it. I never had any interest in business. I opened Ultramar because you ordered me to."

"I prefer my collaborators to make a profit instead of stealing," the Benefactor explained. "Profits help the country, they create jobs, produce wealth, raise the morale of the people. But stealing demoralizes it. I imagine that since the sanctions things are going badly for Ultramar too."

"Practically paralyzed. I don't care, Excellency. Now my twenty-four hours a day are dedicated to keeping our enemies from destroying this regime and killing you."

He spoke without emotion, in the same opaque, neutral tone he normally used to express himself.

"Should I conclude that you admire me as much as you do that asshole Castro?" Trujillo asked, searching out those small, evasive eyes.

"I don't admire you, Excellency," Colonel Abbes murmured, lowering his eyes. "I live for you. Through you. If you'll permit me, I am your watchdog."

It seemed to the Benefactor that when Abbes García said these words, his voice had trembled. He knew Abbes was in no way emotional, not fond of the effusiveness that was so frequent in the mouths of his other courtiers, and so he continued to scrutinize him with his knifelike gaze.

"If I'm killed, it will be by someone very close, a traitor in the family, so to speak," he said, as if talking about someone else. "For you, it would be a great misfortune."

"And for the country, Excellency?"

"That's why I'm still in the saddle," Trujillo agreed. "Otherwise I would have retired, as I was advised to do by my Yankee friends who were sent down here by President Eisenhower: William Pawley, General Clark, Senator Smathers. 'Go down in history as a magnanimous statesman who turned the helm over to younger men.' That's what Roosevelt's friend Smathers told me. It was a message from the White House. That's why they came. To ask me to leave and to offer me asylum in the United States. 'Your patrimony will be safe there.' Those assholes confuse me with Batista, with Rojas Pinilla and Pérez Jiménez. They'll only get me out when I'm dead."

The Benefactor became distracted again, thinking about Guadalupe, Lupe to her friends, the fat, mannish Mexican Johnny Abbes married during that mysterious, adventurous period of his life in Mexico when he was sending detailed reports to Razor on the activities of the Dominican exiles, and at the same time frequenting revolutionary circles, like the one made up of Fidel Castro, Che Guevara, and the July 26 Cubans, who were preparing the expedition of the *Granma*, and people like Vicente Lombardo Toledano, closely connected to the Mexican government, who had been his protector. The Generalissimo had never had time to question him calmly about that period in his life, when the colonel discovered his vocation and talent for espionage and clandestine operations. A juicy life, no doubt about it, full of anecdotes. Why had he ever married that awful woman?

"There's something I always forget to ask you," he said with the vulgarity he used when speaking to his collaborators. "How did you ever marry such an ugly woman?"

He did not detect the slightest sign of surprise on Abbes García's face.

"It wasn't for love, Excellency."

"I always knew that," said the Benefactor, smiling. "She isn't rich, so you didn't do it for money."

"It was gratitude. Lupe saved my life once. She's killed for me.

When she was Lombardo Toledano's secretary and I had just come to Mexico. Thanks to Vicente I began to understand politics. Much of what I've done wouldn't have been possible without Lupe, Excellency. She doesn't know the meaning of fear. And until now her instincts have never failed."

"I know she's tough, and knows how to fight, and carries a pistol and goes to whorehouses like a man," said the Generalissimo, in excellent humor. "I've even heard that Puchita Brazobán saves girls for her. But what intrigues me is that you've been able to make babies with that freak."

"I try to be a good husband, Excellency."

The Benefactor began to laugh, the sonorous laughter of other days.

"You can be amusing when you want to be," he congratulated him. "So you took her out of gratitude. And you can get it up whenever you want to."

"In a manner of speaking, Excellency. The truth is, I don't love Lupe and she doesn't love me. At least not in the way people understand love. We're united by something stronger. Dangers shared shoulder to shoulder, staring death in the face. And lots of blood, on both of us."

The Benefactor nodded. He understood what he meant. He would have liked to have a wife like that hag, damn it. He wouldn't have felt so alone when he had to make certain decisions. It was true, there were no ties like blood. That must be why he felt so tied to this country of ingrates, cowards, and traitors. Because in order to pull it out of backwardness, chaos, ignorance, and barbarism, he had often been stained with blood. Would these assholes thank him for it in the future?

Again he felt demoralized and crushed. Pretending to check his watch, he glanced out of the corner of his eye at his trousers. No stain at all on the crotch or on his fly. Knowing that did not raise his spirits. Again the memory of the girl at Mahogany House crossed his mind. An unpleasant episode. Would it have been better to shoot her on the spot, while she was looking at him with those eyes? Nonsense. He never had fired a gun gratuitously, least of all for things in bed. Only when there was no alternative, when it was absolutely necessary to move this country forward, or to wash away an insult.

"If you'll permit me, Excellency."

"Yes?"

"President Balaguer announced last night on the radio that the government would free a group of political prisoners."

"Balaguer did what I ordered him to do. Why?"

"I'll need a list of those who'll be freed. So we can give them haircuts, shave them, dress them in decent clothes. I imagine they'll be interviewed by the press."

"I'll send you the list as soon as I look it over. Balaguer thinks these gestures are useful in diplomacy. We'll see. In any case, he made a good presentation."

He had Balaguer's speech on his desk. He read the underlined paragraph aloud: "The work of His Excellency Generalissimo Dr. Rafael L. Trujillo Molina has achieved a solidity that allows us, after thirty years of peaceful order and consecutive leadership, to offer America an example of the Latin American capacity for the conscious exercise of true representative democracy."

"Nicely written, isn't it?" he remarked. "That's the advantage of having a well-read poet as President of the Republic. When my brother was in office, the speeches Blacky gave could put you to sleep. Well, I know you can't stand Balaguer."

"I don't mix my personal likes or dislikes with my work, Excellency."

"I've never understood why you don't trust him. Balaguer is the most inoffensive of my collaborators. That's why I've put him where he is."

"I think his manner, his being so discreet, is a strategy. Deep down he isn't a man of the regime, he works only for Balaguer. Maybe I'm wrong. As for the rest of it, I haven't found anything suspicious in his conduct. But I wouldn't put my hands to the fire for his loyalty."

Trujillo looked at his watch. Two minutes to six. His meeting with Abbes García did not last more than an hour unless there were exceptional circumstances. He stood, and the head of the SIM followed suit.

"If I change my mind about the bishops, I'll let you know," he said by way of dismissal. "Have the plan ready, in any case."

"It can be put into effect the moment you decide. With your permission, Excellency."

As soon as Abbes García left the office, the Benefactor went to look at the sky through the window. Not a glimmer of light yet.

6 "Ah, now I know who it is," said Antonio de la Maza.

He opened the car door, still holding the sawed-off rifle in his hand, and climbed out onto the highway. None of his companions—Tony, Estrella Sadhalá, and Amadito—followed him; from inside the vehicle they watched his robust silhouette, outlined against shadows the faint moonlight barely illuminated, as he moved toward the small Volkswagen that had parked near them, its headlights turned off.

"Don't tell me the Chief changed his mind," Antonio exclaimed by way of greeting as he put his head in the window and brought his face up close to the driver and only occupant, a man in a suit and tie, gasping for breath and so fat it didn't seem possible he could have gotten into the car, where he seemed trapped.

"Not at all, Antonio," Miguel Ángel Báez Díaz reassured him, his hands clutching the wheel. "He's going to San Cristóbal no matter what. He's been delayed because after his walk on the Malecón he took Pupo Román to San Isidro Air Base. I came to put your mind at ease, I could imagine how impatient you were. He'll show up any minute now. Be ready."

"We won't fail, Miguel Ángel, I hope you people won't either."

They talked for a moment, their faces very close together, the fat man holding the wheel and De la Maza constantly looking toward the road from Ciudad Trujillo, afraid the automobile would suddenly materialize and he wouldn't have time to get back to his car.

"Goodbye, good luck with everything," said Miguel Ángel Báez Díaz.

He drove away, heading back to Ciudad Trujillo, his headlights still turned off. Standing on the road, feeling the cool air and listening to the waves breaking a few meters away—he felt drops on his face and scalp, where his hair was beginning to thin—Antonio watched the car disappear in the distance, blending into the night where the lights of the city and its restaurants, filled with people, were twinkling. Miguel Ángel seemed confident. There was no doubt, then: he would come, and on this Tuesday, May 30, 1961, Antonio would at last fulfill the vow he had sworn on the family ranch in Moca, before his father, his brothers and sisters, his brothers- and sisters-in-law, four years and four months ago, on January 7, 1957, the day they buried Tavito.

He thought about how close the Pony was, and how good it would be to have a glass of rum with lots of ice, sitting on one of the rush-bottomed stools at the little bar, as he had so often in recent days, and feel the alcohol going to his head, distracting him, distancing him from Tavito and the bitterness, the frustration, the fever that had been his life since the cowardly murder of his younger brother, the one closest to him, the one he loved best. "Especially after the terrible lies they made up about him, to kill him a second time," he thought. He returned slowly to the Chevrolet. It was a brand-new car that Antonio had imported from the United States and souped up and refined, explaining at the garage that as a landowner, and the manager of a sawmill in Restauración, on the Haitian border, he spent a good part of the year traveling and needed a faster, more reliable car. The time had come to test out this late-model Chevrolet, capable, thanks to adjustments to the cylinders and engine, of reaching two hundred kilometers an hour in a few moments, something the Generalissimo's automobile was in no condition to do. He sat down again next to Antonio Imbert.

"Who was it?" said Amadito from the back seat.

"Those are things you don't ask," muttered Tony Imbert without turning around to look at Lieutenant García Guerrero.

"It's no secret now," said Antonio de la Maza. "It was Miguel Ángel Báez. You were right, Amadito. He's definitely going to San Cristóbal tonight. He was delayed, but he won't leave us hanging."

"Miguel Ángel Báez Díaz?" Salvador Estrella Sadhalá whistled. "He's involved too? You couldn't ask for more. He's the ultimate Trujillista. Wasn't he vice president of the Dominican Party? He's one of the men who walk every day with the Goat along the Malecón, kissing his ass, and go with him every Sunday to the Hipódromo."

"He walked with him today too." De la Maza nodded. "That's why he knows he's coming."

There was a long silence.

"I know we have to be practical, that we need them," Turk said with a sigh. "But I swear it makes me sick that somebody like Miguel Ángel is our ally now."

"Now the saint, the puritan, the little angel with clean hands has been heard from." Imbert made an effort to joke. "You see now, Amadito, why it's better not to ask, better not to know who else is in this?"

"You talk as if all of us hadn't been Trujillistas too, Salvador," Antonio de la Maza growled. "Wasn't Tony governor of Puerto Plata? Isn't Amadito a military adjutant? Haven't I managed the Goat's sawmills in Restauración for the past twenty years? And the construction company where you work, doesn't it belong to Trujillo too?"

"I take it back." Salvador patted De la Maza's arm. "I talk too much and say stupid things. You're right. Anybody could say about us what I just said about Miguel Ángel. I didn't say anything and you didn't hear anything."

But he had said it, because despite his serene, reasonable air that everyone liked so much, Salvador Estrella Sadhalá was capable of saying the cruelest things, driven by a spirit of justice that would suddenly take possession of him. He had said them to Antonio, his lifelong friend, in an argument when De la Maza could have shot him. "I wouldn't sell my brother for a couple of bucks." Those words, which kept them apart, not seeing or talking to each other for more than six months, came back to Antonio from time to time like a recurring nightmare. Then he had to have a lot of rum, one drink after the other. Though with inebriation came those blind rages that made him belligerent and drove him to provoke a fight, punching and kicking anybody near him.

He had turned forty-seven a few days earlier and was one of the oldest in the group of seven men stationed on the highway to San Cristóbal, waiting for Trujillo. In addition to the four in the Chevrolet, Pedro Livio Cedeño and Huáscar Tejeda Pimentel sat two kilometers further on, in a car lent by Estrella Sadhalá, and a kilometer past them, alone in his own vehicle, was Roberto Pastoriza Neret. Their plan was to cut Trujillo off, and in a barrage of fire from the front and the rear, leave him no escape. Pedro Livio and Huáscar must be as edgy as the four of them. And Roberto even worse, with no one to talk to and keep up his spirits. Would he come? Yes, he would come. And the long calvary that Antonio's life had been since the murder of Tavito would end.

The moon, round as a coin and accompanied by a blanket of stars, gleamed and turned the crests of the nearby coconut palms silver; Antonio watched them sway to the rhythm of the breeze. In spite of everything this was a beautiful country, damn it. It would be even more beautiful after they had killed the devil who in thirty-one years had violated and poisoned it more than anything else it had suffered in its history of Haitian occupation, Spanish and American invasions, civil wars, battles among factions and caudillos, and in all the catastrophes—earthquakes, hurricanes—that had assailed Dominicans from the sky, the sea, or the center of the earth. More than anything else, what he could not forgive was that just as he had corrupted and brutalized this country, the Goat had also corrupted and brutalized Antonio de la Maza.

He hid his turmoil from his companions by lighting another cigarette. Without removing the cigarette from his lips, he exhaled smoke from his mouth and nose, caressing the sawed-off rifle, thinking about the steel-reinforced bullets prepared especially for tonight's business by his Spanish friend Bissié, whom he had met through another conspirator, Manuel de Ovín Filpo, and who was a weapons expert and a magnificent shot. Almost as good as Antonio de la Maza, who, since childhood, on the family land at Moca, had always amazed parents, brothers and sisters, relatives, and friends with his shooting. That was why he occupied the privileged seat, to the right of Imbert: so he could shoot first. The group, who argued so much about everything, agreed immediately on that: Antonio de la Maza and Lieutenant García Guerrero, the best marksmen, should carry the rifles supplied to the conspirators by the CIA and sit on the right so they could hit the target with their first shot.

One of the things that made Moca and his family proud was that from the very beginning—1930—the De la Mazas had been anti-Trujillista. Naturally. In Moca everyone, from the most privileged landowner to the poorest peon, was Horacista, because President Horacio Vázquez came from Moca and was the brother of Antonio's mother. Starting on the first day, the De la Mazas viewed with suspicion and antipathy the intrigues employed by the brigadier general at the head of the National Police—created by the Americans during the occupation, it became the Dominican Army when they left—Rafael Leonidas Trujillo, to bring down Don Horacio Vázquez and, in 1930, in the first crooked elections in his long history of electoral fraud, have himself elected President of the Republic. When this occurred, the De la Mazas did what patrician families and regional caudillos traditionally did when they didn't like the government: they took to the mountains with men armed and financed out of their own pockets.

For almost three years, with short-lived intervals of peace, from the time he was seventeen until he was twenty, Antonio de la Maza—an athlete, a tireless horseman, a passionate hunter, high-spirited, bold, and in love with life—along with his father, uncles, and brothers, fought Trujillo's forces with guns, though without much effect. Gradually Trujillo's men dissolved the armed bands, inflicting some defeats but above all buying off their lieutenants and supporters until, weary and almost ruined, the De la Mazas finally accepted the government's peace offers and returned to Moca to work their semi-abandoned land. Except for the indomitable, pigheaded Antonio. He smiled, remembering his stubbornness at the end of 1932 and the beginning of 1933 when, with fewer than twenty men, among them his brothers Ernesto and Tavito, who was still a boy, he attacked police stations and ambushed government patrols. The times were so unusual that despite the military activity, the three brothers could almost always sleep at their family home in Moca several days a month. Until the ambush on the outskirts of Tamboril, when the soldiers killed two of his men and wounded Ernesto, and Antonio himself.

From the Military Hospital in Santiago he wrote to his father, Don Vicente, saying that he regretted nothing and asking that the family please not humble itself by asking Trujillo for clemency. Two days after giving the letter to the head nurse, along with a generous tip to make sure it reached Moca, an Army van came to take him, handcuffed and with a guard, to Santo Domingo. (The Congress of the Republic would not change the name of the ancient city until three years later.) To the surprise of young Antonio de la Maza, the military vehicle, instead of depositing him in prison, took him to Government House, which in those days was near the old cathedral. They removed his handcuffs and led him to a carpeted room, where he found General Trujillo, in uniform, and impeccably shaved and combed.

It was the first time he had seen him.

"You need balls to write a letter like this." The Head of State made it dance in his hand. "You've shown that you have them, making war on me for almost three years. That's why I wanted to see your face. Is it true what they say about your marksmanship? We ought to compete some time and see if it's better than mine."

Twenty-eight years later, Antonio recalled that high-pitched, cutting voice, that unexpected cordiality diluted by a touch of irony. And those penetrating eyes whose gaze he—with all his pride—could not endure.

"The war is over. I've put an end to the power of the regional caudillos, including the De la Mazas. Enough shooting. We have to rebuild the country, which is falling to pieces. I need the best men beside me. You're impulsive and you know how to fight, don't you? Good. Come and work with me. You'll have a chance to do some shooting. I'm offering you a position of trust in the military adjutants assigned to guard me. That way, if I disappoint you one day, you can put a bullet in me."

"But I'm not a soldier," stammered the young De la Maza.

"From this moment on you are," said Trujillo. "Lieutenant Antonio de la Maza."

It was his first concession, his first defeat at the hands of that master manipulator of innocents, fools, and imbeciles, that astute exploiter of men's vanity, greed, and stupidity. For how many years did he have Trujillo less than a meter away? Just like Amadito these past two years. You would have spared the country, and the De la Maza family, so much tragedy if you had done then what you're going to do now. Tavito would certainly still be alive.

Behind him he could hear Amadito and Turk talking; from time to time, Imbert became involved in the conversation. It probably didn't surprise them that Antonio remained silent; he never had much to say, although his taciturnity had deepened into muteness since the death of Tavito, a cataclysm that affected him in a way he knew was irreversible, turning him into a man with a single fixed idea: killing the Goat.

"Juan Tomás's nerves must be in worse shape than ours," he heard

Turk say. "Nothing's more horrible than waiting. But is he coming or not?"

"Any minute now," Lieutenant García Guerrero pleaded. "Trust me, damn it."

Yes, at this moment General Juan Tomás Díaz must have been in his house in Gazcue biting his nails, asking himself if it had finally happened, the thing that Antonio and he had dreamed about, stroked, plotted, kept alive and secret for precisely four years and four months. That is, since the day when, following that damn interview with Trujillo, and with Tavito's body recently buried, Antonio jumped in his car and at a hundred twenty kilometers an hour drove to see Juan Tomás on his ranch in La Vega.

"For the sake of twenty years of friendship, help me, Juan Tomás. I have to kill him! I have to avenge Tavito!"

The general put his hand over his friend's mouth. He looked around, indicating with a gesture that the servants could hear them. He took him behind the stables, where they usually did target practice.

"We'll do it together, Antonio. To avenge Tavito and so many other Dominicans for the shame we carry inside us."

Antonio and Juan Tomás had been close friends since the time De la Maza had been one of the Benefactor's military adjutants. The only good thing he could remember of the two years when as a lieutenant, then as a captain, he shared the Generalissimo's life, accompanying him on his trips into the interior, on his departures from Government House to go to the Congress, the Hipódromo, receptions and performances, political meetings and amorous trysts, visits and appointments with associates, allies, and cronies, public, private, and ultrasecret meetings. Without ever becoming a staunch Trujillista, as Juan Tomás was back then, and though secretly harboring some of the rancor every Horacista felt toward the person who had ended the political career of President Horacio Vázquez, Antonio could not resist the magnetism that radiated from the tireless man who could work for twenty hours and then, after two or three hours of sleep, begin at dawn the next day as fresh as an adolescent. The man who, according to popular legend, did not sweat, did not sleep, never had a wrinkle on his uniform, his tuxedo, or his street clothes, and who, during the years Antonio was part of his iron guard, had, in effect, transformed this country. Not only because of the highways, bridges, and industries he built, but also because in every sphere—political, military, institutional, social, economic—he was amassing such extraordinary power that all the dictators the Dominican Republic had endured in its entire history as a republic—including Ulises Heureaux (Lilís), who had once seemed so merciless—were pygmies compared to him.

In Antonio's case, respect and fascination never turned into admiration, never became the abject, servile love other Trujillistas professed for their leader. Including Juan Tomás, who, since 1957, had explored with him all the possible ways they could rid the Dominican Republic of the figure who was crushing it and sucking it dry, but in the 1940s was a fanatical follower of the Benefactor, capable of committing any crime for the man whom he considered the nation's savior, the statesman who had returned to Dominican control the customs service formerly administered by the Yankees, resolved the problem of foreign debt to the United States and earned the title, granted to him by the Congress, of Restorer of Financial Independence, and created a modern, professional Armed Forces, the best-equipped in the Caribbean. During those years, Antonio would not have dared to speak ill of Trujillo to Juan Tomás Díaz, who scaled the ranks of the Army until he became a three-star general and obtained command of the Military Region of La Vega, where he was caught off guard by the invasion of July 14, 1959, which was the beginning of his fall into disgrace. After that happened, Juan Tomás no longer had any illusions about the regime. When they were alone, when he was sure nobody could hear him, when they were hunting in the hills of Moca or La Vega, during family dinners on Sundays, he confessed to Antonio that everything mortified him—the assassinations, the disappearances, the tortures, the precariousness of life, the corruption, the surrender of body, soul, and conscience by millions of Dominicans to a single man.

Antonio de la Maza had never been a heartfelt Trujillista. Not as a military adjutant, and not later, when after asking for the Chief's permission to leave the military, he worked for him in civilian life, managing the Trujillo family's sawmills in Restauración. He clenched his teeth in disgust: he had never been able to stop working for him. As a soldier or as a civilian, for more than twenty years he had contributed to the fortune and power of the Benefactor and Father of the New Nation. It was the great failure in his life. He never knew how to free himself from the snares Trujillo set for him. Hating him with all his might, he had continued to serve him, even after Tavito's death. That was the reason for Turk's insult: "I wouldn't sell my brother for a couple of bucks." He hadn't sold Tavito. He had dissembled and swallowed his rancor. What else could he do? Let himself be killed by Johnny Abbes's *caliés* so he could die with a clear conscience? It wasn't a clear conscience that Antonio wanted. He wanted revenge for himself and for Tavito. And to get it he had swallowed all the shit in the world during these past four years, even having to hear one of his closest friends say what a good many people, he was sure, repeated behind his back.

He hadn't sold Tavito. His younger brother had been a dear friend. Unlike Antonio, the ingenuous, boyishly innocent Tavito had been a convinced Trujillista, one of those who thought of the Chief as a superior being. They often argued about it, because it irritated Antonio when his younger brother repeated, like a refrain, that Trujillo was heaven's gift to the Republic. Well, it was true, the Generalissimo had done favors for Tavito. Thanks to his orders Tavito had been accepted into the Air Force and learned to fly—his dream since childhood—and then was hired as a pilot for Dominican Airlines, which allowed him to make frequent trips to Miami, something his younger brother loved because he could fuck blondes there. Before that, Tavito had been in London, as military attaché, and in a drunken argument had shot and killed Luis Bernardino, the Dominican consul. Trujillo saved him from prison by claiming he had diplomatic immunity and ordered the court in Ciudad Trujillo, where he was tried, to absolve him. Yes, Tavito had his reasons for feeling grateful to Trujillo and, as he told Antonio, for being "ready to give my life for the Chief and do anything he orders me to." A prophetic statement, damn it.

"Yes, you gave your life for him," Antonio thought as he smoked his cigarette. The affair in which Tavito became embroiled in 1956 had smelled bad to him from the start. His brother came to tell him about it, because Tavito told him everything. Even this, which had the air of one of those murky operations that had filled Dominican history since Trujillo's rise to power. But Tavito, the dumb shit, instead of feeling uneasy, covering his ears, being alarmed at the mission he had been entrusted with—picking up a drugged and masked individual in Montecristi, who was taken off a plane that had come from the United States, and flying him in a small, unregistered Cessna to the Fundación

Ranch in San Cristóbal—was delighted, taking it as a sign that the Generalissimo trusted him. Not even when the press in the United States expressed outrage, and the White House began to pressure the Dominican government to facilitate the investigation into the abduction, in New York, of Professor Jesús de Galíndez, a Spanish Basque, did Tavito show the slightest concern.

"This Galíndez business looks very serious," Antonio warned him. "That's the guy you took from Montecristi to Trujillo's ranch, who else could it be. They kidnapped him in New York and brought him here. Keep your mouth shut. Forget all about it. You're risking your life, Tavito."

Now Antonio de la Maza had a good idea of what happened to Jesús de Galíndez, one of the Spanish Republicans to whom Trujillo, in the kind of contradictory political operation that was his specialty, gave asylum in the Dominican Republic at the end of the Civil War. Antonio hadn't met this professor, but many of his friends had, and from them he learned that he had worked for the government in the State Department of Labor and at the School of Diplomacy, attached to Foreign Relations. In 1946 he left Ciudad Trujillo and settled in New York, where he began to help Dominican exiles and write against the Trujillo regime, which he knew from the inside.

In March 1956, Jesús de Galíndez, who had become an American citizen, disappeared after being seen, for the last time, coming out of a subway station on Broadway, in the heart of Manhattan. A few weeks earlier, publication had been announced of his book on Trujillo; he had submitted it as his doctoral dissertation at Columbia University, where he was already teaching. The disappearance of an obscure Spanish exile, in a city and a country where so many people disappeared, would have passed unnoticed, and no one would have paid attention to the outcry from Dominican exiles, if Galíndez had not been an American citizen and, above all, if he had not worked for the CIA, a fact that was revealed when the scandal broke. The powerful machinery that Trujillo had in the United States—journalists, congressmen, lobbyists, lawyers, and promoters—could not contain the explosion of indignation in the press, beginning with *The New York Times*, and among many representatives in Congress, at the possibility that a tinhorn Caribbean dictator would dare to abduct and murder an American citizen on American soil.

In the weeks and months that followed the disappearance of Galíndez, whose body was never found, the investigation by the press and the FBI unequivocally proved the regime's complete responsibility. A short while before it happened, General Espaillat, Razor, had been named Dominican consul in New York. The FBI identified compromising inquiries regarding Galíndez by Minerva Bernardino, the Dominican ambassador to the UN and a woman close to Trujillo. Even more serious was the FBI's identification of a small plane with a false registration, flown by a pilot without a proper license, that took off illegally on the night of the kidnapping from a small airport on Long Island, heading for Florida. The pilot was named Murphy, and from that time on he lived in the Dominican Republic, working for Dominican Airlines. Murphy and Tavito flew together and had become good friends.

Antonio learned all this in bits and pieces (censorship did not allow the Dominican press and radio to mention the subject) in broadcasts from Puerto Rico, Venezuela, or the Voice of America, which could be picked up on shortwave, or in copies of the *Miami Herald* or *The New York Times* that filtered into the country in the bags and uniforms of pilots and airline attendants.

Seven months after the disappearance of Galíndez, Murphy's name suddenly appeared in the international press as the pilot of the plane that had taken an anesthetized Galíndez out of the United States and brought him to the Dominican Republic, and Antonio, who had met Murphy through Tavito—the three of them had shared a paella washed down with wine from La Rioja in the Casa de España on Calle de Padre Billini—jumped into his van in Tirolí, near the Haitian border, and with the accelerator down to the floor and his brain about to burst with grim conjectures, drove to Ciudad Trujillo. He found Tavito in his house, calmly playing bridge with his wife, Altagracia. In order not to worry his sister-in-law, Antonio took him to a noisy club, Típico Najayo, where the music of the Ramón Gallardo Combo and its singer Rafael Martínez allowed for conversation that could not be overheard by the wrong ears. After ordering kid stew and two bottles of Presidente beer, and with no further preamble, Antonio advised Tavito to request asylum at an embassy. His younger brother burst into laughter: what bullshit. He didn't even know that Murphy's name was in every American newspaper. He wasn't worried. His confidence in Trujillo was as prodigious as his naiveté.

"I'll have to tell that gringo all about it," a horrified Antonio heard him say. "He's selling his things, he's decided to go back to the States to get married. He's engaged to a girl in Oregon. If he goes there now it would be like putting his head in the lion's mouth. Nothing will happen to him here. The Chief rules here, Antonio."

Antonio did not allow him to joke. Without raising his voice or attracting the attention of nearby tables, with muted fury at so much innocence, he tried to make him understand:

"Don't you get it, asshole? This is serious. The Galíndez kidnapping has put Trujillo in a very delicate situation with the Yankees. Everybody involved in the kidnapping is at risk. Murphy and you are very dangerous witnesses. And you maybe more than Murphy. Because you're the one who took Galíndez to the Fundación Ranch, to Trujillo's own house. Where's your head?"

"I didn't take Galíndez," his brother insisted, and he clinked his glass against Antonio's. "I took some guy I didn't know, and he was dead drunk. I don't know anything. Why don't you trust the Chief? Didn't he trust me with a really important mission?"

When they said goodbye that night, at the door of Tavito's house, he had finally, on the insistence of his older brother, said okay, he would think over his suggestion. And not to worry: he'd keep his mouth shut.

It was the last time Antonio saw him alive. Three days after their conversation, Murphy disappeared. When Antonio came back to Ciudad Trujillo, Tavito had been arrested. He was being held incommunicado in La Victoria. Antonio went in person to request an audience with the Generalissimo, but the Chief would not receive him. He tried to speak to Colonel Cobián Parra, head of the SIM, but he had become invisible, and shortly afterward, on Trujillo's orders, a soldier killed him in his office. In the next forty-eight hours, Antonio called or visited all the leaders and high officials in the regime whom he knew, from the President of the Senate, Agustín Cabral, to the president of the Dominican Party, Álvarez Pina. All of them had the same uneasy expression, all of them said that the best thing he could do, for his own security and theirs, was to stop calling and seeing people who could not help him and whom he was also putting in danger. "It was like banging your head against the wall," Antonio later told General Juan Tomás Díaz. If Trujillo had received him, he would have begged, he would have gone down on his knees, anything to save Tavito.

Not long after this, at dawn, a SIM car carrying armed *caliés* in civilian clothes stopped at the door of Tavito de la Maza's house. They took his body out of the vehicle and carelessly threw it into the heartsease in the little garden at the entrance. And as they were driving away they yelled at Altagracia, who had come to the door in her nightgown and was looking at the corpse in horror:

"Your husband hung himself in jail. We brought him back so you could give him a decent burial."

"But not even that was the worst thing," thought Antonio. No, seeing Tavito's corpse, the rope of his alleged suicide still around his neck, his body tossed out like a dog's at the entrance to his house by the thuggish killers who were the *caliés* of the SIM, that wasn't the worst. Antonio had repeated this to himself dozens, hundreds of times over these four and a half years, as he devoted his days and nights, and the remnants of lucidity and intelligence he still possessed, to planning the revenge that—God willing—would become a reality tonight. The worst had been Tavito's second death just days after the first one, when, making use of its entire informational and publicity apparatus— *El Caribe* and *La Nación*, the Dominican Voice television and radio stations, the radio stations of the Voice of the Tropics and Caribbean Radio, and a dozen small regional newspapers and radio stations—the regime, in one of its cruelest masquerades, published a letter allegedly written by Octavio de la Maza explaining his suicide. His remorse for having killed with his own hands his friend and colleague at Dominican Airlines, the pilot Murphy! Not satisfied with ordering his murder, the Goat, to wipe out all clues in the Galíndez story, added the macabre refinement of turning Tavito into a killer. In this way he got rid of two troublesome witnesses. To make everything even viler, Tavito's handwritten letter explained why he killed Murphy: the American was a homosexual. Murphy had so pursued Antonio's younger brother, with whom he had fallen in love, that Tavito, reacting with all the energy of a real man, erased the stain to his honor by killing the degenerate and hid his crime by pretending it was an accident.

He had to bend over where he sat in the Chevrolet, pressing the sawed-off rifle against his stomach, to hide the spasm he had just felt. His wife kept telling him to go to the doctor, the pains might be an ulcer or something even more serious, but he refused. He didn't need doctors to tell him that his body had deteriorated in recent years, reflecting the bitterness in his spirit. After what happened to Tavito, he had lost all hope, all enthusiasm, all love for this life or the next. Only the idea of revenge kept him active; he lived only to keep the vow he had sworn aloud, terrifying the neighbors in Moca who had come to sit with the De la Mazas—parents, brothers and sisters, brothers- and sisters-in-law, nieces and nephews, sons and daughters, grandchildren, aunts and uncles—during the wake.

"I swear to God I'll kill the son of a bitch who did this with my own hands!"

Everybody knew he was referring to the Benefactor, to the Father of the New Nation, to Generalissimo Dr. Rafael L. Trujillo Molina, whose funeral wreath of fresh, fragrant flowers was the most elaborate in the viewing room at the mortuary. The De la Maza family did not dare to refuse it or remove it from the room; it was so visible that everyone who came to cross themselves and say a prayer next to the coffin knew that the Chief had sent his condolences for the tragic death of this aviator, "one of the most faithful, loyal, and brave of my followers," according to the sympathy card.

On the day following his burial, two military adjutants from the Palace got out of a Cadillac with an official license plate in front of the De la Maza house in Moca. They had come for Antonio.

"Am I under arrest?"

"Not at all," First Lieutenant Roberto Figueroa Carrión quickly explained. "His Excellency wishes to see you."

Antonio didn't bother to put a pistol in his pocket. He assumed that before he went into the National Palace, if they really were taking him there and not to La Victoria or La Cuarenta, or if they didn't have orders to throw him over some cliff along the road, they would disarm him. He didn't care. He knew how strong he was, and he also knew that his strength, doubled by his hatred, would be enough to kill the tyrant, as he had sworn to do the night before. He pondered that decision, resolved to carry it out, knowing they would kill him before he could escape. He would pay that price if he could put an end to the despot who had ruined his life and the life of his family.

When he got out of the official car, the adjutants escorted him to the Benefactor's office without anyone searching him. The officers must have had precise instructions: as soon as the unmistakable high-pitched voice said, "Come in," First Lieutenant Roberto Figueroa Carrión and his companion left, allowing him to go in alone. The office was in semidarkness because of the partially closed shutters on the window facing the garden. The Generalissimo, sitting at his desk, wore a uniform that Antonio did not recognize: a long white tunic, with tails and gold buttons and large epaulets with gold-colored fringe on his chest, where a multicolored fan of medals and decorations was hanging. He wore light blue flannel trousers with a white stripe down the sides. He must have been getting ready to attend some military ceremony. The light from the desk lamp illuminated the broad, carefully shaved face, meticulously arranged gray hair, and the small brush mustache that copied Hitler's (whom, Antonio had heard the Chief say once, he admired, "not for his ideas but for the way he wore a uniform and presided over parades"). That fixed, direct gaze bored into Antonio as soon as he came through the door. Trujillo spoke after observing him for a long time:

"I know you think I had Octavio killed and that his suicide was a farce set up by the Intelligence Service. I had you come to tell you personally that you're wrong. Octavio was a man of the regime. He was always a loyal Trujillista. I've just appointed a commission, under the leadership of the Attorney General of the Republic, Francisco Elpidio Beras. With broad powers to question everyone, military and civilian. If the story of his suicide is a lie, the guilty parties will pay."

He spoke without animosity and without inflection, looking into Antonio's eyes in the direct, peremptory manner with which he always spoke to subordinates, both friends and enemies. Antonio remained motionless, more determined than ever to attack the hypocrite and wring his neck without giving him time to call for help. As if to make the job easier for him, Trujillo stood and walked toward him with slow, solemn steps. His black shoes shone even brighter than the waxed wood in his office.

"I also authorized the FBI to come here and investigate the death of this Murphy," he added in the same sharp tone. "It's a violation of our sovereignty, of course. Would the gringos allow our police to go and investigate the murder of a Dominican in New York, or Washington, or Miami? Let them come. Let the world know we have nothing to hide."

He was a meter away. Antonio could not endure Trujillo's unmoving gaze, and he blinked incessantly.

"My hand does not tremble when I have to kill," he added, after a pause. "Governing sometimes demands that you become stained with blood. I've often had to do that for this country. But I am a man of honor. I do justice to those who are loyal, I don't have them killed. Octavio was loyal, a man of the regime, a proven Trujillista. That's why I took a risk and kept him out of prison when he went too far in London and killed Luis Bernardino. Octavio's death will be investigated. You and your family can participate in the commission's deliberations."

He turned and, in the same unhurried way, went back to his desk. Why didn't he attack when he had him so close? He was still asking himself the question four and a half years later. Not because he believed a word of what he was saying. That was part of the melodrama that Trujillo was so fond of and that the dictatorship superimposed on its crimes, like a sarcastic supplement to the tragic deeds it was built on. Why, then? It wasn't fear of dying, because fear of dying was never one of the many defects he acknowledged in himself. Since the time he was an insurgent and fought the dictator with a small band of Horacistas, he had risked his life many times. It was something more subtle and indefinable than fear: it was the paralysis, the numbing of determination, reason, and free will, which this man, groomed and adorned to the point of absurdity, with his thin high-pitched voice and hypnotist's eyes, imposed on Dominicans, poor or rich, educated or ignorant, friends or enemies, and it was what held Antonio there, mute, passive, listening to those lies, the lone observer of the hoax, incapable of acting on his desire to attack him and put an end to the witches' Sabbath that the history of the country had become.

"Furthermore, as proof that the regime considers the De la Mazas a loyal family, this morning you have been granted the concession for highway construction between Santiago and Puerto Plata."

He paused again, wet his lips with the tip of his tongue, and concluded with a phrase that also said the interview had ended:

"In this way you'll be able to help Octavio's widow. Poor Altagracia must be having a difficult time. Give her my best, and your parents too."

Antonio left the National Palace more stupefied than if he had been drinking all night. Had that been him? Had he heard with his own ears what that son of a bitch said? Had he accepted explanations from Trujillo, even a business deal, a mess of pottage that would allow him to pocket thousands of pesos, so that he would swallow his bitterness and become an accomplice—yes, an accomplice—to Tavito's murder? Why hadn't he dared even to accuse him, to say he knew very well that the body thrown at his sister-in-law's door had been murdered on his orders, like Murphy before him, and that he had also created, with his melodramatic mind, the masquerade of the gringo pilot's homosexuality and Tavito's remorse for having killed him.

Instead of returning to Moca that morning, Antonio, without really knowing how, found himself in a cheap cabaret, El Bombillo Rojo, at the corner of Vicente Noble and Barahona, whose owner, Loco Frías, organized dance contests. He consumed vast quantities of rum, lost in thought, hearing as if from a distance merengues with a Cibao flavor ("San Antonio," "Con el Alma," "Juanita Morel," "Jarro Pichao," among others), and at a certain moment, without any explanation, he tried to hit the maracas player in the band. His drunkenness blurred the target, he punched the air, fell to the floor, and could not get up again.

When he reached Moca a day later, pale, exhausted, and with his clothes in ruins, his father, Don Vicente, his brother, Ernesto, his mother, and his wife, Aída, were in the family house, waiting for him, horrified. It was his wife who spoke in a trembling voice:

"Everybody's saying that Trujillo shut you up with the highway from Santiago to Puerto Plata. I don't know how many people have called."

Antonio remembered his surprise when he heard Aída rebuke him in front of his parents and Ernesto. She was the model Dominican wife, quiet, obliging, long-suffering, who put up with his drunkenness, his affairs with women, his fighting, the nights he spent away from home, and always welcomed him with a smile, raising his spirits, willing to believe his excuses when he bothered to give her any, and finding comfort in Mass every Sunday, in novenas, confessions, and prayers, for the troubles that filled her life.

"I couldn't let myself be killed just for the sake of a gesture," he said, dropping into the old rocking chair where Don Vicente nodded off at siesta time. "I pretended I believed his explanations, that I let myself be bought off."

He spoke, feeling the weariness of centuries, the eyes of his wife, of Ernesto and his parents, burning into his brain.

"What else could I do? Don't think badly of me, Papa. I swore I'd avenge Tavito. I'll do it, Mama. You'll never have to be ashamed of me again, Aída. I swear it. I swear it again, to all of you."

Any moment now he would keep his oath. In ten minutes, or one, the Chevrolet would appear, the one the old fox used every week to go to Mahogany House in San Cristóbal, and, according to their carefully drawn plan, the murderer of Galíndez, of Murphy, Tavito, and the Mirabal sisters, of thousands of Dominicans, would fall, cut to ribbons by the bullets of another of his victims, Antonio de la Maza, whom Trujillo had also killed with a method that was slower and more perverse than when he had his prey shot, beaten to death, or fed to the sharks. He had killed him in stages, taking away his decency, his honor, his self-respect, his joy in living, his hopes and desires, turning him into a sack of bones tormented by the guilty conscience that had been destroying him gradually for so many years.

"I'm going to stretch my legs," he heard Salvador Estrella Sadhalá say. "They're cramped from sitting so long."

He saw Turk get out of the car and take a few steps along the edge of the highway. Was Salvador feeling as much anguish as he? No doubt about it. And Tony Imbert and Amadito as well. And, up ahead, Roberto Pastoriza, Huáscar Tejeda, and Pedro Livio Cedeño. Gnawed by the fear that something or someone would prevent the Goat from keeping this appointment. But it was with him that Trujillo had old accounts that needed to be settled. He had not harmed any of his six companions, any of the dozens of others who, like Juan Tomás Díaz, were involved in the conspiracy, as much as he had harmed Antonio. He looked through the window: Turk was shaking each leg energetically. He could see that Salvador held his revolver in his hand. He watched him return to the car and take his place in the back seat, next to Amadito.

"Well, if he doesn't come we'll go to the Pony and have a cold beer," he heard him say morosely.

After their fight, he and Salvador did not see each other for months. They would both be at the same social gathering and not say hello. Their break heightened the torment in which he lived. When the conspiracy was fairly well developed, Antonio had the courage to show up at 21 Mahatma Gandhi and go directly to the living room where Salvador was sitting.

"It's useless for us to scatter our efforts," he said by way of greeting. "Your plans to kill the Goat are childish. You and Imbert should join us. Our plan is worked out and can't fail."

Salvador looked into his eyes and said nothing. He made no hostile gesture and did not throw him out of his house.

"I have the support of the gringos," Antonio explained, lowering his voice. "I've spent two months discussing the details at the embassy. Juan Tomás Díaz has also been talking to Consul Dearborn's people. They'll give us weapons and explosives. We have high-ranking officers involved. You and Tony should join us."

"There are three of us," Turk said finally. "Amadito García Guerrero became part of it a few days ago."

Their reconciliation was only relative. They had not had another serious argument during the months when the plan to kill Trujillo was made, unmade, remade, with a different form and a different date every month, every week, every day, because of the vacillations of the Yankees. The planeload of weapons originally promised by the embassy was reduced, in the end, to three rifles that were given to him not long ago by his friend Lorenzo D. Berry, the owner of Wimpy's Supermarket, who, to his astonishment, turned out to be the CIA's man in Ciudad Trujillo. In spite of these cordial meetings, when the only topic was the plan in perpetual transformation, the old, fraternal communication was not reestablished between them—the jokes and confidences, the interweaving of shared intimacies that existed, Antonio knew, among Turk, Imbert, and Amadito, and from which he had been excluded ever since the argument. Another piece of misery to hold the Goat responsible for: he had lost his friend forever.

His three companions in the car, and the other three waiting up ahead, may have been the people who knew least about the conspiracy. It was possible they suspected certain other accomplices, but if something went wrong and they fell into Johnny Abbes García's hands, and the *caliés* took them to La Cuarenta and subjected them to their usual tortures, then Turk, Imbert, Amadito, Huáscar, Pastoriza, and Pedro Livio would not be able to implicate too many people. General Juan Tomás Díaz, Luis Amiama Tió, two or three others. They knew almost nothing about the rest, who included the most important figures in the government, Pupo Román, for example—head of the Armed Forces, the regime's number-two man—and myriad ministers, senators, civilian officials, and high-ranking military officers who were informed about their plans, had participated in their preparation or knew about them indirectly, and had let it be known or understood or guessed through intermediaries (as in the case of Balaguer himself, the theoretical President of the Republic) that once the Goat was eliminated, they would be prepared to cooperate in the political rebuilding, the eradication of the last dregs of Trujillism, the opening, the civilian-military junta that, with the support of the United States, would guarantee order, block the Communists, call for elections. Would the Dominican Republic finally be a normal country, with an elected government, a free press, a system of justice worthy of the name? Antonio sighed. He had worked so hard for that and still he couldn't bring himself to believe it. In fact, he was the only one who knew like the back of his hand the entire web of names and complicities. Often, as one infuriating secret conversation followed another, and everything they had done collapsed and they had to start building again out of nothing, he had felt exactly like a spider at the center of a labyrinth of threads that he himself had spun, trapping a crowd of individuals who did not know each other. He was the only one who knew them all. Only he knew each person's degree of involvement. And there were so many! Not even he could remember how many now. It was a miracle that with this country being what it was, and the Dominicans being how they were, there had been no betrayal to wreck the entire scheme. Perhaps God was on their side, as Salvador believed. The precautions had worked, all the others knowing very little except their final objective, not knowing the means, the circumstances, the moment. No more than three or four people knew that the seven of them were here tonight, knew whose hands would execute the Goat.

Sometimes he was overwhelmed at the thought that if Johnny Abbes arrested him, he would have the only one who could identify everyone involved. He was determined not to be captured alive, to save the last bullet for himself. And he had also taken the precaution of concealing in the hollow heel of his shoe a strychnine-based poison pill prepared for him by a pharmacist in Moca, who thought it was for killing a wild dog that had been wreaking havoc in the henhouses on the ranch. They wouldn't get him alive, he wouldn't give Johnny Abbes the pleasure of watching him writhe in the electric chair. When Trujillo was dead, it would be a real pleasure to finish off the head of the SIM. There would be more than enough volunteers. Most likely, when he found out about the Chief's death, Abbes would disappear. He must have made plans; he had to know how much he was hated, how many people wanted revenge. Not only the opposition; ministers, senators, members of the military said so openly.

Antonio lit another cigarette and smoked, biting down on the tip to relieve his tension. Traffic had stopped altogether; for some time not a truck or a car had passed in either direction.

The truth was, he said to himself, exhaling smoke from his mouth and nose, he didn't give a shit what happened later. The crucial thing was what happened now. Seeing him dead so he would know that his life had not been useless, that he hadn't passed through this world like a worthless creature.

"That bastard is never coming, damn it," a furious Tony Imbert exclaimed beside him.

7 The third time that Urania insists he take a mouthful, the invalid opens his mouth. When the nurse returns with the glass of water, Señor Cabral is relaxed and, as if distracted, docilely accepts the mouthfuls of pap his daughter offers him, and drinks half a glass of water in little sips. A few drops roll down to his chin. The nurse wipes his face carefully.

"Good, very good, you ate up your fruit like a good boy," she congratulates him. "You're happy with the surprise your daughter gave you, aren't you, Señor Cabral?"

The invalid does not deign to look at her.

"Do you remember Trujillo?" Urania asks the nurse point-blank.

The woman stares at her, disconcerted. She is wide in the hips, sour-looking, with prominent eyes. Her hair, dyed a rusty blond, is dark at the roots. At last she responds:

"How would I remember? I was only four or five when he was killed. I don't remember anything except what I heard in my house. I know your papa was a very important man in those days."

Urania nods.

"Senator, minister, everything," she murmurs. "But, in the end, he fell into disgrace."

The old man looks at her in alarm.

"Well, I mean"—the nurse is trying to be agreeable—"he might have been a dictator and everything else they say about him, but people seemed to live better back then. Everybody had jobs and there wasn't so much crime. Isn't that right, señorita?"

"If my father can understand you, he must be happy to hear you say that."

"Of course he understands me," says the nurse, who is already at the door. "Don't you, Señor Cabral? Your papa and I have long conversations. All right, just call if you need me."

She goes out, closing the door.

Perhaps it was true that because of the disastrous governments that came afterward, many Dominicans missed Trujillo now. They had forgotten the abuses, the murders, the corruption, the spying, the isolation, the fear: horror had become myth. "Everybody had jobs and there wasn't so much crime."

"There was crime, Papa." She looks into the invalid's eyes, and he begins to blink. "Maybe there weren't so many thieves breaking into houses, or so many muggers on the streets grabbing wallets, watches, and necklaces. But people were killed and beaten and tortured, people disappeared. Even the people closest to the regime. His son, for instance, the handsome Ramfis, he committed endless abuses. How you trembled at the thought of him noticing me!"

Her father did not know, because Urania never told him, that she and her classmates at Santo Domingo Academy, and perhaps all the girls of her generation, dreamed about Ramfis. With his thin mustache in the style of a Mexican movie star, his Ray-Ban sunglasses, his well-tailored suits and the variety of uniforms he wore as head of the Dominican Air Force, his big dark eyes and athletic build, his solid-gold watches and rings and his Mercedes-Benzes, he seemed favored by the gods: rich, powerful, good-looking, healthy, strong, happy. You remember it very clearly: when the sisters couldn't see or hear you, you and your classmates showed one another your collections of photographs of Ramfis Trujillo, in civilian clothes, in uniform, in a bathing suit, wearing a tie, a sport shirt, a tuxedo, a riding habit, leading the Dominican polo team, or sitting at the controls of his plane. You pretended you had seen him, talked to him at the club, the exhibition, the party, the parade, the charity fair, and when you dared to say it—all of you blushing, nervous, knowing it was a sin in word and thought and that you'd have to confess it to the chaplain—you whispered to each other how wonderful, how marvelous it would be to be loved, kissed, embraced, caressed by Ramfis Trujillo.

"You can't imagine how often I dreamed about him, Papa."

Her father does not laugh. He gives another little start and opens his eyes wide when he hears the name of Trujillo's older son. His favorite, and for that very reason, his greatest disappointment. The Father of the New Nation would have liked his firstborn—"Was he his son, Papa?"—to have his appetite for power, to be as energetic and as much of an executive as he was. But Ramfis had inherited none of his virtues or defects, except, perhaps, his frenzied fornicating, his need to take women to bed to convince himself of his own virility. He lacked political ambition, any kind of ambition; he was indolent, prone to depression and neurotic introversion, besieged by complexes, anxieties, and tortuous mood swings, when his behavior zigzagged between hysterical outbursts and long periods of ennui that he drowned in drugs and alcohol.

"Do you know what the Chief's biographers say, Papa? That he became like that when he found out his mother wasn't married to Trujillo when he was born. They say he began to suffer from depression when he learned that his real father was Dr. Dominici, or the Cuban Trujillo had killed, Doña María Martínez's first lover, back when she never dreamed she'd be the Bountiful First Lady and was just another fast-living party girl they called Españolita. You're laughing? I don't believe it!"

He may be laughing. Or it may merely be his facial muscles relaxing. In any case, this is not the face of someone enjoying himself but of a person who has just yawned or howled and is left slack-jawed, with eyes half closed, nostrils dilated, gullet wide, revealing a dark, toothless hole.

"Do you want me to call the nurse?"

The invalid closes his mouth, puffs out his face, and recovers his attentive, alarmed expression. He remains motionless, shrunken and waiting. Urania is distracted by the sudden clamor of shrieking parrots that fills the bedroom, then stops as suddenly as it began. The brilliant sun shines on roofs and windowpanes and begins to heat the room.

"Do you know something? Despite all the hatred I had, and still have, for your Chief, and his family, and everything that smells of Trujillo, when I think of Ramfis or read something about him, I can't help feeling sad; I'm sorry for the man."

He had been a monster like everyone else in that family of monsters. What else could he have been, being his father's son, brought up and educated as he was? What else could the son of Heliogabalus, or Caligula, or Nero have been? What else could a boy have been who, at the age of seven, was named a colonel in the Dominican Army by decree—"Did you present him in Congress or was it Senator Chirinos, Papa?"—and promoted at the age of ten to general, in a public ceremony the diplomatic corps was obliged to attend at which all the top-ranking military paid him homage? Etched in Urania's mind is a photograph in the album that her father kept in an armoire in the living room—can it still be there?—showing the elegant Senator Agustín Cabral ("Or were you a minister then, Papa?"), wearing an impeccable swallowtail coat under a brutal sun, bent in a respectful bow as he greets the boy in the general's uniform, who, standing on a small canopied podium, has just reviewed the troops and is accepting congratulations from a line of ministers, legislators, and ambassadors. At the rear of the platform, the smiling faces of the Benefactor and the Bountiful First Lady, his proud mama.

"What else could he have been but the parasite, drunkard, rapist, good-for-nothing, criminal, mentally unbalanced man he was? My friends and I at Santo Domingo didn't know any of that when we were in love with Ramfis. But you knew, Papa. That's why you were so afraid he would notice me and take a liking to your little girl, that's why you looked the way you did the time he kissed me and paid me a compliment. I didn't understand a thing!"

The invalid blinks, two times, three times.

Because unlike her classmates whose girlish hearts throb for Ramfis Trujillo and who invent what they have seen with him and said to him, who pretend he has smiled at them and complimented them, it really did happen to Urania. During the inauguration of the outstanding event held to celebrate twenty-five years of the Trujillo Era, the Fair for Peace and Brotherhood in the Free World, which began on December 20, 1955, and would run through 1956, and cost—"No one ever knew the exact amount, Papa"—between twenty-five and seventy million dollars, between a fourth and a half of the national budget. Those images are very vivid to Urania, the excitement and feeling of wonder flooding the entire country because of that memorable fair: Trujillo was throwing himself a party, and he brought to Santo Domingo ("To Ciudad Trujillo, excuse me, Papa") Xavier Cugat's orchestra, the chorus line from the Lido in Paris, the American skaters of the Ice Capades, and, on the 800,000 square meters of the fairground, he erected seventy-one buildings, some of marble, alabaster, and onyx, to house the delegations from the forty-two countries of the Free World that attended, a choice collection of personalities, notably President Juscelino Kubitschek of Brazil and the purple figure of Francis Cardinal Spellman, Archbishop of New York. The crowning events of the commemoration were the promotion of Ramfis to the rank of lieutenant general, for outstanding service to the nation, and the enthroning of Her Gracious Majesty Angelita I, Queen of the Fair, who arrived by boat, announced by all the sirens in the Navy and all the bells in all the churches of the capital, wearing her crown of precious jewels and her delicate gown of tulle and lace created in Rome by the Fontana sisters, two celebrated modistes who used forty-five meters of Russian ermine to create the costume with a train three meters long and a robe that copied the one worn by Elizabeth II of England at her coronation. Among the ladies-in-waiting and the pages, wearing an exquisite long dress of organdy, and silk gloves, and carrying a bouquet of roses, among the other girls and boys who are the cream of Dominican society, is Urania. She is the youngest attendant in the court of young people who escort Trujillo's daughter, under a triumphant sun and through the crowd that applauds the poet and Chief of Staff, Don Joaquín Balaguer, when he sings the praises of Her Majesty Angelita I and places the Dominican people at the feet of her grace and beauty. Feeling very much a young lady, Urania listens to her father, in formal attire, as he reads a panegyric to the accomplishments of these twenty-five years, achieved thanks to the tenacity, vision, and patriotism of Trujillo. She is immensely happy. ("I was never so happy again as I was that day, Papa.") She believes she is the center of attention. Now, in the very center of the fair, they unveil the bronze statue of Trujillo, in a morning coat and academic robes, professorial diplomas in his hand. Suddenly—like a gold ribbon around that magical morning—Urania discovers Ramfis Trujillo at her side, looking at her with his silken eyes, wearing his full-dress uniform.

"And who is this pretty young thing?" The brand-new lieutenant general smiles at her. Urania feels warm, slender fingers lifting her chin. "What's your name?"

"Urania Cabral," she stammers, her heart pounding.

"How pretty you are, and more important, how pretty you're going to be," and Ramfis bends over and his lips kiss the hand of the girl who hears the congratulatory clamor of sighs and jokes from the other pages and ladies-in-waiting of Her Majesty Angelita I. The Generalissimo's son has walked away. She cannot contain her joy. What will her friends say when they find out that Ramfis, Ramfis himself, has called her pretty, touched her cheek and kissed her hand, as if she really were a young lady.

"How appalled you were when I told you, Papa. How furious you were. It's funny, isn't it?"

Her father's anger at learning that Ramfis had touched her made Urania suspect for the first time that everything might not have been as perfect in the Dominican Republic as everyone said, especially Senator Cabral.

"What's the harm in his telling me I'm pretty and kissing my hand, Papa?"

"All the harm in the world," and her father raises his voice, frightening her, for he never reprimands her with that admonishing forefinger raised above his head. "Never again! Listen carefully, Uranita. If he approaches you, run away. Don't greet him, don't talk to him. Get away. It's for your own good."

"But, but . . ." The girl is utterly bewildered.

They have just returned from the Fair for Peace and Brotherhood in the Free World, she still has on the exquisite dress of a lady-in-waiting in the entourage of Her Majesty Angelita I, and her father still wears the tailcoat in which he delivered his speech before Trujillo, President Blacky Trujillo, diplomats, ministers, guests, and the thousands upon thousands of people flooding the flag-draped avenues, streets, and buildings of the fair. Why is he acting like this?

"Because Ramfis, that boy, that man is . . . evil." Her father makes an effort not to say everything he would like to. "With girls, with little girls. Don't repeat this to your friends at school. Or to anybody. I'm telling you because you're my daughter. It's my obligation. I have to take care of you. For your own good, Uranita, do you understand? Yes, you do, you're so intelligent. Don't let him near you, don't let him talk to you. If you see him, run over to me. If you're with me, he won't do anything to you."

You don't understand, Urania. You're as pure as a lily, no wickedness in you yet. You tell yourself that your father is jealous. He doesn't want anybody else to kiss you or say you're pretty, only him. Senator Cabral's reaction indicates that by this time the handsome Ramfis, the romantic Ramfis, has begun to do those nasty things to little girls, big girls, and women that will enhance his reputation, a reputation every Dominican male, highborn or low, aspires to. Great Cocksman, Horny-as-a-Goat, Tireless Fucking Machine. You'll start to hear about it soon, in the classrooms and courtyards of Santo Domingo, the academy for upper-class girls, with its Dominican sisters from the United States and Canada, modern uniforms, students who don't look like novices because they dress in pink, blue, and white and wear thick socks and saddle shoes (black and white), which gives them a sporty, contemporary air. But not even they are safe when Ramfis goes on his forays, alone or with his cronies, hunting for a sweet piece of ass on the streets, in the parks, clubs, bars, or private houses of his great Dominican fiefdom. How many Dominican women did the good-looking Ramfis seduce, abduct, and rape? He doesn't give native girls Cadillacs or mink coats, the gifts he presents to Hollywood stars after he fucks them or in order to fuck them. Because, in contrast to his prodigal father, the elegant Ramfis is, like Doña María, a miser. He fucks Dominican girls free of charge, for the honor of their being fucked by the crown prince, the captain of the nation's invincible polo team, the lieutenant general, the head of the Air Force.

You begin finding out all about it in the students' whispered exchanges of gossip, fantasies, and exaggerations mixed with realities, behind the sisters' backs, during recreational periods, believing and not believing, attracted and repulsed, until, at last, the earthquake occurs at school, in Ciudad Trujillo, because this time the victim of his papa's darling boy is one of the most beautiful girls in Dominican society, the daughter of an Army colonel. The radiant Rosalía Perdomo, with the long blond hair, sky-blue eyes, translucent skin, who plays the part of the Virgin Mary in Passion plays, shedding tears like a genuine Mater Dolorosa when her Son expires. There are many versions of what happened. Ramfis met her at a party, saw her at the Country Club, at a festival, looked her way at the Hipódromo, and he besieged her, called, wrote, and made a date with her for that Friday afternoon, after the practice that Rosalía stayed for because she was on the school's volleyball team. Many classmates see her when she leaves—Urania doesn't remember if she saw her, it's not impossible—and instead of taking the school bus she gets into Ramfis's car, which is waiting for her a few meters from the door. He isn't alone. Papa's darling boy is never alone, he is always accompanied by two or three friends who celebrate him, adulate him, serve him, and prosper at his expense. Like his brother-in-law, Angelita's husband Pechito, another good-looking kid, Colonel Luis José León Estévez. Was his younger brother with them? The homely, stupid, unattractive Radhamés? No doubt. Were they already drunk? Or do they get drunk while they do what they do to the golden, snow-white Rosalía Perdomo? Surely they don't wait until the girl begins to bleed. Later they conduct themselves like gentlemen, but first they rape her. Ramfis, being who he is, must have been the one to deflower the exquisite morsel. Then comes everybody else. Do they go by age or by closeness to the firstborn? Do they gamble on the order? How would they have done it, Papa? And at the height of their fun, the last thing they expect, a hemorrhage.

Instead of throwing her in a ditch somewhere in the countryside, which is what they would have done if instead of being a Perdomo, a white, blond, rich girl from a respected Trujillista family, Rosalía had been a girl with no name and no money, they behave with consideration. They take her to the door of Marión Hospital, where, fortunately or unfortunately for Rosalía, the doctors save her. And also spread the story. They say poor Colonel Perdomo never recovers from the shock of knowing that Ramfis Trujillo and his friends happily violated his beloved daughter, between lunch and supper, as if they were killing time watching a movie. Her mother, devastated by shame and grief, never goes out again. She isn't even seen at Mass.

"Is that what you were afraid of, Papa?" Urania pursues the invalid's eyes. "That Ramfis and his friends would do to me what they did to Rosalía Perdomo?"

"He understands," she thinks, falling silent. His father's gaze is fixed on her; at the back of his eyes there is a mute entreaty: be quiet, stop opening wounds, digging up memories. She doesn't have the slightest intention of complying. Isn't that why you've come to this country when you swore you'd never return?

"Yes, Papa, that must be why I've come," she says so quietly her voice is barely audible. "To give you a bad time. Though with the stroke, you took your precautions. You tore unpleasant things out of your memory. And my, our, unpleasantness, did you erase that too? I didn't. Not for a day. Not a single day in thirty-five years, Papa. I never forgot and I never forgave you. That's why when you called me at Siena Heights or at Harvard, I would hear your voice and hang up and not let you finish. "Uranita, is that you . . . ?" Click. "Uranita, listen to me . . ." Click. That's why I never answered any of your letters. Did you write a hundred? Two hundred? I tore them all up or burned them. Pretty hypocritical, those little notes of yours. You always talked in circles, in allusions, in case other eyes saw them, in case other people learned the story. Do you know why I could never forgive you? Because you were never really sorry. After so many years of serving the Chief, you had lost your scruples, your sensitivity, the slightest hint of rectitude. Just like your colleagues. Just like the whole country, perhaps. Was that a requirement for staying in power and not dying of disgust? To become heartless, a monster like your Chief. To be unfeeling and self-satisfied, like the handsome Ramfis after raping Rosalía and leaving her to bleed in the doorway of Marión Hospital."

The Perdomo girl did not return to school, of course, but her delicate Virgin Mary face continued to inhabit the classrooms, halls, and courtyards of Santo Domingo Academy, the rumors, whispers, fantasies that her misfortune provoked lasted for weeks, months, even though the sisters had forbidden them to mention the name of Rosalía Perdomo. But in the homes of Dominican society, even in the most Trujillista families, her name was mentioned over and over again, an ominous premonition, a terrible warning, above all in houses with girls and young ladies of marriageable age, and the story inflamed the fear that the handsome Ramfis (who was, moreover, married to a divorced woman, Octavia—Tantana—Ricart!) would suddenly discover the little girl, the big girl, and have a party with her, one of those parties that the spoiled heir had regularly with whatever girl he wanted, because who was going to challenge the Chief's oldest son and his circle of favorites?

"It was because of Rosalía Perdomo that your Chief sent Ramfis to the military academy in the United States, wasn't it, Papa?"

To the Fort Leavenworth Military Academy in Kansas City, in 1958. To get him away from Ciudad Trujillo for a couple of years, because, they said, the story of Rosalía Perdomo had irritated even His Excellency. Not for moral reasons but for practical ones. This idiotic boy, instead of becoming knowledgeable about affairs and preparing himself as the Chief's firstborn, devoted his life to dissipation, to polo, to getting drunk with an entourage of bums and parasites and doing clever things like raping the daughter of one of the families most loyal to Trujillo and causing her to hemorrhage. A spoiled, pampered boy. Send him to the Fort Leavenworth Military Academy in Kansas City!

Hysterical laughter overcomes Urania, and the invalid, disconcerted by this sudden outburst, shrinks as if wanting to disappear inside himself. Urania laughs so hard her eyes fill with tears. She wipes them away with her handkerchief.

"The cure was worse than the disease. Instead of a punishment, the handsome Ramfis's little trip to Fort Leavenworth turned out to be a reward.

"It must have been funny, wasn't it, Papa? This little Dominican officer comes for an elite course of study in a select class of American officers and shows up with the rank of lieutenant general, dozens of medals, a long military career behind him (he had started at the age of seven), an entourage of aides-de-camp, musicians, and servants, a yacht anchored in San Francisco Bay, and a fleet of automobiles. What a surprise for all those captains, majors, lieutenants, sergeants, instructors, professors. He came to Fort Leavenworth to study, and the tropical bird displayed more medals and titles than Eisenhower ever had. How should they treat him? How could they permit him to enjoy such prerogatives without discrediting the academy and the U.S. Army? Could they look the other way when every other week the heir apparent would escape spartan Kansas for boisterous Hollywood, where, with his friend Porfirio Rubirosa, he went on millionaire's sprees with famous actresses, which the scandal sheets and gossip columns were thrilled to report? The most famous columnist in Los Angeles, Louella Parsons, revealed that Trujillo's son gave a top-of-the-line Cadillac to Kim Novak and a mink coat to Zsa Zsa Gabor. At a session of the House of Representatives, a Democratic congressman estimated that those gifts cost the equivalent of the annual military aid that Washington graciously supplied to the Dominican Republic, and he asked if this was the best way to help poor countries defend themselves against Communism, the best way to spend the American people's money.

"Impossible to avoid a scandal. In the United States, not in the Dominican Republic, where not a word was published or spoken about Ramfis's diversions. But up there, say what you like, there is such a thing as public opinion and a free press, and politicians are crushed if they expose a weak flank. And so, at the request of Congress, military aid was cut off. Do you remember that, Papa? The academy discreetly informed the State Department, which even more discreetly informed the Generalissimo that there wasn't the remotest possibility that his boy would complete the course, and since his service record was so deficient, it was preferable for him to withdraw rather than suffer the humiliation of being expelled from the Fort Leavenworth Military Academy.

"His papa didn't like it at all when they treated poor Ramfis so badly, did he, Papa? All he did was sow some wild oats and look how the puritanical gringos reacted! In retaliation your Chief wanted to remove the American naval and military missions, and he called the ambassador to register his protest. His closest advisers, Paíno Pichardo, you, Balaguer, Chirinos, Arala, Manuel Alfonso, had to perform miracles to convince him that a break would be enormously prejudicial. Do you remember? The historians say you were one of the men who kept relations with Washington from being poisoned by Ramfis's exploits. But you were only partially successful, Papa. From that time on, after those excesses, the United States realized that this ally had become an embarrassment and it was prudent to find someone more presentable. But how did we end up talking about your Chief's dear boys, Papa?"

The invalid raises and lowers his shoulders, as if saying, "How do I know? You tell me." Did he understand, then? No. At least, not all the time. The stroke didn't completely wipe out his ability to comprehend; it must have been reduced to five or ten percent of normal. That limited, impoverished brain, moving in slow motion, was surely capable of retaining and processing the information his senses perceived, at least for a few minutes or seconds, before it clouded over again. Which is why his eyes, his face, his gestures, like that movement of his shoulders, suddenly suggest that he is listening, that he understands what you are saying. But only in fragments, spasms, flashes, without any sequential coherence. Don't kid yourself, Urania. He understands for a couple of seconds and then he forgets. You're not communicating with him. You're still talking to yourself, as you've done every day for more than thirty years.

She isn't sad or depressed. She is saved from that, perhaps, by the sun coming in the windows and illuminating objects with a brilliant light, outlining them in all their detail, exposing defects, discolorations, age. How shabby, abandoned, and old the bedroom—the house—is now, of the once powerful President of the Senate, Agustín

Cabral. What made you think of Ramfis Trujillo? She has always been fascinated by the strange directions memory takes, the geographies it creates in response to mysterious stimuli and unforeseen associations. Ah, yes, it has to do with the piece you read in *The New York Times* the night before you left the United States. The article was about the younger brother, the stupid, ugly Radhamés. What a report! What an ending. The journalist had made a thorough investigation. Radhamés had lived, penniless, for some years in Panama, engaged in suspicious activities, nobody knew exactly what, until he vanished. The disappearance occurred the previous year, and none of the efforts of his relatives and the Panamanian police—his small room in Balboa was searched, and his meager belongings were still there—turned up any clues. Until, finally, one of the Colombian drug cartels let it be known in Bogotá, with the syntactical pomp characteristic of the Athens of America, that "the Dominican citizen Don Radhamés Trujillo Martínez, a resident of Balboa in our sister Republic of Panama, has been executed in an unnamed location in the Colombian jungle after unequivocally demonstrating dishonorable conduct in the fulfillment of his obligations." *The New York Times* reported that for years a derelict Radhamés had apparently earned his living serving the Colombian Mafia. Wretched work, no doubt, judging by the modest circumstances in which he lived: acting as a gofer for the bosses, renting apartments for them, driving them to hotels, airports, brothels, or, perhaps, acting as an intermediary for money laundering. Did he try to steal a few dollars to make his life a little better? Since he was so short on brains, they caught him right away. They abducted him to the forests of Darién, where they were lords and masters. Perhaps they tortured him with the same kind of ferocity used by him and Ramfis in 1959, when they tortured and killed the invaders of Constanza, Maimón, and Estero Hondo, and in 1961, when they tortured and killed the people involved in the events of May 30.

"A just ending, Papa." Her father, who has been dozing, opens his eyes. "Whoever lives by the sword, dies by the sword. It was true in the case of Radhamés, if he really did die like that. Because nothing has been confirmed. The article also said that there are those who swear he was an informant for the DEA while he worked for the Colombian mafiosi, and that for services rendered, the agency changed his face and put him under their protection. Rumors, conjectures. In any event, what an ending for the darling children of your Chief and the Bountiful First Lady. The handsome Ramfis killed in a car accident in Madrid. An accident, some say, arranged by the CIA and Balaguer to stop the firstborn, who was conspiring in Madrid, prepared to invest millions to recover the family fiefdom. Radhamés transformed into a poor devil murdered by the Colombians for trying to steal the dirty money he helped to launder, or for being an agent of the DEA. And Angelita, Her Majesty Angelita I, whose lady-in-waiting I was, do you know where she is now? In Miami, brushed by the wings of the divine dove. A born-again Christian. In one of the thousands of evangelical sects driven by madness, idiocy, anguish, fear. That's how the queen of this country has ended up. In a clean little house in very bad taste, a hybrid of gringo and Caribbean vulgarity, devoted to missionary work. They say she can be seen on the street corners of Dade County, in Latino and Haitian neighborhoods, singing hymns and exhorting passersby to open their hearts to the Lord. What would the Heroic Father of the New Nation say to all that?"

Again the invalid raises and lowers his shoulders, and blinks, and becomes lethargic. He lowers his eyelids and curls up, ready for a little nap.

It's true, you've never felt hatred for Ramfis, Radhamés, or Angelita, nothing like what Trujillo and the Bountiful First Lady still inspire in you. Because, somehow, the three children have paid in degradation or violent deaths for their part in the family's crimes. And you've never been able to avoid a certain benevolent feeling toward Ramfis. Why, Urania? Perhaps because of his emotional crises, his depressions and fits of madness, the mental instability his family always concealed and which, following the murders he ordered in June 1959, obliged Trujillo to commit him to a psychiatric hospital in Belgium. In all of Ramfis's actions, even the cruelest, there was something caricatured, fraudulent, pathetic. Like his spectacular gifts to the Hollywood actresses Porfirio Rubirosa fucked free of charge (when he wasn't making them pay him). Or the way he had of botching the plans devised for him by his father. Hadn't it been grotesque, for instance, when Ramfis ruined the reception given in his honor by the Generalissimo to compensate for his failure at Fort Leavenworth? He had the Congress—"Did you propose the law, Papa?"—name Ramfis Head of the Joint Chiefs of Staff of the Armed Forces, and, on his return, he was to be recognized as such at a military review on the Avenida, at the foot of the obelisk. Everything was arranged, and the troops in formation, on that morning when the yacht *Angelita*, which the Generalissimo sent to pick him up in Miami, entered the port on the Ozama River, and Trujillo himself, accompanied by Joaquín Balaguer, went to the docking berth to welcome him and drive him to the parade. What astonishment, what disappointment, what confusion overwhelmed the Chief when he boarded the yacht and discovered the calamitous condition, the slobbering incapacity in which a shipboard orgy had left poor Ramfis. He could barely stand, he was incapable of speaking. His slack, recalcitrant tongue emitted grunts instead of words. His bulging eyes were glassy, his clothes streaked with vomit. And his cronies, and the women who accompanied them, were in even worse shape. Balaguer described it in his memoirs: Trujillo turned white and trembled with indignation. He ordered the cancellation of the military parade and Ramfis's swearing-in as Head of the Joint Chiefs of Staff. And, before he left, he picked up a glass and proposed a toast meant as a symbolic slap in the face of the worthless drone (his inebriation prevented him from understanding): "Here's to work, the only thing that will bring prosperity to the Republic."

Urania is overcome by another attack of hysterical laughter, and the invalid opens his eyes in terror.

"Don't be afraid." Urania becomes serious. "I can't help laughing when I imagine the scene. Where were you at that moment, when your Chief discovered his boy drunk, surrounded by his drunken whores and buddies? On the platform on the Avenida, dressed in your morning coat, waiting for the new Head of the Joint Chiefs of Staff of the Armed Forces? What explanation was given? The parade is canceled because General Ramfis is suffering from delirium tremens?"

She laughs again under the profound gaze of the invalid.

"A family to laugh at and cry over, not to be taken seriously," Urania murmurs. "Sometimes you must have been ashamed of all of them. And felt fear and remorse, when you allowed yourself to, though that kind of audacity would be kept very secret. I'd like to know what you would have thought of the melodramatic fates met by the Chief's darling children. Or the sordid story of the final years of Doña María Martínez, the Bountiful First Lady, the terrible, the vengeful, who screamed her demand that Trujillo's assassins have their eyes put out and be skinned alive. Do you know that in the end she was eroded by arteriosclerosis? That the grasping woman secretly got all those millions and millions of dollars away from the Chief? And had all the numbers to the secret accounts in Switzerland and hid them from her children? With good reason, no doubt. She was afraid they'd steal her millions and bury her in an old-age home, where she'd spend her final years not being any trouble to them. She, with her hardening arteries, was the one who had the last laugh. I would have given anything to see the Bountiful First Lady in Madrid, stupefied by misfortune and losing her memory, but maintaining, from the depths of her avarice, enough lucidity not to reveal to her dear children the numbers of the Swiss accounts. And to see the efforts the poor things made—in Madrid, in the house of homely, stupid Radhamés, or in Miami, in Angelita's house, before she turned to mysticism—to have her remember where she had scribbled them down or hidden them. Can you picture it, Papa? How they must have hunted, and pulled open, and broken, and slashed, looking for the hiding place. They took her to Miami, they brought her back to Madrid. And they never found it. She took her secret to the grave. What do you think of that, Papa? Ramfis managed to squander a few million that he got out of the country in the months following his father's death, because the Generalissimo (was this true, Papa?) insisted on not taking a penny out of the country in order to oblige his family and followers to die here, to face the consequences. But Angelita and Radhamés were out on the street. And thanks to her hardening arteries, the Bountiful First Lady died poor too, in Panama, where Kalil Haché buried her, taking her to the cemetery in a taxi. She left the family's millions to the Swiss bankers! To cry over or to laugh at, but in no case to be taken seriously. Isn't that so, Papa?"

She laughs again, until tears come to her eyes. As she dries them, she struggles against a fragment of depression growing inside her. The invalid observes her, accustomed to her presence. He no longer seems interested in her monologue.

"Don't think I've become a hysteric," she says with a sigh. "Not yet, Papa. What I'm doing now, digging up the past, rooting around in memories, is something I never do. This is my first vacation in years. I don't like vacations. When I was a girl here, I used to like them. But I never did again, not after I went to Adrian, thanks to the sisters. I've spent my life working. I never took a vacation at the World Bank. Or at the law firm in New York. I don't have time to go around giving monologues on Dominican history."

It's true, your life in Manhattan is exhausting. Every hour is accounted for, starting at nine, when you walk into your office at 47th and Madison. By then you've run for three-quarters of an hour in Central Park, if the weather is good, or done aerobics at the Fitness Center on the corner, where you have a membership. Your morning is a series of interviews, reports, discussions, consultations, research in the archives, working lunches in a private dining room at the office or at a nearby restaurant, and your afternoon is just as busy and frequently does not end until eight. Weather permitting, you return home on foot. You prepare a salad and open a container of yogurt before watching the news on television, you read for a while and go to bed, so tired that the letters in the book or the images on the screen begin to dance before ten minutes have passed. There is always one trip a month, sometimes two, within the United States or to Latin America, Europe, or Asia; and recently to Africa as well, where some investors are finally daring to risk their money, and for that they come to the firm for legal advice. That's your specialty: the legal aspect of financial operations in companies anywhere in the world. A specialty you came to after working for many years in the Legal Department of the World Bank. The trips are more fatiguing than your days in Manhattan. Flying five, ten, twelve hours, to Mexico City, Bangkok, Tokyo, Rawalpindi, or Harare, and going immediately to give or listen to reports, discuss figures, evaluate projects; changing landscapes and climates, from heat to cold, from humidity to drought, from English to Japanese, Spanish, Urdu, Arabic, and Hindi, using interpreters whose mistakes can cause erroneous decisions. Which is why her five senses are always alert, in a state of concentration that leaves her drained, so that at the inevitable receptions she can barely stifle her yawns.

"When I have a Saturday and Sunday to myself, I'm happy to stay home, reading Dominican history," she says, and it seems to her that her father nods. "A rather peculiar history, it's true. But I find it restful. It's my way of not losing my roots. Even though I've lived there twice as long as I lived here, I haven't turned into a gringa. I still talk like a Dominican, don't I, Papa?"

Is there an ironic little glimmer in the invalid's eyes?

"Well, more or less a Dominican, one from up there. What do you expect from somebody who has lived more than thirty years with gringos, who goes for weeks without speaking Spanish? Do you know, I was sure I'd never see you again? I wasn't going to come back, not even to bury you. It was a firm decision. I know you'd like to know why I changed my mind. Why I'm here. The truth is, I don't know. I did it on impulse. I didn't think much about it. I asked for a week's vacation and here I am. I must have come for something. Maybe it was you. To find out how you were. I knew you were sick, that after the stroke it was no longer possible to talk to you. Would you like to know what I'm feeling? What I felt when I came back to the house of my childhood? When I saw the ruin you've become?"

Her father is paying attention again. He is waiting, with curiosity, for her to continue. What do you feel, Urania? Bitterness? A certain melancholy? Sadness? The old anger reborn? "The worst thing is that I don't think I feel anything," she thinks.

The front doorbell rings. It keeps chiming, vibrating in the heat-filled morning.

8 The hair that was missing on his head jutted aggressively out of his ears in jet-black clumps, a kind of grotesque compensation for the baldness of the Constitutional Sot. Had he given him that nickname too, before he rebaptized him, in his heart of hearts, as the Walking Turd? Probably. Since his youth he had been good at making up nicknames. Many of the savage labels he stamped on people became part of their very flesh and eventually replaced their real names. That's what had happened to Senator Henry Chirinos. No one in the Dominican Republic, except for the newspapers, called him by name; they used only his devastating epithet: the Constitutional Sot. He had the habit of stroking the greasy bristles that nested in his ears, and though the Generalissimo, obsessed with cleanliness, had forbidden him to do so in his presence, he was doing it now, and, to make matters worse, he was alternating one revolting act with another: smoothing the hairs in his nose. He was nervous, very nervous. The Benefactor knew why: he was bringing him a negative report on his enterprises. But responsibility for things going badly did not lie with Chirinos; it was the fault of the sanctions imposed by the OAS, which were strangling the country.

"If you keep picking at your nose and ears, I'll call in the adjutants and put you behind bars," he said in a bad temper. "I've forbidden you to do those disgusting things here. Are you drunk?"

The Constitutional Sot started in his chair, which faced the Benefactor's desk. He moved his hands away from his face.

"I haven't had a drop of alcohol," he apologized in confusion. "You know I don't drink during the day, Chief. Just in the evening, and at night."

He wore a suit that the Generalissimo thought of as a monument to bad taste: grayish green, with glints of iridescence; like everything he put on, it looked as if he had squeezed his fat body into the suit with a shoehorn. Jiggling on his white shirt was a bluish tie with yellow dots, where the harsh gaze of the Benefactor detected grease spots. He thought with distaste that he had gotten the stains while eating, because Senator Chirinos ate by taking enormous mouthfuls, wolfing them down as if he feared his neighbors would snatch away his plate, and chewing with an open mouth, spraying a shower of food all around him.

"I swear there's not a drop of alcohol in my body," he repeated. "Just the black coffee I had for breakfast."

Probably it was true. When he saw him come into the office a moment ago, balancing his elephantine body and advancing very slowly, testing the floor before putting down his foot, he thought he was intoxicated. No; he must have somatized all his drinking; even when he was sober, he carried himself with the trembling uncertainty of an alcoholic.

"You're pickled in alcohol: even when you don't drink you look drunk," he said, examining him from head to foot.

"It's true," Chirinos quickly acknowledged, making a theatrical gesture. "I am a *poète maudit*, Chief. Like Baudelaire and Rubén Darío."

He had ashen skin, a double chin, thin, greasy hair, and little eyes set deep behind puffy lids. His nose, flattened since the accident, was like a boxer's, and his almost lipless mouth added a perverse quality to his brash ugliness. He had always been so disagreeably ugly that ten years earlier, after the car crash that he miraculously survived, his friends thought plastic surgery would improve his looks. It only made them worse.

That he was still a man trusted by the Benefactor, a member of his narrow circle of intimates that included Virgilio Álvarez Pina, Paíno Pichardo, Egghead Cabral (now in disgrace), or Joaquín Balaguer, was proof that when it was time to choose his collaborators, the Generalissimo did not let himself be guided by personal likes or dislikes. In spite of the repugnance his physical appearance, slovenliness, and bad manners always inspired in the Chief, from the beginning of his regime Henry Chirinos had been favored with the delicate tasks that Trujillo entrusted to people who were not only reliable but capable. And he was one of the most capable of the men accepted into that exclusive club. An attorney who served as a constitutionalist, while still very young he had been, along with Agustín Cabral, the principal author of the Constitution ordered by Trujillo in the early days of the Era, and of all the amendments made since then. He had also composed the most important institutional and ordinary laws, and written almost all the legal decisions adopted by the Congress to legitimize the needs of the regime. There was no one like him for giving, in parliamentary speeches filled with Latin phrases and quotations that were often in French, the appearance of juridical necessity to the most arbitrary decisions of the Executive, or for refuting, with devastating logic, every proposal that Trujillo disapproved of. His mind, organized like a legal code, immediately found a technical argument to provide a veneer of legality to any decision made by Trujillo, whether it was a ruling by the Treasury or the Supreme Court, or a law passed by Congress. A good part of the legal web of the Era had been spun by the perverse skill of this great pettifogger (that's what he had been called once, in Trujillo's presence, by Senator Agustín Cabral, his close friend and enemy within the circle of favorites).

Because of these attributes, the perpetual parliamentarian Henry Chirinos had been everything one could be during the thirty years of the Era: deputy, senator, Minister of Justice, member of the Constitutional Tribunal, ambassador plenipotentiary and chargé d'affaires, governor of the Central Bank, president of the Trujillonian Institute, member of the Central Council of the Dominican Party, and, for the past few years, the position that required the greatest confidence, supervisor of the Benefactor's business operations. As such, Agriculture, Commerce, and Finance were subordinate to him. Why entrust such enormous responsibility to a confirmed alcoholic? Because, in addition to being a shyster, he knew about economics. He had done well as the head of the Central Bank, and in Finance, for a few months. And because, in recent years, due to ambushes from all sides, the Benefactor needed someone in the post who was absolutely reliable and could be told about the family's entanglements and disputes. And for that, this alcoholic greaseball was invaluable.

How did it happen that an uncontrollable drinker had not lost his skill in legal intrigue, or his capacity for work, the only one, perhaps, after the fall into disgrace of Anselmo Paulino, that the Benefactor could compare to his own? The Walking Turd could work ten or twelve hours without stopping, drink himself blind, and the next day be in his office in Congress, in the Ministry, or in the National Palace, fresh and lucid, dictating legal reports to the stenographers or expounding with florid eloquence on political, legal, economic, and constitutional matters. Besides all that, he wrote acrostic, celebratory poems, historical articles and books, and was one of the best-sharpened pens used by Trujillo to distill the poison of "The Public Forum" in *El Caribe*.

"How are the businesses doing?"

"Very badly, Chief." Senator Chirinos took a deep breath. "At this rate, they'll soon be at death's door. I'm sorry to tell you this, but you don't pay me to deceive you. If the sanctions aren't lifted soon, it'll be catastrophic."

He opened his bulky briefcase, took out rolls of papers, and notebooks, and proceeded to analyze the principal enterprises, beginning with the plantations of the Dominican Sugar Corporation and continuing with Dominican Air, the cement factory, the lumber companies and the sawmills, the import-export offices and commercial establishments. The music of names and figures lulled the Generalissimo, who was barely listening: Atlas Commercial, Caribbean Motors, Tobacco Products S.A., Dominican Cotton Consortium, Chocolate Manufacturing Company, Dominican Footwear Manufacturers, Granulated Salt Distributors, Vegetable Oil Processors, Dominican Cement Factory, Dominican Record Production, Dominican Battery Factory, Sack and Cordage Company, Read Iron Works, El Marino Iron Works, Dominican-Suisse Manufacturing, Dairy Processing, Altagracia Liquor Industries, National Glass Industries, National Paper Industries, Dominican Mills, Dominican Paints, Retreading Plant, Quisqueya Motors, Salt Refinery, Dominican Textile Mills, San Rafael Insurance, Real Estate Corporation, *El Caribe* newspaper. The Walking Turd left for last the businesses in which the Trujillo family had minority interests, barely mentioning that there was no "positive movement" here either. He said nothing that the Benefactor did not already know: what was not paralyzed by a lack of investment and replacement parts was operating at a third, even a tenth, of capacity. The catastrophe had already arrived, in spades. But at least—the Benefactor sighed—what the gringos thought would be the final blow had not succeeded: cutting off his supply of oil and replacement parts for cars and planes. Johnny

Abbes García had arranged for fuel to come in through Haiti, crossing the border as contraband. The surcharge was high but the consumer didn't pay for it; the regime was absorbing the subsidy. The State could not tolerate this hemorrhaging for much longer. Because of the restrictions on foreign currency and the paralysis of exports and imports, its economic life had come to a standstill.

"Practically speaking, there is no income in any of the enterprises, Chief. Only expenditures. Since they were flourishing before, they can survive for now. But not indefinitely."

He sighed melodramatically, as he did when he gave a funeral eulogy, another of his great specialties.

"Let me remind you that not a single worker, farmer, or employee has been laid off, even though the economic war has gone on for more than a year. These enterprises provide sixty percent of the jobs in the country. Think of how serious this is. Trujillo cannot go on supporting two-thirds of Dominican families when all of his businesses are half paralyzed because of the sanctions. And so . . ."

"And so . . ."

"Either you give me authorization to reduce personnel in order to cut costs, hoping for better times . . ."

"Do you want an explosion of thousands of unemployed workers?" Trujillo categorically cut him off. "Add a social problem to the ones I already have?"

"There is an alternative, one that has been used in exceptional circumstances," Senator Chirinos replied with a Mephistophelian little smile. "And isn't this one? Well, then. The State, in order to guarantee employment and economic activity, assumes control of strategic enterprises. The State nationalizes, say, a third of manufacturing firms and a half of farming and livestock enterprises. There are still enough funds for that in the Central Bank."

"What the hell do I gain by that?" an irritated Trujillo interrupted. "What do I gain if dollars move from the Central Bank to an account in my name?"

"What you gain is that from now on, the damage signified by three hundred enterprises operating at a loss doesn't come out of your pocket, Chief. I repeat, if this goes on, they'll all be bankrupt. My advice is technical. The only way to avoid the dissolution of your patrimony because of the economic blockade is to transfer the losses to the State. It isn't good for anybody if you're ruined, Chief."

Trujillo had a feeling of fatigue. The sun was growing hotter, and like all visitors to his office, Senator Chirinos was perspiring. From time to time he wiped his face with a blue handkerchief. He too would have liked the Generalissimo to have an air conditioner. But Trujillo detested the fake air that chilled you, the false atmosphere. He tolerated only a fan, on extremely hot days. Besides, he was proud of being the man-who-never-sweats.

He was silent for a moment, meditating, and his face soured.

"You're another one who thinks, in the back of your piggish brain, that I take over farms and businesses for profit," he said in a weary tone. "Don't interrupt. If you don't know me yet, after so many years at my side, what can I expect from the rest? They believe I'm interested in power in order to get rich."

"I know very well that isn't so, Chief."

"Do you need me to explain it again, for the hundredth time? If those businesses didn't belong to the Trujillo family, those jobs wouldn't exist. And the Dominican Republic would still be the backward African country it was when I picked it up and put it on my shoulders. You haven't realized that yet."

"I realize that perfectly, Chief."

"Are you stealing from me?"

Chirinos gave another start, and the ashen color of his face darkened. He blinked in alarm.

"What are you saying, Chief? As God is my witness . . ."

"I know you aren't," Trujillo reassured him. "And why don't you steal, even though you have the power to make or break us financially? Out of loyalty? Maybe. But more than anything else, out of fear. You know that if you steal from me and I find out, I'd turn you over to Johnny Abbes, and he'd take you to La Cuarenta, sit you on the Throne, and burn you to a crisp before he threw you to the sharks. All the things that tickle the overheated imaginations of the head of the SIM and the little team he's put together. That's why you don't steal from me. And that's why the managers, administrators, accountants, engineers, veterinarians, foremen, et cetera, et cetera, in the companies you oversee, that's why they don't steal from me either. That's why their work is conscientious and efficient, that's why the enterprises have prospered and multiplied and turned the Dominican Republic into a modern, prosperous country. Do you understand?"

"Of course, Chief." The Constitutional Sot gave another start. "You're absolutely right."

"On the other hand," Trujillo continued, as if he hadn't heard him, "you'd steal everything you could lay your hands on if you were doing the work you do for the Vicini family, the Valdéz family, the Armenteros family, instead of the Trujillo family. And you'd steal even more if the enterprises belonged to the State. Then you'd really line your pockets. Now can your brain grasp the reason for all the businesses, all the land, all the livestock?"

"To serve the nation, I know that better than anybody, Excellency," Senator Chirinos swore. He was frightened, and Trujillo could see it in the way he clutched the briefcase tight against his belly, and the increasingly unctuous manner in which he spoke. "I didn't mean to suggest anything to the contrary, Chief. God forbid!"

"But, it's true, not all the Trujillos are like me." The Benefactor eased the tension with a disillusioned expression. "My brothers, my wife, my children, none of them has the passion for this country that I do. They're a greedy bunch. Worst of all, these days they waste my time, forcing me to make sure they don't ignore my orders."

He adopted the belligerent, direct gaze he used to intimidate people. The Walking Turd shrank into his seat.

"Ah, I see, one of them has disobeyed," he murmured.

Senator Henry Chirinos nodded, not daring to speak.

"Did they try to take out currency again?" he asked, his voice turning cold. "Who was it? The old woman?"

The flabby face, dripping with perspiration, nodded again, as if against its will.

"She called me aside last night, during the poetic soiree." He hesitated and thinned his voice until he had almost extinguished it. "She said she was thinking about you, not about herself or the children. To make sure you have a peaceful old age, if something happens. I'm sure it's true, Chief. She adores you."

"What did she want?"

"Another transfer to Switzerland." The senator choked up. "Only a million this time."

"I hope for your sake you didn't go along with it," Trujillo said dryly.

"I didn't," stammered Chirinos, his apprehension deforming his words, his body shaken by a light tremor. "The captain gives the orders, not the soldier. And with all the respect and devotion Doña María deserves, my first loyalty is to you. This is a very delicate situation for me, Chief. Because of my refusals, I'm losing Doña María's friendship. For the second time in a week I've had to turn down a request of hers."

Was the Bountiful First Lady another one who thought the regime would collapse? Four months ago she had told Chirinos to transfer five million dollars to Switzerland; now it was another million. She thought that any day now they would have to run, that they needed hefty overseas accounts to enjoy a golden exile. Like Pérez Jiménez, Batista, Rojas Pinilla, or Perón, that trash. The old miser. As if their backs weren't more than covered. For her, it was never enough. She had been greedy when she was young, and had gotten worse with age. Was she going to take those accounts with her to the next world? It was the one area in which she dared to defy her husband's authority. Twice this week. She was plotting behind his back, that was it, pure and simple. That was how she bought the house in Spain, without Trujillo's knowing anything about it, after their official visit to Franco in 1954. That was how she opened and fed numbered accounts in Switzerland and New York, which he learned about eventually, sometimes by accident. In the past, he hadn't paid much attention to it, limiting himself to cursing her a few times and then shrugging his shoulders at the whims of an old, menopausal woman to whom, because she was his legitimate wife, he owed some consideration. Now, it was different. He had given categorical orders that no Dominican, including the Trujillo family, could take a single peso out of the country as long as the sanctions were in effect. He was not going to allow the rats to flee, trying to escape a ship that really would sink if the entire crew, beginning with the officers and the captain, ran away. No, damn it. Relatives, friends, enemies—they all stayed here, with everything they owned, to fight or leave their bones on the field of honor. Like the Marines, damn it. Stupid old bitch! How much better it would have been if he had left her and married one of the magnificent women he had held in his arms; the beautiful, docile Lina Lovatón, for example; he had sacrificed her, too, for this ungrateful country. He'd have to tell off the Bountiful First Lady this afternoon, remind her that Rafael Leonidas Trujillo Molina wasn't Batista, or that pig Pérez Jiménez, or that hypocrite Rojas Pinilla, or even the slick-haired General Perón. He wasn't going to spend his last years as a retired statesman overseas. He'd live until his final moment in this country, which, thanks to him, had stopped being a tribe, a mob, a caricature, and become a Republic.

He noticed that the Constitutional Sot was still trembling. Foam had gathered at the corners of his mouth. His little eyes, behind the two lumps of fat that were his eyelids, opened and closed frantically.

"There's something else. What is it?"

"Last week, I reported that we had managed to avoid their blocking the payment from Lloyds of London for sugar sold in Great Britain and the Netherlands. Not too much. About seven million dollars, of which four go to your enterprises and the rest to the Vicini mills and the Romana Plantation. Following your instructions, I asked Lloyds to transfer those monies to the Central Bank. This morning they indicated that the order had been countermanded."

"Who countermanded it?"

"General Ramfis, Chief. He telegraphed a request that the entire amount be sent to Paris."

"And Lloyds of London is full of dumb shits who follow counterorders from Ramfis?"

The Generalissimo spoke slowly, making an effort not to explode. This stupid crap was taking up too much of his time. And besides, it hurt him to have all his family's defects laid bare in front of strangers, no matter how trusted they were.

"They haven't processed General Ramfis's request yet, Chief. They're confused, that's why they called me. I reiterated that the money should be sent to the Central Bank. But, since General Ramfis has your authorization and has withdrawn funds on other occasions, it would be a good idea to let Lloyds know that there was a misunderstanding. A question of appearances, Chief."

"Call him and tell him to apologize to Lloyds. Today."

Chirinos shifted uneasily in his seat.

"If you order me to, I'll do it," he whispered. "But allow me to make a request, Chief. From your old friend. From the most faithful of your servants. I've already earned the ill will of Doña María. Don't turn me into your older son's enemy too."

The discomfort he felt was so visible that Trujillo smiled.

"Call him, don't be afraid. I won't die yet. I'm going to live ten more years and complete my work. It's the time I need. And you'll stay with me, until the last day. You're ugly, drunk, and dirty, but you're one of my best collaborators." He paused, and looking at the Walking Turd as tenderly as a beggar looking at his mangy dog, added something extraordinary, coming from him: "I only wish one of my brothers or sons was worth as much as you, Henry."

The senator was overwhelmed and did not know how to respond.

"What you have said compensates for all my sleepless nights," he stammered, bending his head.

"You're lucky you never married, that you don't have a family," Trujillo continued. "You must have thought it was a misfortune not to have any children. Bullshit! The great mistake of my life has been my family. My brothers, my own wife, my children. Have you ever seen disasters like them? Their only horizon is booze, pesos, and fucking. Is there one of them capable of continuing my work? Isn't it a shame that at a time like this, Ramfis and Radhamés are playing polo in Paris instead of standing at my side?"

Chirinos listened with downcast eyes, not moving, his face somber, expressing solidarity, not saying a word, undoubtedly afraid of compromising his future if he let slip a remark against the Chief's sons and brothers. It was unusual for the Generalissimo to give himself over to such bitter reflections; he never talked about his family, not even to intimates, and certainly not in such harsh terms.

"The order stands," he said, changing his tone and the subject at the same time. "Nobody, least of all a Trujillo, takes money out of the country while the sanctions are in effect."

"Understood, Chief. In fact, even if they wanted to they couldn't. Unless they carry out their dollars in suitcases, there are no transactions with foreign countries. Financial activity is at a standstill. Tourism has disappeared. Our reserves are dwindling every day. Do you flatly reject the State's taking over some enterprises? Not even the ones in the worst shape?"

"We'll see." Trujillo yielded slightly. "Leave your proposal with me, I'll study it. Anything else that's urgent?"

The senator consulted his notebook, bringing it close to his eyes. He adopted a tragicomic expression.

"There's a paradoxical situation in the United States. What shall we do with our so-called friends? The congressmen, politicians, and lobbyists who receive stipends for defending our country. Manuel Alfonso kept them up until he got sick. After that, they stopped. Some people have made discreet requests for payment."

"Who ordered them to be suspended?"

"Nobody, Chief. It's a good question. The accounts dedicated to that purpose, in New York, are dwindling too. They can't be added to, given the circumstances. It comes to several million pesos a month. Will you continue to be so generous with gringos who can't help us lift the sanctions?"

"I always knew they were leeches." The Generalissimo made a contemptuous gesture. "But they're also our only hope. If the political situation changes in the United States, they can use their influence to have the sanctions eased or lifted. And, in the short term, they can get Washington to at least pay us for the sugar already received."

Chirinos did not look hopeful. He shook his head solemnly.

"Even if the United States agreed to hand over what they've held back, it wouldn't do much good, Chief. What's twenty-two million dollars? Money for basic investment and the importation of crucial commodities for just a few weeks. But if you've made up your mind, I'll inform Consuls Mercado and Morales to resume payments to those parasites. By the way, Chief. The funds in New York might be frozen. If the proposal of three members of the Democratic Party is successful, they'll freeze the accounts of nonresident Dominicans in the United States. I know they appear as corporate accounts at Chase Manhattan and Chemical. But suppose the banks don't respect our confidentiality? Allow me to suggest that we transfer them to a country that's more secure. Canada, for example, or Switzerland."

The Generalissimo felt a hollow in his stomach. It wasn't anger that produced acid, it was disappointment. In the course of his long life, he had never wasted time licking his wounds, but what was happening now with the United States, the country to whom his regime had always given its vote at the UN no matter why it was needed, that really upset him. What had been the point of giving a royal welcome and a medal to every Yankee who set foot on the island?

"It's hard to understand the gringos," he murmured. "I can't get it into my head that they're treating me this way."

"I never trusted those jerks," echoed the Walking Turd. "They're all alike. You can't even say that this harassment is Eisenhower's fault. Kennedy is hounding us too."

Trujillo pulled himself together—"Back to work, damn it," he thought—and changed the subject again.

"Abbes García has everything ready to get that bastard Bishop

Reilly out from behind the nuns' skirts," he said. "He has two proposals. Deport him, or have the people lynch him and teach a lesson to plotting priests. Which do you prefer?"

"Neither one, Chief." Senator Chirinos recovered his self-assurance. "You know my opinion. We have to soften the conflict. The Church is two thousand years old, and nobody has ever defeated it. Look at what happened to Perón when he challenged it."

"He told me that himself, sitting right where you are now," Trujillo acknowledged. "Is that your advice? To bend over for those sons of bitches?"

"You should corrupt them with gifts and concessions, Chief," explained the Constitutional Sot. "Or maybe scare them, but don't do anything irreparable, and leave the door open for a reconciliation. What Johnny Abbes proposes would be suicide. Kennedy would send the Marines in a heartbeat. That's my opinion. You'll make the decision, and it will be the right one. I'll defend it with pen and tongue. As always."

The poetic flights that the Walking Turd was prone to amused the Benefactor. This latest one pulled him out of the dejection that was beginning to get the better of him.

"I know," he said with a smile. "You're loyal and that's why I appreciate you. Tell me, confidentially. How much do you have overseas in case you need to get out right away?"

For the third time the senator became agitated, as if his seat had turned into a bucking horse.

"Very little, Chief. Well, relatively speaking, I mean."

"How much?" Trujillo insisted, affectionately. "And where?"

"About four hundred thousand dollars," he admitted rapidly, lowering his voice. "In two separate accounts. In Panama. Opened before the sanctions, of course."

"That's peanuts," Trujillo admonished him. "With the posts you've held, you should have been able to save more."

"I'm not a saver, Chief. Besides, you know I never cared about money. I've always had all I needed to live."

"To drink, you mean."

"To dress well, to eat well, to drink well, and to buy the books I want," the senator agreed, looking at the ceiling and the crystal lamp in the office. "Thank God, with you I've always had interesting work to do. Should I repatriate that money? I'll do it today if you tell me to."

"Leave it where it is. If I need a hand when I'm in exile, you can help me out."

He laughed, in good humor. But as he laughed he suddenly recalled the scared little girl at Mahogany House, a compromising, accusatory witness who ruined his mood. It would have been better to shoot her, hand her over to the guards, let them raffle her off, or share her. The memory of that stupid little face watching him suffer reached all the way into his soul.

"Who's taken the most precautions?" he asked, hiding his distress. "Who has the most money overseas? Paíno Pichardo? Álvarez Pina? Egghead Cabral? Modesto Díaz? Balaguer? Who's accumulated the most? Because none of you believed me when I said the only way I'd leave here was in a coffin."

"I don't know, Chief. But if you'll permit me, I doubt that any of them has much money outside the country. For a very simple reason. Nobody ever thought the regime could end, that we'd find ourselves obliged to leave. Who would ever think that one day the earth could stop moving around the sun?"

"You would," Trujillo replied sarcastically. "That's why you took your miserable pesos to Panama, figuring I wouldn't last forever, that one of the conspiracies might succeed. You've given yourself away, asshole."

"I'll repatriate my savings this afternoon," Chirinos protested, gesticulating. "I'll show you the deposit slips from the Central Bank. Those savings have been in Panama a long time. My diplomatic missions allowed me to put something away. For cash outlays on the trips I make in your service, Chief. I've never padded the expenses the position required."

"You're scared, you think what happened to Egghead might happen to you." Trujillo was still smiling. "It's a joke. I've forgotten the secret you told me. Come on, tell me some gossip before you go. Bedroom gossip, not politics."

The Walking Turd smiled with relief. But as soon as he began telling him that the talk of Ciudad Trujillo right now was the beating the German consul gave his wife because he thought she was cheating on him, the Benefactor became distracted. How much money had his closest collaborators taken out of the country? If the Constitutional Sot had done it, they all had. Was it only four hundred thousand he had tucked away? It had to be more. All of them, in the darkest corner of their souls, had lived in fear that the regime would collapse. Bah, they were trash. Loyalty was not a Dominican virtue. He knew that. For thirty years they had worshiped him, applauded him, deified him, but the first time the wind changed, they would reach for their daggers.

"Who invented the slogan of the Dominican Party, using the initials of my name?" he asked unexpectedly. "Rectitude, Liberty, True Work, Morality. Was it you or Egghead?"

"Yours truly, Chief," Senator Chirinos exclaimed proudly. "On the tenth anniversary. It caught on, and twenty years later it's on all the streets and squares in the country. And in the overwhelming majority of the homes."

"It ought to be in the minds and memories of Dominicans," said Trujillo. "Those words summarize everything I've given them."

And at that moment, like the blow of a club to his head, he was seized by doubt. By certainty. It had happened. Dissembling, not listening to the praises of the Era that Chirinos had embarked on, he lowered his head, as if concentrating on an idea, focused his eyes, and looked, filled with anxiety. His bones turned to water. There it was: the dark stain covered his fly and part of his right leg. It must have been recent, it was still damp, at this very moment his insensible bladder was still leaking. He didn't feel it, he wasn't feeling it. A lashing rage shook him. He could dominate men, bring three million Dominicans to their knees, but he could not control his bladder.

"I can't listen to any more gossip, I don't have time," he lamented, not looking up. "Go on and take care of Lloyds, don't let them pay that money to Ramfis. Tomorrow, at the same time. Goodbye."

"Goodbye, Chief. If you'll permit me, I'll see you this afternoon, on the Avenida."

As soon as he heard the Constitutional Sot close the door, he called Sinforoso. He told him to bring another suit, also gray, and a change of underwear. He stood, and moving quickly, bumping into a sofa, he locked himself in the bathroom. He felt faint with disgust. He took off the trousers, shorts, and undershirt soiled by his involuntary urination. His shirt was not stained, but he took it off as well and then sat on the bidet. He soaped himself carefully. As he was getting dried he cursed once again the dirty trick his body was playing on him. He was waging war against many enemies, he could not constantly be distracted by his fucking bladder. He sprinkled talcum powder on his genitals and between his legs, and sat down on the toilet to wait for Sinforoso.

His meeting with the Walking Turd had left him troubled. What he told the senator was true: unlike his hoodlum brothers, and the Bountiful First Lady, an insatiable vampire, and his children, parasites sucking him dry, he had never cared very much about money. He used it in the service of power. Without money he would not have been able to make his way at first, for he had been born into a very modest family in San Cristóbal, which meant that as a boy he had to get what he needed, any way he could, to dress decently. Later, money helped him to be more efficient, to remove obstacles, to buy, attract, or bribe the people he needed and punish those who interfered with his work. Unlike María, who, when they were still lovers, thought up the idea of a laundry for constabulary guards and since then dreamed only of hoarding money, he liked to give it away.

If he hadn't been like that, would he have given gifts to the people, those countless presents every October 24, so that Dominicans could celebrate the Chief's birthday? How many millions of pesos had he spent over the years on sacks of caramels, chocolates, toys, fruits, dresses, trousers, shoes, bracelets, necklaces, soft drinks, blouses, records, guayaberas, brooches, magazines for the interminable processions that came to the Palace on the Chief's birthday? And how many more on gifts for his compadres and godchildren at the collective baptisms in the Palace chapel, when, for the past three decades, once and even twice a week, he became godfather to at least a hundred infants? Millions and millions of pesos. A productive investment, of course. An inspiration, in the first year of his government, that came from his profound knowledge of Dominican psychology. To establish that relationship, to be compadres with a campesino, a laborer, a craftsman, a merchant, was to guarantee the loyalty of the poor man and poor woman whom he embraced after the baptism of his godchild and whom he presented with two thousand pesos. Two thousand when times were good. As the list of his godchildren grew to twenty, fifty, a hundred, two hundred a week, the gifts—due in part to howls of protest from Doña María and also to the decline in the Dominican economy following the Fair for Peace and Brotherhood in the Free World in 1955—had gradually shrunk to fifteen hundred, a thousand, five hundred, two hundred, a hundred pesos for each godchild. Now, the Walking Turd was insisting that the collective baptisms be suspended or the gift be symbolic, a loaf of bread or ten pesos for each godchild, until the sanctions ended. Damn the Yankees!

He had founded enterprises and established businesses to create jobs and progress for the country and have the resources to give away presents left and right and keep the Dominicans happy.

And with his friends, collaborators, employees, hadn't he been as magnificent as Petronius in *Quo Vadis*? He had showered them with money, giving generous gifts for birthdays, weddings, births, jobs well done, or simply to show that he knew how to reward loyalty. He had presented them with pesos, houses, land, stocks, he had made them partners in his farms and enterprises, he had created businesses for them so they could earn good money and not plunder the State.

He heard a discreet knock at the door. Sinforoso, with the suit and underwear. He handed them over with lowered eyes. He had been with him more than twenty years; he had been his orderly in the Army, and the Chief had promoted him to majordomo and taken him to the Palace. He feared nothing from Sinforoso. He was deaf, dumb, and blind regarding everything that had to do with Trujillo, and he had the sense to know that where certain intimate subjects were concerned, such as his involuntary urinations, the slightest betrayal would deprive him of all he had—a house, a little cattle farm, a car, a large family—and, perhaps, even his life. The suit and underwear, hidden in a bag, would not attract anyone's attention, for the Benefactor was in the habit of changing clothes several times a day in his private office.

He dressed while Sinforoso—husky, his hair in a crew cut, impeccably groomed in his uniform of black trousers, white shirt, and white jacket with gold buttons—picked up the clothing scattered on the floor.

"What should I do with those two terrorist bishops, Sinforoso?" he asked as he was buttoning his trousers. "Expel them from the country? Send them to jail?"

"Kill them, Chief," Sinforoso answered without hesitation. "Everybody hates them, and if you don't do it, the people will. Nobody can forgive the Yankee and the Spaniard who came to this country to bite the hand that feeds them."

The Generalissimo had stopped listening. He would have to reprimand Pupo Román. That morning, after receiving Johnny Abbes and the Ministers of Foreign Affairs and of the Interior, he had gone to San Isidro Air Base to meet with the heads of the Air Force. And he saw something that turned his stomach: right at the entrance, a few meters from the guard post, under the flag and seal of the Republic, a pipe was spewing out filthy black water that had formed a quagmire at the edge of the highway. He ordered the car to stop. He got out and walked to the spot. It was a pipe carrying thick, stinking sewage—he had to put his handkerchief over his nostrils—and, of course, it had attracted a swarm of flies and mosquitoes. The waste kept flowing, inundating the area, poisoning the air and soil of the leading Dominican garrison. He felt rage, burning lava flooding his body. He controlled his first impulse, to return to the base and curse the officers who were present and demand if this was the image they were trying to give to the Armed Forces: an institution overrun by stinking water and vermin. But he immediately decided that he had to take the warning to the head man. And make Pupo Román in person swallow a little of the liquid shit pouring out of that sewage pipe. He decided to call him right away. But when he got back to his office, he forgot to do it. Was his memory beginning to fail, just like his bladder? Damn. The two things that had responded best throughout his whole life were failing now that he was seventy.

When he was clean and dressed, he returned to his desk and picked up the telephone that communicated automatically with Armed Forces headquarters. It did not take long to hear the voice of General Román:

"Yes, hello? Is that you, Excellency?"

"Come to the Avenida this afternoon," he said, very curtly, by way of greeting.

"Of course, Chief." General Román sounded alarmed. "Would you prefer me to come right now to the Palace? Has something happened?"

"You'll find out what's happened," he said, slowly, imagining the nervousness of his niece Mireya's husband, on hearing how dryly he spoke to him. "Any news?"

"Everything normal, Excellency," General Román said hurriedly. "I was receiving the routine regional reports. But if you prefer . . ."

"On the Avenida," he cut him off. And hung up.

It cheered him to imagine the sizzling questions, suppositions, fears, suspicions he had put into the head of that asshole who was the

Minister of the Armed Forces. What did they say about me to the Chief? What gossip, what slander have my enemies told him? Have I fallen into disgrace? Did I fail to carry out one of his orders? He would be in hell until the evening.

But this thought occupied him for only a few seconds, and once again the humiliating memory of the girl filled his mind. Anger, sadness, nostalgia mixed together in his spirit and kept him in a state of turmoil. And then it occurred to him: "A cure equal to the disease." The face of a beautiful woman, exploding with pleasure in his arms, thanking him for the joy he had given her. Wouldn't that erase the frightened little face of that idiot? Yes: he'd go tonight to San Cristóbal, to Mahogany House, and wipe away the affront in the same bed and with the same weapons. This decision—he touched his fly in a kind of exorcism—raised his spirits and stiffened his resolve to continue with the day's schedule.

9 "What's new with Segundo?" asked Antonio de la Maza.

Leaning against the steering wheel, Antonio Imbert replied, not turning around:

"I saw him yesterday. They let me visit him every week now. A short visit, half an hour. Sometimes the fucking warden of La Victoria decides to cut the visits to fifteen minutes. Just to be a son of a bitch."

"How is he?"

How could someone be who, trusting in a promise of amnesty, left Puerto Rico, where he had a good job working for the Ferré family in Ponce, and returned to his country only to discover that they were waiting to try him for the alleged crime of a unionist that had been committed in Puerto Plata years earlier, and sentence him to thirty years in prison? How could a man feel who, if he had killed, did it for the regime, and was repaid by Trujillo's leaving him to rot in a dungeon for the past five years?

But this was not his answer, because Imbert knew that Antonio de la Maza had not asked the question out of interest in his brother Segundo but only to break the interminable waiting. He shrugged:

"Segundo has balls. If he's having a tough time he doesn't show it. Sometimes he even gets a kick out of cheering me up."

"You didn't tell him anything about this."

"Of course not. To be on the safe side, and not to give him false hopes. Suppose it fails?"

"It won't fail," Lieutenant García Guerrero interjected from the back seat. "The Goat is coming."

Was he? Tony Imbert looked at his watch. He still might come, no reason to lose hope. He never lost patience, and hadn't for many years. When he was young he did, unfortunately, and that led him to do things he regretted with every cell in his body. Like the telegram he sent in 1949, crazed with anger at the landing of anti-Trujillistas, led by Horacio Julio Ornes, on the beach at Luperón in the province of Puerto Plata, when he was governor. "Give the order and I'll burn Puerto Plata, Chief." The words he regretted most in his life. He saw them printed in every newspaper, for the Generalissimo wanted all Dominicans to know how much of a dedicated, fanatical Trujillista the young governor was.

Why did Horacio Julio Ornes, Félix Córdoba Boniche, Tulio Hostilio Arvelo, Gugú Henríquez, Miguelucho Feliú, Salvador Reyes Valdéz, Federico Horacio, and the rest choose Puerto Plata on that long-ago June 19 in 1949? The expedition was a resounding failure. One of the two invading airplanes could not even fly the distance and returned to the island of Cozumel. The Catalina, carrying Horacio Julio Ornes and his companions, landed on the water near the muddy coast of Luperón, but before the expeditionary force could climb out, a Coast Guard cutter fired on the plane and destroyed it. In a few hours Army patrols captured the invaders. That permitted the kind of farcical show Trujillo liked so much. He granted amnesty to the prisoners, including Horacio Julio Ornes, and in a show of power and magnanimity allowed them to go into exile again. But as he was making this gesture of generosity for the outside world, the governor of Puerto Plata, Antonio Imbert, and his brother, Major Segundo Imbert, military commander of the province, were stripped of their rank, imprisoned, and beaten, and a merciless reprisal was carried out against supposed accomplices, who were arrested, tortured, and often shot in secret. "Accomplices who weren't accomplices," he thinks. "They thought everybody would rise up when they saw them land. In fact, nobody was with them." Too many innocents had to pay for their fantasy.

How many innocents would have to pay if tonight's plan failed? Antonio Imbert was not as optimistic as Amadito or Salvador Estrella Sadhalá; when they learned from Antonio de la Maza that General José René (Pupo) Román, head of the Armed Forces, was involved in the plot, they became convinced that once Trujillo was dead, everything would go like clockwork: the military, obeying Román's orders, would detain the Goat's brothers, kill Johnny Abbes and the die-hard Trujillistas, and install a civilian-military junta. The people would take to the streets and, overjoyed at gaining their freedom, exterminate the *caliés*. Would things turn out that way? Disillusionment, ever since the stupid ambush to which Segundo fell victim, had made Antonio Imbert allergic to premature enthusiasm. He wanted to see Trujillo's corpse lying at his feet; the rest of it mattered less to him. Ridding the country of that man was the main thing. When that obstacle was out of the way, even if things didn't go so well at first, at least a door would be opened. And that justified what they were doing tonight, even if none of them survived.

No, Tony had not said a word about the conspiracy to his brother Segundo on his weekly visits to him at La Victoria. They talked about the family, about baseball and boxing, and Segundo told him stories about the prison routine, but they avoided the only important topic. On his last visit, as he was saying goodbye, Antonio whispered: "Things are going to change, Segundo." A word to the wise. Had he guessed? After a series of crushing blows, Segundo, like Tony, had gone from enthusiastic Trujillista to a man disaffected with the regime to conspirator, and long ago had concluded that the only way to put an end to the tyranny was by killing the tyrant; everything else was useless. You had to eradicate the person in whom all the strands of the dread spiderweb converged.

"What would have happened if the bomb had exploded on Máximo Gómez when the Goat was taking his walk?" Amadito fantasized.

"Trujillista fireworks in the sky," replied Imbert.

"I could have been one of the firecrackers if I had been on duty," the lieutenant said with a laugh.

"I would have sent a huge wreath of roses to your funeral," said Tony.

"What a plan," Estrella Sadhalá remarked. "Blowing up the Goat and all his cronies. Heartless!"

"Well, I knew you wouldn't be part of his escort," said Imbert. "Besides, when that happened I hardly knew you, Amadito. Now I would have to give it a little more thought."

"That's a relief," said the lieutenant, thanking him.

They had been waiting on the road to San Cristóbal for more than an hour, and had tried several times to have a conversation, or to joke, as they were doing now, but those efforts had petered out and each man enclosed himself again in his own torments, hopes, or memories. At one point Antonio de la Maza turned on the radio, but as soon as he heard the honeyed voice on the Voice of the Tropics announcing a program on spiritualism, he turned it off.

Yes, in the failed plan to kill the Goat two and a half years earlier, Antonio Imbert had been prepared to blow up, along with Trujillo, many of the toadies who escorted him every afternoon on his walk from the house of Doña Julia, the Sublime Matriarch, along Máximo Gómez and the Avenida, to the obelisk. Weren't the men who accompanied him the dirtiest and most bloodstained? It would be a service to the country to eradicate so many of his henchmen at the same time as the tyrant.

He prepared the assault alone, not even telling his best friend, Salvador Estrella Sadhalá, because even though Turk was an anti-Trujillista, Tony was afraid he would disapprove because of his Catholicism. He planned it and thought it out in his own mind, bringing to it all the resources at his disposal, convinced that the fewer the people involved, the greater its chances for success. Not until the final stage did he include in his project two boys from what would later be called the June 14 Movement; at that time, it was a clandestine group of young professionals and students trying to organize in order to take action, though they didn't know what kind, against tyranny.

His plan was simple and practical. It took advantage of the maniacal discipline that Trujillo brought to his routine activities, in this case his evening walk along Máximo Gómez and the Avenida. He studied the terrain carefully, going back and forth along the avenue lined with the residences of the regime's top men, past and present. The ostentatious house of Héctor (Blacky) Trujillo, his brother's puppet president for two terms. The pink mansion of Mama Julia, the Sublime Matriarch, whom the Chief visited every afternoon before setting out on his walk. The house of Luis Rafael Trujillo Molina, nicknamed Kid, who was mad for cockfights. And the houses of General Arturo (Razor) Espaillat, and of Joaquín Balaguer, the current puppet president, which stood next to the nuncio's residence. The elegant dwelling that once belonged to Anselmo Paulino was now one of Ramfis Trujillo's houses. The mansion of the Goat's daughter, the beautiful Angelita, and her husband, Colonel Luis José (Pechito) León Estévez. The residence of the Cáceres Troncoso family, and the palatial home of the Vicini tycoons. Adjoining Máximo Gómez was a ball field that Trujillo built for his sons across from Radhamés Manor and the lot once occupied by the house of General Ludovino Fernández, whom the Goat had ordered killed. Separating the mansions were large open spaces filled with weeds and protected by green-painted wire fences erected along the edge of the sidewalk. On the right side of the street, where the entourage always walked, there were vacant lots surrounded by the same wire fencing, which Antonio Imbert had spent many hours studying.

He chose the piece of fence that started at Kid Trujillo's house. On the pretext of replacing part of the fencing around Ready-Mix, the cement factory where he was manager (it belonged to Paco Martínez, the Bountiful First Lady's brother), he bought several dozen meters of wire fencing and the metal poles that were placed every fifteen meters to hold the fence taut. He verified personally that the poles were hollow and could be filled with sticks of dynamite. Since Ready-Mix owned two quarries on the outskirts of Ciudad Trujillo, from which raw materials were extracted, it was easy for him, on his periodic visits, to take away sticks of dynamite and hide them in his own office: he always came in before anyone else and left after the last employee had gone home.

When everything was ready, he told his plan to Luis Gómez Pérez and Iván Tavares Castellanos. Younger than he, they were at the university, studying law and engineering, respectively. They belonged to his cell of the clandestine anti-Trujillista groups; after observing them for many weeks, he decided they were serious, trustworthy, and eager to take action. Both accepted enthusiastically. They agreed not to say a word to their comrades, with whom they met in groups of eight or ten, always in a different location, to discuss the best way to mobilize the people against the dictatorship.

With Luis and Iván, who turned out to be even better than he had hoped, Tony filled the poles with sticks of dynamite, and placed the caps after testing them with a remote control. To be certain of their timing, they practiced in the empty lot of the factory after the workers and clerical staff had left, to see how long they needed to take down a piece of existing fence and put up a new one, replacing the old posts with ones full of dynamite. Less than five hours. Everything was ready on June 12. They planned to act on June 15, when Trujillo returned from a trip to Cibao. They had at their disposal a dump truck that would knock down the piece of fence at dawn, so they would have a pretext—wearing the blue overalls of Municipal Services—to replace it with the armed one. They marked two points, each less than fifty paces from the explosion, where, with Imbert to the right and Luis and Iván to the left, they would activate the remote controls in quick succession, the first blast to kill Trujillo at the moment he passed in front of the poles, and the second to make sure he was dead.

And then, on June 14, 1959, the eve of the day they had decided on, in the mountains of Constanza, it happened—the unexpected landing of an airplane from Cuba, painted with the colors and insignia of the Dominican Air Force and carrying anti-Trujillista guerrillas, followed a week later by landings on the beaches of Maimón and Estero Hondo. The arrival of that small detachment, which included the bearded Cuban comandante Delio Gómez Ochoa, sent a chill down the spine of the regime. It was a rash, uncoordinated attempt. The clandestine groups had absolutely no information regarding what was being prepared in Cuba. The support of Fidel Castro for the uprising against Trujillo had been, since the fall of Batista six months earlier, an obsessive topic at their meetings. They counted on that help in every plan they put together and then took apart, and for which they were amassing hunting rifles, revolvers, old shotguns. But no one Imbert knew was in touch with Cuba or had any idea that June 14 would see the arrival of dozens of revolutionaries; after putting the handful of guards at the Constanza airport out of commission, they fled to the nearby mountains, only to be hunted down like rabbits in the days that followed, and killed on the spot or taken to Ciudad Trujillo, where, on Ramfis's orders, almost all of them were murdered (but not the Cuban Gómez Ochoa and his adopted son, Pedrito Mirabal, whom the regime, in another of its theatrical gestures, returned some time later to Fidel Castro).

And no one could have suspected the magnitude of the repression the government would unleash after the landing. In the ensuing weeks and months, it intensified rather than subsided. The *caliés* seized all suspects and took them to the SIM, where they were subjected to torture—castration, bursting their eardrums, gouging out their eyes, sitting them on the Throne—to force them to name names. La Victoria, La Cuarenta, and El Nueve were overflowing with young people of both sexes—students, professionals, and office workers—many of them the children or relatives of men in the government. Trujillo was dumbfounded: was it possible that the children, grandchildren, nieces and nephews of the people who had benefited most from the regime were plotting against him? They were shown no consideration despite their family names, white faces, and middle-class trappings.

Luis Gómez Pérez and Iván Tavares Castellanos fell into the hands of the *caliés* of the SIM on the morning of the day scheduled for the attack. With his customary realism, Antonio Imbert knew he had no possibility of seeking asylum: all the embassies were surrounded by lines of uniformed police, soldiers, and *caliés*. He calculated that, under torture, Luis, Iván, or anyone else from the clandestine groups would mention his name and the *caliés* would come for him. Then, just as he did tonight, he knew exactly what to do: welcome them with lead. He would try to send a few of them into the next world before he was cut to ribbons. He was not going to let them pull out his nails with pliers, cut out his tongue, or sit him in the electric chair. Kill him, yes; abuse him, never.

On some pretext or other he sent his wife, Guarina, and his daughter, Leslie, who knew nothing of his activities, to the farm of some relatives in La Romana, and with a glass of rum in his hand, he sat down to wait. He had a loaded revolver, with the safety off, in his pocket. But the *caliés* did not come that day, or the next, or the one after that, to his house, or to his office at Ready-Mix, where he continued to show up punctually with all the sangfroid he could muster. Luis and Iván had not betrayed him, and neither had the people he knew in the clandestine groups. Miraculously, he escaped a repression that struck at the guilty and the innocent, filled the prisons, and for the first time in the twenty-nine years of the regime, terrorized the families of the middle class, Trujillo's traditional mainstays and the source of most of the prisoners, members of what was called, in response to the frustrated invasion, the June 14 Movement. Tony's cousin Ramón (Moncho) Imbert Rainieri was one of its leaders.

Why did he escape? Because of the courage of Luis and Iván, no doubt—two years later they were still in the dungeons of La Victoria— and the courage, no doubt, of other girls and boys in June 14 who forgot to name him. Perhaps they considered him merely an onlooker, not an activist. Tony Imbert was so shy that he rarely opened his mouth at the meetings Moncho took him to for the first time; he would only listen, or offer a monosyllabic opinion. And it was unlikely he was in the files of the SIM except as the brother of Major Segundo Imbert. His service record was clean. He had spent his life working for the regime—as an inspector general on the railroad, governor of Puerto Plata, general supervisor of the National Lottery, director of the office that issued identity papers—and as manager at Ready-Mix, a factory that belonged to Trujillo's son-in-law. Why would they suspect him?

Very cautiously, in the days following June 14, he stayed at the factory at night, dismantled the sticks of dynamite and returned them to the quarries, while he pondered how and with whom he would carry out the next plan to do away with Trujillo. He confessed everything that had happened (and failed to happen) to his dearest friend, Salvador (Turk) Estrella Sadhalá, who berated Tony for not including him in the Máximo Gómez plot. Salvador had reached the same conclusion on his own: nothing would change as long as Trujillo was alive. They began to propose and discard possible methods of attack, but said nothing in front of Amadito, the third man in their trio: it was hard to believe that a military adjutant would want to kill the Benefactor.

Not long afterward, the traumatic episode in Amadito's career occurred—in order to obtain his promotion, he had to kill a prisoner (his ex-fiancée's brother, he believed)—that brought him into the game. It would soon be two years since the landings at Constanza, Maimón, and Estero Hondo. One year, eleven months, and fourteen days, to be exact. Antonio Imbert looked at his watch. He probably wasn't coming.

So many things had happened in the Dominican Republic, in the world, and in his personal life. So many. The massive dragnets of January 1960, into which so many boys and girls of the June 14 Movement fell, among them the Mirabal sisters and their husbands. Trujillo's break with his old accomplice, the Catholic Church, after the Pastoral Letter of January 1960, in which the bishops denounced the dictatorship. The attempt against President Betancourt of Venezuela, in June 1960, that mobilized so many countries against Trujillo, including his great ally the United States, which voted in favor of sanctions on August 6, 1960, at the conference in Costa Rica. And, on November 25, 1960—Imbert felt the inevitable piercing in his chest every time he recalled that dismal day—the murder of the three sisters, Minerva, Patria, and María Teresa Mirabal, and their driver, in La Cumbre, in the northern mountain range, on their way home from visiting Minerva's and Maria Teresa's husbands, imprisoned in the Fortress of Puerto Plata.

The entire Dominican Republic learned about the killing in the rapid, mysterious way that news circulated from mouth to mouth and house to house and in a few hours reached the most remote corners of the country, though not a line appeared in the press, and often, as it circulated, the news transmitted by human tom-tom was colored, diminished, exaggerated until it turned into myth, legend, fiction, with almost no connection to real events. He recalled that night on the Malecón, not very far from where he was now, six months later, waiting for the Goat—to avenge the Mirabal sisters too. They were sitting on the stone railing, as they did every night—he, Salvador, Amadito, and, on this occasion, Antonio de la Maza—to enjoy the cool breeze and to talk, away from prying ears. What had happened to the Mirabal sisters set their teeth on edge, it turned their stomachs as they discussed the deaths of the three incredible women, high in the mountains, in an alleged car accident.

"They kill our fathers, our brothers, our friends. And now they're killing our women. And here we sit, resigned, waiting our turn," he heard himself say.

"Not resigned, Tony," Antonio de la Maza objected. He had come from Restauración, and had brought the news of the death of the Mirabal sisters, which he had heard along the way. "Trujillo will pay. A plan's in motion. But it has to be done right."

At that time, an attempt was being planned in Moca, during a visit by Trujillo to the land of the De la Maza family, on one of the trips through the country that he had been making since the condemnation by the OAS and the imposition of economic sanctions. A bomb would go off in the main church, consecrated to the Sacred Heart of Jesus, and a rain of rifle fire would fall on Trujillo from the balconies, terraces, and clock tower as he spoke on the platform erected in the atrium to a crowd gathered around the statue of St. John Bosco, partially covered by heartsease. Imbert himself inspected the church and volunteered to hide in the clock tower, the most dangerous place in the church.

"Tony knew the Mirabals," Turk explained to Antonio. "That's why he's so upset."

He knew them, though he couldn't say they were friends. He had occasionally met the three sisters, and Minerva's and Patria's husbands, Manolo Tavares Justo and Leandro Guzmán, at the meetings at which the June 14 Movement was organized, taking the historic Trinitaria de Duarte as their model. The three women were leaders of the small, enthusiastic, but disorganized and inefficient organization that the repression was destroying. They had made an impression on him because of the conviction and boldness they brought to an unequal and uncertain struggle, Minerva Mirabal in particular. It happened to everyone who met her and heard her give opinions, hold discussions, offer proposals, or make decisions. Though he hadn't thought about it earlier, after the killing Tony Imbert told himself that until he knew Minerva Mirabal, it had never occurred to him that a woman could dedicate herself to things as manly as planning a revolution, obtaining and hiding weapons, dynamite, Molotov cocktails, knives, bayonets, talking about assassination attempts, strategy, and tactics, and dispassionately discussing whether, in the event they fell into the hands of the SIM, activists ought to swallow poison to avoid the risk of betraying their comrades under torture.

Minerva spoke about these things, and about the best way to engage in clandestine propaganda or recruit university students, and everyone listened to her. Because of her intelligence and the clarity with which she spoke. Her firm convictions and eloquence gave her words a strength that was contagious. And she was beautiful as well, with black hair and eyes, delicate features, finely drawn nose and mouth, and dazzling white teeth that contrasted with the bluish cast of her skin. Very beautiful, yes. There was something powerfully feminine in her, a delicacy, a natural flirtatiousness in her movements and smiles, despite the somber clothing she wore to meetings. Tony did not recall ever seeing her in makeup. Yes, very beautiful, but—he thought—none of the men would ever have dared to pay her one of those compliments, say one of those playful, witty things that were normal, natural—obligatory—for Dominican men, especially if they were young, and united by the intense brotherhood created by shared ideals, illusions, and dangers. Something in Minerva Mirabal's self-assured presence kept men from taking the informal liberties they allowed themselves with other women.

By then, she was already a legend in the small world of the clandestine struggle against Trujillo. Which of the things they said about her were true, which were exaggerated, which invented? No one would have presumed to ask her, no one wanted to receive that deep, scornful look or one of those cutting replies with which she sometimes silenced an opponent. They said that as a teenager she dared to rebuff Trujillo himself by refusing to dance with him, and for that reason her father was deposed as mayor of Ojo de Agua and sent to prison. Others suggested that it was more than a rebuff, that she had slapped him because while they were dancing he fondled her and said something obscene, a possibility that many rejected ("She wouldn't be alive, he would have killed her or had her killed on the spot"), but not Antonio Imbert. From the first time he saw and heard her, he did not doubt for a second that if the slap wasn't the truth, it could have been. It was enough to see and hear Minerva Mirabal for only a few minutes (talking, for example, with icy naturalness about the need to prepare activists psychologically to resist torture) to know she was capable of slapping even Trujillo if he showed a lack of respect. She had been arrested several times, and stories were told about her fearlessness, first in La Cuarenta, and then in La Victoria, where she went on a hunger strike, withstood solitary confinement on bread and worm-infested water, and where, they said, she was savagely mistreated. She never spoke of her time in prison, or about the torture, or about the calvary her family had lived since it was known she was an anti-Trujillista: they had been hounded, had their few goods confiscated, and been placed under house arrest. The dictatorship allowed Minerva to study the law so that when she finished—a well-planned vengeance—it could deny her a professional license—that is, condemn her to not working, to not earning a living, to feeling frustrated in the prime of her youth, having studied five years for nothing. But none of that made her bitter; she went on tirelessly, encouraging everyone, an engine that would not stop, a prelude—Imbert often told himself—to the young, beautiful, enthusiastic, idealistic country the Dominican Republic would be one day.

He was embarrassed as he felt his eyes filling with tears. He lit a cigarette and took several drags, blowing the smoke toward the ocean, where moonlight glimmered and played. There was no breeze now. Occasionally, the headlights of a car appeared in the distance, coming from Ciudad Trujillo. The four would sit up straight, crane their necks, tensely scrutinize the darkness, but each time, when the car was twenty or thirty meters away, they discovered it wasn't the Chevrolet and slumped back in their seats, disappointed.

The one who controlled his emotions best was Imbert. He had always been quiet, but in recent years, since the idea of killing Trujillo had taken possession of him and, like a hermit crab, fed on all his energy, his silence had intensified. He had never had many friends; in the last few months, his life had been bounded by his office at Ready-Mix, his home, and his daily meetings with Estrella Sadhalá and Lieutenant García Guerrero. Following the death of the Mirabal sisters, clandestine meetings had practically ceased. The repression crushed the June 14 Movement. Those who escaped withdrew into family life, trying to go unnoticed. From time to time a question would torment him: "Why wasn't I arrested?" Uncertainty made him feel ill, as if he were guilty of something, as if he were responsible for how much others had suffered at the hands of Johnny Abbes while he continued to enjoy his freedom.

A very relative freedom, it's true. When he understood the kind of regime he was living under, the kind of government he had served since he was a young man, and was still serving—what else was he doing as manager at one of the clan's factories?—he felt like a prisoner. Perhaps it was to rid himself of the feeling that all his steps were controlled, every path he took and all his movements tracked, that the idea of eliminating Trujillo took hold so firmly in his consciousness. His disenchantment with the regime was gradual, long, and secret, beginning much earlier than the political difficulties of his brother Segundo, who had been even more of a Trujillista than he. Who around him had not been a Trujillista for the past twenty, twenty-five years? They all thought the Goat was the savior of the Nation, the man who ended the caudillo wars, did away with the threat of a new invasion from Haiti, called a halt to a humiliating dependency on the United States—which controlled customs, prohibited a Dominican currency, and approved the budget—and, whether they were willing or not, brought the country's best minds into the government. Compared to that, what did it matter if Trujillo fucked any woman he wanted? Or swallowed up factories, farms, and livestock? Wasn't he increasing Dominican prosperity? Hadn't he given this country the most powerful Armed Forces in the Caribbean? For twenty years Tony Imbert had said and defended these things. That was what turned his stomach now.

He couldn't remember how it began, the first doubts, conjectures, discrepancies that led him to wonder if everything really was going so well, or if, behind the facade of a country that under the severe but inspired leadership of an extraordinary statesman was moving ahead at a quickstep, lay a grim spectacle of people destroyed, mistreated, and deceived, the enthronement, through propaganda and violence, of a monstrous lie. Drops falling tirelessly, one after the other, boring a hole in his Trujillism. When he was no longer governor of Puerto Plata, deep in his heart he stopped being a Trujillista; he had become convinced the regime was dictatorial and corrupt. He told no one, not even Guarina. The face he showed the world was still Trujillista, and even though his brother Segundo had gone into exile in Puerto Rico, the regime, as a demonstration of its magnanimity, continued to give positions to Antonio, even—what greater proof of confidence?—in the Trujillo family enterprises.

It had been this malaise of so many years' duration—thinking one thing and doing something that contradicted it every day—that led him, in the secret recesses of his mind, to condemn Trujillo to death, to convince himself that as long as Trujillo lived, he and many other Dominicans would be condemned to this awful queasy sickness of constantly having to lie to themselves and deceive everyone else, of having to be two people in one, a public lie and a private truth that could not be expressed.

The decision did him good; it raised his morale. His life stopped being a mortifying duplicity when he could share his true feelings with someone else. His friendship with Salvador Estrella Sadhalá was like a gift from heaven. With Turk he could talk freely against everything around him; his moral integrity, the sincerity with which he tried to accommodate his behavior to the religion he professed with a devotion Tony had never seen in anyone else, made Salvador his model as well as his best friend.

Shortly after they became close friends, Imbert began to frequent clandestine groups, thanks to his cousin Moncho. Although he left the meetings with the feeling that these girls and boys were risking their freedom, their futures, their lives but would not find an effective way to fight Trujillo, the hour or two he spent with them after arriving at a strange house—a different one each time, taking a thousand detours, following messengers identified with different code names—gave him a reason for living, cleared his conscience, and centered his life.

Guarina was dumbstruck when finally, so that some calamity would not take her completely by surprise, Tony began revealing to her that, contrary to all appearances, he was no longer a Trujillista and was even working in secret against the government. She did not try to dissuade him. She did not ask what would happen to their daughter, Leslie, if he was arrested and sentenced to thirty years in prison, like Segundo, or, even worse, if they killed him.

His wife and daughter did not know about tonight; they thought he was playing cards at Turk's house. What would happen to them if this failed?

"Do you trust General Román?" he said hurriedly, to force himself to think about something else. "Are you sure he's one of us?" Pupo Román, married to Trujillo's niece, was the brother-in-law of Generals José and Virgilio García Trujillo, the Chief's favorite nephews.

"If he weren't with us, we'd all be in La Cuarenta by now," said Antonio de la Maza. "He's with us as long as we meet his conditions: he has to see the body."

"It's hard to believe," Tony murmured. "What does the Minister of the Armed Forces stand to gain from this? He has everything to lose."

"He hates Trujillo more than you and I do," replied De la Maza. "And so do many of the men at the top. Trujillism is a house of cards. It'll collapse, you'll see. Pupo has commitments from a lot of men in the military; they're only waiting for his orders. He'll give them, and tomorrow this will be a different country."

"If the Goat comes," Estrella Sadhalá grumbled in the back seat.

"He'll come, Turk, he'll come," the lieutenant repeated one more time.

Antonio Imbert sank again into his thoughts. Would his country wake tomorrow to find itself liberated? He wanted that with all his strength, but even now, minutes before they would act, it was hard for him to believe. How many people were in the conspiracy besides General Román? He never wanted to find out. He knew about four or five, but there were many more. Better not to know. He always thought it crucial that the conspirators know as little as possible so as not to put the operation at risk. He had listened with interest to everything Antonio de la Maza told them about the commitment the head of the Armed Forces had made to assume power if they executed the tyrant. In this way the Goat's close relatives and the leading Trujillistas would be captured or killed before they could unleash a series of reprisals. Just as well that his two boys, Ramfis and Radhamés, were in Paris. How many people had Antonio de la Maza talked to? At times, in the endless meetings of the past few months to revise the plan, Antonio had let slip allusions, references, half-spoken words that suggested there were many people involved. Tony had taken caution to the extreme of cutting Salvador off one day when he began to say in indignation that he and Antonio de la Maza, at a meeting in the house of General Juan Tomás Díaz, had argued with a group of conspirators who objected to bringing Imbert into the plot. They didn't think he was safe because of his Trujillista past; somebody recalled the famous telegram to Trujillo, offering to burn Puerto Plata. ("It will follow me to my death and beyond," he thought.) Turk and Antonio had protested, saying they would put their hands to the fire for Tony, but he would not allow Salvador to continue:

"I don't want to know, Turk. After all, why would people who don't know me ever trust me? They're right, I've worked my whole life for Trujillo, directly or indirectly."

"And what do I do?" replied Turk. "What do thirty or forty percent of Dominicans do? Aren't we all working for the government or its businesses? Only the very rich can allow themselves the luxury of not working for Trujillo."

"Not them either," he thought. The rich too, if they wanted to go on being rich, had to ally themselves with the Chief, sell him part of their businesses or buy part of his, and contribute in this way to his greatness and power. With half-closed eyes, lulled by the gentle sound of the sea, he thought of what a perverse system Trujillo created, one in which all Dominicans sooner or later took part as accomplices, a system which only exiles (not always) and the dead could escape. In this country, in one way or another, everyone had been, was, or would be part of the regime. "The worst thing that can happen to a Dominican is to be intelligent or competent," he had once heard Agustín Cabral say ("A very intelligent and competent Dominican," he told himself) and the words had been etched in his mind: "Because sooner or later Trujillo will call upon him to serve the regime, or his person, and when he calls, one is not permitted to say no." He was proof of this truth. It never occurred to him to put up the slightest resistance to his appointments. As Estrella Sadhalá always said, the Goat had taken from people the sacred attribute given to them by God: their free will.

In contrast to Turk, religion had never occupied a central place in the life of Antonio Imbert. He was Catholic in the Dominican way, he had gone through all the religious ceremonies that marked people's lives—baptism, confirmation, first communion, Catholic school, marriage in the Church—and he undoubtedly would be buried with the sermon and blessing of a priest. But he had never been a particularly conscientious believer, never been concerned with the implications of his faith in everyday life, never bothered to verify if his behavior complied with the commandments, as Salvador did in a way that he found debilitating.

But what he said about free will affected him. Perhaps this was why he decided that Trujillo had to die. So that he and other Dominicans could recover their ability to at least accept or reject the work they did to earn a living. Tony did not know what that was like. Perhaps as a child he knew, but he had forgotten. It must be nice. Your cup of coffee or glass of rum must taste better, the smoke of your cigar, a swim in the ocean on a hot day, the movie you see on Saturday, the merengue on the radio, everything must leave a more pleasurable sensation in your body and spirit when you had what Trujillo had taken away from Dominicans thirty-one years ago: free will.

10 At the sound of the bell, Urania and her father become rigid, looking at each other as if caught in some mischief. Voices on the ground floor and an exclamation of surprise. Hurried steps coming up the stairs. The door opens almost at the same time that they hear an impatient knock, and a bewildered face peers in; Urania immediately recognizes her cousin Lucinda.

"Urania? Urania?" Her large protruding eyes examine her from top to bottom, from bottom to top, then she opens her arms and walks toward her as if to verify whether or not she is a hallucination.

"It's me, Lucindita." Urania embraces the younger daughter of her Aunt Adelina, the cousin who is her own age, her classmate at school.

"Uranita! I can't believe it! You're here? Let me take a look at you! What's going on? Why didn't you call me? Why didn't you come to the house? Have you forgotten how much we love you? Don't you remember your Aunt Adelina, and Manolita? And me, you ungrateful thing?"

She is so surprised, so full of questions, so curious—"My God, girl, how could you spend thirty-five years—thirty-five, right?—without coming home and seeing your family? Oh, Uranita! You must have so much to tell us!"—that she doesn't give her time to answer her questions. That's one way she hasn't changed much. Even as a little girl she chattered like a parrot, Lucindita the enthusiastic one, the inventive and playful one. The cousin she always liked best. Urania remembers her in her dress uniform, white skirt and navy-blue jacket, and in the everyday pink-and-blue outfit: an agile, plump little girl in bangs, with braces on her teeth and a smile on her lips. Now she is a stout matron, her face taut and smooth with no sign of a face-lift, wearing a simple flowered dress. Her only adornment is a pair of long, flashing gold earings. Suddenly she interrupts her affectionate questioning of Urania, goes over to the invalid, and kisses him on the forehead.

"What a nice surprise your daughter gave you, Uncle Agustín. You didn't expect your little girl to come back to life and pay you a visit. It's a happy time, isn't it, Uncle Agustín?"

She kisses him again on the forehead and just as abruptly forgets about him. She sits next to Urania on the edge of the bed. She takes her by the arm, looks at her, examines her, overwhelms her again with exclamations and questions:

"You look so good, girl. We're the same age, right? And you look ten years younger. It's not fair! It must be because you never married and had children. Nothing like a husband and kids to ruin your looks. What a figure, what skin! You look like a kid, Urania!"

She begins to recognize in her cousin's voice the nuances, the accents, the music of the little girl she played with so often in the courtyards of Santo Domingo Academy, and to whom she so often had to explain geometry and trigonometry.

"A whole lifetime of not seeing each other, Lucindita, of not knowing anything about each other," she exclaims at last.

"It's your fault, you ungrateful thing." Her cousin lectures her with affection, but now her eyes blaze with the question, the questions, that uncles, aunts, and cousins must have asked one another so often in the early years, after the sudden departure of Uranita Cabral, at the end of May 1961, for the distant town of Adrian, Michigan, where Siena Heights Preparatory School and College had been established by the same order of Dominican nuns that administered Santo Domingo Academy in Ciudad Trujillo. "I never understood it, Uranita. You and I were such good friends besides being cousins, we were so close. What happened to make you suddenly turn away from us? From your papa, your aunts and uncles, your cousins. Even from me. I wrote twenty or thirty letters and not a word from you. For years I sent you postcards, birthday cards, and so did Manolita and my mama. What did we ever do to you? What made you so angry that for thirty-five years you never wrote, never even set foot in your own country?"

"The foolishness of youth, Lucindita." Urania laughs and takes her hand. "But now, as you can see, I'm over it, and here I am."

"Are you sure you're not a ghost?" Her cousin pulls back to look at her, and shakes her head in disbelief. "Why come like this, not letting anybody know? We would have met you at the airport."

"I wanted to surprise you," Urania lies. "It was a last-minute decision. An impulse. I threw a couple of things in a suitcase and caught a plane."

"In the family, we were sure you'd never come back again." Lucinda becomes serious. "Uncle Agustín too. I have to tell you, he suffered a lot. Because you didn't want to talk to him, wouldn't answer him on the phone. He was desperate, he used to cry about it to my mama. He never got over your treating him like that. I'm sorry, I don't know why I'm telling you this, I don't want to interfere in your life, Urania. It's because we were always so close. Tell me about yourself. You live in New York, right? I know things are going well for you. We've followed your career, you're a legend in the family. You work in a very important office, don't you?"

"Well, there are bigger law firms than ours."

"It doesn't surprise me that you've been so successful in the United States," Lucinda exclaims, and Urania detects an acid note in her cousin's voice. "Everybody saw it coming from the time you were a little girl, you were so intelligent and studious. Mother Superior said so, and Sister Helen Claire, Sister Francis, Sister Susana, and especially Sister Mary, you were always her pet: Uranita Cabral, an Einstein in skirts."

Urania bursts out laughing. Not so much because of what her cousin says as for the way she says it: with eloquence and humor, talking with her mouth, eyes, hands, her whole body, all at the same time and with the effusive high spirits typical of Dominican speech. Something she learned about, by way of contrast, thirty-five years earlier, when she came to Adrian, Michigan, and suddenly found herself surrounded by people who spoke only English.

"When you left and didn't even say goodbye to me, I was so sad I almost died," her cousin says, sorrowful about those long-ago times. "Nobody in the family understood anything. But what does this mean? Uranita goes to the United States and doesn't even say goodbye! We pestered Uncle Agustín with questions, but he seemed to be in the dark too. 'The nuns offered her a scholarship, it was too good an opportunity to miss.' Nobody believed him."

"That's how it was, Lucindita." Urania looks at her father, who once again is motionless and attentive, listening to them. "There was a chance to study in Michigan, and not being a fool, I took it."

"That part I understand," her cousin reiterates, "and I know you deserved a scholarship. But why leave as if you were running away? Why break with your family, your father, your country?"

"I was always a little crazy, Lucindita. And really, even though I didn't write, I thought about all of you a lot. Especially you."

A lie. You didn't miss anyone, not even Lucinda, your cousin and classmate, your confidante and accomplice in mischief. You wanted to forget her too, and Manolita, Aunt Adelina, and your father, this city and this country, during those early months in faraway Adrian, on that beautiful campus of neat gardens with their begonias, tulips, magnolia trees, borders of rosebushes, and tall pines whose resinous scent drifted into the room you shared during your first year with four roommates, among them Alina, the black girl from Georgia, your first friend in that new world so different from the one where you had spent your first fourteen years. Did the Dominican nuns at Adrian know why you had left as if you were "running away"? Did they find out from Sister Mary, the director of studies at Santo Domingo? They had to know. If Sister Mary hadn't given them some background, they wouldn't have given you the scholarship so quickly. The sisters were models of discretion, because in the two years Urania spent at Siena Heights Prep and the four years following at Siena Heights College, none of them ever made the slightest allusion to the story that tore at your memory. As for the rest, they never repented of having been so generous: you were the first graduate of that school to be accepted at Harvard and earn a degree with honors from the most prestigious university in the world. Adrian, Michigan! You haven't been back in so many years. It must have changed from the provincial town of farmers who went into their houses at sunset and left the streets empty, families whose horizons ended at neighboring towns that seemed like twins—Clinton and Chelsea—and whose greatest diversion was attending the famous barbecued chicken festival in Manchester. A clean city, Adrian, and pretty, especially in winter when the snow hid the straight, narrow streets where people could ice-skate and ski, under white puffs of cotton that children made into snowmen and that you, entranced, watched falling from the sky, and where you would have died of bitterness, and perhaps of boredom, if you hadn't devoted yourself so furiously to studying.

Her cousin has not stopped talking.

"And a little while after that they killed Trujillo, and the calamities began. Do you know the *caliés* went into the academy? They beat the sisters, Sister Helen Claire's face was covered with cuts and bruises, and they killed Badulaque, the German shepherd. They almost burned down our house because we were related to your papa. They said that Uncle Agustín sent you to the United States because he guessed what was going to happen."

"Well, he wanted to get me away from here," Urania interrupts. "Even though he had fallen into disgrace, he knew the anti-Trujillistas would settle accounts with him."

"I understand that too," Lucinda murmurs. "But not your refusing to have anything more to do with us."

"And since you always had a good heart, I'll bet you're not still angry with me," Urania says with a laugh. "Right, Lucindita?"

"Of course not," her cousin agrees. "If you knew how much I begged my papa to send me to the United States. To be with you, at Siena Heights. I had persuaded him, I think, when the disaster came. Everybody began attacking us, telling horrible lies about the family just because my mother was the sister of a Trujillista. Nobody remembered that at the end Trujillo treated your papa like a dog. You were lucky not to be here during those months, Uranita. We were scared to death. I don't know how Uncle Agustín stopped them from burning his house. But sometimes they threw stones at him."

She is interrupted by a timid knock at the door.

"I don't mean to interrupt," the nurse says, pointing at the invalid. "But it's time."

Urania looks at her, not understanding.

"To do his business," Lucinda explains, glancing at the chamber pot. "He's as regular as a clock. He's so lucky: I have problems with my stomach and live on prunes. Nerves, they say. Well, let's go to the living room."

As they walk down the stairs, the memory returns to Urania of her months and years in Adrian, the austere library with stained-glass windows, beside the chapel and adjacent to the refectory, where she spent most of her time when she wasn't in classes and seminars. Studying, reading, scrawling in notebooks, writing essays, summarizing books, in the methodical, intense, absorbed way that her teachers valued so highly and that filled some classmates with admiration and infuriated others. It wasn't a desire to learn and succeed that kept you in the library but the yearning to become distracted, intoxicated, lost in those subjects—sciences or literature, it was all the same—so you wouldn't think, so you could drive away your Dominican memories.

"But you're wearing gym clothes," Lucinda observes when they're in the living room, near the window that faces the garden. "Don't tell me you've done aerobics this morning."

"I went for a run on the Malecón. And on my way back to the hotel, my feet brought me here, dressed in these clothes. I arrived a couple of days ago, and wasn't sure if I'd come to see him or not. If it would be too much of a shock for him. But he hasn't even recognized me."

"Of course he recognized you." Her cousin crosses her legs and takes a pack of cigarettes and a lighter out of her purse. "He can't talk, but he knows who comes in, and he understands everything. Manolita and I see him almost every day. My mama can't, not since she broke her hip. If we miss one day, he puts on a long face the next time."

She sits looking at Urania in a way that makes her predict: "Another string of reproaches." Doesn't it make you sad that your father is spending his final years alone, in the hands of a nurse, visited only by two nieces? Isn't it your job to be with him and give him affection? Do you think that giving him a pension means you've done your duty? It's all in Lucinda's bulging eyes. But she doesn't dare say it. She offers Urania a cigarette, and when her cousin refuses, she exclaims:

"You don't smoke, of course. I thought you wouldn't, living in the United States. They're psychotic about tobacco up there."

"Yes, really psychotic," Urania admits. "They've banned smoking in the office. It doesn't matter to me, I never smoked."

"The perfect girl," Lucindita says with a laugh. "Listen, darling, you can tell me, did you ever have any vices? Did you ever do any of those crazy things everybody else does?"

"Some." Urania laughs. "But I can't tell you about them."

As she talks to her cousin, she examines the living room. The furniture is the same, its shabbiness shows that; the armchair has a broken leg and a wedge of wood props it up; the frayed upholstery is torn and has lost its color, which, Urania recalls, was a pale brownish red. Worse than the furniture are the walls: damp spots everywhere, and in many places parts of the outside wall are visible. The curtains have disappeared, though the wooden rods and rings where they hung are still there.

"You're upset by how bad your house looks." Her cousin exhales a mouthful of smoke. "Ours is the same, Urania. The family was ruined when Trujillo died, that's the truth. They threw my papa out of the Tobacco Company and he never found another job. Because he was your father's brother-in-law, just because of that. Well, Uncle Agustín had it even worse. They investigated him, made all kinds of accusations, brought lawsuits against him. Even though he had fallen into disgrace with Trujillo. They couldn't prove anything, but his life was ruined too. It's lucky you're doing well and can help him. Nobody in the family could. We were all flat broke, on our uppers. Poor Uncle Agustín! He wasn't like so many others who made accommodations. He was a decent, honest man, and that's why he was ruined."

Urania listens gravely, her eyes encourage Lucinda to go on but her mind is in Michigan, at Siena Heights, reliving those years of obsessive, redemptive study. The only letters she read and answered were from Sister Mary. Affectionate, discreet letters that never mentioned what had happened, though if Sister Mary had—she was the only person in whom Urania had confided, the one who came up with the brilliant solution of getting her out of there and sending her to Adrian, the one who threatened Senator Cabral until he agreed—she would not have been angry. Would it have been a relief to unburden herself occasionally in a letter to Sister Mary, to mention the phantom that gave her no peace?

Sister Mary wrote to her about the school, she told her about the great events and turbulent months that followed the assassination of Trujillo, the departure of Ramfis and the rest of the family, the changes in government, the violence and disorder in the streets, she expressed interest in her studies and congratulated her on her academic achievements.

"How is it you never got married?" Lucindita undresses her with a look. "It couldn't be for lack of opportunity. You still look good. I'm sorry, but you know, Dominican women are very nosy."

"I really don't know why," Urania says with a shrug. "Maybe I didn't have the time, Lucinda. I've always been too busy; first studying, then working. I'm used to living alone and couldn't share my life with a man."

She hears herself talking and can't believe what she's saying. Lucinda, on the other hand, doesn't doubt what she hears.

"Girl, you did the right thing." She grows sad. "You tell me what good it did me to get married. Pedro, that bum, left me with two little girls. One day he moved out and never sent a penny. I've had to raise two girls doing the most boring things: renting houses, selling flowers, giving classes to drivers, and they're really fresh, you have no idea. I never studied for anything, it was the only work I could find. I wish I were like you, Uranita. You have a profession and earn a living in the capital of the world, you have an interesting job. You're better off not being married. But you must have had your share of affairs, right?"

Urania feels her cheeks burning, and her blush makes Lucinda laugh:

"Aha, aha, look at you. You have a lover! Tell me about him. Is he rich? Good-looking? Gringo or Latino?"

"A gentleman with graying temples, very elegant," Urania improvises. "Married, with children. We see each other on weekends, if I'm not traveling. A nice relationship, with no commitments."

"Girl, I'm so jealous!" Lucinda claps her hands. "It's my dream. An old man who's rich and distinguished. I'll have to go to New York to find one, here all the old men are disasters: fat as pigs and dead broke."

In Adrian she couldn't avoid attending some parties, going out with boys and girls, pretending to flirt with some freckled farmer's son who talked about horses or dangerous climbs up snow-covered mountains in winter, but she would return to the dormitory so exhausted by all the pretending she had to do that she looked for reasons to avoid diversion. She developed a repertory of excuses: exams, projects, visits, ailments, pressing deadlines for turning in papers. During her years at Harvard, she didn't recall ever going to a party, or a bar, or dancing, not even once.

"Manolita had terrible luck in her marriage too. Not because her husband was a womanizer, like mine. Esteban wouldn't harm a fly. But he's useless, he loses every job he gets. Now he's working at one of the tourist hotels they built in Punta Canas. He earns a miserable salary, and my sister sees him maybe once or twice a month. Is that what you call a marriage?"

"Do you remember Rosalía Perdomo?" Urania interrupts.

"Rosalía Perdomo?" Lucinda searches her memory, half closing her eyes. "The truth is, I don't . . . Oh, sure! The Rosalía who had that trouble with Ramfis Trujillo? Nobody ever saw her again. They must have sent her overseas."

Urania's admission to Harvard Law School was celebrated at Siena Heights as a great event. Until she had been accepted, she hadn't realized how much prestige the university had in the United States, how reverently everyone referred to those who had graduated, studied, or taught there. It happened in the most natural way; if she had planned it, it couldn't have been easier. She was in her last year. The guidance counselor, after congratulating her on her academic work; asked what professional plans she had, and Urania replied, "I like the law." "A career where you can earn a lot of money," Dr. Dorothy Sallison responded. But Urania had said "law" because it was the first thing that came to mind, she could have just as easily said medicine, economics, or biology. You had never thought about your future, Urania; you were so paralyzed by the past it never occurred to you to think about what lay ahead. Dr. Sallison reviewed various options with her and they chose four prestigious universities: Yale, Notre Dame, Chicago, and Stanford. One or two days after completing the applications, Dr. Sallison called her: "Why not Harvard too? You have nothing to lose." Urania remembers traveling to interviews, the nights in religious hostels, arranged for by the Dominican sisters. And the joy of Dr. Sallison, the nuns, and her classmates as she received acceptances from all the universities, including Harvard. They gave her a party, where she was obliged to dance.

Her six years in Adrian allowed her to survive, something she thought she would never be able to do. Which is why she was still profoundly grateful to the Dominican sisters. And yet Adrian, in her memory, was a somnambulistic, uncertain time, the only concrete thing the infinite hours in the library, when she worked to keep from thinking.

Cambridge, Massachusetts, was different. There she began to live again, to discover that life was worth living, that studying was not only therapy but a joy, the most glorious of diversions. How she had relished the classes, the lectures, the seminars! Overwhelmed by the abundance of possibilities (in addition to studying law, she audited a course in Latin American history, a seminar on the Caribbean, a series on Dominican social history), she found there were not enough hours in the day or weeks in the month to do everything that appealed to her.

Years of intensive work, and not only intellectual. In her second year at Harvard, her father let her know, in one of those letters she never answered, that in view of how badly things were going, he found himself obliged to cut the five hundred dollars a month he was sending her down to two hundred. She obtained a student loan, and her studies were assured. But to meet her frugal needs, in her free hours she worked as a cashier at a supermarket, a waitress at a Boston pizzeria, a clerk at a pharmacy, and—her least tedious job—as a companion and reader to a paraplegic millionaire of Polish origin, Mr. Melvin Makovsky, to whom, from five to eight in the evening, in his Victorian brownstone house on Massachusetts Avenue, she read voluminous eighteenth- and nineteenth-century novels (*War and Peace*, *Moby Dick*, *Bleak House*, *Pamela*) and who, after she had been his reader for three months, unexpectedly proposed marriage.

"A paraplegic?" Lucinda's large eyes open wide.

"Seventy years old," Urania says. "And very rich. He proposed marriage, that's right. So I could keep him company and read to him, that's all."

"You were a fool, Urania." Lucindita was scandalized. "You would have inherited a fortune, you'd be a millionaire."

"You're right, it would have been a terrific deal."

"But you were young, idealistic, and you believed a girl should marry for love." Her cousin makes her explanations easy. "As if any of that lasts. I missed a chance too, with a doctor who was rolling in money. He was crazy about me. But he was dark-skinned, they said his mother was Haitian. I'm not prejudiced, but suppose my child was a throwback and came out black as coal?"

She liked studying so much, she felt so happy at Harvard, that she planned to complete a Ph.D. and go into teaching. But she didn't have the money. Her father was in an increasingly difficult situation, in her third year he cut off her already reduced monthly allowance, and she needed to get a degree and begin earning money as soon as she could to pay off her student loans and support herself. The prestige of Harvard Law School was immense; when she began to send out applications, she was called to a good number of interviews. She decided on the World Bank. She was sorry to leave; during her years in

Cambridge, she acquired her "perverse hobby": reading and collecting books on the Trujillo Era.

In the shabby living room there is another photograph of her graduation—a morning of brilliant sun that lit up the Yard, festive with canopies, elegant clothing, the many-colored mortarboards and robes of professors and graduates—identical to the one that Senator Cabral has in his bedroom. How did he get it? She certainly didn't send it to him. Of course, Sister Mary. She'd sent this photograph to Santo Domingo Academy. For, until the nun's death, Urania maintained a correspondence with her. That charitable soul must have kept Senator Cabral informed about Urania's life. She remembers Sister Mary looking at the sea, leaning against the stone balustrade on the top floor of the academy building facing southeast—off-limits to students, it was where the nuns lived; at that distance, from the courtyard where the two German shepherds, Badulaque and Brutus, raced around the tennis courts, the volleyball courts, and the swimming pool, her lean silhouette seemed smaller.

It's hot, and she drips perspiration. She has never felt anything like this volcanic heat even in steamy New York summers, which are offset by the chill of air conditioning. This was a different kind of heat: the heat of her childhood. And she had never heard that extravagant symphony of blowing horns, voices, music, barking, squealing brakes, which came in through the windows and obliged her and her cousin to raise their voices.

"Is it true that Johnny Abbes put Papa in prison when they killed Trujillo?"

"Didn't he tell you about it?" her cousin asks in surprise.

"I was already in Michigan," Urania reminds her.

Lucinda nods, with an apologetic half-smile.

"Of course he did. Those men went crazy. Ramfis, Radhamés, the Trujillistas. They began killing and locking up people left and right. Well, I really don't remember much about it. I was a little girl and didn't care anything about politics. Uncle Agustín had been distanced from Trujillo, and they must have thought he was involved in the plot. They held him in that awful prison, La Cuarenta, the one that Balaguer tore down, there's a church there now. My mama went to talk to Balaguer, to plead with him. They kept him locked up for a few days until they proved he wasn't part of the conspiracy. Later, the President gave him a miserable little job that seemed like a joke: as an official in the Civil Government of the Third District."

"Did he say anything about how he was treated in La Cuarenta?"

Lucinda exhales smoke that hides her face for a moment.

"Maybe to my parents, but not to me or Manolita, we were very young. It hurt Uncle Agustín that they thought he could have betrayed Trujillo. For years he protested the injustice that had been done to him."

"The Generalissimo's most loyal servant," mocks Urania. "For a man capable of committing monstrous crimes for Trujillo to be suspected of complicity with his assassins—that really was an injustice!"

She stops because of the reproach she sees on her cousin's round face.

"I don't know why you talk about monstrous crimes," she murmurs in astonishment. "Maybe my uncle was wrong to be a Trujillista. Now they say he was a dictator and all. Your father served him in good faith. Even though he held such high posts, he didn't take advantage of them. Did he? He's spending his final years as poor as a dog; without you, he'd be in an old-age home."

Lucinda tries to control the irritation that has overwhelmed her. She takes a final drag on her cigarette, and since she has no place to put it out—there are no ashtrays in the dilapidated living room—she tosses it out the window into the withered garden.

"I know very well that my papa didn't serve Trujillo out of self-interest." Urania cannot avoid a trace of sarcasm. "That doesn't seem extenuating to me. It's more like an aggravating circumstance."

Her cousin looks at her, uncomprehending.

"The fact that he did what he did out of admiration, out of love for him," Urania explains. "Of course he must have been offended when Ramfis, Abbes García, and the rest suspected him. He almost went mad with despair when Trujillo turned his back on him."

"Well, maybe he was wrong," her cousin repeats, her eyes begging her to change the subject. "At least recognize that he was a very decent man. He didn't make accommodations, like so many others, who went on living the good life with every government, especially the three run by Balaguer."

"I wish he had served Trujillo out of self-interest, to steal or have power," Urania says, and again she sees perplexity and displeasure in Lucinda's eyes. "Anything, rather than seeing him whimper because

Trujillo wouldn't grant him an audience, because letters appeared in 'The Public Forum' insulting him."

It is a persistent memory, one that tormented her in Adrian and in Cambridge, in somewhat attenuated form stayed with her through all her years at the World Bank in Washington, D.C., and that still assaults her in Manhattan: the helpless Senator Agustín Cabral pacing frantically in this very living room, asking himself what intrigue had been mounted against him by the Constitutional Sot, the unctuous Joaquín Balaguer, the cynical Virgilio Álvarez Pina, or Paíno Pichardo, to make the Generalissimo wipe out his existence overnight. Because what existence could a senator and ex-minister have when the Benefactor did not answer his letters or permit him to appear in Congress? Was the history of Anselmo Paulino repeating itself in him? Would the *caliés* come for him in the middle of the night and bury him in some dungeon? Would *La Nación* and *El Caribe* come out with vile reports of his thefts, embezzlements, betrayals, crimes?

"Falling into disgrace was worse for him than if they had killed the person he loved best."

Her cousin listens to her with increasing discomfort.

"Was that why you got so angry, Uranita?" she says at last. "Over politics? But I remember very clearly that you had no interest at all in politics. When those two girls nobody knew came in at midyear, for example. Everybody said they were *caliesas* and nobody talked about anything else, but you were bored by political gossip and told us all to shut up."

"I've never been interested in politics," Urania agrees. "You're right, why talk about things that happened thirty years ago?"

The nurse appears on the stairs. She comes down drying her hands on a blue cloth.

"All cleaned up and powdered like a baby," she announces. "You can go up whenever you want. I'm going to prepare Don Agustín's lunch. Can I fix something for you too, señora?"

"No, thank you," says Urania. "I'm going back to the hotel to shower and change."

"Well, tonight you'll come to the house for supper. You'll give my mama such a nice surprise. I'll call Manolita too, she'll be so happy." Lucinda puts on a mournful face. "You'll be shocked, Uranita. Do you remember how big and pretty the house was? Only half of it is left. When Papa died, we had to sell the garden along with the garage and the servants' quarters. Well, enough of that. Seeing you has made me remember my childhood. We were happy then, weren't we? It never occurred to us that everything would change, that lean years would come. Well, I'm going, Mama hasn't had her lunch yet. You'll come for supper, won't you? You won't disappear for another thirty-five years? You must remember the house, on Calle Santiago, about five blocks from here."

"I remember it very well." Urania stands and embraces her cousin. "This neighborhood hasn't changed at all."

She accompanies Lucinda to the front door and says goodbye with another hug and a kiss on the cheek. When she sees her walking away in her flowered dress, along a street boiling in the sun, where the response to frantic barking is the cackling of hens, she is filled with anguish. What are you doing here? What have you come to find in Santo Domingo, in this house? Will you go to have supper with Lucinda, Manolita, and Aunt Adelina? The poor thing must be a fossil, just like your father.

She climbs the stairs, slowly, putting off seeing him again. She is relieved to find him asleep, huddled in his chair; his eyes are wrinkled, his mouth open, and his rachitic chest rises and falls in a rhythmic pattern. "Just a piece of a man." She sits on the bed and contemplates him. Studies him, reads him. They imprisoned him too, when Trujillo died. Believing he was one of the Trujillistas who conspired with Antonio de la Maza, General Juan Tomás Díaz and his brother Modesto, Antonio Imbert, and company. How frightening and how frightful for you, Papa. She had learned many years later, in a passing reference in an article about the events of 1961 in the Dominican Republic, that her father had also been caught in the dragnet. But she never knew the details. As far as she could remember, Senator Cabral did not allude to the experience in the letters she never answered. "That anyone could imagine, even for a second, that you planned to assassinate Trujillo, must have hurt you as much as falling into disgrace without knowing why." Did Johnny Abbes himself interrogate him? Ramfis? Pechito León Estévez? Did they sit him on the Throne? Was her father linked in some way to the conspirators? True, he had made superhuman efforts to regain Trujillo's favor, but what did that prove? Many conspirators kissed Trujillo's ass until moments before they killed him. It very well might be that Agustín Cabral, a good friend of Modesto Díaz, had been informed of the plan. Even Balaguer knew about it, according to some. If the President of the Republic and the Minister of the Armed Forces had heard about it, why not her father? The conspirators knew that the Chief had ordered the fall from grace of Senator Cabral several weeks earlier; nothing strange about their thinking of him as a possible ally.

From time to time her father emits a quiet snore. When a fly settles on his face, he drives it away, not waking, with a movement of his head. How did you find out they had killed him? On May 30, 1961, you were already in Adrian. She was beginning to shake off the heaviness, the exhaustion that kept her disengaged from the world and from herself, in a kind of somnambulism, when the sister in charge of the dormitory came to the room that Urania shared with four other girls and showed her the headline in the newspaper she held in her hand: TRUJILLO KILLED. "I'll lend it to you," she said. What did you feel? She would swear she felt nothing, that the news slid over her without piercing her consciousness, like everything else she heard and saw around her. It's possible you didn't even read the article, didn't look past the headline. She recalls, however, that days or weeks later, in a letter from Sister Mary, there were details about the crime, about the *caliés* breaking into the academy to take away Bishop Reilly, about the lawlessness and uncertainty they were living through. But not even that letter from Sister Mary could pull her out of the profound indifference to everything and everyone Dominican into which she had fallen and from which she was freed only years later, by a course on Antillean history at Harvard.

This sudden decision to come to Santo Domingo, to visit your father, does it mean you're cured? No. You must have felt happy, been moved, at seeing Lucinda again, she was so close to you, your companion in rounds of vermouth, and at the matinees at the Olimpia and Elite movie theaters, on the beach or at the Country Club, and you must have felt sorry for the apparent mediocrity of her life, her lack of hope that it would improve. No. She didn't make you happy, she didn't move you, she didn't make you feel sorry. She bored you because of that sentimentality and self-pity you find so objectionable.

"You're an iceberg. You really don't seem Dominican. I'm more Dominican than you are." Well, well; imagine remembering Steve Duncan, her colleague at the World Bank. 1985 or 1986? Around then. They had been in Taipei that night, having supper together in the Grand Hotel, shaped like a Hollywood pagoda, where they were staying; through its windows the city looked like a blanket of fireflies. For the third, fourth, or tenth time, Steve proposed marriage and Urania, more categorically than before, told him no. Then, in surprise, she saw Steve's ruddy face contort. She couldn't contain her laughter.

"Don't tell me you're going to cry, Steve. For love of me? Or have you had too much whiskey?"

Steve did not smile. He sat looking at her for a long time, without answering, and then he said those words: "You're an iceberg. You really don't seem Dominican. I'm more Dominican than you are." Well, well; the redhead fell in love with you, Urania. Whatever happened to him? A wonderful person, with a degree in economics from the University of Chicago, his interest in the Third World encompassed its problems of development, its languages, and its women. He finally married a Pakistani, an official of the Bank in the area of communications.

Are you an iceberg, Urania? Only with men. And not with all of them. With those whose glances, movements, gestures, tones of voice announce a danger. When you can read, in their minds or instincts, the intention to court you, to make advances. With them, yes, you do make them feel the arctic cold that you know how to project around you, like the stink skunks use to frighten away an enemy. A technique you handle with the mastery you've brought to every goal you set for yourself: studies, work, an independent life. "Everything except being happy." Would she have been happy if, applying her will, her discipline, she had eventually overcome the unconquerable revulsion and disgust caused by men who desired her? You could have gone into therapy, seen a psychologist, an analyst. They had a remedy for everything, even finding men repugnant. But you never wanted to be cured. On the contrary, you don't consider it a disease but a character trait, like your intelligence, your solitude, your passion for doing good work.

Her father's eyes are open, and he looks at her with a certain fear.

"I was thinking about Steve, a Canadian at the World Bank," she says in a quiet voice, scrutinizing him. "Since I didn't want to marry him, he told me I was an iceberg. An accusation that would offend any Dominican woman. We have a reputation for being ardent, unbeatable in love. I earned a reputation for being just the opposite: prudish, indifferent, frigid. What do you think of that, Papa? Just now, for my cousin Lucinda, I had to invent a lover so she wouldn't think badly of me."

She falls silent because she notices that the invalid, shrinking in his chair, seems terrified. He no longer shakes off the flies that walk undisturbed across his face.

"A subject I would have liked us to talk about, Papa. Women, sex. Did you have affairs after Mama died? I never noticed anything. You didn't seem like a womanizer. Did power satisfy you so much you didn't need sex? It happens, even in this hot country. It happened to our perpetual President, Don Joaquín Balaguer, didn't it? A bachelor at the age of ninety. He wrote love poems, and there are rumors he had a daughter he never recognized. I always had the impression that sex never interested him, that power gave him what other men got in bed. Was that the case with you, Papa? Or did you have discreet adventures? Did Trujillo invite you to his orgies at Mahogany House? What happened there? Did the Chief, like Ramfis, amuse himself by humiliating his friends and courtiers, forcing them to shave their legs, shave their bodies, make themselves up like old queens? Did he do those charming things too? Did he do them to you?"

Senator Cabral has turned so pale that Urania thinks: "He's going to faint." To let him recover, she moves away. She goes to the window and looks out. She feels the strength of the sun on her head, on the feverish skin of her face. She is sweating. You ought to go back to the hotel, fill the tub with bubbles, take a long, cool bath. Or go down and dive into the tiled pool and then try the Dominican buffet at the restaurant in the Hotel Jaragua, they'll have beans with rice and pork. But you don't feel like doing that. You'd rather go to the airport, take the first plane to New York, and resume your life at the busy law firm, and in your apartment at 73rd and Madison.

She sits down again on the bed. Her father closes his eyes. Is he sleeping or pretending to sleep because of the fear you inspire in him? You're giving the poor invalid a bad time. Is that what you wanted? To frighten him, inflict a few hours of terror on him? Do you feel better now? Weariness has overwhelmed her, and since her eyes are beginning to close, she gets to her feet.

In a mechanical way she goes to the large armoire of dark wood that takes up one whole wall of the room. It is half empty. On wire hangers she sees a dark gray suit, yellowing like the skin of an onion, and a few shirts, washed but not ironed; two of them are missing buttons. Is this all that is left of the wardrobe of the President of the Senate, Agustín Cabral? He had been an elegant man. Meticulous in his person and dress, the way the Chief liked men to be. What had happened to his dinner jackets, his dress tails, his dark suits made of English worsted, the white ones of finest linen? The servants must have stolen them, the nurses, the impoverished relatives.

Weariness is stronger than her will to stay awake. Finally, she lies down on the bed and closes her eyes. Before she falls asleep, she thinks that the bed smells of old man, old sheets, very old dreams and nightmares.

11 "A question, Excellency," said Simon Gittleman, flushed from the glasses of champagne and wine, or, perhaps, emotion. "Of all the steps you have taken to make this country great, which was the most difficult?"

He spoke excellent Spanish, with a very faint accent, nothing like the caricatured language full of errors and incorrect intonations mouthed by so many gringos who had paraded through the offices and reception rooms of the National Palace. Simon's Spanish had improved a good deal since 1921, when Trujillo, a young lieutenant in the National Guard, was accepted as a student at the Officers' Training School at Haina and had the Marine as an instructor; back then, he mouthed a barbaric Spanish peppered with curses. Gittleman had asked the question in so loud a voice that conversations stopped and twenty heads—curious, smiling, grave—turned toward the Benefactor, waiting for his reply.

"I can answer your question, Simon." Trujillo adopted the measured, hollow voice he used on solemn occasions. He fixed his eyes on the crystal chandelier with the petal-shaped bulbs, and added: "The second of October 1937, in Dajabón."

Rapid glances were exchanged among the guests at the luncheon given by Trujillo for Simon and Dorothy Gittleman, following the ceremony in which the former Marine received the Juan Pablo Duarte Order of Merit. When Gittleman expressed his thanks, his voice broke. Now, he tried to guess what His Excellency was alluding to.

"Ah, the Haitians!" His slap on the table made the fine crystal goblets, platters, glasses, and decanters ring. "The day Your Excellency decided to cut the Gordian knot of the Haitian invasion."

Everyone had glasses of wine, but the Generalissimo drank only water. He was solemn, absorbed in his memories. The silence thickened. Hieratic and theatrical, the Generalissimo raised his hands and showed them to his guests:

"For the sake of this country, I have stained these with blood," he stated, emphasizing each syllable. "To keep the blacks from colonizing us again. There were tens of thousands of them, and they were everywhere. If I hadn't, the Dominican Republic would not exist today. The entire island would be Haiti, as it was in 1840. The handful of white survivors would be serving the blacks. That was my most difficult decision in thirty years of government, Simon."

"We followed your orders and traveled the entire length of the border." The young deputy Henry Chirinos leaned over the enormous map displayed on the President's desk and pointed: "If this continues, there will be no future for the Dominican Republic, Excellency."

"The situation is more serious than you were told, Excellency." The slender index finger of the young deputy Agustín Cabral caressed the dotted red line that moved in S curves from Dajabón down to Pedernales. "Thousands and thousands of them, working on plantations, in empty fields, in settlements. They've displaced Dominican laborers."

"They work free of charge, not for wages, but for food. Since there's nothing to eat in Haiti, a little rice and beans is plenty for them. They cost less than donkeys and dogs."

Chirinos made a gesture and let his friend and colleague continue:

"Talking to the ranchers and plantation owners is useless, Excellency," Cabral explained. "They reply by patting their pockets. What do I care if they're Haitians if they can harvest the cane and work for almost nothing? Patriotism won't make me go against my own interests."

He stopped speaking and looked at Deputy Chirinos, who took up the argument:

"All through Dajabón, Elías Piña, Independencia, and Pedernales, instead of Spanish all you hear are the African grunts of Creole."

He looked at Agustín Cabral, who resumed speaking immediately:

"Voodoo, Santería, African superstitions are uprooting the Catholic religion that, like language and race, distinguishes our nationality."

"We've seen parish priests weeping in despair, Excellency," young Deputy Chirinos said, his voice quavering. "Pre-Christian savagery is taking over the country of Diego Colón, Juan Pablo Duarte, and Trujillo. Haitian sorcerers have more influence than priests, medicine men more than pharmacists and physicians."

"The Army didn't do anything?" Simon Gittleman took a sip of wine. One of the white-uniformed waiters quickly refilled his glass.

"The Army does what the Chief orders, Simon, you know that." Only the Benefactor and the former Marine were speaking. The others listened as their heads turned from one to the other. "The gangrene had moved very high. Montecristi, Santiago, San Juan, Azua, they were all teeming with Haitians. The plague was spreading and no one did anything. They were waiting for a statesman with vision, one whose hand would not tremble."

"Imagine a hydra with countless heads, Excellency." Young Deputy Chirinos's poetic turns of phrase were accompanied by extravagant gestures. "These laborers steal work from Dominicans who, in order to survive, sell their little plots of ground, their farms. Who buys the land? The newly prosperous Haitians, naturally."

"It is the second head of the hydra, Excellency," young Deputy Cabral specified. "They take work from nationals and, piece by piece, appropriate our sovereignty."

"And our women too." His voice thickened, and young Henry Chirinos gave off a whiff of lechery: his reddish tongue appeared like a snake between his thick lips. "Nothing attracts black flesh more than white. Haitian violations of Dominican women are an everyday occurrence."

"Not to mention robberies and attacks on property," insisted young Agustín Cabral. "Gangs of criminals cross the Masacre River as if there were no customs, checkpoints, or patrols. The border is like a sieve. The gangs demolish villages and farms like swarms of locusts. Then they drive the livestock back into Haiti, along with everything they can find to eat, wear, or adorn themselves with. That region is no longer ours, Excellency. We have lost our language there, our religion, our race. It now forms part of Haitian barbarism."

Dorothy Gittleman barely spoke Spanish and must have been bored with this conversation regarding something that occurred twenty-four years earlier, but she nodded very seriously from time to time, looking at the Generalissimo and her husband as if following every syllable of what they were saying. She had been seated between the puppet president, Joaquín Balaguer, and the Minister of the Armed

Forces, General José René (Pupo) Román. She was a small, fragile, upright old woman rejuvenated by the pink tones of her summer dress. During the ceremony, when the Generalissimo had said that the Dominican people would not forget the solidarity displayed by the Gittlemans during this difficult time, when so many governments were stabbing them in the back, she too had shed a few tears.

"I knew what was going on," Trujillo declared. "But I wanted proof, so there would be no doubts. I didn't make a decision even after I received an on-site report from the Constitutional Sot and Egghead. I decided to go there myself. I traveled the length of the border on horseback, accompanied by volunteers from the University Guard. I saw it with my own eyes: they had invaded us again, just as they had in 1822. Peacefully, this time. Could I allow the Haitians to remain in my country for another twenty-two years?"

"No patriot would have allowed it," exclaimed Senator Henry Chirinos, raising his glass. "Least of all Generalissimo Trujillo. A toast to His Excellency!"

Trujillo continued as if he hadn't heard:

"Could I allow what happened during those twenty-two years of occupation to happen again, allow blacks to murder, rape, and cut the throats of Dominicans, even in churches?"

Seeing the failure of his toast, the Constitutional Sot wheezed, drank some wine, and began to listen again.

"During the entire trip along the border with the University Guard, the cream of our youth, I examined the past," the Generalissimo continued, with increasing emphasis. "I recalled the slaughter in the church at Moca. The burning of Santiago. The march to Haiti by Dessalines and Cristóbal, with nine hundred prominent men from Moca who died along the way or were given as slaves to the Haitian military."

"More than two weeks since we presented our report and the Chief hasn't done a thing." Young Deputy Chirinos was agitated. "Is he going to make a decision, Egghead?"

They had both accompanied Trujillo on his trip along the border, with the hundred volunteers from the University Guard, and they had just reached the city of Dajabón, breathing more heavily than their horses. The two of them, despite their youth, would have preferred to rest their saddle-weary bones, but His Excellency was holding a reception for Dajabón society and they would never offend him. There they were, suffocating with the heat in their stiff-collared shirts and tunics, in the decorated town hall, where Trujillo, as fresh as if he had not been riding since dawn, and wearing an impeccable blue-and-gray uniform studded with medals and gold braid, moved among the various groups with a glass of Carlos I in his right hand, accepting their tributes. Then he caught sight of a young officer in dust-covered boots who burst into the flag-draped room.

"You showed up at that gala reception, sweating and in your field uniform." The Benefactor abruptly turned his gaze toward the Minister of the Armed Forces. "What disgust I felt!"

"I came to make a report to the head of my regiment, Excellency," General Román said in confusion, after a silence during which his memory struggled to identify that long-ago episode. "Last night a gang of Haitian criminals slipped across the border. Early this morning they attacked three farms in Capotillo and Parolí and stole all the cattle. And left three men dead."

"You risked your career, appearing before me in that condition," the Generalissimo reproached him with retroactive irritation. "All right. It's the straw that broke the camel's back. The Ministers of War and Government, and all the military present, come here. The rest of you, please step aside."

He had raised his thin, piercing voice to a hysterical pitch, as he used to when he gave instructions in the barracks. He was obeyed immediately, in the midst of voices buzzing like wasps. The military formed a dense circle around him; gentlemen and ladies withdrew to the walls, leaving an empty space in the center of the room decorated with streamers, paper flowers, and little Dominican flags. A resolute President Trujillo gave the order:

"Beginning at midnight, the forces of the Army and the police will proceed to exterminate without mercy every person of Haitian nationality who is in Dominican territory illegally, except for those on the sugar plantations." He cleared his throat and his gray gaze moved around the circle of officers: "Is that clear?"

The heads nodded, some with an expression of surprise, others with glints of savage joy in their eyes. They clicked their heels when they left.

"Head of the Dajabón Regiment: detain and put on bread and water the officer who presented himself here in that disgraceful condition. Let the party continue. Enjoy yourselves!"

On Simon Gittleman's face, admiration mixed with nostalgia.

"His Excellency never hesitated when it was time to act," said the former Marine to the entire table. "I had the honor of training him at the school in Haina. From the first moment I knew he would go far. But I never imagined it would be this far."

He laughed, and amiable chuckles echoed him.

"They never trembled," Trujillo repeated, displaying his hands again. "Because I gave the order to kill only when it was absolutely necessary for the good of the country."

"I read somewhere, Your Excellency, that you ordered the soldiers to use machetes, not guns. Was that to save ammunition?" Simon Gittleman asked.

"To sugarcoat the pill, anticipating international reaction," Trujillo corrected him slyly. "If they only used machetes, the operation could appear to be a spontaneous action by campesinos, without government intervention. We Dominicans are lavish, we've never skimped on anything, least of all ammunition."

The entire table celebrated the witticism with laughter. Simon Gittleman as well. But then he returned to the same subject.

"Is it true about the parsley, Your Excellency? That to distinguish Dominicans from Haitians you made all the blacks say *perejil*? And the ones who couldn't pronounce it properly had their heads cut off?"

"I've heard that story." Trujillo shrugged. "It's just idle gossip."

He lowered his head, as if a profound thought suddenly demanded a great effort of concentration. It hadn't happened; his eyes were still sharp and they did not detect the telltale stain on his fly or between his legs. He gave a friendly smile to the former Marine:

"Like the stories about the number of dead," he said mockingly. "Ask the people sitting at this table and you'll hear all kinds of figures. For example, you, Senator, how many were there?"

Henry Chirinos's dark face came to attention, swelling with satisfaction at being the first one the Chief asked.

"Difficult to know." He gestured, as he did when giving speeches. "It has been greatly exaggerated. Between five and eight thousand, at most."

"General Arredondo, you were in Independencia at the time, cutting throats. How many?"

"About twenty thousand, Excellency," replied the obese General

Arredondo, who looked caged inside his uniform. "In the Independencia zone alone there were several thousand. The senator underestimated the number. I was there. No less than twenty thousand."

"How many did you kill personally?" the Generalissimo joked, and another wave of laughter ran around the table, making the chairs creak and the crystal sing.

"What you said about idle gossip is the absolute truth, Excellency," the rotund officer said with a start, and his smile turned into a grimace. "Now they blame everything on us. False, all false. The Army obeyed orders. We began to separate the illegals from the others. But the people wouldn't let us. Everybody began to hunt down Haitians. Campesinos, merchants, and officials revealed their hiding places, and they hung them and beat them to death. They burned them, sometimes. In many places, the Army had to intervene to stop the excesses. There was a lot of resentment against them for their thieving and plundering."

"President Balaguer, you were one of the negotiators with Haiti following those events," said Trujillo, continuing his survey. "How many were there?"

The small, gray figure of the President of the Republic, half swallowed up by his chair, stretched his benign head forward. After observing the gathering from behind his nearsighted man's glasses, the soft, well-modulated voice emerged, the one that recited poems at poetry competitions, celebrated the crowning of Miss Dominican Republic (he was always the Royal Poet), made speeches to the crowds on Trujillo's political tours, or expounded on the government's policies in the National Assembly.

"The exact figure could never be determined, Excellency." He spoke slowly, with a professorial air. "A prudent estimate is between ten and fifteen thousand. In our negotiations with the Haitian government, we agreed on a symbolic figure: 2,750. In this way, each affected family would, in theory, receive a hundred pesos of the 275,000 in cash paid by Your Excellency's government as a gesture of goodwill and for the sake of Haitian-Dominican harmony. But, as you will remember, that is not what happened."

He fell silent, a hint of a smile on his round little face narrowing the small, pale eyes behind his thick glasses.

"Why didn't the compensation reach the families?" asked Simon Gittleman.

"Because the President of Haiti, Sténio Vincent, was a thief and kept the money." Trujillo laughed. "Only 275,000? As I recall, we agreed on 750,000 to make them stop protesting."

"That is true, Excellency," Dr. Balaguer replied immediately, with the same calm, perfect diction, "750,000 pesos were agreed on, but only 275,000 in cash. The remaining half million was to be remitted in annual payments of 100,000 pesos over a period of five years. However, and I remember this quite clearly, I was interim Minister of Foreign Affairs at the time, and I and Don Anselmo Paulino, who advised me during the negotiations, imposed a clause according to which the payments were contingent upon the presentation, before an international tribunal, of the death certificates issued for the 2,750 recognized victims during the first two weeks of October 1937. Haiti never fulfilled this requirement. And consequently the Dominican Republic was exempted from paying the remaining sum. Reparations never went beyond the initial remittance. Your Excellency made the payment out of your own patrimony, so that it did not cost the Dominican state a cent."

"A small amount to end a problem that might have wiped us out," concluded Trujillo, who was serious now. "It's true, some innocent people died. But we Dominicans recovered our sovereignty. Since then our relations with Haiti have been excellent, thank God."

He wiped his lips and took a sip of water. They had begun to serve coffee and to offer liqueurs. He did not drink coffee, and never drank alcohol at lunch, except in San Cristóbal, on the Fundación Ranch or in Mahogany House, in the company of intimates. Along with the images his memory brought back of those bloody weeks in October 1937, when his office received reports of the horrifying dimensions the hunting down of Haitians had reached along the border and throughout the entire country, the hateful figure again appeared of that stupid, terrified girl watching his humiliation. He felt insulted.

"Where is Senator Agustín Cabral, the famous Egghead?" Simon Gittleman gestured toward the Constitutional Sot: "I see Senator Chirinos but not his inseparable partner. What happened to him?"

The silence lasted many seconds. The diners raised their little cups of coffee to their mouths, sipped, and looked at the tablecloth, the floral arrangements, the crystal, the chandelier hanging from the ceiling.

"He is no longer a senator and he does not set foot in this Palace," the Generalissimo declaimed with the slowness characteristic of his cold rages. "He is alive, but as far as this regime is concerned, he has ceased to exist."

The former Marine was uncomfortable as he drained his glass of cognac. He must be close to eighty years old, the Generalissimo estimated. He carried his years magnificently: he kept himself erect and slim, with thinning hair in a crew cut, not an ounce of fat or loose skin on his neck, energetic in his gestures and movements. The web of fine wrinkles that surrounded his eyelids and extended down his weather-beaten face betrayed his age. He grimaced and tried to change the subject.

"How did Your Excellency feel when you gave the order to eliminate thousands of illegal Haitians?"

"Ask your former President Truman how he felt when he gave the order to drop the atomic bomb on Hiroshima and Nagasaki. Then you'll know what I felt that night in Dajabón."

Everyone celebrated the Generalissimo's sally. The tension provoked by the former Marine when he mentioned Agustín Cabral was dissipated. Now it was Trujillo who steered the conversation in another direction.

"A month ago, the United States suffered a defeat at the Bay of Pigs. The Communist Fidel Castro captured hundreds of men. What consequences will it have in the Caribbean, Simon?"

"That expedition of Cuban patriots was betrayed by President Kennedy," he murmured sorrowfully. "They were sent to the slaughterhouse. The White House prohibited the air cover and artillery support they had been promised. The Communists used them for target practice. But, if you'll permit me, Your Excellency. I was glad it happened. It will be a lesson to Kennedy, whose government is infiltrated by fellow travelers. Maybe he'll decide to get rid of them. The White House won't want another failure like the Bay of Pigs. Which reduces the danger of his sending Marines to the Dominican Republic."

As he said these final words, the former Marine became emotional and made a noticeable effort to maintain his self-control. Trujillo was surprised: had his old instructor from Haina been on the verge of tears at the idea of a landing by his comrades in arms to overthrow the Dominican regime?

"Excuse my weakness, Your Excellency," Simon Gittleman murmured, regaining his composure. "You know I love this country as if it were my own."

"This country is yours, Simon," said Trujillo.

"The idea that because of leftist influences, Washington might send Marines to fight the government that is the United States' best friend, seems diabolical to me. That is why I spend time and money trying to open my countrymen's eyes. That is why Dorothy and I have come to Ciudad Trujillo, to fight alongside Dominicans if the Marines land."

A burst of applause that made the plates, glasses, and silverware resound greeted the Marine's impassioned speech. Dorothy smiled, nodding in solidarity with her husband.

"Your voice, Mr. Simon Gittleman, is the true voice of the United States," the Constitutional Sot said in exaltation, firing a salvo of saliva. "A toast to this friend, this man of honor. To Simon Gittleman, gentlemen!"

"One moment." The thin, high-pitched voice of Trujillo ripped the fervent atmosphere into shreds. The other guests looked at him, disconcerted, and Chirinos remained holding his glass in the air. "To our friends, our sister and brother, Dorothy and Simon Gittleman!"

Overwhelmed, the couple expressed their thanks to those present with smiles and nods.

"Kennedy won't send in the Marines, Simon," said the Generalissimo, when the echoes of the toast died down. "I don't think he's that stupid. But if he does, the United States will suffer its second Bay of Pigs. Our Armed Forces are more modern than Castro's. And here, with me leading them, they will fight to the last Dominican."

He closed his eyes, wondering if his memory would allow him to recall the citation exactly. Yes, he had it, it came to him, complete, from the commemoration of the twenty-ninth anniversary of his first election. He recited it, and was listened to in reverential silence:

" 'Whatever surprises the future may hold in store for us, we can be certain that the world may see Trujillo dead, but not a fugitive like Batista, an escapee like Pérez Jiménez, or a prisoner before the bar like Rojas Pinilla. The Dominican statesman follows a different ethic and comes from a different lineage.' "

He opened his eyes and sent a pleased gaze around the table, and his guests, after listening to the citation with great attention, made gestures of approval.

"Who wrote the words I've just quoted?" asked the Benefactor.

They examined each other, looking around with curiosity, misgiving, alarm. Finally, their eyes converged on the amiable round face, abashed by modesty, of the diminutive writer upon whom the first magistracy of the Republic had fallen when Trujillo forced his brother Blacky to resign in the vain hope of avoiding the OAS sanctions.

"I marvel at the memory of Your Excellency," Joaquín Balaguer whispered, displaying excessive humility, as if stunned by the honor being shown him. "It makes me proud that you remember a modest speech of mine delivered on the third of August last."

Behind his lashes, the Generalissimo observed how the faces of Virgilio Álvarez Pina, the Walking Turd, Paíno Pichardo, and all the generals contorted with envy. They were suffering. They were thinking that the timid, discreet poet, the shy professor and jurist, had just won a few points in their eternal competition to receive the favors of the Chief, to be recognized, mentioned, chosen, distinguished over the rest. He felt tenderness for his diligent scions, whom he had maintained for thirty years in a state of perpetual insecurity.

"Those are not mere words, Simon," the Benefactor affirmed. "Trujillo is not one of those leaders who abandon power when the bullets fly. I learned what honor is at your side, in the Marines. I learned that one is a man of honor at every moment. And men of honor don't run. They fight, and if they have to die, they die fighting. Not Kennedy or the OAS, not Betancourt the repulsive black faggot or Fidel Castro the Communist, none of them is going to make Trujillo run from the country that owes everything it is to him."

The Constitutional Sot began to clap, but when many hands were lifted to follow suit, Trujillo's gaze cut short the applause.

"Do you know what the difference is between those cowards and me, Simon?" he continued, looking into the eyes of his old instructor. "I was trained in the Marine Corps of the United States of America. I've never forgotten it. You taught me, in Haina and in San Pedro de Macorís. Do you remember? Those of us from that first class of the Dominican National Police are made of iron. Rancorous people said DNP stood for 'Dominican Niggers Panic.' The truth is, that class of men changed the country, they created it. I'm not surprised at what you're doing for this nation. Because you're a real Marine, like me, a loyal man. Who dies without bowing his head, looking at the sky, like Arabian horses. Simon, no matter how badly your country behaves, I bear it no grudge. Because I owe what I am to the Marines."

"One day the United States will regret being ungrateful to its Caribbean partner and friend."

Trujillo took a few sips of water. Conversations resumed. The waiters offered more coffee, more cognac and other liqueurs, cigars. The Generalissimo listened to Simon Gittleman again:

"How is this trouble with Bishop Reilly going to end, Your Excellency?"

He made a contemptuous gesture:

"There is no trouble, Simon. The bishop has taken the side of our enemies. The people were angry, he became frightened, and he ran to hide behind the nuns at Santo Domingo Academy. What he's doing there with so many women is his business. We've placed guards there so he won't be lynched."

"It would be good if this could be resolved soon," the former Marine insisted. "In the United States, many ill-informed Catholics believe the statements made by Monsignor Reilly. That he's being threatened, that he had to take refuge because of a campaign of intimidation, all the rest of it."

"It's not important, Simon. Everything will be straightened out and our relations with the Church will be excellent again. Don't forget that my government has always been filled with devout Catholics, and that Pius XII awarded me the Great Cross of the Papal Order of St. Gregory." And abruptly he changed the subject: "Did Petán take you to visit the Dominican Voice?"

"Of course," replied Simon Gittleman; Dorothy nodded, with a broad smile.

The center that belonged to his brother, General José Arismendi (Petán) Trujillo, had begun twenty years earlier with a small radio station. The Voice of Yuna had grown into a formidable complex, the Dominican Voice, the first television station, the largest radio station, the best cabaret and musical theater on the island (Petán insisted it was the best in the Caribbean, but the Generalissimo knew it had not managed to unseat the Tropicana in Havana). The Gittlemans had been impressed by the magnificent facilities; Petán himself had been their guide, and he had them attend the rehearsal for the Mexican ballet that would perform tonight at the cabaret. Petán wasn't a bad person if you dug deep enough; when the Benefactor needed him, he could always count on him and his picturesque private army, "the mountain fire beetles." But, like his other brothers, he had done him more harm than good: because of him and a stupid fight, he had been forced to intervene, and, to maintain the principle of authority, eliminate that magnificent giant—and his classmate at the Haina Officers' Training School besides—General Vázquez Rivera. One of his best officers—a Marine, damn it—who had always served him loyally. But the family, even if it was a family of parasites, failures, fools, and scoundrels, came before friendship and political gain: this was a sacred commandment in his catalogue of honor. Without abandoning his own line of thought, the Generalissimo listened to Simon Gittleman telling him how surprised he had been to see the photographs of film, show business, and radio celebrities from all over the Americas who had come to the Dominican Voice. Petán had them displayed on the walls of his office: Los Panchos, Libertad Lamarque, Pedro Vargas, Ima Súmac, Pedro Infante, Celia Cruz, Toña la Negra, Olga Guillot, María Luisa Landín, Boby Capó, Tintán and his brother Marcelo. Trujillo smiled: what Simon didn't know was that Petán, besides brightening the Dominican night with the stars he brought in, also wanted to fuck them, the way he fucked all the girls, single or married, in his small empire of Bonao. The Generalissimo let him do what he wanted there as long as he didn't go too far in Ciudad Trujillo. But that crazy prick Petán sometimes fucked around in the capital, convinced that the performers hired by the Dominican Voice were obliged to go to bed with him if he wanted them to. Sometimes he was successful; other times, there was a scandal, and he—he was always the one—had to put out the fire, making a millionaire's gifts to artists who had been offended by that moronic delinquent; Petán had no manners with ladies. Ima Súmac, for example, an Incan princess with an American passport. Petán's brashness forced the intervention of the ambassador of the United States. And the Benefactor, distilling bile, paid damages to the Incan princess and obliged his brother to apologize. The Benefactor sighed. With the time he had wasted filling in the deep holes that opened before the feet of his horde of relatives, he could have built a second country.

Yes, of all the outrages committed by Petán, the one he would never forgive was that stupid fight with the head of the Army General Staff. The giant Vázquez Rivera had been Trujillo's good friend since they trained together in Haina; he possessed an uncommon strength that he cultivated by practicing every sport. He was one of the officers who contributed to the realization of Trujillo's dream: transforming the Army, born of the small National Police, into a professional, disciplined, efficient force, a replica in miniature of the U.S. Army. And then, when it had been accomplished, the stupid fight. Petán held the rank of major and served in the leadership of the Army General Staff. He disobeyed an order when he was drunk, General Vázquez Rivera reprimanded him, and Petán became insulting. The giant took off his insignia, pointed to the courtyard, and suggested they forget about rank and resolve the matter with their fists. It was the most ferocious beating of Petán's life, and with it he paid for all the ones he had given to so many poor bastards. Saddened, but convinced that the family's honor obliged him to act as he did, Trujillo demoted his friend and sent him to Europe on a merely symbolic mission. A year later, the Intelligence Service informed him of the resentful general's subversive plans: he was visiting garrisons, meeting with former subordinates, hiding arms on his small farm in Cibao. He had him arrested, sent to the military prison at the mouth of the Nigua River, and some time later secretly condemned to death by a military tribunal. To drag him to the gallows, the commander of the fortress had to use twelve prisoners serving sentences for common crimes. So there would be no witnesses to the titanic end of General Vázquez Rivera, Trujillo ordered the twelve outlaws shot. Despite the time that had passed, he sometimes felt, as he did now, a certain nostalgia for that companion of his heroic years, the one he had to sacrifice because Petán was an imbecile and a troublemaker.

Simon Gittleman was explaining that the committees he had established in the United States had begun collecting money for a major campaign: that very day they would publish full-page advertisements in *The New York Times*, *The Washington Post*, *Time*, the *Los Angeles Times*, and all the publications that were attacking Trujillo and supporting the OAS sanctions, to refute the accusations and argue in favor of reopening relations with the Dominican regime.

Why had Simon Gittleman asked about Agustín Cabral? He made an effort to control the irritation that overpowered him as soon as he thought about Egghead. There could be no evil intent. If anyone admired and respected Trujillo, it was the former Marine, dedicated body and soul to defending his regime. He must have mentioned the name through an association of ideas, when he saw the Constitutional Sot and recalled that Chirinos and Cabral were—in the eyes of someone who was not privy to the workings of the regime—inseparable companions. Yes, they had been. Trujillo often gave them joint assignments. As he had in 1937, when he named them Director General of Statistics and Director General of Migration and sent them to travel along the border and report on the infiltration of Haitians. But the friendship between the two men was always relative: it ceased as soon as consideration or flattery from the Chief came into play. It amused Trujillo—an exquisite, secret game that he could permit himself—to observe the subtle maneuvers, the secretive stabbings, the Florentine intrigues devised against one another by the Walking Turd and Egghead, but also by Virgilio Álvarez Pina and Paíno Pichardo, Joaquín Balaguer and Fello Bonnelly, Modesto Díaz and Vicente Tolentino Rojas, and everyone else in his close circle—to displace a comrade, move ahead, be closer to and deserve greater attention, a closer hearing, more jokes, from the Chief. "Like women in a harem competing to be the favorite," he thought. And in order to keep them always on the alert, to keep them from becoming moth-eaten and to avoid routine and ennui, he alternated them on the list, sending one, then the other, into disgrace. He had done it with Cabral: distanced him, made him aware that everything he was, everything he was worth, everything he had, he owed to Trujillo, that without the Benefactor he was nobody. A trial he had forced all his collaborators, close or distant, to endure. Egghead had handled it badly and become desperate, like a woman in love abandoned by her man. Because he wanted to straighten things out too soon, he was making serious mistakes. He would have to swallow a lot more shit before he came back into existence.

Could it be that Cabral, knowing Trujillo was going to decorate the former Marine, had begged Gittleman to intercede on his behalf? Was that the reason he had mentioned, in so inopportune a way, the name of someone who was out of favor with the regime, as every Dominican who read "The Public Forum" knew? Well, perhaps Simon Gittleman didn't read *El Caribe*.

His blood froze: urine was coming out. He felt it, he thought he could see the yellow liquid pouring out of his bladder without asking permission of that useless valve, that dead prostate incapable of containing it, then moving toward his urethra, running merrily through it and coming out in search of air and light, through his underwear, his fly, the crotch of his trousers. He felt faint. He closed his eyes for a few seconds, shaken by indignation and impotence. Unfortunately, instead of Virgilio Álvarez Pina, he had Dorothy Gittleman on his right and Simon on his left, and they couldn't help him. Virgilio could. He was president of the Dominican Party, but, in fact, since Dr. Puigvert, brought in secret from Barcelona, had diagnosed the damn infection in his prostate, his really important function had been to act quickly when one of these acts of incontinence occurred, to spill a glass of water or wine on the Benefactor and then beg a thousand pardons for his clumsiness, or, if it happened on a podium or during a parade, to place himself like a screen in front of the stained trousers. But the imbeciles in charge of protocol had placed Virgilio Álvarez four seats away. Nobody could help him. When he stood up he would suffer the horrific mortification of letting the Gittlemans and some of the guests see that he had pissed in his pants without realizing it, like an old man. Rage kept him from moving, from pretending he was going to take a drink and spilling the glass or pitcher that was in front of him.

Very slowly, looking around with a distracted air, he began to move his right hand toward the glass full of water. Very, very slowly, he drew it toward him until it was on the edge of the table, so that the slightest movement would tip it over. Suddenly he remembered that the first daughter born in Aminta Ledesma to his first wife, Flor de Oro—that mad little thing with the body of a woman and the soul of a man who changed husbands as often as she changed shoes—habitually wet her bed until she was in high school. He had the courage to take another peek at his trousers. Instead of the mortifying sight, the stain he was expecting, he discovered—his sight was still formidable, just like his memory—that his fly and pant legs were dry. Completely dry. It had been a false impression, motivated by his fear, his panic at "passing water," as they said about women in labor. He was overwhelmed by happiness and optimism. The day, which had begun with bad humor and gloomy presentiments, had just become beautiful, like the coastline when the sun came out after a storm.

He stood, and, like soldiers obeying a command, everyone followed suit. As he bent down to help Dorothy Gittleman to her feet, he decided, with all the strength of his soul: "Tonight, in Mahogany House, I'll make a girl cry out, the way I did twenty years ago." It seemed to him that his testicles were coming to a boil and his penis beginning to stiffen.

12 Salvador Estrella Sadhalá was thinking that he would never see Lebanon, and the thought depressed him. From the time he was a boy he had dreamed that one day he would visit Upper Lebanon, and Basquinta, the town, perhaps a village, that had been the home of the Sadhalá family and from which, at the end of the last century, his mother's forebears had been expelled for being Catholics. Salvador grew up hearing from Mama Paulina about the adventures and misfortunes of the prosperous merchants the Sadhalás had been in Lebanon: how they lost everything, how Don Abraham Sadhalá and his family suffered as they fled the persecutions the Muslim majority inflicted on the Christian minority. They wandered half the world, faithful to Christ and the Cross, until they landed in Haiti and then moved to the Dominican Republic. They settled in Santiago de los Caballeros, and by working with the family's proverbial dedication and honesty, became prosperous and respected again in their adopted country. Though he saw little of his maternal relatives, Salvador, bewitched by the stories of Mama Paulina, always felt himself to be a Sadhalá. Which is why he had dreamed of visiting the mysterious Basquinta that he never found on maps of the Middle East. Why was he certain now that he would never set foot in the exotic country of his ancestors?

"I think I fell asleep," he heard Antonio de la Maza say from the back seat. He saw him rubbing his eyes.

"You all fell asleep," said Salvador. "Don't worry, I'm keeping an eye on the cars coming from Ciudad Trujillo."

"So am I," said Lieutenant Amado García Guerrero, sitting beside him. "It looks like I'm sleeping because I don't move a muscle and blank out my mind. It's a relaxation technique I learned in the Army."

"Are you sure he's coming, Amadito?" Antonio Imbert, sitting at the wheel, challenged him. Turk could hear his tone of reproach. How unfair! As if Amadito were to blame if Trujillo canceled his trip to San Cristóbal.

"Yes, Tony," grumbled the lieutenant, with fanatical certainty. "He's coming."

Turk was no longer so sure; they had been waiting for an hour and a quarter. And probably had lost another day, filled with enthusiasm, anguish, and hope. At the age of forty-two, Salvador was one of the oldest of the seven men stationed in the three cars that lay in wait for Trujillo on the highway to San Cristóbal. He didn't feel old, not at all. His strength was still as remarkable as it had been when he was thirty, and, on the Los Almácigos farm, they said that Turk could kill a donkey with a single punch behind the ear. The power of his muscles was legendary, and known by all those who had put on gloves to box with him in the ring at the Santiago Reformatory, where, thanks to his efforts to teach them sports, he had achieved remarkable results with delinquent and homeless boys. Kid Dynamite came from there, a Golden Gloves winner who became a boxer well known throughout the Caribbean.

Salvador loved the Sadhalá family and was proud of his Arab-Lebanese blood, but the Sadhalás had not wanted him to be born; they had put up fierce opposition when his mother, Paulina, told them she was being courted by Piro Estrella, a mulatto, a soldier, and a politician, three things—Turk smiled—that gave the Sadhalás the chills. The family's resistance drove Piro Estrella to run off with Mama Paulina, take her to Moca, drag the priest to the church at gunpoint, and force him to marry them. Over time, the Sadhalás and the Estrellas reconciled. When Mama Paulina died, in 1936, there were ten Estrella Sadhalá children. General Piro Estrella fathered another seven in his second marriage, so that Turk had sixteen legitimate siblings. What would happen to them if they failed tonight? Above all, what would happen to his brother Guaro, who knew nothing about any of this? General Guarionex Estrella Sadhalá had been head of Trujillo's military adjutants and was currently commander of the Second Brigade in La Vega. If the plot failed, the reprisals against him would be savage. But why would it fail? It had been carefully prepared. As soon as his superior, General José René (Pupo) Román, informed Guarionex that Trujillo was dead and a civilian-military junta was taking power, he would place all the military forces in the north at the service of the new regime. Would it really happen? Discouragement, brought on by waiting, overwhelmed Salvador again.

Half closing his eyes, not moving his lips, he prayed. He did this several times a day, aloud when he woke up and went to bed, in silence the rest of the time. Our Fathers and Hail Marys, but also prayers he improvised according to circumstances. Since his youth he had been in the habit of involving God in his large and small problems, confiding his secrets and asking advice. He begged Him to let Trujillo come, begged that His infinite grace would at last permit them to kill the executioner of Dominicans, the Beast who had now turned his fierce wrath against the Church of Christ and its shepherds. Until recently, Turk had been indecisive about putting Trujillo to death, but since he had received the sign, he could speak to the Lord about tyrannicide with a clear conscience. The sign had been the words read to him by His Holiness's nuncio.

It was because of Father Fortín, a Canadian priest residing in Santiago, that Salvador had the conversation with Monsignor Lino Zanini, and because of that, he was here now. For many years, Father Cipriano Fortín had been his spiritual adviser. Once or twice a month they had long conversations in which Turk opened his heart and his conscience to him; the priest would listen, answer his questions, and express his own doubts. Imperceptibly, political matters began to replace personal ones in their conversations. Why did the Church of Christ support a regime stained with blood? How could the Church shelter with its moral authority a leader who committed abominable crimes?

Turk remembered Father Fortín's embarrassment. He ventured explanations that did not even convince himself: render unto God what is God's and unto Caesar what is Caesar's. Does such a separation even exist for Trujillo, Father? Doesn't he go to Mass, doesn't he receive the blessing and the consecrated host? Aren't there Masses, Te Deums, benedictions for all the government's actions? Don't bishops and priests sanctify acts of tyranny every day? What circumstances allowed the Church to abandon the faithful and identify in this way with Trujillo?

Ever since his childhood, Salvador had known how difficult, how impossible it sometimes was to subject his daily behavior to the commandments of his religion. His principles and beliefs, though firm, had not stopped him from drinking or chasing women. He could never atone enough for having fathered two children out of wedlock before he married Urania Mieses. These errors shamed him, and he had attempted to rectify them, though he had not placated his conscience. Yes, it was very difficult not to offend Christ in one's daily life. He, a poor mortal marked by original sin, was proof of man's innate weaknesses. But how could the Church inspired by God make the mistake of supporting a cruel, merciless man?

Until sixteen months ago—he would never forget that day: Sunday, January 24, 1960—when the miracle occurred. A rainbow in the Dominican sky. January 21 had been the festival of the country's patron saint, Our Lady of Altagracia, and also the date of the most extensive roundup of June 14 members. The Church of Altagracia, on that sunlit morning in Santiago, was packed. Suddenly, from the pulpit, in a firm voice, Father Cipriano Fortín began to read—shepherds of Christ were doing the same in every Dominican church—the Pastoral Letter that shook the Republic. It was a hurricane, even more dramatic than the famous San Zenón storm in 1930, at the beginning of the Trujillo Era, that wiped out the capital city.

In the darkness of the automobile, Salvador Estrella Sadhalá, immersed in the memory of that glorious day, smiled. Hearing Father Fortín read, in his lightly French-accented Spanish, each sentence of the Pastoral Letter that drove the Beast mad with rage, seemed a response to his doubts and anguish. He knew the text so well—after hearing it he had read the letter, which was secretly printed and distributed all over the country—he had almost memorized it. A "shadow of sorrow" marked the festival of the Dominican Virgin. "We cannot remain oblivious to the deep suffering that afflicts so many Dominican homes," the bishops said. Like St. Peter, they wanted "to weep with those who weep." They recalled that "the root and foundation of all rights lie in the inviolate dignity of the human person." A quotation from Pius XII evoked the "millions of human beings who continue to live under oppression and tyranny," for whom "nothing is secure: not their homes, their property, their liberty, nor their honor."

Each sentence made Salvador's heart beat faster. "To whom does the *right to life* belong but to God alone, Creator of life?" The bishops emphasized that from this "primordial right" all others spring: the right to have a family, to work, to transact business, to immigrate (wasn't this a condemnation of the infamous system of having to request police permission each time you left the country?), and the right to one's good name and to not be slandered "on trivial pretexts or in anonymous denunciations . . . for base and despicable motives." The Pastoral Letter reaffirmed that "all men have the right to freedom of conscience, freedom of the press, and free association. . . ." The bishops were sending up prayers "in this time of affliction and uncertainty" that there might be "harmony and peace" and that there might be established in the nation "the sacred rights of human brotherhood."

Salvador was so moved that when he left the church he could not even talk about the Pastoral Letter with his wife or the friends who had gathered at the entrance, stammering with surprise, enthusiasm, or fear at what they had just heard. There was no possible confusion: the Pastoral Letter came from Archbishop Ricardo Pittini and was signed by the five bishops in the country.

Mumbling an excuse, he left his family and, like a sleepwalker, returned to the church. He went to the sacristy. Father Fortín was removing his chasuble. He smiled: "You're proud of your Church now, Salvador, aren't you?" He could not speak. He gave the priest a long embrace. Yes, the Church of Christ had finally come over to the side of the victims.

"The reprisals will be terrible, Father Fortín," he murmured.

They were. But with the regime's perverse capacity for intrigue, it concentrated its revenge on the two foreign bishops and ignored those born on Dominican soil. Monsignor Thomas F. Reilly, in San Juan de la Maguana, an American, and Monsignor Francisco Panal, in La Vega, a Spaniard, were the targets of the ignominious campaign.

In the weeks following the jubilation of January 24, 1960, Salvador considered, for the first time, the need to kill Trujillo. Initially the idea horrified him: a Catholic had to respect the Fifth Commandment. And yet he returned to it, irresistibly, every time he read in *El Caribe* or *La Nación*, or heard on the Dominican Voice, the attacks against Monsignor Panal and Monsignor Reilly: they were agents of foreign powers, sellouts to Communism, colonialists, traitors, vipers. Poor Monsignor Panal! Accusing a priest of being a foreigner when he had spent thirty years doing his apostolic work in La Vega, where he was loved equally by opposing factions. The calumnies hatched by Johnny Abbes—who else could concoct such vileness?—which Turk heard from Father Fortín and the human tom-tom, did away with his scruples. The final straw was the act of sacrilege mounted against Monsignor Panal in the church in La Vega, where the bishop was saying twelve o'clock Mass. The nave was crowded with parishioners, and when Monsignor Panal was reading the day's lesson from Scripture, a gang of heavily made-up, half-naked prostitutes burst into the church and, to the stupefied amazement of the worshipers, approached the pulpit, hurled insults and recriminations at the aged bishop, and accused him of having fathered their children and engaging in sexual perversions. One of them grabbed the microphone and howled: "Recognize the babies you gave us, don't let them die of starvation." When some people finally reacted and tried to remove the whores from the church and protect the bishop, who was staring in disbelief, the *caliés* stormed in—about twenty hoodlums armed with clubs and chains— and attacked the parishioners mercilessly. The poor bishops! They painted their houses with insults. In San Juan de la Maguana, they dynamited the van that Monsignor Reilly used to drive around his diocese, and bombarded his house every night with dead animals, urine, live rats, until he was forced to take refuge in Ciudad Trujillo, in the Santo Domingo Academy. The indestructible Monsignor Panal continued to resist threats, slanders, and insults in La Vega. An old man made of the stuff of martyrs.

It was during this time that Turk came to Father Fortín's house, his large, heavy face transformed.

"What's the matter, Salvador?"

"I'm going to kill Trujillo, Father. I want to know if I'll go to hell." He broke down. "It can't go on. What they're doing to the bishops, to the churches, that disgusting campaign on television, on the radio, in the papers. It has to stop, and the only way is to cut off the hydra's head. Will I go to hell?"

Father Fortín calmed him down. He offered him coffee he had just prepared, he took him out for a long walk along the laurel-lined streets of Santiago. A week later he announced that the papal nuncio, Monsignor Lino Zanini, would grant him a private audience in Ciudad Trujillo. Turk felt intimidated when he presented himself at the nunciature's elegant mansion on Avenida Máximo Gómez. From the very first moment, this prince of the Church put the timid giant, constrained by the shirt and tie he had worn for his audience with the Pope's representative, at ease.

How elegant Monsignor Zanini was, how well-spoken! No doubt he was a real prince. Salvador had heard many stories about the nuncio, and liked him because they said Trujillo hated him. Was it true that Perón had left the country, after spending seven months here as an exile, when he learned of the arrival of His Holiness's new nuncio? Everybody said he had hurried to the National Palace: "Be careful, Excellency. With the Church you can't win. Remember what happened to me. It wasn't the military that overthrew me, it was the priests. This nuncio the Vatican is sending you is like the one they sent me when my difficulties with the crows began. Watch out for him!" And the former Argentine dictator packed his bags and fled to Spain.

After that encounter, Turk was ready to believe anything good said about Monsignor Zanini. The nuncio led him to his office, offered him a cold drink, encouraged him to let out what he was carrying inside, with affable comments in a Spanish spoken with Italian music that had the effect of an angelic melody on Salvador. The nuncio heard him say that he could no longer endure what was happening, that the regime's actions against the Church and its bishops were driving him mad. After a long pause, he grasped the nuncio's ringed hand:

"I'm going to kill Trujillo, Monsignor. Will there be forgiveness for my soul?"

His voice broke. He sat, his eyes lowered, his breathing agitated. He felt Monsignor Zanini's paternal hand on his back. When, at last, he raised his eyes, the nuncio was holding a book by St. Thomas Aquinas. His fresh face smiled at him with a roguish air. One of his fingers was pointing to a passage on the open page. Salvador leaned forward and read: "God looks with favor upon the physical elimination of the Beast if a people is freed thereby."

He left the nunciature in a trance. He walked for a long time along Avenida George Washington, at the edge of the sea, feeling a tranquillity of spirit he had not known for years. He would kill the Beast, and God and His Church would forgive him; staining his hands with blood would wash away the blood the Beast was spilling in his homeland.

But would he come? He felt the awful tension that waiting had caused in his companions. Nobody opened his mouth, or even moved. He could hear them breathing: Antonio Imbert, in long, quiet inhalations as he clutched the wheel; Antonio de la Maza, panting rapidly, did not take his eyes from the road; and, beside him, the regular, deep breathing of Amadito, whose face was turned as well toward Ciudad Trujillo. His three friends probably held their weapons in their hands, as he did. Turk felt the butt of the Smith & Wesson .38, bought some time ago at a friend's hardware store in Santiago. Amadito, in addition to his .45 pistol, was carrying an M-1 rifle—part of the ludicrous Yankee contribution to the conspiracy—and, like Antonio, one of the two 12-gauge Browning shotguns, the barrels cut down by a Spaniard, Miguel Ángel Bissié, a friend of Antonio de la Maza, in his workshop. They were loaded with special projectiles that another Spanish friend of Antonio's, Manuel de Ovín Filpo, a former artillery officer, had prepared for them with the assurance that each shell had enough killing power to pulverize an elephant. God willing. It was Salvador who proposed that the CIA's carbines be used by Lieutenant García Guerrero and Antonio de la Maza, and that they occupy the right-hand seats next to the windows. They were the best shots, they should be the first to shoot at the closest distance. But would he come, would he come?

Salvador Estrella Sadhalá's gratitude and admiration for Monsignor Zanini increased when, a few weeks after their conversation in the nunciature, he learned that the Sisters of Mercy had decided to transfer Gisela, his sister who was a nun—Sor Paulina—from Santiago to Puerto Rico. Gisela, his pampered little sister, Salvador's favorite. Even more so since she had embraced the religious life. On the day she made her vows and adopted Mama Paulina's name, huge tears ran down Turk's cheeks. Whenever he could spend time with Sor Paulina, he felt redeemed, comforted, more spiritual, touched by the serenity and joy emanating from his beloved sister, the tranquil certainty with which she lived her life of service to God. Had Father Fortín told the nuncio how frightened he was about what might happen to his sister if the regime discovered that he was conspiring? Not for a moment did he believe that the transfer of Sor Paulina to Puerto Rico was coincidental. It was a wise and generous decision by the Church of Christ to place a pure, innocent young woman, whom Johnny Abbes's killers would devour, beyond the reach of the Beast. It was one of the regime's customs that most angered Salvador: venting its wrath on the families of those it wanted to punish, on their parents, children, brothers and sisters, confiscating all they had, imprisoning them, taking away their jobs. If the plan failed, the reprisals against his sisters and brothers would be implacable. Not even his father, General Piro Estrella, the Benefactor's good friend, who gave banquets in Trujillo's honor at his ranch in Las Lavas, would be excused. He had weighed all of this, over and over again. He had made his decision. And it was a relief to know that criminal hands could not touch Sor Paulina in her convent in Puerto Rico. From time to time she sent him a letter filled with affection and good humor, written in her clear, upright hand.

In spite of his religious devotion, it had never occurred to Salvador to do what Giselita had done and enter an order. It was a vocation he admired and envied, but one from which the Lord had excluded him. He never would have been able to keep the vows, especially the one of chastity. God had made him too earthbound, too willing to surrender to the instincts that a shepherd of Christ had to annihilate in order to fulfill his mission. He had always liked women; even now, when he led a life of marital fidelity with only occasional slips that tore at his conscience for a long time afterward, the presence of a brunette with a narrow waist and rounded hips, a sensual mouth and flashing eyes—the typical Dominican beauty with mischief in her glance, her walk, her talk, the movements of her hands—aroused Salvador and inflamed him with fantasies and desires.

These were temptations he usually resisted. His friends often made fun of him, in particular Antonio de la Maza, who, after Tavito's murder, had turned to the wild life, because Turk refused to join them on their all-night visits to brothels, or to the houses where the madams had young girls rumored to be virgins. True, sometimes he succumbed. And then the bitterness lasted many days. For some time he had held Trujillo responsible when he gave in to these temptations. It was the fault of the Beast that so many Dominicans turned to whores, drinking binges, and other dissipations in order to ease their anguish at leading a life without a shred of liberty or dignity, in a country where human life was worth nothing. Trujillo had been one of Satan's most effective allies.

"That's him!" roared Antonio de la Maza.

And Amadito and Tony Imbert:

"It's him! That's him!"

"Pull out, damn it!"

Antonio Imbert already had, and the Chevrolet that had been

parked facing Ciudad Trujillo whirled around, tires screeching—Salvador thought of a police movie—and headed for San Cristóbal, following Trujillo's car along the dark, deserted highway. Was it him? Salvador didn't see, but his companions seemed so certain it had to be him that it had to be him. His heart pounded in his chest. Antonio and Amadito lowered the windows, and as Imbert, who leaned over the wheel like a rider making his horse jump, accelerated, the wind was so strong that Salvador could barely keep his eyes open. He protected them with his free hand—the other was holding the revolver—as their distance from the red taillights gradually diminished.

"Are you sure it's the Goat's Chevrolet, Amadito?" he shouted.

"I'm sure, I'm sure," the lieutenant cried. "I recognized the driver, Zacarías de la Cruz. Didn't I tell you he would come?"

"Step on it, damn it," Antonio de la Maza repeated for the third or fourth time. He had put his head, and the sawed-off barrel of his carbine, out the window.

"You were right, Amadito," Salvador heard himself shout. "He came, and without an escort, just like you said."

The lieutenant held his rifle in both hands. He leaned to one side, his back was turned, and with his finger on the trigger, he rested the butt of the M-1 on his shoulder. "Thank you, God, in the name of your Dominican children," Salvador prayed.

Antonio de la Maza's Chevrolet Biscayne raced along the highway, gaining on the light blue Chevrolet Bel Air that Amadito García Guerrero had described to them so many times. Turk identified the official black-and-white license plate, number 0–1823, and the cloth curtains on the windows. It was, yes, it was, the car the Chief used to go to his Mahogany House in San Cristóbal. Salvador had been having a recurrent nightmare about the Chevrolet Biscayne that Tony Imbert was driving. In it, they were driving just as they were now, under a moonlit, star-filled sky, and suddenly this brand-new car, specially prepared for pursuit, began to decelerate, to go more slowly, until, with all of them cursing, it stopped dead. And Salvador watched the Benefactor's automobile disappear into the darkness.

The Chevrolet Bel Air continued to speed—it must have been going more than a hundred kilometers an hour—and was clearly outlined in the high beams that Imbert turned on. Salvador had heard in detail the story of this vehicle ever since, following Lieutenant García Guerrero's proposal, they had agreed to ambush Trujillo on his weekly drive to San Cristóbal. It was evident that their success would depend on a fast car. Antonio de la Maza had a passion for cars. At Santo Domingo Motors they were not surprised that someone whose job near the Haitian border required him to drive hundreds of kilometers a week would want a special automobile. They recommended a Chevrolet Biscayne and ordered it for him from the United States. It had arrived in Ciudad Trujillo three months ago. Salvador remembered the day they took it out for a test drive, and how they laughed when they read in the brochure that this car was identical to the ones used by the New York police to pursue criminals. Air conditioning, automatic transmission, hydraulic brakes, and a 350 cc eight-cylinder engine. It cost seven thousand dollars and Antonio had said, "Pesos have never been put to better use." They tested it on the outskirts of Moca, and the brochure did not exaggerate: it could reach a hundred sixty kilometers an hour.

"Careful, Tony," he heard himself say after a jolt that must have dented a fender. Antonio and Amadito did not seem to notice; their weapons and heads were still leaning out the windows, waiting for Imbert to pass Trujillo's car. They were less than twenty meters away, the wind was choking him, and Salvador did not take his eyes off the closed curtains on the back window. They would have to shoot blindly, riddle the entire seat with bullets. He prayed to God that the Goat was not accompanied by one of those unfortunate women he often took to his Mahogany House.

As if, suddenly, it had noticed that they were in pursuit, or as if its sporting instinct refused to let any other car pass, the Chevrolet Bel Air pulled ahead a few meters.

"Step on it, damn it," ordered Antonio de la Maza. "Faster, damn it!"

In a few seconds the Chevrolet Biscayne made up the distance and kept drawing closer. And the others? Why hadn't Pedro Livio and Huáscar Tejeda shown up? They were in the Oldsmobile—it also belonged to Antonio de la Maza—only a couple of kilometers away, and they should have intercepted Trujillo's car by now. Did Imbert forget to turn the headlights on and off three times in a row? Fifí Pastoriza in Salvador's old Mercury, waiting two kilometers beyond the Oldsmobile, had not appeared either. They already had driven two, three, four, or more kilometers. Where were they?

"You forgot the signals, Tony," shouted Turk. "We left Pedro Livio and Fifí behind."

They were about eight meters from Trujillo's car, and Tony was trying to pass, flashing the headlights and blowing the horn.

"Step on it, faster!" roared Antonio de la Maza.

They drove even closer, but the Chevrolet Bel Air, indifferent to Tony's signals, would not leave the center of the highway. Where the hell was the Oldsmobile with Pedro Livio and Huáscar? Where was his Mercury with Fifí Pastoriza? Finally, Trujillo's car moved to the right. It left them enough room to pass.

"Step on it, step on it," Antonio de la Maza pleaded hysterically.

Tony Imbert accelerated and in a few seconds they were beside the Chevrolet Bel Air. The side curtains were also closed, so that Salvador did not see Trujillo, but he had a clear view, through the driver's window, of the heavy, coarse face of the famous Zacarías de la Cruz at the moment his eardrums seemed to burst with the explosion of simultaneous shots from Antonio and Amadito. The cars were so close that when the back window of the other automobile shattered, pieces of glass hit them and Salvador felt tiny stings on his face. As if he were having a hallucination, he saw Zacarías's head move in a strange way, and, a moment later, Salvador fired over Amadito's shoulder.

It did not last very long, and now—the squeal of the tires made his skin crawl—a violent braking left Trujillo's car behind them. Turning his head, he saw through the rear window that the Chevrolet Bel Air was swerving as if it would turn over before it came to a stop. It did not make a turn, it did not try to escape.

"Stop, stop!" Antonio de la Maza was shouting. "Put it in reverse, damn it!"

Tony knew what he was doing. He had braked at almost the same time as Trujillo's bullet-ridden car, but he took his foot off the brake when the vehicle gave a violent jolt, as if it were about to overturn, and then he braked again until the Chevrolet Biscayne stopped. Without wasting a second he turned the car—no other vehicle was coming—in the opposite direction, and then drove toward Trujillo's automobile, which had stopped, absurdly, with its headlights on, less than a hundred meters away, as if it were waiting for them. When they had driven half the distance, the lights of the parked car turned off, but Turk could still see it in Tony Imbert's high beams.

"Heads down, get down," said Amadito. "They're going to shoot."

The glass in the window on his left shattered. Salvador felt pinpricks on his face and neck, and was thrown forward by the car's braking. The Biscayne screeched, swerved, drove off the road before it stopped. Imbert turned off the headlights. Everything was in darkness. Salvador heard shouts around him. When had he, Amadito, Tony, and Antonio jumped onto the highway? The four of them were out of the car, hiding behind the fenders and open doors, firing toward Trujillo's car, toward where it ought to be. Who was shooting at them? Was someone else with the Goat besides the driver? Because, no doubt about it, somebody was firing, the bullets resonated all around, chinked as they pierced the metal of the car, and had just wounded one of his friends.

"Turk, Amadito, cover us," said Antonio de la Maza. "Tony, let's finish it."

Almost at the same time—his eyes were beginning to make out profiles and silhouettes in the tenuous bluish light—he saw two crouching figures running toward Trujillo's automobile.

"Don't fire, Turk," said Amadito; with one knee on the ground, he aimed his rifle. "We have them. Keep an eye open. We don't want him to get past if he tries to run away."

For five, eight, ten seconds, the silence was absolute. As if in a nightmare, Salvador noticed that on the lane to his right, two cars were speeding toward Ciudad Trujillo. A moment later, another explosion of rifle and revolver fire. It lasted a few seconds. Then the booming voice of Antonio de la Maza filled the night:

"He's dead, damn it!"

He and Amadito began to run. Seconds later, Salvador stopped, craned his head over the shoulders of Tony Imbert and Antonio de la Maza, who, one with a lighter and the other with matches, were examining the blood-soaked body dressed in olive green, the face destroyed, that lay on the asphalt in a puddle of blood. The Beast was dead. He did not have time to give thanks to God, he heard the sound of running and was certain he heard shots, there, behind Trujillo's car. Without thinking, he raised his revolver and fired, convinced they were *caliés* or military adjutants coming to the aid of the Chief, and very close by he heard the moans of Pedro Livio Cedeño, who had been hit by his bullets. It was as if the earth had opened up, as if, from the bottom of the abyss, he could hear the sound of the Evil One laughing at him.

13 "You really don't want a little more arepa?" Aunt Adelina insists affectionately. "Go on, have some. When you were little, every time you came to the house you asked for corn cake. Don't you like it anymore?"

"Of course I like it, Aunt Adelina," Urania protests. "But I've never eaten so much in my life. I won't be able to sleep a wink."

"All right, we'll just leave it here in case you want a little more later," says a resigned Aunt Adelina.

Her firm voice and mental lucidity contrast with how decrepit she looks: bent, almost bald—patches of scalp can be seen through her white hair—her face puckered into a thousand wrinkles, dentures that shift when she eats or speaks. She is a shrunken little woman, half lost in the rocking chair where Lucinda, Manolita, Marianita, and the Haitian maid settled her after carrying her downstairs. Her aunt was determined to have supper in the dining room with her brother Agustín's daughter, who had suddenly reappeared after so many years. She speaks energetically, and in her small, deep-set eyes there is a flashing intelligence. "I never would have recognized her," thinks Urania. Or Lucinda, and certainly not Manolita, whom she last saw when she was eleven or twelve and who is now a prematurely aged matron with wrinkles on her face and neck, and hair badly dyed a rather vulgar blue-black. Marianita, Lucinda's daughter, must be about twenty: thin, very pale, her hair almost in a crew cut, and melancholy eyes. She doesn't stop looking at Urania, as if she were under a spell. What has her niece heard about her?

"I can't believe it's you, that you're really here." Aunt Adelina fixes her penetrating eyes on her. "I never thought I'd see you again."

"Well, Aunt Adelina, here I am. It makes me so happy."

"Me too, darling. You must have made Agustín even happier. My brother had resigned himself to never seeing you again."

"I don't know, Aunt Adelina." Urania puts up her defenses, foresees recriminations and indiscreet questions. "I spent all day with him, and I don't think he even recognized me."

Her two cousins react in unison:

"Of course he recognized you, Uranita," declares Lucinda.

"He can't speak, so it's hard to tell," Manolita concurs. "But he understands everything, his mind still works."

"He's still Egghead," says Aunt Adelina with a laugh.

"We know because we see him every day," Lucinda continues. "He recognized you, and your coming back made him happy."

"I hope so, Lucinda."

A silence that is prolonged, glances that cross the old table in the narrow dining room, with a china closet that Urania vaguely recognizes, and religious pictures on faded green walls. Nothing is familiar here either. In her memory, the house of her Aunt Adelina and Uncle Aníbal, where she came to play with Manolita and Lucinda, was large, bright, elegant, and airy; this is a cave crowded with depressing furniture.

"Breaking my hip separated me from Agustín forever." She shakes her small fist, the fingers deformed by sclerosis. "Before it happened, I used to spend hours with him. We had long conversations. He didn't need to talk for me to understand what he wanted to say. My poor brother! I would have brought him here. But where would I put him, in this rat hole?"

She speaks angrily.

"The death of Trujillo was the beginning of the end for the family," Lucindita says with a sigh. And then she becomes alarmed. "I'm sorry, Urania. You hate Trujillo, don't you?"

"It started before that," Aunt Adelina corrects her, and Urania becomes interested in what she is saying.

"When, Grandma?" Lucinda's oldest daughter asks in a thin little voice.

"With the letter in 'The Public Forum,' a few months before they killed Trujillo," Aunt Adelina declares; her eyes pierce the emptiness. "In January or February of 1961. We gave the news to your papa, early in the morning. Aníbal was the first to read it."

"A letter in 'The Public Forum'?" Urania is searching, searching through her memories. "Ah, yes."

"I assume it's nothing important, a foolish mistake that will be straightened out," his brother-in-law said on the phone; he sounded so agitated, so vehement, so false, that Senator Agustín Cabral was taken aback: what was wrong with Aníbal? "Haven't you read *El Caribe*?"

"They've just brought it in, I haven't opened it yet."

He heard a nervous little cough.

"Well, there's a letter, Egghead." His brother-in-law tried to be casual, lighthearted. "It's all nonsense. Clear it up as soon as you can."

"Thanks for calling me." Senator Cabral said goodbye. "My love to Adelina and the girls. I'll stop by to see them."

Thirty years in the highest echelons of political power had made Agustín Cabral a man familiar with imponderables—traps, ambushes, trickery, betrayals—and so, learning there was a letter attacking him in "The Public Forum," the most widely read, and widely feared, section in *El Caribe* because it was fed from the National Palace and served as a political barometer for the entire country, did not unnerve him. It was the first time he had appeared in the infernal column; other ministers, senators, governors, or officials had been burned in its flames, but not him, until now. He went back to the dining room. His daughter, in her school uniform, was eating breakfast: mangú—plantain mashed with butter—and fried cheese. He kissed the top of her head ("Hi, Papa"), sat down across from her, and while the maid poured his coffee, he slowly, carefully opened the folded paper lying on a corner of the table. He turned the pages until he reached "The Public Forum":

To the Editor:

I am writing out of civic duty to protest the affront to Dominican citizens and to the unrestricted freedom of expression which the government of Generalissimo Trujillo guarantees to this Republic. I refer to the fact that until now, your respected and widely read pages have not disclosed something that everyone knows, which is that Senator Agustín Cabral, nicknamed Egghead (for what reason?) was stripped of the Presidency of the Senate when it was determined that he was guilty of irregularities as the Minister of Public Works, a post he occupied until a short while ago. It is also known that because this regime is scrupulous in questions of probity and the use of public

funds, an investigative committee to look into apparent mismanage-
ment and collusion—illegal commissions, acquisition of obsolete mate-
rials at elevated prices, misleading inflation of budgets, in which the
senator would have been involved in the course of his duties as minis-
ter—has been named to examine the charges against him.

Doesn't the Trujillista citizenry have the right to be informed
with regard to such serious matters?

Respectfully,

> *Telésforo Hidalgo Saíno, Engineer*
> *Calle Duarte no. 171*
> *Ciudad Trujillo*

"I have to run, Papa," Senator Cabral heard, and without a single gesture that would belie his apparent calm, he moved the newspaper aside to kiss the girl. "I won't be on the school bus, I'm staying to play volleyball. Some friends and I will walk home."

"Be careful at the intersections, Uranita."

He drank his orange juice and had an unhurried cup of steaming, freshly brewed coffee, but did not taste the mangú or fried cheese or toast with honey. Again he read every word, every syllable, of the letter in "The Public Forum." It undoubtedly had been fabricated by the Constitutional Sot, a pen pusher who delighted in sneak attacks but only when ordered by the Chief; nobody would dare to write, let alone publish, a letter like this without Trujillo's authorization. When was the last time he saw him? The day before yesterday, on his walk. He hadn't been called to walk beside him, the Chief spent the whole time talking to General Román and General Espaillat, but he greeted him with the customary civility. Or did he? He sharpened his memory. Had he noticed a certain hardness in that fixed, intimidating gaze, which seemed to tear through appearances and reach deep into the soul of the person he was scrutinizing? A certain dryness when he responded to his greeting? The beginning of a frown? No, he didn't remember anything unusual.

The cook asked if he'd be home for lunch. No, only for supper, and he nodded when Aleli suggested the menu. When he heard the official car of the Senate Presidency pulling up to the door of his house, he looked at his watch: exactly eight o'clock. Thanks to Trujillo, he had discovered that time is gold. Like so many others, since his youth he had made the Chief's obsessions his own: order, exactitude, discipline, perfection. Senator Agustín Cabral had said it in a speech: "Thanks to His Excellency, the Benefactor, we Dominicans have discovered the wonders of punctuality." Putting on his jacket, he went out to the street: "If I had been dismissed, the official car would not have come for me." His assistant, Humberto Arenal, an Air Force lieutenant who had never hidden his connections to the SIM, opened the door for him. His official car, with Teodosio at the wheel. His assistant. There was nothing to worry about.

"He never found out why he fell into disgrace?" Urania asks in astonishment.

"Never with any certainty," Aunt Adelina explains. "There were plenty of suppositions, but that's all. For years Agustín asked himself what he had done to make Trujillo so angry overnight. And turn a man who had served him his whole life into a pariah."

Urania observes Marianita's disbelief as she listens to them.

"They sound like things that happened on another planet, don't they, Marianita?"

The girl blushes.

"It's just that it seems so incredible, Aunt Urania. Like something in *The Trial*, the Orson Welles movie they showed at the Cinema Club. Anthony Perkins is tried and executed, and he never finds out why."

Manolita has been fanning herself with both hands, but she stops in order to interject:

"They said he fell into disgrace because somebody made Trujillo believe it was Uncle Agustín's fault that the bishops refused to proclaim him Benefactor of the Catholic Church."

"They said a thousand things," exclaims Aunt Adelina. "The doubt was the worst part of his calvary. The family was being ruined and nobody knew what Agustín had been accused of, what he had done or failed to do."

No other senator was there when Agustín Cabral entered the Senate at a quarter past eight, as he did every morning. The guards gave him the proper salute, and the ushers and clerks he passed in the halls on the way to his office said good morning with their usual effusiveness. But the uneasiness felt by his two secretaries, Isabelita and Paris Goico, a young lawyer, was reflected in their faces.

"Who died?" he joked. "Are you worried about the letter in 'The

Public Forum'? We'll clear up that nasty business right now. Call the editor of *El Caribe*, Isabelita. At home—Panchito doesn't go to his office before noon."

He sat down at his desk, glanced at the pile of documents, his correspondence, the day's schedule prepared by the efficient Parisito. "The letter was dictated by the Chief," he thought. A little snake slid down his spine. Was it one of those melodramas that amused the Generalissimo? In the midst of tensions with the Church and a confrontation with the United States and the OAS, was he in the mood for one of his bravura performances from the past, when he had felt all-powerful, unthreatened? Was this the time for circuses?

"He's on the line, Don Agustín."

He picked up the receiver and waited a few seconds before speaking.

"Did I wake you, Panchito?"

"What an idea, Egghead." The journalist's voice sounded normal. "I'm up at the crack of dawn, like a capon rooster. And I sleep with one eye open, just in case. What's up?"

"Well, as you can imagine, I'm calling about the letter this morning in 'The Public Forum,' " Senator Cabral said hoarsely. "Can you tell me anything about it?"

The answer came in the same light, jocular tone, as if they were talking about something trivial.

"It came recommended, Egghead. I wasn't going to print something like that without checking. Believe me, given our friendship, it didn't make me happy to publish it."

"Yes, yes, sure," he murmured to himself. He mustn't lose his composure for a single instant.

"I intend to rectify the slander," he said softly. "I haven't been dismissed from anything. I'm calling you from the office of the President of the Senate. And that alleged committee investigating my management of the Ministry of Public Works, that's another lie."

"Send me your rectification right away," Panchito replied. "I'll do everything I can to publish it, it's the least I can do. You know the esteem I have for you. I'll be at the paper from four o'clock on. My love to Uranita. Take care of yourself, Agustín."

As soon as he hung up, he began to have his doubts. Had he done the right thing in calling the editor of *El Caribe*? Wasn't it a false move that betrayed his concern? What else could Panchito have said? He received letters for "The Public Forum" directly from the National Palace and printed them, no questions asked. He looked at his watch: a quarter to nine. He had time; the meeting of the Senate executive committee was at nine-thirty. He dictated his rectification to Isabelita with the same austere clarity he used in all his writing. A brief, dry, fulminating letter: he continued as President of the Senate and no one had questioned his scrupulous management at the Ministry of Public Works, entrusted to him by the regime presided over by that eponymous Dominican, His Excellency Generalissimo Rafael Leonidas Trujillo, Benefactor and Father of the New Nation.

When Isabelita left to type the letter, Paris Goico came into the office.

"The meeting of the Senate executive committee has been canceled, Don Agustín."

He was young and didn't know how to dissemble; his mouth hung open and his face was livid.

"Without consulting me? By whom?"

"The Vice President of the Senate, Don Agustín. He just told me so himself."

He weighed what he had just heard. Could it be a separate incident, unrelated to the letter in "The Public Forum"? Parisito waited in distress, standing beside the desk.

"Is Dr. Quintanilla in his office?" His secretary nodded, and he rose to his feet. "Tell him I'm on my way to see him."

"It can't be that you don't remember, Uranita," her Aunt Adelina admonished her. "You were fourteen years old. It was the most serious thing that had happened in the family, even worse than the accident that killed your mother. And you didn't know anything about it?"

They'd had coffee and tea. Urania tried a mouthful of arepa. They sat around the dining-room table, talking in the wan light of a small floor lamp. The Haitian servant, as silent as a cat, had cleared the table.

"I remember how Papa suffered, of course I do, Aunt Adelina," Urania explains. "I forget the details, the daily incidents. He tried to hide it from me at first. 'There are some problems, Uranita, they'll be resolved soon.' I didn't imagine that from then on my life would turn upside down."

She feels the eyes of her aunt, her cousins, her niece, burning into her. Lucinda says what they are all thinking:

"Some good came out of it for you, Uranita. You wouldn't be where you are now if it hadn't. But for us, it was a disaster."

"And most of all, for my poor brother," her aunt says accusingly. "They stabbed him in the back and left him to bleed for another thirty years."

A parrot shrieks above Urania's head, startling her. She hadn't realized it was there until now; the bird is agitated, moving from side to side on its wooden bar inside a large cage with heavy blue bars. Her aunt, cousins, and niece burst into laughter.

"This is Samson." Manolita introduces him. "He's upset because we woke him. He's a sleepyhead."

The parrot helps to ease the atmosphere.

"I'm sure if I understood what he was saying, I'd learn a lot of secrets," Urania jokes, pointing at Samson.

Senator Agustín Cabral is in no mood for smiling. He responds with a solemn nod to the honeyed greeting of Dr. Jeremías Quintanilla, Vice President of the Senate; he has just burst into his office, and with no preliminaries, he rebukes him:

"Why have you canceled the meeting of the Senate executive committee? Isn't that the responsibility of the President? I demand an explanation."

The heavy, cocoa-colored face of Senator Quintanilla nods repeatedly, while his lips, in a cadenced, almost musical Spanish, attempt to placate him:

"Of course, Egghead. Don't be angry. Everything except death has a reason."

A plump man in his sixties, with puffy eyelids and a wet mouth, he is wearing a blue suit and a glistening tie with silver stripes. He smiles persistently, and Agustín Cabral sees him remove his glasses, wink at him, roll his eyes, revealing the gleaming whites, then step toward him, take his arm, and pull him as he says, very loudly:

"Let's sit here, we'll be more comfortable."

He doesn't lead him to the heavy, tiger-foot chairs in his office but to a balcony with half-opened doors. He obliges him to go out with him so they can talk in the open air, across from the droning hum of the ocean, away from indiscreet ears. The sun is strong; the brilliant morning is ablaze with engines and horns from the Malecón, and the voices of street peddlers.

"What the hell's going on, Monkey?" Cabral whispers.

Quintanilla is still holding his arm and is now very serious. In his eyes he can detect a vague feeling of solidarity or compassion.

"You know very well what's going on, Egghead, don't be stupid. Didn't you realize that three or four days ago the papers stopped calling you a 'distinguished gentleman' and demoted you to 'señor'?" Monkey Quintanilla murmurs in his ear. "Didn't you read *El Caribe* this morning? That's what's going on."

For the first time since reading the letter in "The Public Forum," Agustín Cabral is afraid. It's true: yesterday or the day before somebody at the Country Club joked that the society page in *La Nación* had deprived him of "distinguished gentleman," which was usually a bad omen: those kinds of warnings amused the Generalissimo. This was serious. A storm. He had to use all his experience and intelligence not to drown in it.

"Did the order to cancel the meeting of the executive committee come from the Palace?" he whispers. The Vice President, leaning over, has his ear against Cabral's mouth.

"Where else would it come from? There's more. All committees in which you participate are canceled. The directive says: 'Until the status of the President of the Senate is regularized.' "

He is silent. It has happened. The nightmare is happening, the one that came periodically to drag down his triumphs, his ascent, his political achievements: he has been estranged from the Chief.

"Who sent it to you, Monkey?"

Quintanilla's chubby face tightens in alarm, and Cabral finally understands Monkey's agitation. Is the Vice President going to say he cannot commit an act of such disloyalty? Abruptly, he makes his decision:

"Henry Chirinos." He takes his arm again. "I'm sorry, Egghead. I don't think there's much I can do, but if I can, you can count on me."

"Did Chirinos tell you what I'm accused of?"

"He only gave me the order and made a speech: 'I know nothing. I am the humble messenger of a higher decision.' "

"Your papa always suspected that the schemer was Chirinos, the Constitutional Sot," Aunt Adelina recalls.

"That fat repulsive nigger was one of the people who made the best accommodation," Lucindita interrupts. "From Trujillo's bed and board to Balaguer's minister and ambassador. Do you see what kind of country this is, Uranita?"

"I remember him very well, I saw him in Washington a few years ago, when he was ambassador," says Urania. "He often came to the house when I was little. He seemed like one of Papa's intimate friends."

"And Aníbal's, and mine," adds Aunt Adelina. "He would come here with all his flattery, he'd recite his poems for us. He was always quoting books, pretending to be educated. He invited us to the Country Club once. I didn't want to believe he had betrayed his lifelong friend. Well, that's what politics is, you make your way over corpses."

"Uncle Agustín had too much integrity, he was too good, that's why they turned on him."

Lucindita waits for her to corroborate this, to protest the injustice done to him. But Urania does not have the strength to pretend. She merely listens, with an air of regret.

"But my husband, may he rest in peace, behaved like a gentleman, he gave your papa all his support." Aunt Adelina gives a sarcastic little laugh. "What a Quixote he was! He lost his job at the Tobacco Company and never found work again."

Samson the parrot lets loose another flood of shouts and noises that sound like curses. "Quiet, lazybones," Lucindita scolds him.

"Just as well we haven't lost our sense of humor, girls," exclaims Manolita.

"Find Senator Henry Chirinos and tell him I want to see him right away, Isabel," Senator Cabral says as he enters his office. And addressing Paris Goico: "Apparently he's the one who cooked up this mess."

He sits down at his desk, prepares to review again the day's schedule, but becomes aware of his circumstances. Does it make sense to sign letters, resolutions, memoranda, notes, as the President of the Senate of the Republic? It's doubtful he still is. The worst thing would be to show signs of discouragement to his subordinates. Put the best face on a bad situation. He picks up the papers and is beginning to reread the first page when he notices that Parisito is still there. His hands are trembling:

"President Cabral, I wanted to tell you," he stammers, devastated by emotion. "Whatever happens, I'm with you. In everything. I know how much I owe you, Dr. Cabral."

"Thank you, Goico. You're new to this world, and you'll see things that are worse. Don't worry. We'll weather the storm. And now, let's get to work."

"Senator Chirinos is expecting you at his house, Senator Cabral."

Isabelita is speaking as she comes into the office. "He answered himself. Do you know what he said? 'The doors of my house are open day and night to my great friend Senator Cabral.'"

When he leaves the Congress building, the guards salute him as usual. The black, funereal car is still there. But his assistant, Lieutenant Humberto Arenal, has disappeared. Teodosio, the driver, opens the door for him.

"Senator Henry Chirinos's house."

The chauffeur nods, not saying a word. Later, when they are driving along Avenida Mella, on the edge of the colonial city, he looks at him in the rearview mirror and says:

"Since we left Congress, we've been followed by a Beetle full of *caliés*, Senator."

Cabral turns around: fifteen or twenty meters behind them is one of the unmistakable black Volkswagens of the Intelligence Service. In the blinding morning light he can't tell how many *caliés* are inside. "Now I'm escorted by people from the SIM instead of my assistant," he thinks. As the car enters the crowded, narrow streets of the colonial city, lined with little one- and two-story houses with bars at the windows and stone entrances, he tells himself that the matter is even graver than he supposed. If Johnny Abbes is having him followed, he may have decided to arrest him. The story of Anselmo Paulino repeated. What he had feared so much. His brain is a red-hot forge. What did he do? What had he said? What mistake did he make? Whom had he seen recently? They were treating him like an enemy of the regime. Him, him!

The car stopped at the corner of Salomé Ureña and Duarte, and Teodosio opened the door for him. The Beetle parked a few meters behind them but no *calié* got out. He was tempted to go over and ask them why they were following the President of the Senate, but he restrained himself: what good would it do to challenge some poor bastards who were only obeying orders?

Senator Henry Chirinos's old two-story house with its little colonial balcony and jalousied windows resembled its owner; time, age, and neglect had deformed it and made it asymmetrical; it had widened excessively in the middle, as if it had grown a belly and were about to explode. A long time ago it must have been a solid, noble house; now it was dirty, neglected, and seemed on the verge of collapse. Splotches and stains defaced the walls, and spiderwebs hung from the roof. The door was opened as soon as he knocked. He climbed a lugubrious, groaning staircase with a greasy banister, and on the first landing the butler opened a creaking glass door: he recognized the large library, the heavy velvet drapes, the tall cases filled with books, the thick, faded carpet, the oval pictures, and the silvery threads of cobwebs catching the beams of sunlight that penetrated the shutters. It smelled of age and rank humors, and the heat was infernal. He remained standing and waited for Chirinos. The number of times he had been here, over so many years, for meetings, agreements, negotiations, conspiracies, all in the service of the Chief.

"Welcome to your house, Egghead. A sherry? Sweet or dry? I recommend the fino amontillado. It's chilled."

Wearing pajamas and wrapped in a flamboyant green flannel robe with silk binding that accentuated the rotundity of his body, with a huge handkerchief in the pocket, and on his feet, backless bedroom slippers misshapen by his bunions, Senator Chirinos smiled at him. His uncombed, thinning hair, the mucus on his puffy face, his purplish lids and lips, the dried saliva at the corners of his mouth, revealed to Senator Cabral that he had not yet bathed. He allowed him to pat his shoulder and lead him to the ancient easy chairs with silk antimacassars over the backs, without responding to the effusions of his host.

"We've known each other for many years, Henry. We've done many things together. Good things, and some bad. No two people in the regime have been as close as you and I. What's going on? Why did the sky start falling in on me this morning?"

He had to stop talking because the butler came in, an old, bent mulatto as ugly and slovenly as his employer, carrying a glass decanter into which he had poured the sherry, and two glasses. He left them on the table and hobbled out of the room.

"I don't know." The Constitutional Sot touched his own chest. "You probably don't believe me. You probably think I've schemed, instigated, provoked what's happening to you. By my mother's memory, the most sacred thing in this house, I don't know. Since I found out yesterday afternoon, I've been utterly dumbfounded. Wait, wait, a toast. To this mess being resolved quickly, Egghead!"

He spoke with animation and emotion, with his heart in his hand and the sugary sensibility of heroes on the radio soap operas that HIZ imported, before the Castro revolution, from CMQ in Havana. But Agustín Cabral knew him: he was a first-rate actor. It might be true or false, he had no way to find out. He took a small, unwilling sip of sherry, for he never drank alcohol in the morning. Chirinos smoothed the hairs in his nostrils.

"Yesterday, at a meeting with the Chief, he suddenly ordered me to instruct Monkey Quintanilla, as Vice President of the Senate, to cancel all meetings until the vacancy in the Presidency had been filled," he continued, gesticulating. "I don't know, I thought you had an accident, a heart attack. 'What happened to Egghead, Chief?' 'That's what I'd like to know,' he replied, with that gruffness that freezes your bones. 'He's no longer one of us, he's gone over to the enemy.' I couldn't ask any more questions, his tone was categorical. He sent me to carry out his order. And this morning, like everyone else, I read the letter in 'The Public Forum.' Again, I swear to you on the memory of my sainted mother: that's all I know."

"Did you write the letter in 'The Public Forum'?"

"I write Spanish correctly," the Constitutional Sot said in indignation. "That ignoramus committed three syntactical errors. I've marked them."

"Who was it, then?"

The fat-enclosed eyes of Senator Chirinos poured out compassion as they looked at him:

"What the hell difference does it make, Egghead? You're one of the intelligent men in this country, don't play dumb with me, I've known you since you were a boy. The only thing that matters is that for some reason you've made the Chief angry. Talk to him, ask his forgiveness, give him explanations, promise to make amends. Regain his confidence."

He picked up the glass decanter, refilled his glass, and drank. There was less noise from the street than at Congress. Because of the thick colonial walls, or because the narrow streets in the center of the city discouraged cars.

"Ask his forgiveness, Henry? What have I done? Don't I devote my days and nights to the Chief?"

"Don't tell me. Convince him. I already know. Don't be discouraged. You know how he is. Basically, a magnanimous man. A deep sense of justice. If he weren't suspicious, he wouldn't have lasted thirty-one years. There's been a mistake, a misunderstanding. It ought to be resolved. Ask him for an audience. He knows how to listen."

As he spoke, he waved his hand, savoring every word his ashen lips expelled. He looked even more obese seated than when he was standing: his enormous belly had pushed open his robe and pulsated in a rhythmic ebb and flow. Cabral imagined those intestines dedicated, for so many hours a day, to the arduous task of absorbing and digesting the masses of food swallowed by that voracious maw. He regretted being here. Did he think the Constitutional Sot would help him? If he hadn't actually devised this, in his heart of hearts he was celebrating it as a great victory over someone who, despite all appearances, had always been his rival.

"Thinking it over, racking my brains," Chirinos added, with a conspiratorial air, "I think the reason may be the disappointment the Chief felt when the bishops refused to proclaim him Benefactor of the Catholic Church. You were on the commission that failed to achieve that."

"There were three of us, Henry! Balaguer, and Paíno Pichardo too, as Minister of the Interior and Religious Practice. The negotiations took place months ago, right after the Pastoral Letter. Why would I get all the blame?"

"I don't know, Egghead. In fact, it seems pretty farfetched. I can't see any reason either why you should fall into disgrace. Sincerely, after all, we've been friends for so many years."

"We've been something more than friends. We've been together, behind the Chief, in every decision that transformed this country. We're living history. We set traps for each other, gave each other low blows, played dirty tricks to gain an advantage. But total annihilation seemed out of the question. This is different. I can end up ruined, discredited, in prison. Without knowing why! If you've cooked this up, congratulations. It's a masterpiece, Henry!"

He had risen to his feet. He spoke calmly, impersonally, almost didactically. Chirinos stood up too, leaning on one of the arms of the chair to hoist his weight. They were very close, almost touching. Cabral saw a quotation from Tagore in a small, square frame on the wall, between the shelves of books: *An open book is a mind that speaks; closed, a friend who waits; forgotten, a soul that forgives; destroyed, a heart that weeps.* "He's pretentious in everything he does, touches, says, and feels," he thought.

"Frankness deserves frankness in return." Chirinos brought his face close to Agustín Cabral, who was dazed by the stink that accompanied his words. "Ten years ago, five years ago, I wouldn't have hesitated to concoct anything that got you out of the way, Agustín. And you would have done the same to me. Including annihilation. But now? To what end? Do we have some account left to settle? No. We're no longer in competition, Egghead, you know that as well as I do. How much oxygen is left to a dying cause? For the last time: I have nothing to do with what's happening to you. My hope, my wish, is that you resolve it. Difficult days are coming, and it's to the regime's advantage if you're there to help withstand the onslaught."

Senator Cabral nodded. Chirinos patted his shoulder.

"If I go down to the *caliés* who are waiting for me and tell them what you've said, that the regime is suffocating, that it's a dying cause, you'll be keeping me company," he murmured, instead of saying goodbye.

"You won't do that." The great dark mouth of his host laughed. "You're not like me. You're a true gentleman."

"What happened to him?" Urania asks. "Is he still alive?"

Aunt Adelina laughs, and the parrot Samson, who seemed to be asleep, reacts with another series of shrieks. When he stops, Urania can hear the rhythmic creak of the rocking chair where Manolita is sitting.

"Weeds don't die," her aunt explains. "He's still in his lair in the colonial city, at the corner of Salomé Ureña and Duarte. Lucindita saw him a little while ago, walking with a cane in Independencia Park, in his house slippers."

"Some kids were running after him and shouting: 'The bogeyman, the bogeyman!'" Lucinda laughs. "He's uglier and more repulsive than ever. He must be over ninety, right?"

Have they had enough after-dinner conversation so that she can leave? Urania hasn't felt comfortable all night. She's been tense, waiting for the attack. This is the only family she has left and she feels more distant from them than from the stars. And she's beginning to be irritated by Marianita's large eyes constantly staring at her.

"Those were terrible days for the family." Aunt Adelina keeps harping on the same subject.

"I remember my papa and Uncle Agustín whispering together in this living room," says Lucindita. "And your papa was saying: 'But my God, what could I have done to the Chief to make him treat me this way?'"

She is silenced by a dog barking wildly near the house; two more, five more, respond. Through a small skylight in the ceiling, Urania can see the moon: round, yellow, splendid. There were no moons like that in New York.

"What upset him most was your future if something happened to him." Aunt Adelina's look is heavy with reproach. "When they took over his bank accounts, he knew it was hopeless."

"His bank accounts!" Urania nods. "That was the first time my papa talked to me about it."

She was already in bed and her father came in without knocking. He sat at the foot of her bed. In shirtsleeves, very pale, he looked thinner, more fragile, older. He hesitated over every syllable.

"This business is going very badly, darling. You have to be prepared for anything. So far, I've kept the gravity of the situation from you. But, today, well, you must have heard something at school."

The girl nodded solemnly. She wasn't worried; her confidence in him was limitless. How could anything bad happen to a man who was so important?

"Yes, Papa, there were letters against you in 'The Public Forum,' accusing you of crimes. Nobody will believe it, it's so silly. Everybody knows you're incapable of doing bad things."

Her father embraced her, through the quilt.

It was more serious than slanders in the newspaper. They had removed him from the Presidency of the Senate. A congressional committee was looking into mismanagement and misuse of public funds during his tenure as minister. For days the Beetles of the SIM had been following him; there was one outside the front door right now, with three *caliés* inside. This past week he had received notifications of expulsion from the Trujillonian Institute, the Country Club, the Dominican Party, and this afternoon, when he went to withdraw money from the bank, the final blow. The manager, his friend Josefo Heredia, informed him that his two accounts had been frozen for the duration of the congressional investigation.

"Anything can happen, Uranita. They can confiscate this house, throw us out on the street. Even into prison. I don't mean to frighten you. Maybe nothing will happen. But you ought to be prepared. And be brave."

She listened to him, stunned; not because of what he was saying but because of the weakness of his voice, the hopelessness of his expression, the fear in his eyes.

"I'll pray to the Virgin," she said. "Our Lady of Altagracia will help us. Why don't you talk to the Chief? He's always liked you. He'll give an order, and everything will be settled."

"I've requested an audience and he won't even respond, Uranita. I go to the National Palace and the secretaries and aides barely greet me. And President Balaguer doesn't want to see me, and neither does the Minister of the Interior; that's right, Paíno Pichardo. I'm the living dead, my dear. Maybe you're right, maybe the only thing we can do is trust in the Virgin."

His voice broke. But when the girl sat up to embrace him, he regained his composure. He smiled at her:

"You had to know about this, Uranita. If anything happens to me, go to your aunt and uncle. Aníbal and Adelina will take care of you. It may be a test. Sometimes the Chief does things like this, to test his collaborators."

"Accusing a man like him of mismanagement," Aunt Adelina says with a sigh. "Except for that little house on Gazcue, he never had anything. No estates, no companies, no investments. Except for his savings, the twenty-five thousand dollars he doled out to you while you were studying up there. The most honorable politician and the best father in the world, Uranita. And, if you'll permit some interference in your private life from this doddering old aunt, you didn't act properly with him. I know you support him and pay for the nurse. But do you know how much you made him suffer when you wouldn't answer a single letter or come to the phone when he called? Aníbal and I often saw him crying over you, right here in this house. Now, after so much time has gone by, Urania, can I ask why?"

Urania reflects, enduring the censorious look of the old woman bent like a hook in her chair.

"Because he wasn't as good a father as you think, Aunt Adelina," she says at last.

Senator Cabral had the taxi drop him at the International Clinic, four blocks from the Intelligence Service, which was also located on Avenida México. When he was about to give the address to the driver, he felt a strange rush of shame and embarrassment, and instead of telling him to go to the SIM, he mentioned the clinic. He walked the four blocks slowly; the domains of Johnny Abbes were probably the only important places in the regime he had never visited, until now. The Beetle full of *caliés* followed him openly, in slow motion, right next to the sidewalk, and he could see the turning heads and alarmed expressions of passersby when they became aware of the emblematic Volkswagen. He recalled that when he was on the Budget Committee in Congress, he argued in favor of the appropriation to import the hundred Beetles in which Johnny Abbes's *caliés* now cruised the entire country looking for enemies of the regime.

At the drab, anonymous building, uniformed and plainclothes police armed with submachine guns, guarding the entrance behind barbed wire and sandbags, let him pass without searching him or demanding identification. Inside, César Báez, one of Colonel Abbes's adjutants, was waiting for him. Husky, pockmarked, with curly red hair, he offered a sweating hand and led him along narrow corridors, where men with pistols in holsters hanging over their shoulders or dangling under their armpits were smoking, arguing, or laughing in smoke-filled cubicles that had bulletin boards covered with memos on the walls. It smelled of sweat, urine, and feet. A door opened. There was the head of the SIM. Cabral was surprised at the monastic spareness of the office, the walls bare of pictures or posters except for the one behind the colonel, which was a portrait in parade uniform—three-cornered feathered hat, his chest gleaming with medals—of the Benefactor. Abbes García, in civilian clothes, wore a short-sleeved summer shirt and had a cigarette dangling from his mouth. In his hand he held the red handkerchief that Cabral had seen so often.

"Good morning, Senator." He extended a soft, almost feminine hand. "Have a seat. We have few amenities here, you must forgive us."

"I'm grateful to you for seeing me, Colonel. You're the first. No one, not the Chief or President Balaguer, not a single minister, has replied to my requests for an audience."

The small, somewhat hunchbacked, potbellied figure nodded. Above the double chin, thin mouth, and flabby cheeks, Cabral could see the colonel's deep-set, watery eyes darting like quicksilver. Could he be as cruel as they said?

"Nobody wants to risk contagion, Señor Cabral," Johnny Abbes said coldly. It occurred to the senator that if snakes could talk, they would have that same, sibilant voice. "Falling into disgrace is an infectious disease. How can I help you?"

"Tell me what I'm accused of, Colonel." He paused to take a breath and appear more composed. "My conscience is clear. Since the age of twenty I've devoted my life to Trujillo and to the country. There's been some mistake, I swear it."

The colonel silenced him with a movement of the soft hand holding the red handkerchief. He put out his cigarette in a brass ashtray:

"Don't waste your time giving me explanations, Dr. Cabral. Politics is not my field, I'm concerned with security. If the Chief refuses to see you because he's unhappy with you, write to him."

"I already have, Colonel. I don't even know if they've given him my letters. I took them to the Palace personally."

Johnny Abbes's bloated face distended slightly:

"Nobody would hold back a letter addressed to the Chief, Senator. He's probably read them, and if you've been sincere, he'll respond." He paused, constantly watching him with his nervous eyes, and added, rather defiantly: "I see you've noticed the color of my handkerchief. Do you know the reason? It's a Rosicrucian teaching. Red is a good color for me. You probably don't believe in Rosicrucianism, you must think it's primitive superstition."

"I don't know anything about the Rosicrucian religion, Colonel. I have no opinion in that regard."

"Now I don't have the time, but when I was a young man I read a lot about Rosicrucianism. I learned a number of things. How to read a person's aura, for example. Right now yours is the aura of someone scared to death."

"I am scared to death," Cabral replied immediately. "For days your men have been following me constantly. Tell me, at least, if you're going to arrest me."

"That doesn't depend on me," said Johnny Abbes, casually, as if the matter were not important. "If I'm ordered to, I will. The escort is to discourage you from seeking asylum. If you try that, then my men will arrest you."

"Asylum? But, Colonel, seeking asylum, as if I were an enemy of the regime? I've been a part of the regime for thirty years."

"With your friend Henry Dearborn, the head of the mission the Yankees left us," Colonel Abbes continued, sarcastically.

Astonishment silenced Agustín Cabral. What did he mean?

"The American consul, my friend?" he stammered. "I've seen Mr. Dearborn only two or three times in my life."

"He's an enemy of ours, as you know," Abbes García went on. "When the OAS imposed sanctions, the Yankees left him here so he could keep on plotting against the Chief. For the past year, every conspiracy has passed through Dearborn's office. And despite that, you, the President of the Senate, recently attended a cocktail party at his house. Do you remember?"

Agustín Cabral's amazement increased. Was that it? Having attended a cocktail party at the house of the chargé d'affaires appointed by the United States when they closed their embassy?

. "The Chief ordered Minister Paíno Pichardo and me to attend that cocktail party," he explained. "To sound out his government's plans. I've fallen into disgrace because I obeyed an order? I submitted a written report about the gathering."

Colonel Abbes García shrugged his rounded shoulders in a puppet-like movement.

"If it was an order from the Chief, forget what I said," he conceded, with a touch of irony.

His attitude betrayed a certain impatience, but Cabral did not leave. He was encouraged by the foolish hope that this talk might bear some fruit.

"You and I have never been friends, Colonel," he said, forcing himself to speak normally.

"I can't have friends," Abbes García replied. "It would prejudice my work. My friends and enemies are the friends and enemies of the regime."

"Please let me finish," Agustín Cabral continued. "But I've always respected you, and recognized the exceptional service you render the nation. If we've had any differences . . ."

The colonel seemed to be raising a hand to silence him, but it was only to light another cigarette. He inhaled greedily and calmly exhaled smoke through his mouth and nose.

"Of course we've had differences," he acknowledged. "You were one of those who fought hardest against my theory that in view of the Yankee betrayal, we had to approach the Russians and the Eastern bloc. You, along with Balaguer and Manuel Alfonso, have been trying to convince the Chief that reconciliation with the Yankees is possible. Do you still believe that bullshit?"

Was this the reason? Had Abbes García stabbed him in the back?

Had the Chief accepted that idiotic idea? Were they distancing him so they could move the regime closer to the Communists? It was useless to go on humiliating himself before a specialist in torture and assassination who, as a result of the crisis, now dared to think of himself as a political strategist.

"I still believe we have no alternative, Colonel," he affirmed, with conviction. "What you propose, and you'll forgive my frankness, is an illusion. The U.S.S.R. and its satellites will never accept a rapprochement with the Dominican Republic, the bulwark of anti-Communism in Latin America. The United States won't accept it either. Do you want another eight years of American occupation? We have to come to some understanding with Washington or it will mean the end of the regime."

The colonel allowed his cigarette ash to fall to the floor. He took one puff after the other, as if he were afraid someone would take away his cigarette, and from time to time he wiped his forehead with the flame-colored handkerchief.

"Your friend Henry Dearborn doesn't think so, unfortunately." He shrugged again, like a cheap comic. "He keeps trying to finance a coup against the Chief. Well, there's no point to this discussion. I hope your situation is resolved and I can remove your escort. Thank you for the visit, Senator."

He did not offer his hand. He merely nodded his fat-cheeked face, partially obscured in a wreath of smoke, with the photograph of the Chief in grand parade uniform in the background. Then the senator recalled the quotation from Ortega y Gasset that was written in the notebook he always carried in his pocket.

The parrot Samson also seems petrified by Urania's words; he is as still and mute as Aunt Adelina, who has stopped fanning herself and opened her mouth. Lucinda and Manolita are looking at her, disconcerted. Marianita doesn't stop blinking. Urania has the absurd thought that the beautiful moon she sees through the window approves of what she has said.

"I don't know how you can say that about your father," her Aunt Adelina responds. "In all my days I never knew anyone who sacrificed more for a daughter than my poor brother. Were you serious when you called him a bad father? He worshiped you, and you were his torment. So you wouldn't suffer, he didn't marry again after your mother died, even though he was widowed so young. Who's responsible for your being lucky enough to study in the United States? Didn't he spend every cent he had on you? Is that what you call being a bad father?"

You mustn't say anything, Urania. She's an old woman, spending her final years, months, weeks immobilized and embittered, she's not to blame for something that happened so long ago. Don't answer her. Agree with her, pretend. Make some excuse, say goodbye, and forget about her forever. Calmly, without any belligerence at all, she says:

"He didn't make those sacrifices out of love for me, Aunt Adelina. He wanted to buy me. Salve his guilty conscience. Knowing it would do no good, that whatever he did, he would live the rest of his days feeling as vile and evil as he really was."

When he left the offices of the Intelligence Service on the corner of Avenida México and Avenida March 30, it seemed that the police on guard gave him pitying looks, and that one of them, staring into his eyes, meaningfully caressed the San Cristóbal submachine gun he carried over his shoulder. He felt suffocated, and somewhat faint. Did he have the quotation from Ortega y Gasset in his notebook? So opportune, so prophetic. He loosened his tie and removed his jacket. Taxis passed by but he didn't hail any of them. Would he go home? And feel caged, and rack his brains as he came down to his study from his bedroom or went up again to his bedroom, passing through the living room, asking himself a thousand times what had happened? Why was the rabbit being pursued by invisible hunters? They had taken away his office at the Congress, and the official car, and his membership at the Country Club, where he could have taken refuge, had a cool drink, and seen from the bar a landscape of well-tended gardens and distant golfers. Or he could visit a friend, but did he have any left? Everyone he had called on the phone sounded frightened, reticent, hostile: he was harming them by wanting to see them. He walked aimlessly, his jacket folded under his arm. Could the cocktail party at Henry Dearborn's house be the reason? Impossible. At a meeting of the Council of Ministers, the Chief decided that he and Paíno Pichardo would attend, "to explore the terrain." How could he punish him for obeying? Perhaps Paíno suggested to Trujillo that at the cocktail party he had seemed overly cordial to the gringo. No, no, no. Impossible that for something so trivial and stupid the Chief would trample on a man who had served him with more devotion and less self-interest than anyone.

He walked as if he were lost, changing direction every few blocks.

The heat made him perspire. It was the first time in many years he had wandered the streets of Ciudad Trujillo. A city he had seen grow, transformed from a small town in ruins, devastated by the San Zenón hurricane of 1930, into the beautiful, prosperous, modern metropolis it was now, with paved streets, electric lights, broad avenues filled with new cars.

When he looked at his watch it was a quarter past five. He had been walking for two hours, and he was dying of thirst. He was on Casimiro de Moya, between Pasteur and Cervantes, a few meters from a bar: El Turey. He went in, sat down at the first table. He ordered an ice-cold Presidente. It wasn't air-conditioned but there were fans, and the shade felt good. The long walk had calmed him. What would happen to him? And to Uranita? What would happen to the girl if they put him in jail, or if, in a fit of rage, the Chief ordered him killed? Would Adelina be prepared to rear her, be her mother? Yes, his sister was a good, generous woman. Uranita would be another daughter to her, like Lucindita and Manolita.

He tasted the beer with pleasure as he turned the pages in his notebook, looking for the quotation from Ortega y Gasset. The cold liquid, sliding down his throat, produced a feeling of well-being. Don't lose hope. The nightmare could disappear. Didn't that sometimes happen? He had sent three letters to the Chief. Frank, heartfelt letters, baring his soul. Begging his forgiveness for whatever mistake he might have committed, swearing he would do anything to make amends and redeem himself if, by some inadvertent, thoughtless act, he had offended him. He had reminded him of his long years of service and absolute honesty, as demonstrated by the fact that now, when his accounts at the Reserve Bank had been frozen—some two hundred thousand pesos, his life's savings—he was out on the street, with only the little house in Gazcue to live in. (He concealed only the twenty-five thousand dollars deposited in the Chemical Bank of New York, which he kept for an emergency.) Trujillo was magnanimous, that was true. He could be cruel, when the country required it. But generous, too, as magnificent as that Petronius in *Quo Vadis?* he was always quoting. Any day now he would summon him to the National Palace or to Radhamés Manor. They'd have one of those theatrical explanations, the kind the Chief liked so much. Everything would be settled. He would say that, for him, Trujillo had been not only the Chief, the statesman, the founder of the Republic, but a human model, a father. The nightmare would come to an end. His former life would rematerialize, as if by magic. The quotation from Ortega y Gasset appeared at the corner of a page, written in his tiny hand: "Nothing that a man has been, is, or will be, is something he has been, is, or will be forever; rather, it is something he *became* one day and *will stop being* the next." He was a living example of the precariousness of existence as postulated in that philosophy.

On one of the walls in El Turey, a poster announced that the piano music of Maestro Enriquillo Sánchez would begin at seven o'clock. Two tables were occupied by couples whispering to one another and exchanging romantic looks. "Accusing me, me, of being a traitor," he thought. A man who, for Trujillo's sake, had renounced pleasures, diversions, money, love, women. On a nearby chair, someone had left a copy of *La Nación*. He picked up the paper, and just for something to do with his hands, leafed through the pages. On page three, a panel announced that the illustrious and very distinguished ambassador Don Manuel Alfonso had just returned after traveling abroad for reasons of health. Manuel Alfonso! No one had more direct access to Trujillo; the Chief favored him and entrusted to him his most intimate affairs, from his wardrobe and perfumes to his romantic adventures. Manuel was a friend, and he owed him favors. He might be the key.

He paid and left. The Beetle wasn't there. Had he evaded them without intending to, or had the persecution stopped? A feeling of gratitude, of jubilant hope, blossomed in his chest.

14 The Benefactor walked into the office of Dr. Joaquín Balaguer at five o'clock, as he had every Monday through Friday for the past nine months, ever since August 3, 1960, when, in an attempt to avoid OAS sanctions, he had his brother Héctor (Blacky) Trujillo resign the Presidency of the Republic and replaced him with the affable, diligent poet and jurist, who rose to his feet and came forward to greet him:

"Good afternoon, Excellency."

After the luncheon for the Gittlemans, the Generalissimo rested for half an hour, changed his clothes—he was wearing a lightweight suit of white linen—and tended to routine matters with his four secretaries until just five minutes ago. He walked in scowling and came straight to the point, not hiding his anger:

"Did you authorize Agustín Cabral's daughter to leave the country a couple of weeks ago?"

The myopic eyes of the tiny Dr. Balaguer blinked behind thick glasses.

"Yes, I did, Excellency. Uranita Cabral, yes. The Dominican nuns gave her a scholarship to their academy in Michigan. The girl had to leave immediately to take some tests. The head of the school explained it to me, and Archbishop Ricardo Pittini took an interest in the matter. I thought this small gesture might build bridges to the hierarchy. I explained it all in a memorandum, Excellency."

The diminutive man spoke with his usual mild amiability and a slight smile on his round face, pronouncing the words with the perfection of a radio actor or a professor of phonetics. Trujillo scrutinized him, trying to uncover in his expression, the shape of his mouth, his evasive eyes, the smallest sign, the slightest allusion. In spite of his infinite mistrust, he saw nothing; obviously, the puppet president was too astute a politician to allow his face to betray him.

"When did you send me that memorandum?"

"A couple of weeks ago, Excellency. Following the intervention of Archbishop Pittini. I told him that since the girl's trip was urgent, I would grant her permission unless you had any objection. When I received no answer from you, I went ahead. She already had an American visa."

The Benefactor sat down facing Balaguer's desk and indicated to him that he should do the same. He felt comfortable in this office on the second floor of the National Palace; it was spacious, airy, sober, with shelves full of books, shining floor and walls, and a desk that was always immaculate. You could not call the puppet president an elegant man (how could he be with a miniature rounded body that made him not merely short, but almost a midget?), but he dressed as correctly as he spoke, respected protocol, and was a tireless worker for whom holidays and schedules did not exist. The Chief noticed his alarm; Balaguer had realized that by granting permission to Egghead's daughter, he might have committed a serious error.

"I only saw your memorandum half an hour ago," he said reproachfully. "It might have been lost. But that would surprise me. My papers are always in very good order. None of my secretaries saw it until now. So one of Egghead's friends, afraid I would deny her permission, must have mislaid it."

Dr. Balaguer's expression changed to one of consternation. He leaned his body forward and partially opened that mouth from which there emerged soft arpeggios and delicate trills when he recited poetry, and high-flown, even impassioned sentences when he gave political speeches.

"I will carry out a thorough investigation to learn who took the memorandum to your office and to whom it was given. Undoubtedly I moved too quickly. I should have spoken to you personally. I beg you to forgive this mistake on my part." His small, plump hands, nails trimmed short, opened and closed in contrition. "The truth is, I thought it a trivial matter. You had indicated, at the Council of Ministers, that Egghead's situation did not extend to his family."

He silenced him with a movement of his head.

"What's not trivial is that for a few weeks somebody hid that memorandum from me," he said curtly. "There is a traitor or an incompetent on the secretarial staff. I hope it's a traitor, incompetents do more damage."

He sighed, somewhat fatigued, and thought of Dr. Enrique Lithgow Ceara: had the man really intended to kill him, or had he simply made a mistake? Through two of the windows in the office he could see the ocean; big white-bellied clouds covered the sun, and in the ashen afternoon the surface of the water looked rough and agitated. Large waves pounded the irregular coastline. Though he had been born in San Cristóbal, far from the sea, the sight of foaming waves and the surface of the water disappearing into the horizon was his favorite view.

"The nuns gave her a scholarship because they know Cabral's in disgrace," he murmured in annoyance. "Because they think that now he'll work for the enemy."

"I assure you that is not the case, Excellency." The Generalissimo could see that Dr. Balaguer hesitated as he chose his words. "Mother María, Sister Mary, and the head of Santo Domingo Academy do not have a high opinion of Agustín. Apparently he did not get along with the girl, and she was suffering at home. They wanted to help her, not him. They assured me she is an exceptionally gifted student. I was hasty in signing the permission, and I am sorry. More than anything else, I did it to try to ease relations with the Church. This conflict seems dangerous to me, Excellency, but you already know my opinion."

He silenced him again with an almost imperceptible gesture. Had Egghead already betrayed him? Feeling himself marginalized, abandoned, with no responsibilities and no financial means, drowning in uncertainty, had he been pushed into the ranks of the enemy? He hoped not; he was an old collaborator, he had rendered good services in the past and perhaps could render them in the future.

"Have you seen Egghead?"

"No, Excellency. I followed your instructions not to receive him or answer his calls. He wrote me several letters, which you have already seen. Through Aníbal, his brother-in-law, who is at the Tobacco Company, I know he is very distressed. 'On the verge of suicide,' he told me."

Had it been frivolous to put an efficient servant like Cabral to the test at this difficult time for the regime? Perhaps.

"We've wasted enough time on Agustín Cabral," he said. "The Church, the United States. Let's start there. What's going to happen with Bishop Reilly? How long is he going to stay with the nuns at Santo Domingo and play the martyr?"

"I have spoken at length with the archbishop and the nuncio in this regard. I insisted that Monsignor Reilly must leave Santo Domingo Academy, that his presence there is intolerable. I believe I have convinced them. They ask that the bishop's safety be guaranteed, that the campaign in *La Nación*, *El Caribe*, and the Dominican Voice come to an end. And that he be allowed to return to his diocese in San Juan de la Maguana."

"Don't they also want you to grant him the Presidency of the Republic?" the Benefactor asked. The mere mention of the name Reilly or Panal made his blood boil. What if the head of the SIM was right after all? Suppose they definitively lanced that focal point of infection? "Abbes García suggests I put Reilly and Panal on a plane back to their countries. Expel them as undesirables. What Fidel Castro is doing in Cuba with the Spanish priests and nuns."

The President did not say a word or make the smallest gesture. He waited, absolutely still.

"Or allow the people to punish that pair of traitors," he continued, after a pause. "They're longing to do it. I've seen that on the tours I've made recently. In San Juan de la Maguana, in La Vega, they can barely control themselves."

Dr. Balaguer acknowledged that the people, if they could, would lynch them. They were resentful of these purple-clad priests and their ingratitude toward someone who had done more for the Catholic Church than all the governments of the Republic since 1844. But the Generalissimo was too wise and too much of a realist to follow the rash, impolitic advice of the head of the SIM, which, if carried out, would have the most unfortunate consequences for the nation. He spoke without haste, in a cadence that, combined with his pure elocution, was extremely soothing.

"You're the person in the regime who despises Abbes García most," he interrupted. "Why?"

Dr. Balaguer had his answer ready on his lips.

"The colonel is a technician in questions of security, and he provides a good service to the State," he replied. "But, in general, his political judgments are reckless. Because of the respect and admiration I feel for Your Excellency, I permit myself to entreat you to reject those ideas. The expulsion or, even worse, the death of Reilly and Panal would bring another military invasion. And the end of the Trujillo Era."

Because his tone was so gentle and cordial, and the music of his words so agreeable, it seemed as if the things Dr. Joaquín Balaguer said did not possess the firm opinions, the rigor, that the tiny man on occasion—this was one of those times—permitted himself with the Chief. Was he going too far? Had he succumbed, like Egghead, to the idiocy of believing himself safe, and did he also need a dose of reality? A curious character, Joaquín Balaguer. He had been at his side since 1930, when Trujillo sent two guards for him at the small Santo Domingo hotel where he was living, and took him to his house for a month so that he could help him in the election campaign; he had as an ephemeral ally Estrella Ureña, the leader from Cibao, and the young Balaguer was his ardent partisan. The invitation and a half hour's conversation were enough for the twenty-four-year-old poet, professor, and lawyer, a native of the shabby little village of Navarrete, to be transformed into an unconditional Trujillista, a competent, discreet servant in all the diplomatic, administrative, and political posts he had conferred on him. In spite of their thirty years together, the truth was that this person, so unobtrusive that Trujillo once baptized him the Shadow, was still something of a mystery to him, though the Chief boasted of having a bloodhound's nose for men's characters. He did, however, harbor the certainty that Balaguer lacked ambitions. Unlike the other men in his intimate group, whose appetites he could read like an open book in their behavior, their initiatives, and their flattery, Joaquín Balaguer always gave the impression of aspiring only to what he wished to give him. In his diplomatic posts in Spain, France, Colombia, Honduras, and Mexico, or in the Ministries of Education and Foreign Affairs, or in the Presidency, he seemed completely fulfilled, even overwhelmed by missions far beyond his dreams and aptitudes, and which, for that very reason, he strove resolutely to carry out. But—it suddenly occurred to the Benefactor—because of his humility the tiny bard and legal scholar had always been at the top, yet, unlike the others, and thanks to his inconsequentiality, he had never endured periods of disgrace. Which was why he was puppet president. In 1957, when a Vice President had to be chosen from the list headed by his brother Blacky Trujillo, the Dominican Party followed his orders and selected Rafael Bonnelly, the ambassador to Spain. The Generalissimo decided suddenly to replace that aristocrat with the insignificant Balaguer, using a decisive argument: "He has no ambitions." But now this intellectual lacking in ambition, with his delicate manner and refined speech, held the highest office in the nation and allowed himself to rail against the head of the Intelligence Service. He would have to take him down a peg or two someday.

Balaguer remained motionless and mute, not daring to interrupt the Benefactor's reflections, hoping he would deign to speak to him. He did, finally, without returning to the subject of the Church:

"I've always used formal address with you, haven't I? The only one of my collaborators I call *usted*. Haven't you noticed?"

The round little face blushed.

"I have, Excellency," he murmured, shamefaced. "I always ask myself if you avoid *tú* because you have less confidence in me than in my colleagues."

"I only realized it now," Trujillo added in surprise. "And you never call me Chief, like the others. All the years we've been together, and you're still something of a mystery to me. I never could discover any human weakness in you, Dr. Balaguer."

"I am full of them, Excellency," the President said with a smile. "But instead of paying me a compliment, you seem to be reproaching me."

The Generalissimo was not joking. He crossed and uncrossed his legs, not moving his piercing gaze away from Balaguer. He passed his hand over his brush mustache and parched lips, and scrutinized him steadily.

"There's something inhuman in you," he said, as if the object of his remarks were not present. "You don't have a man's natural appetites. As far as I know, you don't like women and you don't like boys. Your life is more chaste than the nuncio's, your neighbor on Avenida Máximo Gómez. Abbes García couldn't find any mistress or girlfriend, and no whores either. Which means that sex doesn't interest you. Or money. You hardly have any savings; except for the house where you live, you don't own property, or stocks, and you have no investments, at least not here. You haven't been involved in the intrigues, the deadly wars that bleed my collaborators dry, though they all plot against you. I had to force ministries and embassies on you, the Vice Presidency, even the Presidency. If I removed you now and sent you off to some damn little post in Montecristi or Azua, you'd go and be just as content. You don't drink, you don't smoke, you don't eat, you don't chase women, money, or power. Is that the way you really are? Or is it a strategy with a hidden agenda?"

Dr. Balaguer's clean-shaven face flushed again. His soft voice did not falter when he declared:

"Ever since I first met Your Excellency, on that April morning in 1930, my only vice has been serving you. That was when I learned that by serving Trujillo I was serving my country. This has enriched my life more than a woman, or money, or power could have done. I will never find the words to thank Your Excellency for allowing me to work at your side."

Bah, the usual flattery, the kind any Trujillista who was less well-read might have said. For a moment, he had imagined that the diminutive, inoffensive man would open his heart, as in the confessional, and reveal his sins and fears, his animosities and dreams. He probably didn't have a secret life, or any existence other than the one everybody could see: he was a functionary, frugal, hardworking, tenacious, and unimaginative, who gave shape, in beautiful orations, proclamations, letters, agreements, speeches, and diplomatic negotiations, to the ideas of the Generalissimo; a poet who produced acrostics and odes to the beauty of Dominican women and the Dominican landscape that embellished poetic festivals, special anniversaries, Miss Dominican Republic pageants, and patriotic celebrations. A little man without his own light, like the moon, who was illuminated by Trujillo, the sun.

"I know you have been a good colleague," the Benefactor declared. "Yes, ever since that morning in 1930. I sent for you at the suggestion of Bienvenida, my wife at the time. A relative of yours, wasn't she?"

"My cousin, Excellency. That lunch decided my life. You invited me to accompany you on your election campaign. You did me the honor of asking me to introduce you at meetings in San Pedro de Macorís, the capital, and La Romana. It was my debut as a political speaker. At that moment, my destiny took another direction. My vocation had been literature, the classroom, the lecture hall. Thanks to you, politics came to the forefront."

A secretary knocked at the door, asking permission to enter. Balaguer consulted the Generalissimo with a glance, and gave his authorization. The secretary—well-cut suit, small mustache, hair smoothed with brillantine—brought in a memorandum signed by five hundred seventy-six prominent residents of San Juan de la Maguana, requesting "that the return to this prelature of Monsignor Reilly, the felonious bishop, be prevented." A commission led by the mayor and the local head of the Dominican Party wanted to deliver it personally to the President. Would he receive them? Again he consulted the Benefactor, who nodded.

"Ask them to be good enough to wait," Balaguer said. "I shall receive those gentlemen as soon as I finish my meeting with His Excellency."

Could Balaguer be as devout a Catholic as people said? Countless jokes circulated about his bachelorhood and the pious, intense manner he adopted at Masses, Te Deums, and processions; he had seen him come up to take communion with his hands together and his eyes lowered. When he built the house where he lived with his sisters, on Máximo Gómez, next to the nuncio's residence, Trujillo had the Walking Turd write a letter to "The Public Forum" that ridiculed their proximity and asked what kind of relationship existed between the diminutive lawyer and the envoy of His Holiness. Because of his reputation for piety and his excellent relations with the priests, he entrusted him with designing the regime's policy toward the Catholic Church. He did it very well; until Sunday, January 24, 1960, when the Pastoral Letter from those bastards was read in every parish, the Church had been a solid ally. The Concordat between the Dominican Republic and the Vatican, which Balaguer negotiated and Trujillo signed in Rome, in 1954, provided formidable support for his regime and his own presence in the Catholic world. The poet and legal scholar must have suffered because of this year-and-a-half-long confrontation between the government and the crows. Could he really be so devout? He always maintained that the regime had to get along with the bishops, the priests, the Vatican, for pragmatic, political reasons, not religious ones: the approbation of the Catholic Church legitimized the actions of the regime to the Dominican people. What had happened to Perón must not happen to Trujillo: Perón's government began to crumble when the Church turned against him. Was he right? Would the hostility of those eunuchs in cassocks be the end of Trujillo? Before he let that happen, Panal and Reilly would be fattening the sharks at the bottom of the cliffs.

"I'm going to say something that will please you, Mr. President," he said abruptly. "I don't have time to read the bullshit intellectuals write. All those poems and novels. Matters of state are too demanding. Even though he's worked so many years with me, I've never read anything by Marrero Aristy. I didn't read *Over*, or the articles he wrote about me, or his *Dominican History*. And I haven't read the hundreds of books dedicated to me by poets, playwrights, and novelists. I haven't even read the stuff my wife writes. I don't have time for that, or for seeing movies, or listening to music, or going to the ballet or to cockfights. And I've never trusted artists. They're spineless and have no sense of honor, they tend to be traitors and are very servile. I haven't read your verses or essays either. I barely opened your book on Duarte, *The Christ of Liberty*, that you sent to me with such an affectionate dedication. But there's one exception. A speech you gave seven years ago. At the Fine Arts, when you were inducted into the Academy of the Language. Do you remember it?"

The little man had turned even brighter red. He radiated an exalted light of indescribable joy:

" 'God and Trujillo: A Realistic Interpretation,' " he murmured, lowering his lids.

"I've read it many times," said the high-pitched, mellifluous voice of the Benefactor. "I know whole paragraphs by heart, like poems."

Why this revelation to the puppet president? It was a weakness, and he never gave in to them. Balaguer could boast about it, feel important. Things weren't going so well that he could afford to to lose another collaborator in so short a time. It reassured him to recall that perhaps the greatest attribute of this puny little man was that not only did he know what was advisable but, even more important, he ignored what was inadvisable. He would not repeat this, in order not to earn the homicidal enmity of the other courtiers. Balaguer's speech had moved him deeply and often led him to wonder if it might not express a profound truth, one of those unfathomable divine decisions that mark the destiny of a people. That night, the Benefactor had paid little attention to the opening paragraphs of the address read by the new academician, dressed in a cutaway coat worn with little flair, from the stage of the Theater of Fine Arts. (He wore tails too, as did all the men in the audience; the ladies, glittering with jewels and diamonds, were in long dresses.) It seemed like a summary of Dominican history starting with the landing of Christopher Columbus on Hispaniola. But he began to be interested when, in the educated words and elegant prose of the speaker, a vision, a thesis, started to emerge. The Dominican Republic had survived more than four centuries—four hundred thirty-eight years—of countless adversities, including buccaneers, Haitian invasions, attempts at annexation, the massacre and flight of whites (only sixty thousand remained when it declared its emancipation from Haiti), because of Divine Providence. Until now, the task had been assumed directly by the Creator. But in 1930, Rafael Leonidas Trujillo Molina had relieved God of this arduous mission.

" 'A bold, energetic will that supports, in the march of the Republic toward the fulfillment of its destiny, the protective benevolence of supernatural forces,' " Trujillo recited with half-closed eyes. " 'God and Trujillo: here, in synthesis, is the explanation, first, of the survival of the nation, and second, of the present-day flourishing of Dominican life.' "

He opened his eyes and gave a melancholy sigh. Balaguer, made even smaller by gratitude, listened in rapture.

"Do you still believe that God passed the baton to me? That He delegated to me the responsibility of saving this country?" he asked with an indefinable mixture of irony and interest.

"More than I did then, Excellency," replied the delicate, clear voice. "Trujillo could not have carried out his superhuman mission without transcendental help. You have been, for this nation, an instrument of the Supreme Being."

"Too bad those asshole bishops haven't heard the news," Trujillo said with a smile. "If your theory is true, I hope God makes them pay for their blindness."

Balaguer was not the first to associate divinity with his work. The Benefactor recalled that the law professor, attorney, and politician Don Jacinto B. Peynado (whom he had made puppet president in 1938, when the massacre of Haitians had resulted in international protests against his third reelection) had placed a large luminous sign on the door of his house: "God and Trujillo." And then identical signs began to be displayed on many homes in the capital city and in the interior.

No, it hadn't been the words but the arguments justifying that association that had struck Trujillo as an overwhelming truth. It wasn't easy to feel the weight of a supernatural hand on his shoulders. Reissued every year by the Trujillonian Institute, Balaguer's speech was required reading in schools, and the central text in the Civics Handbook, used to educate high school and university students in the Trujillista Doctrine and composed by a trio of men he had selected: Balaguer, Egghead Cabral, and the Walking Turd.

"I've often thought about that theory of yours, Dr. Balaguer," he confessed. "Was it a divine decision? Why me? Why was I chosen?"

Dr. Balaguer wet his lips with the tip of his tongue before answering:

"The decisions of the Divinity are ineluctable," he said unctuously. "What must have been taken into account were your exceptional talent for leadership, your capacity for work, and, above all, your love for this country."

Why was he wasting time on this bullshit? He had urgent matters to attend to. And yet, it was very strange, he felt a need to prolong this vague, reflective, personal conversation. Why with Balaguer? Within the circle of his collaborators, he had shared the fewest intimate moments with him. He never invited him to the private suppers in San Cristóbal, at Mahogany House, where the liquor flowed and excesses were sometimes committed. Perhaps because, in that entire horde of intellectuals and writers, he was the only one who had not yet disappointed him. And because he was famous for his intelligence (although, according to Abbes García, a dirty aura surrounded the President).

"I've always had a low opinion of intellectuals and writers," he repeated. "On the scale of merit, the military occupy first place. They do their duty, they don't get involved in intrigues, they don't waste time. Then the campesinos. In the bateys and huts, on the sugar plantations, that's where the healthy, hardworking, honorable people of this country are. Then the bureaucrats, entrepreneurs, businessmen. Writers and intellectuals come last. Even below the priests. You're an exception, Dr. Balaguer. But the rest of them! A pack of dogs. They received the most favors and have done the most harm to the regime that fed and clothed them and showered them with honors. Those Spanish refugees, for example, like José Almoina or Jesús de Galíndez. We gave them asylum and work. And from groveling and begging for handouts they moved to writing slander and lies. And Osorio Lizarazo, that Colombian cripple you brought here? He came to write my biography, praised me to the skies, lived like a king, then went back to Colombia with his pockets full and became an anti-Trujillista."

Another of Balaguer's virtues was knowing when not to speak, when to become a sphinx before whom the Generalissimo could permit himself to vent his feelings. Trujillo fell silent. He listened, trying to hear the sound of the metallic surface, with its parallel foaming lines, that he glimpsed through the windows. But he could not hear the murmur of the ocean, it was drowned out by the noise of car engines.

"Do you think Ramón Marrero Aristy betrayed us?" he asked abruptly, turning toward the quiet presence, the other participant in the conversation. "Do you think he gave information to that gringo from *The New York Times* so he could attack us?"

Dr. Balaguer never failed to be surprised by Trujillo's sudden compromising and dangerous questions, which trapped other men. He had a solution for these occasions:

"He swore he did not, Excellency. With tears in his eyes, sitting right where you are sitting, he swore to me on his mother and all the saints that he was not Tad Szulc's informant."

Trujillo reacted with an irritated gesture:

"Was Marrero going to come here and confess he had sold out? I'm asking your opinion. Did he betray us or not?"

Balaguer also knew when he could not avoid taking the leap: another of his virtues that the Benefactor recognized.

"With sorrow in my heart, because of the intellectual and personal esteem I felt for Ramón, I believe he did, that he was the one who talked to Tad Szulc," he said in a very low, almost inaudible voice. "The evidence was overwhelming, Excellency."

He had reached the same conclusion. During thirty years in government—and before that, when he was a constabulary guard, and even earlier, as an overseer on a sugar plantation—he had become accustomed to not wasting time looking back and regretting or celebrating decisions he had already made, but what happened with Ramón Marrero Aristy, that "ignorant genius," as Max Henríquez Ureña had called him, that writer and historian for whom he had developed real affection, showering him with honors, money, and posts—columnist and editor of *La Nación* and Minister of Labor—and whose *History of the Dominican Republic*, in three volumes, he had paid for out of his own pocket, sometimes came to mind and left him with the taste of ashes in his mouth.

If there was anyone for whom he would have put his hands to the fire, it was the author of the most widely read Dominican novel at home and abroad—*Over*, about the La Romana sugar plantation—which had even been translated into English. An unshakable Trujillista; as editor of *La Nación* he proved it, defending Trujillo and the regime with clear ideas and bold prose. An excellent Minister of Labor, who got along wonderfully with unionists and employers. Which is why, when the journalist Tad Szulc of *The New York Times* announced that he was coming to the Dominican Republic to write a series of articles about the country, he entrusted Marrero Aristy with the task of accompanying him. He traveled everywhere with Szulc and arranged the interviews he asked for, including one with Trujillo. When Tad Szulc returned to the United States, Marrero Aristy escorted him as far as Miami. The Generalissimo never expected the articles in *The New York Times* to be an apology for his regime. But he also did not expect that they would expose the corruption of the "Trujillista satrapy," or that Tad Szulc would lay out with so much precision the facts, dates, names, and figures regarding properties owned by the Trujillo family and the businesses that had been awarded to relatives, friends, and collaborators. Only Marrero Aristy could have given him the information. He was sure his Minister of Labor would not set foot in Ciudad Trujillo again. He was surprised when he sent a letter from Miami to the paper in New York, refuting Tad Szulc, and even more surprised when he had the audacity to return to the Dominican Republic. He came to the National Palace. He cried and said he was innocent; the Yankee had eluded his watchful eye and talked in secret to their adversaries. It was one of the few times that Trujillo lost control of his nerves. Disgusted by his sniveling, he slapped him so hard that Marrero Aristy lost his footing, finally stopped talking, and stepped back, horrified. The Benefactor cursed him, calling him a traitor, and when the head of the military adjutants killed him, he ordered Johnny Abbes to resolve the problem of the corpse. On July 17, 1959, the Minister of Labor and his chauffeur drove over a precipice in the Cordillera Central on their way to Constanza. He was given an official funeral, and at the cemetery Senator Henry Chirinos emphasized the political accomplishments of the deceased and Dr. Balaguer delivered a literary eulogy.

"In spite of his betrayal, I was sorry when he died," said Trujillo, with sincerity. "He was young, barely forty-six, he still had a lot to offer."

"The decisions of the Divinity are ineluctable," the President repeated, without a shred of irony.

"We've gotten off the subject," Trujillo responded. "Do you see any possibility of settling things with the Church?"

"Not immediately, Excellency. The dispute has become poisonous. To be perfectly frank, I fear it will go from bad to worse if you do not order Colonel Abbes to have *La Nación* and Caribbean Radio moderate their attacks on the bishops. Only today I received a formal complaint from the nuncio and Archbishop Pittini regarding yesterday's assault on Monsignor Panal. Did you read it?"

He had the clipping on his desk and he read it to the Benefactor, in a respectful manner. Caribbean Radio's editorial, reproduced in *La Nación*, asserted that Monsignor Panal, the Bishop of La Vega, "formerly known as Leopoldo de Ubrique," was a fugitive from Spain and listed in the files of Interpol. It accused him of filling "the bishop's residence in La Vega with women before he turned his fevered brain to terrorism," and now, "since he fears a legitimate popular reprisal, he hides behind pathologically religious women with whom, it seems, he enjoys unrestrained sexual relations."

The Generalissimo laughed heartily. The things Abbes García thought up! The last time that Spaniard, who was as old as Methuselah, had a hard-on must have been twenty or thirty years ago; accusing him of fucking pious hags in La Vega was very optimistic; what he probably did was feel up the altar boys, like all those lecherous, faggot priests.

"The colonel sometimes exaggerates," he remarked with a smile.

"I have also received another formal complaint from the nuncio and the curia," Balaguer continued, very seriously. "Regarding the campaign launched on May 17 in the press and on the radio against the friars of San Carlos Borromeo, Excellency."

He picked up a blue folder that held newspaper articles with glaring headlines. "Terrorist Franciscan-Capuchin monks" were making and storing homemade bombs in their church. Neighbors had discovered this after the accidental explosion of one of the devices. *La Nación* and *El Caribe* were demanding that the forces of law and order turn their attention to this den of terrorists.

Trujillo passed a bored glance over the clippings.

"Those priests don't have the balls to make bombs. The most they do is attack with sermons."

"I know the abbot, Excellency. Brother Alonso de Palmira is a saintly man, devoted to his apostolic mission and respectful of the government. Absolutely incapable of a subversive act."

He paused briefly, and in the same cordial tone of voice he would have used in after-dinner conversation, laid out an argument that the Generalissimo had often heard Agustín Cabral make. In order to rebuild bridges to the hierarchy, the Vatican, and the priests—the immense majority of whom still supported the regime out of fear of atheistic Communism—it was indispensable that this daily campaign of accusations and diatribes end, or at least become more moderate, for it allowed their enemies to portray the regime as anti-Catholic. Dr. Balaguer, with his unfailing courtesy, showed the Generalissimo a protest from the U.S. State Department concerning the persecution of the sisters at Santo Domingo Academy. The President had replied by explaining that the police guard was there to protect the nuns against hostile acts. But, in fact, it really was harassment. For example, every night Colonel Abbes García's men played popular Trujillista merengues over loudspeakers directed at the school, depriving the sisters of sleep. They had done the same thing earlier, at the residence of Monsignor Reilly in San Juan de la Maguana, and were still doing it in La Vega, to Monsignor Panal. A reconciliation with the Church was still possible. But this campaign was moving the crisis toward a complete rupture.

"Talk to the Rosicrucian and convince him," Trujillo said with a shrug. "He's the priest-hater; he's sure it's too late to placate the Church and that the priests want to see me exiled, arrested, or dead."

"I assure you that is not the case, Excellency."

The Benefactor paid no attention to him. He said nothing as he scrutinized the puppet president with penetrating eyes that disconcerted and frightened. The little lawyer normally resisted the visual inquisition longer than others, but now, after a few minutes of being stripped bare by an audacious gaze, he began to betray some discomfort: his eyes opened and closed unceasingly behind his thick spectacles.

"Do you believe in God?" Trujillo asked with a certain uneasiness: he bored into him with his cold eyes, demanding a frank answer. "In a life after death? In heaven for the good people and hell for the bad? Do you believe in that?"

It seemed to him that the diminutive figure of Joaquín Balaguer grew even smaller, crushed by his questions. And that behind him, his own photograph—in formal dress and wearing a feathered tricorn, the presidential sash crossing his chest next to the decoration he prized most, the great Spanish cross of Carlos III—grew to gigantic size inside its gold frame. The puppet president's tiny hands caressed one another, as he said, like a person confessing a secret:

"At times I doubt, Excellency. But years ago I reached this conclusion: there is no alternative. It is necessary to believe. It is not possible to be an atheist. Not in a world like ours. Not if one has a vocation for public service and engages in politics."

"You have the reputation of being very overly pious," Trujillo insisted, moving in his chair. "I've even heard that you never married, and don't have a girlfriend, and don't drink, and don't do business, because you made secret vows. That you're a lay priest."

The bantam executive shook his head: none of that was true. He had not made and never would make any vow; unlike some of his classmates at the Normal School, who tormented themselves wondering if they had been chosen by God to serve Him as shepherds of the Catholic flock, he always knew that his vocation was not the priesthood but intellectual labor and political action. Religion gave him spiritual order, an ethical system with which to confront life. At times he doubted transcendence, he doubted God, but never the irreplaceable function of Catholicism as an instrument for the social restraint of the human animal's irrational passions and appetites. And, in the Dominican Republic, as a constituent force for nationhood, equal to the Spanish language. Without the Catholic faith, the country would fall into chaos and barbarism. As for belief, he followed the recommendation of St. Ignatius Loyola in his Spiritual Exercises: to behave as if one believed, miming the rites and precepts: Masses, prayers, confessions, communions. This systematic repetition of religious form gradually created the content, filling the void—at a certain point—with the presence of God.

Balaguer stopped speaking and lowered his eyes, as if ashamed of having revealed to the Generalissimo the rocky places in his soul, his personal accommodations with the Supreme Being.

"If I'd had any doubts, if I had waited for some sign from heaven before acting, I never would have raised this corpse," said Trujillo. "I had to trust in myself, nobody else, when it was a question of making life and death decisions. At times I may have been wrong, of course."

The Benefactor could tell by Balaguer's expression that he was asking himself who or what he was talking about. He did not tell him that he had in mind the face of Dr. Enrique Lithgow Ceara. He was the first urologist he consulted—recommended by Egghead Cabral as an eminent physician—when he realized he was having difficulty urinating. In the early 1950s, Dr. Marión, after operating on him for a peri-urethral ailment, assured him he would have no more problems. But the same difficulties soon flared up again. After many years and an unpleasant rectal examination, Dr. Lithgow Ceara, putting on the face of a whore or an unctuous sacristan, and spewing incomprehensible jargon to demoralize him ("urethral perineal sclerosis," "urethrographies," "acinous prostatitis"), formulated the diagnosis that would cost him dearly:

"You should place your trust in God, Excellency. Your prostate is cancerous."

His sixth sense told him he was exaggerating or lying. He was convinced of it when the urologist demanded immediate surgery. Too many risks if the prostate was not removed, it could metastasize, the scalpel and chemotherapy would prolong his life for a few years. He was exaggerating or lying because he was a quack or an enemy who was attempting to hasten the death of the Father of the New Nation, and he knew it absolutely when he brought in a famous physician from Barcelona. Dr. Antonio Puigvert denied he had cancer; the enlargement of that damned gland, brought on by age, could be treated with drugs and did not threaten the life of the Generalissimo. A prostatectomy was unnecessary. Trujillo gave the order that same morning and a military adjutant, Lieutenant José Oliva, made certain that the insolent Dr. Lithgow Ceara, with all his venom and bad science, disappeared off the Santo Domingo docks. By the way! The puppet president had not yet signed the promotion of Peña Rivera to captain. He descended from divine existence to the pedestrian matter of rewarding the services of one of the most able thugs recruited by Abbes García.

"I almost forgot," he said, making a gesture of annoyance with his head. "You haven't signed the resolution promoting Lieutenant Peña Rivera to captain for outstanding merit. I sent the file to you a week ago, along with my approval."

The round little face of President Balaguer soured and his mouth tightened; his tiny hands twitched. But he regained his self-control and again assumed his usual tranquil posture.

"I did not sign it because I thought it a good idea to discuss this promotion with you, Excellency."

"There's nothing to discuss." The Generalissimo cut him off harshly. "You received your instructions. Weren't they clear?"

"Of course they were, Excellency. I beg you to hear me out. If my reasons do not convince you, I will sign Lieutenant Peña Rivera's promotion immediately. I have it here, ready for my signature. Because it is a delicate matter, I thought it preferable to discuss it with you personally."

He knew all too well the reasons that Balaguer was going to present to him, and he began to be annoyed. Did this nonentity think he was so old and tired he could disobey an order? He hid his anger and listened, without interrupting. Balaguer performed rhetorical miracles with soft-pedaling words and extremely refined tonalities to make the things he said seem less rash. With all the respect in the world he would take the liberty of advising His Excellency to reconsider his decision to promote, especially for outstanding merit, a man like Lieutenant Victor Alicinio Peña Rivera. He had so negative a record, one so stained with reprehensible actions—perhaps unjustly—that his promotion would be exploited by their enemies, above all in the United States, and represented as compensation for the deaths of Minerva, Patria, and María Teresa Mirabal. Although the courts had established that the sisters and their driver died in an automobile accident, overseas it was depicted as a political murder carried out by Lieutenant Peña Rivera, the head of the SIM in Santiago at the time of the tragedy. The President took the liberty of reminding him of the uproar caused by their adversaries when, by order of His Excellency, on the seventh day of February of the current year, he authorized, by means of a presidential decree, the ceding to Lieutenant Peña Rivera of the house and four-hectare farm which had been expropriated by the State from Patria Mirabal and her husband because of subversive activities. And the outcry had not ended. The committees established in the United States were still protesting, calling the gift of Patria Mirabal's land and house to Lieutenant Peña Rivera payment for a crime. Dr. Joaquín Balaguer urged His Excellency not to give a new pretext to his enemies for repeating the charge that he protected murderers and torturers. Although His Excellency undoubtedly recalled it, he would take the liberty of pointing out that Colonel Abbes García's favorite lieutenant was associated, in the exiles' slanderous campaigns, not only with the death of the Mirabal sisters but with Marrero Aristy's accident, and certain alleged disappearances. Under these circumstances, it seemed imprudent to reward the lieutenant in so public a manner. Why not do it discreetly, with financial compensation or a diplomatic post in a distant country?

When he stopped speaking, he kneaded his hands together. He blinked uneasily, sensing that his careful argumentation had failed, fearing a reprimand. Trujillo restrained the anger boiling up inside him.

"You, President Balaguer, have the good fortune to be concerned only with the best part of politics," he said icily. "Laws, reforms, diplomatic negotiations, social transformations. That's what you've done for thirty-one years. You've been involved in the pleasant, enjoyable aspects of governing. I envy you! I would like to have been only a statesman, a reformer. But governing has a dirty side, and without it what you do would be impossible. What about order? Stability? Security? I've tried to keep you away from unpleasant things. But don't tell me you don't know how peace is achieved. With how much sacrifice and how much blood. Be grateful that I've allowed you to see the other side and devote yourself to the good, while I, Abbes, Lieutenant Peña Rivera, and others kept the country in order so you could write your poems and your speeches. I'm sure that with your acute intelligence, you understand me perfectly."

Joaquín Balaguer nodded. He was pale.

"Let's not talk any more about unpleasant things," the Generalissimo concluded. "Sign the promotion for Lieutenant Peña Rivera, have it appear tomorrow in *The Official Gazette*, and send him congratulations written in your own hand."

"I will, Excellency."

Trujillo passed his hand across his face because he thought he was going to yawn. A false alarm. Tonight, breathing in the fragrance of trees and plants through the open windows of Mahogany House, and seeing the myriad of stars in a coal-black sky, he would caress the body of a naked, affectionate, slightly intimidated girl with all the elegance of Petronius the Arbiter, and he would feel the excitement growing between his legs while he sucked the warm juices of her sex. He would have a big, solid erection, the kind he had in the old days. He would make the girl moan and give her pleasure and he would feel pleasure too, and he would erase the bad memory of that stupid, skinny little bitch.

"I looked over the list of prisoners the government is going to release," he said, in a more neutral tone. "Except for that professor from Montecristi, Humberto Meléndez, there's no objection. Go ahead. Have the families come to the National Palace on Thursday afternoon. They'll meet the freed prisoners there."

"I'll begin the process immediately, Excellency."

The Generalissimo rose to his feet and indicated to the puppet president, who was about to do the same, that he should remain seated. He wasn't leaving yet. He wanted to stretch his legs. He took a few steps away from the desk.

"Will this new release of prisoners placate the Yankees?" he said. "I doubt it. Henry Dearborn will go on encouraging conspiracies. There's another one in the works, according to Abbes. Even Juan Tomás Díaz is involved."

The silence he heard behind him—he heard it, like a heavy, clammy presence—took him by surprise. He whirled around to look at the puppet President: there he was, absolutely still, observing him with his beatific expression. He did not feel reassured. Those intuitions of his had never lied. Could it be that this microscopic creature, this pygmy, knew something?

"Have you heard anything about this new conspiracy?"

He saw him shake his head vigorously.

"I would have reported it right away to Colonel Abbes García, Excellency. As I have always done whenever I hear rumors of anything subversive."

He took two or three more steps, in front of the desk, not saying a word. No, if there was one man in the regime incapable of being involved in a plot, it was the circumspect President. He knew that without Trujillo he would not exist, that the Benefactor was the sap that gave him life, that without him he would vanish forever from politics.

He walked to one of the large windows. For a long while he observed the sea in silence. The clouds had covered the sun and the grayness of the sky and air was streaked with silver; the dark blue water reflected it in places. A small boat moved across the bay, heading for the mouth of the Ozama River; a fishing boat, it must have finished for the day and was returning to dock. It left a foaming wake, and though he could not see them at this distance, he imagined the gulls endlessly shrieking and beating their wings. He looked forward with anticipation to the hour-and-a-half walk he would take, after visiting his mother, along Máximo Gómez and the Avenida, smelling the salt air, soothed by the waves. Don't forget to ream out the head of the Armed Forces for that broken pipe at the entrance to the air base. Let Pupo Román stick his nose in that stinking puddle, then see if the Generalissimo ever finds anything so disgusting again at the front gate of a military installation.

He left the office of President Joaquín Balaguer without saying goodbye.

15 "If we're in this shape when we're together, imagine how Fifí Pastoriza feels all by himself," said Huáscar Tejeda, leaning against the steering wheel of the heavy black four-door Oldsmobile 98 parked at kilometer seven on the highway to San Cristóbal.

"What the hell are we doing here?" raged Pedro Livio Cedeño. "It's a quarter to ten. He isn't coming!"

He squeezed the semiautomatic M-1 carbine on his lap as if he wanted to break it. Pedro Livio was prone to angry outbursts; his bad temper had ruined his military career: he had been cashiered when he was a captain. By then he already knew that his temper had made him so many enemies, he would never move up through the ranks. He was sorry to leave the Army. He had attended a military academy in the United States and graduated with outstanding grades. But the temper that made him blaze like a torch when somebody called him Nigger, and lash out with his fists for any reason at all, put a brake on his promotions in the Army despite his excellent service record. He was expelled for pulling his revolver on a general who admonished him, as an officer, for undue fraternization with the troops. And yet those who knew him, like the man waiting with him, the engineer Huáscar Tejeda Pimentel, also knew that his violent exterior hid a man of fine feelings, capable—he had witnessed it—of crying over the murder of the Mirabal sisters, whom he did not even know.

"Impatience is a killer too, Nigger," Huáscar Tejeda said, attempting a joke.

"Nigger's the whore who bore you."

Tejeda Pimentel tried to laugh, but his friend's immoderate response saddened him. Pedro Livio was hopeless.

"I'm sorry," he heard him apologize a moment later. "My nerves are shot, it's the damned waiting."

"We all feel the same way, Nigger. Shit, I called you Nigger again. Are you going to insult my mother a second time?"

"Not this time." Pedro Livio laughed, finally.

"Why does 'Nigger' make you so angry? You know it's an affectionate name."

"I know, Huáscar. But in the United States, at the academy, when the cadets or the officers called me Nigger they weren't being affectionate, they were racists. I had to make them respect me."

A few vehicles drove past on the highway, heading west, toward San Cristóbal, or east, toward Ciudad Trujillo, but not Trujillo's Chevrolet Bel Air, followed by Antonio de la Maza's Chevrolet Biscayne. Their instructions were simple: as soon as they saw the two cars, which they would recognize by Tony Imbert's signal—flashing the headlights three times—they would cut off the Goat's car with the heavy black Oldsmobile. And he, with the semiautomatic M-1 carbine, for which Antonio had given him extra ammunition, and Huáscar, using his Smith & Wesson 9 mm Model 39 with nine shots, would lay down as much lead in front of the car as Imbert, Amadito, Antonio, and Turk were firing from behind. The Goat would not get past them, but if he did, Fifí Pastoriza, at the wheel of Estrella Sadhalá's Mercury, two kilometers to the west, would be there to cut him off again.

"Does your wife know about tonight, Pedro Livio?" asked Huáscar Tejeda.

"She thinks I'm at Juan Tomás Díaz's house, watching a movie. She's pregnant and . . ."

He saw a speeding car race by, followed at less than ten meters by another car that, in the dark, looked like Antonio de la Maza's Biscayne.

"It's them, isn't it, Huáscar?" He tried to see through the blackness.

"Did you see the headlights flash?" Tejeda Pimentel shouted in excitement. "Did you see them?"

"No, they didn't signal. But it's them."

"What shall we do, Nigger?"

"Drive, drive!"

Pedro Livio's heart had begun to pound with a fury that hardly allowed him to speak. Huáscar turned the Oldsmobile around. The red taillights of the two automobiles were speeding away, and soon they'd lose sight of them.

"It's them, Huáscar, it has to be them. Why the hell didn't they signal?"

The red lights had disappeared; all they saw in front of them was the cone of light from the headlights of the Oldsmobile and a pitch-black night: the clouds had just covered the moon. Pedro Livio—his semiautomatic carbine pointed out the window—thought about his wife, Olga. How would she react when she learned that her husband was one of Trujillo's assassins? Olga Despradel was his second wife. They got along wonderfully, because Olga—unlike his first wife, with whom domestic life had been hell—had infinite patience with his explosions of anger; when he was raging she avoided contradicting him or arguing with him, and she kept the house so neat and clean it made him happy. What a surprise for her. She thought he wasn't interested in politics, though lately he had been very close to Antonio de la Maza, General Juan Tomás Díaz, and Huáscar Tejeda, all of them notorious anti-Trujillistas. Until a few months ago, whenever his friends began to criticize the regime, he would be as silent as a sphinx and nobody could pull an opinion out of him. He didn't want to lose his administrative position at the Dominican Battery Factory, which belonged to the Trujillo family. The company had been doing very well until business took a nosedive because of the sanctions.

Naturally, Olga knew that Pedro Livio resented the regime because his first wife, a rabid Trujillista and close friend of the Generalissimo, who had made her governor of San Cristóbal, used her influence to obtain a court order prohibiting Pedro Livio from seeing his daughter Adanela, whose sole custody had been granted to his ex-wife. Tomorrow Olga might think he became involved in the plot to avenge that injustice. No, that wasn't the reason he was here with his semiautomatic M-1 carbine, chasing down Trujillo. It was—Olga wouldn't understand—because of the murder of the Mirabal sisters.

"Aren't those shots, Pedro Livio?"

"Yes, yes, shots. It's them, damn it! Step on it, Huáscar."

He knew what shots sounded like. What they had heard, disturbing the night, were several bursts of gunfire—the carbines of Antonio and

Amadito, Turk's revolver, and maybe Imbert's—something that filled his spirit, so frustrated by waiting, with exaltation. Now the Oldsmobile was flying down the highway. Pedro Livio put his head out the window but could not make out the Goat's Chevrolet or his pursuers. Then, at a bend in the road, he recognized Estrella Sadhalá's Mercury and, a second later, illuminated by the Oldsmobile's headlights, the thin face of Fifí Pastoriza.

"They forgot Fifí too," said Huáscar Tejeda. "They forgot the signal twice. What assholes!"

Less than a hundred meters away, Trujillo's motionless Chevrolet came into view, pointing to the right of the highway, its headlights on. "There it is!" "It's him, damn it!" shouted Pedro Livio and Huáscar at the moment revolver, carbine, and submachine-gun bullets started flying again. Huáscar turned off the headlights and, less than ten meters from the Chevrolet, he slammed on the brakes. Pedro Livio, who was opening the door of the Oldsmobile, was thrown to the highway before he fired. His whole body was scraped and pounded, and he heard an exultant Antonio de la Maza—"This buzzard won't eat another chicken" or something like that—and the shouting voices of Turk, Tony Imbert, and Amadito, toward whom he began to run blindly as soon as he could get up. He took two or three steps and heard more shots, very close, and a burning sensation stopped him short and knocked him down as he clutched at his lower belly.

"Don't shoot, damn it, it's us," shouted Huáscar Tejeda.

"I'm hit," he groaned, and without any transition, worried, at the top of his voice: "Is the Goat dead?"

"Dead as a doornail, Nigger," Huáscar Tejeda said, at his side. "Look!"

Pedro Livio felt his strength leaving him. He was sitting on the road, surrounded by debris and broken glass. He heard Huáscar Tejeda say that he was going to find Fifí Pastoriza and then the Oldsmobile pulled away. He heard the excited shouting of his friends, but he felt dizzy, incapable of taking part in their conversation; he barely understood what they were saying, because his attention was focused now on the blazing heat in his stomach. His arm was burning too. Had he been hit twice? The Oldsmobile came back. He recognized Fifí Pastoriza's exclamations: "Shit, oh shit, oh God Almighty, oh shit!"

"Let's put him in the trunk," ordered Antonio de la Maza, who spoke with great calm. "We have to bring the corpse to Pupo, then he'll put the Plan in action."

His hands felt wet. That viscous substance could only be blood. His or the Goat's? The asphalt was damp. It hadn't rained, so that must be blood too. Somebody put a hand across his shoulders and asked how he felt. The voice sounded distressed. He recognized Salvador Estrella Sadhalá.

"A bullet in the stomach, I think." Instead of words, what came out were guttural noises.

He could see the silhouettes of his friends carrying something and putting it into the trunk of Antonio's Biscayne. Trujillo! Damn! They'd done it. He didn't feel joy; it was more like relief.

"Where's the driver? Has anybody seen Zacarías?"

"He's dead as a doornail too, back there in the dark," said Tony Imbert. "Don't waste time looking for him, Amadito. We have to get back. The important thing now is to take the body to Pupo Román."

"Pedro Livio's wounded," exclaimed Salvador Estrella Sadhalá.

They had closed the trunk of the Chevrolet, with the corpse inside. Faceless silhouettes surrounded him, patted him on the back, asked, "How do you feel, Pedro Livio?" Were they going to give him the coup de grâce? They had all agreed on that. They wouldn't leave a wounded comrade behind and let him fall into the hands of the *caliés* and be subjected to Johnny Abbes's tortures and humiliations. He recalled the conversation—Luis Amiama Tió was there too—in the garden filled with mangoes, flamboyán, and breadfruit trees that belonged to General Juan Tomás Díaz and his wife, Chana. Everyone had agreed: absolutely no slow deaths. If things went badly and someone was seriously wounded: the coup de grâce. Was he going to die? Were they going to finish him off?

"Get him into the car," ordered Antonio de la Maza. "We'll call a doctor from Juan Tomás's house."

The shadows of his friends were hard at work, moving the Goat's car off the highway. He could hear them panting. Fifí Pastoriza whistled: "Damn, it has more holes than a colander."

When his friends picked him up to put him in the Chevrolet Biscayne, the pain was so intense he passed out. But only for a few seconds, for when he regained consciousness they hadn't left yet. He was in the back seat, Salvador had his arm around his shoulder and had pillowed his head on his chest. He recognized Tony Imbert at the wheel, and Antonio de la Maza beside him. How do you feel, Pedro Livio? He wanted to say: "Better, with that fucker dead," but all that came out was a moan.

"Nigger's in bad shape," Imbert muttered.

Which meant his friends called him Nigger when he wasn't there. What difference did it make? They were his friends, damn it: it hadn't occurred to any of them to give him the coup de grâce. It seemed natural to them to put him in the car, and now they were taking him to Chana and Juan Tomás Díaz's house. The burning in his stomach and arm had eased up. He felt weak and didn't try to speak. He was lucid, he understood what they were saying perfectly. Apparently Tony, Antonio, and Turk were wounded too, but not seriously. Flying debris had opened gashes on Antonio's forehead and the back of Salvador's head. They held handkerchiefs to their cuts. Tony had been grazed on the left breast and said the blood was staining his shirt and pants.

He recognized the National Lottery building. Had they taken the old Sánchez highway to come into the city by a less trafficked route? No, that wasn't the reason. Tony Imbert wanted to stop at the house of his friend Julito Senior, who lived on Avenida Angelita, and telephone General Díaz to let him know they were taking the body to Pupo Román, using the coded sentence they had agreed on earlier: "The squab are ready to go into the oven, Juan Tomás." They stopped in front of a darkened house. Tony got out. They didn't see anyone around. Pedro Livio heard Antonio: his poor Chevrolet had been hit by dozens of bullets and had a flat tire. Pedro Livio had felt it, it made a horrible racket, and the jolting gave him stabbing pains in the stomach.

Imbert came back: nobody was home at Julito Senior's. They'd better go straight to Juan Tomás's house. They started driving again, very slowly; the car tilted and creaked, and they avoided the busy avenues and streets.

Salvador leaned toward him:

"How are you doing, Pedro Livio?"

"Fine, Turk, fine," and he squeezed his arm.

"It won't be long now. At Juan Tomás's house, a doctor will look at you."

What a shame he didn't have the strength to tell his friends not to worry, that he was happy now that the Goat was dead. They had avenged the Mirabal sisters, and poor Rufino de la Cruz, the driver who took them to the Fortress of Puerto Plata to visit their imprisoned husbands; Trujillo had ordered him killed as well to make the farce of the accident more believable. That murder had shaken Pedro Livio in the deepest part of his being and moved him, after November 25, 1960, to join the conspiracy organized by his friend Antonio de la Maza. He had only heard of the Mirabal sisters. But, like many Dominicans, he had been devastated by the tragic end of those girls from Salcedo. Now they were killing defenseless women too, and nobody did a thing about it! Have we sunk so low in the Dominican Republic? Damn it, weren't there any men left in this country? Listening to Antonio Imbert speak so movingly about Minerva Mirabal, he—always reluctant to externalize his feelings—broke down in front of his friends, the only time he had cried as an adult. Yes, there were still men in the Dominican Republic who had balls. The proof was the corpse bouncing around in the trunk.

"I'm dying!" he shouted. "Don't let me die!"

"We're almost there, Nigger." Antonio de la Maza reassured him. "We'll get you fixed up right away."

He made an effort not to pass out. A short while later he recognized the intersection of Máximo Gómez and Avenida Bolívar.

"Did you see that official car?" asked Imbert. "Wasn't that Pupo Román?"

"Pupo's at home, waiting," Antonio de la Maza replied. "He told Amiama and Juan Tomás he wouldn't go out tonight."

A century later, the car stopped. He understood from his friends' conversation that they were at the rear entrance of General Díaz's house. Somebody was opening the gate. They could drive into the courtyard and park in front of the garages. In the dim light of the streetlamps and the lights at the windows, he recognized the garden, filled with trees and flowers that Chana tended so carefully, where he had come on many Sundays, alone or with Olga, for the delicious Dominican lunches the general prepared for his friends. At the same time, it seemed to him that he wasn't himself but an observer, removed from all the activity. This afternoon, when he learned it would be tonight and said goodbye to his wife, pretending he was coming to this house to see a movie, Olga put a peso in his pocket and asked him to bring her back chocolate and vanilla ice cream. Poor Olga! The pregnancy gave her food cravings. Would the shock make her lose the baby? No, God no! This would be a little sister for Luis Mariano, his two-year-old son. Turk, Imbert, and Antonio had climbed out of the car. He was alone, stretched out on the back seat of the Chevrolet in semidarkness. He thought that nothing and no one could save him, that he would die not knowing who won tonight's game between his company team, Hercules Batteries, and the Dominican Aviation Company, which was being played on the baseball field at the National Dominican Brewery.

A violent argument broke out in the courtyard. Estrella Sadhalá was berating Fifí, Huáscar, and Amadito, who had just arrived in the Oldsmobile, for leaving his Mercury on the highway. "Idiots! Assholes! Don't you realize what you've done? You've given me up! You have to go back right now and get my Mercury." A strange situation: to feel that he was and was not there. Fifí, Huáscar, and Amadito reassured Turk: in the rush they became confused and nobody thought about the Mercury, but it didn't matter, General Román would assume power tonight. They had nothing to be afraid of. The whole country would take to the streets to cheer the executioners of the tyrant.

Had they forgotten about him? The authoritative voice of Antonio de la Maza imposed order. Nobody would go back to the highway, it would be crawling with *caliés*. The main thing was to find Pupo Román and show him the body, as he had demanded. There was a problem; Juan Tomás Díaz and Luis Amiama had just stopped by Román's house—Pedro Livio knew the house, it was on the next corner—and Mireya, his wife, said that Pupo had left with General Espaillat "because it seems something happened to the Chief." Antonio de la Maza put their minds at ease: "Don't worry. Luis Amiama, Juan Tomás, and Modesto Díaz have gone to get Bibín, Pupo's brother. He'll help us find him."

Yes, they had forgotten about him. He would die in this bullet-riddled car, next to Trujillo's corpse. He had one of those fits of anger that had been the misfortune of his life, but he calmed down almost immediately. What the hell good does it do you to get mad now, asshole?

He had to close his eyes because a searchlight or powerful flashlight was shining right in his face. Crowded together, he recognized the faces of Juan Tomás Díaz's son-in-law, the dentist Bienvenido García,

Amadito, and was that Linito? Yes, it was Linito, the physician Dr. Marcelino Vélez Santana. They leaned over him, touched him, lifted his shirt. They asked him something he didn't understand. He wanted to say that the pain had eased, wanted to find out how many holes were in his body, but his voice wouldn't come out. He kept his eyes wide open to let them know he was alive.

"We have to take him to the hospital," Dr. Vélez Santana declared. "He's bleeding to death."

The doctor's teeth were chattering as if he were dying of cold. They weren't close friends, Linito wouldn't be trembling like that on his account. It must be because he just found out they had killed the Chief.

"There's internal hemorrhaging"—his voice was trembling too—"at least one bullet penetrated the pericardial region. He needs surgery right away."

They argued. He didn't care about dying. He felt happy in spite of everything. God would forgive him, he was sure. For leaving Olga alone with her six-months-pregnant belly and Luis Marianito. God knew he wouldn't profit by Trujillo's death. Just the opposite; he managed one of his companies, he was a privileged person. By getting involved in this damn thing, he had endangered his job and his family's security. God would understand and forgive him.

He felt a powerful contraction in his stomach, and he screamed. "Easy, take it easy, Nigger," Huáscar Tejeda pleaded. He felt like answering, "Nigger's your mother," but he couldn't. They took him out of the Chevrolet. Bienvenido's face was very close—Juan Tomás's son-in-law, the husband of his daughter Marianela—and so was Dr. Vélez Santana's: his teeth were still chattering. He recognized Mirito, Juan Tomás's chauffeur, and Amadito, who was limping. Taking great precautions, they placed him in Juan Tomás's Opel, parked next to the Biscayne. Pedro Livio saw the moon: it was shining, in what was now a cloudless sky, through the mangoes and heartsease.

"We're going to the International Clinic, Pedro Livio," said Dr. Vélez Santana. "Hold on, hold on just a little longer."

He cared less and less about what was happening to him. He was in the Opel, Mirito was driving, Bienvenido sat in front, and Dr. Vélez Santana was beside him, in the back. Linito had him inhale something with a strong ether smell. "The smell of carnivals." The dentist and the physician encouraged him: "We're almost there, Pedro Livio." And he didn't care about what they were saying, or about what seemed to matter so much to Bienvenido and Linito: "Where did General Román get to?" "If he doesn't show up, we're fucked." Instead of chocolate and vanilla ice cream, Olga would receive the news that her husband was being operated on at the International Clinic, three blocks from the Palace, after executing the killer of the Mirabal sisters. It was only a few blocks from Juan Tomás's house to the hospital. Why was it taking them so long?

Finally the Opel stopped. Bienvenido and Dr. Vélez Santana got out. He saw them knock on the door where a fluorescent light flickered: "Emergencies." A nurse in a white headdress appeared, and then a stretcher. When Bienvenido García and Vélez Santana lifted him from the seat, he felt a stabbing pain: "You're killing me, damn it!" He blinked, blinded by the whiteness of a corridor. They took him up in an elevator. Now he was in a very clean room, with a Virgin at the head of the bed. Bienvenido and Vélez Santana had disappeared; two nurses undressed him and a young man with a small mustache put his face close to his:

"I'm Dr. José Joaquín Puello. How do you feel?"

"Okay, okay," he murmured, happy to have his voice back. "Is it serious?"

"I'm going to give you something for the pain," said Dr. Puello. "While we prepare you for surgery. We have to get that bullet out."

Over the doctor's shoulder he saw a face he knew, with a wide forehead and large, penetrating eyes: Dr. Arturo Damirón Ricart, the proprietor and chief surgeon at the International Clinic. But instead of smiling and good-natured, which is how he usually looked, he seemed distraught. Had Bienvenido and Linito told him everything?

"This injection is to prepare you, Pedro Livio," he said. "Don't worry, you'll be fine. Do you want to call home?"

"Not Olga, she's pregnant, I don't want to scare her. Call my sister-in-law Mary."

His voice sounded firmer. He gave them Mary Despradel's phone number. The pills he had just swallowed, the injection, the bottles of disinfectant the nurses were pouring on his arm and stomach, made him feel better. He no longer thought he was going to pass out. Dr. Damirón Ricart put the receiver in his hand. "Hello? Hello?"

"It's Pedro Livio, Mary. I'm at the International Clinic. An accident. Don't say anything to Olga, don't scare her. They're going to operate."

"Good God, oh my God! I'm coming over there, Pedro Livio."

The doctors examined him, moved him, and he couldn't feel his hands. He was filled with a great serenity. With utter lucidity he told himself that no matter how much of a friend he was, Damirón Ricart would have to inform the SIM that a man with bullet wounds had come to the emergency room, something all clinics and hospitals were obliged to do or risk having their doctors and nurses go to prison. And so, pretty soon, the SIM would be all over the place asking questions. But no. Juan Tomás, Antonio, Salvador, must have shown Pupo the body by now, and Román would have alerted the barracks and announced the civilian-military junta. Perhaps at this very moment the military loyal to Pupo were arresting or exterminating Abbes García and his gang of killers, putting Trujillo's brothers and allies in jail, and the people would be out on the streets, summoned by radios announcing the death of the tyrant. The colonial city, Independencia Park, El Conde, the area around the National Palace, would see a real carnival, celebrating freedom. "Too bad you're on an operating table instead of dancing, Pedro Livio."

And then he saw the weeping, frightened face of his wife: "What is it, darling, what happened, what did they do to you?" He embraced and kissed her, trying to reassure her ("An accident, love, don't be afraid, they're going to operate"). He recognized his sister-in-law and her husband, Mary and Luis Despradel Brache. He was a doctor and was asking Dr. Damirón Ricart about the operation. "Why did you do it, Pedro Livio?" "So our children can be free, Olga." She kept asking questions and did not stop crying. "My God, there's blood all over you." Releasing a torrent of restrained emotions, he grasped his wife's arms, looked into her eyes, and exclaimed:

"He's dead, Olga! He's dead, dead!"

It was like a movie when the image freezes and moves out of time. He wanted to laugh when he saw the incredulous looks that Olga, his in-laws, the nurses and doctors were giving him.

"Be quiet, Pedro Livio," murmured Dr. Damirón Ricart.

They all turned toward the door: in the corridor there was a rush of footsteps, people coming down hard on their heels, not caring about the "Quiet" signs on the walls. The door opened. Pedro Livio instantly recognized, among all the military figures, the flaccid face, receding double chin, and eyes embedded in protuberant flesh of Colonel Johnny Abbes García.

"Good evening," he said, looking at Pedro Livio but speaking to the others. "Please leave. Dr. Damirón Ricart? You stay, Doctor."

"He's my husband," Olga whimpered, her arms around Pedro Livio. "I want to be with him."

"Take her out," Abbes García ordered, not looking at her.

More men had come into the room, *caliés* with revolvers in their belts and soldiers carrying San Cristóbal submachine guns over their shoulders. Half closing his eyes, he saw them take away Olga, who was sobbing ("Don't do anything to her, she's pregnant"), and Mary, and he saw his brother-in-law follow them, not needing to be shoved. The men looked at him with curiosity and some revulsion. He recognized General Félix Hermida and Colonel Figueroa Carrión, whom he had known in the Army. He was Abbes García's right hand in the SIM, they said.

"How is he?" Abbes asked the doctor in a slow, well-modulated voice.

"It's very serious, Colonel," replied Dr. Damirón Ricart. "The bullet must be near the heart, in the epigastrium. We gave him medication to control the hemorrhaging so we could operate."

Many of them had cigarettes, and the room filled with smoke. How he wanted to smoke, to inhale one of those mentholated Salems, with their cooling aroma, that Huáscar Tejeda smoked and Chana Díaz always offered in her house.

Above him, brushing against him, was the bloated face, the tortoise eyes with drooping lids, of Abbes García.

"What happened to you?" he heard him say softly.

"I don't know." He regretted his answer, it couldn't be dumber. But nothing else occurred to him.

"Who shot you?" Abbes García insisted, impassively.

Pedro Livio Cedeño remained silent. Incredible that in all these months of planning Trujillo's execution, they had never thought about a situation like the one he was in now. About some alibi, some excuse, for handling an interrogation. "What assholes!"

"An accident," and again he regretted making up something so stupid.

Abbes García did not become impatient. There was a bristling silence. Pedro Livio felt the heavy, hostile glances of the men around him. The ends of their cigarettes reddened when they raised them to their mouths.

"Tell me about the accident," said the head of the SIM, in the same tone of voice.

"I was leaving a bar and somebody shot me, from a car. I don't know who it was."

"What bar?"

"El Rubio, on Calle Palo Hincado, near Independencia Park."

In a few minutes the *caliés* would find out he had lied. Suppose his friends, when they broke the agreement to give the coup de grâce to anyone who was wounded, had done him no favor at all?

"Where's the Chief?" asked Johnny Abbes. A certain amount of emotion had filtered into his questioning.

"I don't know." His throat was beginning to close; he was losing strength again.

"Is he alive?" asked the head of the SIM. And he repeated: "Where is he?"

Although he felt dizzy again, as if he were going to faint, Pedro Livio noticed that beneath his tranquil appearance, the head of the SIM was boiling with agitation. The hand that carried the cigarette to his mouth moved awkwardly, trying to find his lips.

"In hell, I hope, if there is a hell," he heard himself say. "That's where we sent him."

Abbes García's face, somewhat obscured by smoke, did not change expression this time either; but he opened his mouth, as if he needed air. The silence had thickened. He had to lose all his strength, finally pass out.

"Who?" he asked, very gently. "Who sent him to hell?"

Pedro Livio did not respond. Abbes García was looking into his eyes and Pedro Livio held his gaze, remembering his childhood in Higüey, when they played who-would-blink-first at school. The colonel's hand lifted, took the lit cigarette from his mouth, and with no change of expression he put it out on his face, near his left eye. Pedro Livio did not scream, he did not moan. He closed his eyes. The heat was intense; there was a smell of singed flesh. When he opened them, Abbes García was still there. It had begun.

"These things, if they're not done right, it's better not to do them at all," he heard him say. "Do you know who Zacarías de la Cruz is? The Chief's chauffeur. I just talked to him in the Marión Hospital. He's in worse shape than you, riddled with bullets from head to toe. But he's alive. You see, things didn't work out. You're fucked. You're not going to die either. You're going to live. And tell me everything that happened. Who else was with you on the highway?"

Pedro Livio was sinking, floating, at any moment he would begin to vomit. Hadn't Tony Imbert and Antonio said that Zacarías de la Cruz was dead as a doornail too? Was Abbes García lying to make him give up names? How stupid they had been. They should have made sure the Goat's driver was dead.

"Imbert said that Zacarías was dead," he protested. Curious being yourself and someone else at the same time.

The face of the head of the SIM bent over him. He could feel his breath, heavy with tobacco. His eyes were dark, with yellow flecks. He wished he had the strength to bite those flaccid cheeks. Spit on them, at least.

"He was wrong, he's only wounded," said Abbes García. "Which Imbert?"

"Antonio Imbert," he explained, gnawed by anxiety. "Does that mean he lied to me? Shit, oh shit!"

He could hear footsteps, a movement of bodies, those present crowding around his bed. The smoke blurred their faces. He felt asphyxiated, as if they were stamping on his chest.

"Antonio Imbert and who else?" Colonel Abbes García said in his ear. His skin crawled when he thought that this time he'd put the cigarette out in his eye and blind him. "Is Imbert in charge? Did he organize this?"

"No, no leaders," he stammered, fearful he wouldn't have the strength to finish the sentence. "If there were, it would be Antonio."

"Antonio who?"

"Antonio de la Maza," he explained. "If there were, it would be him, sure. But there aren't any leaders."

There was another long silence. Had they given him sodium pentothal, is that why he was talking so much? But pentothal made you sleepy and he was wide awake, overexcited, eager to tell, to pull out the secrets chewing at him inside. He'd go on answering whatever they asked, damn it. There were murmurs, footsteps on the tiles. Were they leaving? A door opening, closing.

"Where are Imbert and Antonio de la Maza?" The head of the SIM exhaled a mouthful of smoke and it seemed to Pedro Livio that it went into his throat and nose and down to his guts.

"Looking for Pupo, where the hell else would they be?" Would he have the energy to finish the sentence? The astonishment of Abbes García, General Félix Hermida, and Colonel Figueroa Carrión was so great that he made a superhuman effort to explain what they didn't understand: "If he doesn't see the Goat's body, he won't lift a finger."

They had opened their eyes wide and were scrutinizing him with suspicion and dread.

"Pupo Román?" Abbes García had certainly lost his confidence now.

"General Román Fernández?" Figueroa Carrión repeated.

"The head of the Armed Forces?" an agitated General Félix Hermida asked in a shrill voice.

Pedro Livio was not surprised when the hand came down again and put out the lit cigarette in his mouth. An acrid taste of tobacco and ash on his tongue. He did not have the strength to spit out that stinking, burning piece of trash scraping against his gums and palate.

"He's fainted, Colonel," he heard Dr. Damirón Ricart murmur. "If we don't operate, he'll die."

"The one who's going to die is you if you don't revive him," replied Abbes García with muted rage. "Give him a transfusion, whatever, but wake him up. This man has to talk. Revive him or I'll fill you with all the lead in this revolver."

If they were talking like that, he wasn't dead. Had they found Pupo Román? Shown him the body? If the revolution had started, Abbes García, Félix Hermida, and Figueroa Carrión wouldn't be standing around his bed. They'd be arrested or dead, like Trujillo's brothers and nephews. He tried in vain to ask them to explain why they weren't arrested or dead. His stomach didn't hurt; his eyelids and mouth felt on fire because of the cigarette burns. They gave him an injection, they made him inhale from a piece of cotton that smelled of menthol, like Salems. He discovered a bottle filled with serum next to his bed. He could hear them and they thought he couldn't.

"Can it be true?" Figueroa Carrión seemed more terrified than surprised. "The Armed Forces Minister involved in this? It's impossible, Johnny."

"Surprising, absurd, inexplicable," Abbes García corrected him. "Not impossible."

"But why, what for?" General Félix Hermida's voice rose. "What can he hope to gain? He owes everything he is to the Chief, everything he has. This asshole is just throwing out names to confuse us."

Pedro Livio twisted around, trying to sit up so they would know he wasn't groggy or dead, and that he had told the truth.

"You can't still believe this is one of the Chief's tricks to find out who's loyal and who's not, Félix."

"Not anymore," General Hermida acknowledged sadly. "If these sons of bitches have killed him, what the hell's going to happen here?"

Colonel Abbes García slapped his forehead:

"Now I understand why Román made an appointment with me at Army Headquarters. Of course he's involved in this! He wants people close to the Chief near him so he can lock them up before the coup. If I had gone, I'd be dead by now."

"I can't believe it, damn it," General Félix Hermida repeated.

"Send SIM patrols to close Radhamés Bridge," ordered Abbes García. "Don't let anybody in the government, particularly Trujillo's relatives, cross the Ozama or get anywhere near the December 18 Fortress."

"The Minister of the Armed Forces, General José René Román, Mireya Trujillo's husband," General Félix was saying to himself, mindlessly. "I don't understand anything about anything anymore, damn it."

"Believe it until he proves himself innocent," said Abbes García. "Hurry and warn the Chief's brothers. Have them meet in the National Palace. Don't mention Pupo yet. Tell them there are rumors of assassination attempts. Hurry! How is he? Can I question him?"

"He's dying, Colonel," Dr. Damirón Ricart declared. "As a physician, my duty . . ."

"Your duty is to shut up unless you want to be treated like an accomplice." Again Pedro Livio saw at close range the face of the head of the SIM. "I'm not dying," he thought. "The doctor lied so he won't keep putting butts out on my face."

"General Román ordered the Chief killed?" Again, in his nose and mouth, the colonel's pungent breath. "Is that true?"

"They're looking for him to show him the body," he heard himself shout. "That's how he is: seeing is believing. And the briefcase too."

The effort left him exhausted. He was afraid that at this very moment the *caliés* were putting out cigarettes on Olga's face. Poor girl, what a shame. She'd lose the baby, she'd curse the day she ever married ex-Captain Pedro Livio Cedeño.

"What briefcase?" asked the head of the SIM.

"Trujillo's," he replied immediately, articulating clearly. "Covered with blood outside and full of pesos and dollars inside."

"With his initials?" the colonel insisted. "The initials RLTM in gold?"

He couldn't answer, his memory was betraying him. Tony and Antonio found it in the car, they opened it and said it was full of Dominican pesos and dollars. Thousands and thousands. He noticed the agitation of the head of the SIM. Ah, you son of a bitch, the briefcase convinced you it was true, they had killed him.

"Who else is in this?" Abbes García asked. "Give me names. So you can go to the operating room and have the bullets taken out. Who else?"

"Did they find Pupo?" he asked, excited, speaking quickly. "Did they show the body to him? And to Balaguer?"

Again Colonel Abbes García's jaw dropped. There he was, openmouthed with astonishment and apprehension. In some obscure way, he was winning the game.

"Balaguer?" he said slowly, syllable by syllable, letter by letter. "The President of the Republic?"

"Of the civilian-military junta," explained Pedro Livio, struggling to control his nausea. "I was against it. They say it's necessary, to reassure the OAS."

This time, he didn't have time to turn his head and vomit on the floor. Something warm and viscous ran down his neck and dirtied his chest. He saw the head of the SIM move away in disgust. He had severe stomach cramps, and his bones felt cold. He couldn't talk anymore. After a while the colonel's face hung over him again, grimacing with impatience, looking at him as if he wanted to drill into his skull and find out the whole truth.

"Joaquín Balaguer too?"

He could resist his gaze for only a few seconds. He closed his eyes, he wanted to sleep. Or die, it didn't matter. Two or three times he heard the question: "Balaguer? Balaguer too?" He didn't answer or open his eyes. Not even when the intense burning on his right earlobe made him shrink away. The colonel had put out his cigarette and now he was twisting it and breaking it inside his ear. He did not scream, he did not move. Turned into an ashtray for the head of the *caliés*, Pedro Livio, that's how you ended up. Bah, what the hell. The Goat was dead. Sleep. Die. From the deep pit into which he was falling, he could still hear Abbes García: "A plaster saint like him had to be plotting with the priests. It's a conspiracy of the bishops allied with the gringos." There were long silences interspersed with murmurs and, at times, the timid pleading of Dr. Damirón Ricart: if they didn't operate, the patient would die. "But what I want is to die," thought Pedro Livio.

People running, hurried footsteps, a door slamming. The room was crowded again, and among the recent arrivals was Colonel Figueroa Carrión:

"We found a denture on the highway, near His Excellency's Bel Air. His dentist, Dr. Fernando Camino Certero, is examining it now. I woke him myself. In half an hour he'll make his report. At first glance, he thought it was the Chief's."

His voice was mournful. As was the silence in which the others listened to him.

"You didn't find anything else?" Abbes García bit off every word.

"An automatic pistol, forty-five caliber," said Figueroa Carrión. "It will take a few hours to verify the registration. There's an abandoned car, about two hundred meters from the attack. A Mercury."

Pedro Livio told himself that Salvador had been right to get angry with Fifí Pastoriza for leaving his Mercury on the highway. They would identify the owner and soon the *caliés* would be putting out butts on Turk's face.

"Did he say anything else?"

"Balaguer, no less." Abbes García whistled. "Do you realize what that means? The head of the Armed Forces and the President of the Republic. He mentioned a civilian-military junta, with Balaguer at the head to reassure the OAS."

Colonel Figueroa Carrión came out with another "Damn!"

"It's a plan to throw us off the track. Involve important people, compromise everybody."

"Maybe, we'll see," said Colonel Abbes García. "One thing's sure. A lot of people are involved, high-level traitors. And the priests, of course. We have to get Bishop Reilly out of Santo Domingo Academy. Whether he's willing to leave or not."

"Will we take him to La Cuarenta?"

"They'll look for him there as soon as they find out. San Isidro is better. But wait, this is touchy, we have to talk it over with the Chief's brothers. If there's one person who can't be in on the conspiracy, it's General Virgilio García Trujillo. Go and tell him personally."

Pedro Livio heard the footsteps of Colonel Figueroa Carrión moving away. Had he been left alone with the head of the SIM? Was he going to put out more cigarettes on him? But that wasn't what tormented him now. It was realizing that even though they had killed the Chief, things hadn't turned out as planned. Why hadn't Pupo and his soldiers taken power? What was Abbes García doing, ordering the *caliés* to arrest Bishop Reilly? Was this bloodthirsty degenerate still in command? He continued to hover over him; he couldn't see him but there was that hot breath in his nose and mouth.

"A couple more names and I'll let you rest," he heard him say.

"He doesn't hear or see you, Colonel," Dr. Damirón Ricart pleaded. "He's in a coma."

"Then operate," said Abbes García. "And listen carefully, I want him alive. It's his life or yours."

"You can't take much from me," Pedro Livio heard the doctor say with a sigh. "I have only one life, Colonel."

16 "Manuel Alfonso?" Aunt Adelina lifts her hand to her ear, as if she had not heard, but Urania knows the old woman has excellent hearing and is dissembling while she recovers from the shock. Lucinda and Manolita stare at her too, their eyes very wide. Only Marianita does not seem to be affected.

"Yes, him, Manuel Alfonso," Urania repeats. "A name worthy of a Spanish conquistador. Did you know him, Aunt Adelina?"

"I saw him once or twice." The old woman nods, both intrigued and offended. "What does he have to do with the outrageous things you've said about Agustín?"

"He was the playboy who got women for Trujillo," Manolita recalls. "Isn't that right, Mama?"

"Playboy, playboy," shrieks Samson. But this time only her tall, skinny niece laughs.

"He was very good-looking, an Adonis," says Urania. "Before the cancer."

He had been the handsomest Dominican of his generation, but in the weeks, perhaps months, since Agustín Cabral had seen him, the demigod whose elegance and grace made girls turn around to look at him had become a shadow of himself. The senator could not believe his eyes. He must have lost ten or fifteen kilos; emaciated, wasted, he had deep shadows around eyes that had always been proud and smiling—the gaze of a pleasure-taker, the smile of a victor—and now were lifeless. He had heard about the small tumor under his tongue that the dentist happened to find when Manuel, who was still ambassador in Washington, went for his annual cleaning. The news, they said, affected Trujillo as much as if they had discovered a tumor in one of his children, and he remained glued to the telephone during the operation at the Mayo Clinic, in the United States.

"I'm so sorry to bother you when you've just come home, Manuel." Cabral stood up when he saw him come into the small room where he was waiting.

"My dear Agustín, how nice." Manuel Alfonso embraced him. "Can you understand me? They had to take out part of my tongue. But with some therapy I'll speak normally again. Do you understand me?"

"Perfectly, Manuel. I don't notice anything strange in your voice, I assure you."

It wasn't true. The ambassador spoke as if he were chewing pebbles, or was tongue-tied, or had a stammer. The faces he made indicated the effort each word cost him.

"Have a seat, Agustín. Some coffee? A drink?"

"Nothing, thank you. I won't take up much of your time. Again I apologize for bothering you when you're recuperating from surgery. I'm in a very difficult situation, Manuel."

He stopped speaking, embarrassed. Manuel Alfonso put a friendly hand on his knee.

"I can imagine, Egghead. A small country, a huge hell: I even heard the rumors in the United States. You've been stripped of the Presidency of the Senate and they're investigating your management of the ministry."

Illness and suffering had drastically aged the Dominican Apollo whose face, with its perfect white teeth, had intrigued Generalissimo Trujillo on his first official trip to the United States, causing the fortunes of Manuel Alfonso to experience a sudden upturn, as if he were Snow White touched by a magic wand. But he was still an elegant man, dressed like the fashion model he had been in his youth, when he was a Dominican immigrant in New York: suede loafers, cream-colored velour trousers, an Italian silk shirt, and a smart scarf around his neck. A gold ring sparkled on his little finger. He was meticulously shaved, perfumed, and combed.

"I'm so grateful that you've received me, Manuel." Agustín Cabral recovered his poise: he had always been contemptuous of men who felt sorry for themselves. "You're the only one. I've become a pariah. Nobody wants to see me."

"I don't forget services rendered, Agustín. You were always generous, you supported all my nominations in Congress, you did me a thousand favors. I'll do what I can. What are the charges against you?"

"I don't know, Manuel. If I knew, I could defend myself. So far no one will tell me what crime I've committed."

"Yes, very much so, all our hearts beat faster when he was nearby," Aunt Adelina admits impatiently. "But what connection can he have with what you've said about Agustín?"

Urania's throat has become dry, and she takes a few sips of water. Why do you insist on talking about this? What's the point?

"Because Manuel Alfonso was the only one of all his friends who tried to help Papa. I'll bet you didn't know that, any of you."

The three women look at her as if they thought her unbalanced.

"Well, no, I didn't know that," murmurs Aunt Adelina. "He tried to help him when he fell into disgrace? Are you sure?"

"As sure as I am that my papa didn't tell you or Uncle Aníbal about the steps Manuel Alfonso took to get him out of his difficulty."

She stops speaking because the Haitian servant comes into the dining room. She asks, in hesitant, lilting Spanish, if they need her or if she can go to bed. Lucinda dismisses her with a wave of her hand: go on, then.

"Who was Manuel Alfonso, Aunt Urania?" Marianita's barely audible voice inquires.

"A personality, Marianita. Good-looking, from an excellent family. He went to New York to make his fortune and ended up modeling clothes for designers and expensive stores, and appearing on billboards with his mouth open, advertising Colgate, the toothpaste that refreshes and cleans and makes your teeth sparkling white. Trujillo, on a trip to the United States, learned that the handsome young man on the signs was a Dominican hustler. He sent for him and he adopted him. He made him a person of consequence. His interpreter, because he spoke perfect English; his instructor in protocol and etiquette, because he was professionally elegant; and, an extremely important function, the one who selected his suits, ties, shoes, hose, and the New York tailors who dressed him. He kept him up-to-date on the latest trends in men's fashions. And helped him design his uniforms, one of the Chief's hobbies."

"Most of all, he picked his women," Manolita interrupted. "Isn't that right, Mama?"

"What does all of this have to do with my brother?" She shakes a small, angry fist.

"Women were the least of it," Urania continues to inform her niece. "Trujillo couldn't care less because he had all of them. But clothes and accessories, he cared a great deal about them. Manuel Alfonso made him feel exquisite, refined, elegant. Like that Petronius in *Quo Vadis?* he was always quoting."

"I haven't seen the Chief yet, Agustín. I have an audience this afternoon, at his house, at Radhamés Manor. I'll find out what it is, I promise."

He had let him speak without interrupting, limiting himself to nodding and waiting when the senator's spirits fell and bitterness or anguish affected his voice. He told him what had happened, what he had said, done, and thought since the first letter appeared in "The Public Forum" ten days earlier. He poured out his heart to this considerate man, the first who had shown him sympathy since that terrible day; he told him the intimate details of his life, devoted, since the age of twenty, to serving the most important man in Dominican history. Was it fair of him to refuse to listen to someone who had lived in him and for him for the past thirty years? He was prepared to recognize his errors, if he had committed any. To examine his conscience. To pay for his mistakes, if any existed. But the Chief had to at least grant him five minutes.

Manuel Alfonso patted him again on the knee. The house, in a new neighborhood, Arroyo Hondo, was enormous, surrounded by a park, and furnished and decorated in exquisite taste. Infallible in detecting hidden possibilities in people—a faculty that always amazed Agustín Cabral—the Chief had done a good job of gauging the former model. Manuel Alfonso could move easily in the diplomatic world, thanks to his amiability and his gift for dealing with people, and obtain advantages for the regime. He had done so on all his assignments, especially the last one, in Washington, during the most difficult period, when Trujillo stopped being the spoiled darling of Yankee governments and became an embarrassment attacked by the press and many in Congress. The ambassador raised his hand to his face, in a gesture of pain.

"From time to time, it's like a whiplash," he apologized. "It's passing now. I hope the surgeon told me the truth. That they found it in time. A ninety percent guarantee of success. Why would he have lied? The gringos are brutally frank, they don't have our delicacy, they don't sugarcoat the pill."

He stops speaking, because another grimace convulses his devastated face. He reacts immediately, becomes serious, philosophizes:

"I know how you feel, Egghead, what you're going through. It's happened to me a couple of times in my twenty-some years of friendship with the Chief. It didn't go as far as it has with you, but there was a distancing on his part, a coldness I couldn't explain. I remember my worry, the solitude I felt, the sensation of having lost my compass. But everything was resolved, and the Chief honored me again with his confidence. It must be intrigue on the part of some envious man who can't forgive your talent, Agustín. But, as you already know, the Chief is a just man. I'll speak to him this afternoon, you have my word."

Cabral rose to his feet, very moved. There were still decent people left in the Dominican Republic.

"I'll be at home all day, Manuel," he said, shaking his hand warmly. "Don't forget to tell him that I'm prepared to do anything to regain his confidence."

"I thought of him as a Hollywood star, Tyrone Power or Errol Flynn," says Urania. "I was very disappointed when I saw him that night. He wasn't the same person. They had cut out half his throat. He looked like anything but a Don Juan."

Her Aunt Adelina, her cousins, her niece, listen in silence, exchanging glances. Even the parrot Samson seems interested, for he hasn't silenced her with his screeching for some time.

"You're Urania? Agustín's little girl? How you've grown, and how pretty you are! I've known you since you were in diapers. Come over here, my girl, and give me a kiss."

"He dribbled when he talked, he looked retarded. He was very affectionate with me. I couldn't believe that this human wreck was Manuel Alfonso."

"I have to talk with your papa," he said, taking a step toward the interior of the house. "You really are pretty. You'll break a lot of hearts. Is Agustín home? Go on, call him."

"He had spoken to Trujillo and had come to our house from Radhamés Manor to report on what he had done. Papa couldn't believe it. 'The only one who didn't turn his back on me, the only one who offered his hand,' he kept repeating."

"Didn't you just dream that Manuel Alfonso did anything for him?" Aunt Adelina exclaims, disconcerted. "Agustín would have told Aníbal and me right away."

"Let her go on, don't interrupt so much, Mama," Manolita intervenes.

"That night I made a promise to Our Lady of Altagracia if she would help my papa out of his difficulty. Can you imagine what it was?"

"That you'd enter a convent?" Her cousin Lucinda laughs.

"That I'd remain a virgin the rest of my life." Urania laughs.

Her cousins and her niece laugh too, but unwillingly, hiding their embarrassment. Aunt Adelina remains serious, not taking her eyes off her and not hiding her impatience: what else, Urania, what else?

"That child has grown so big and so pretty," Manuel Alfonso repeats as he drops into an armchair across from Agustín Cabral. "She reminds me of her mother. The same languid eyes as your wife, Egghead, the same slim, graceful body."

He thanks him with a smile. He has brought the ambassador to his study instead of receiving him in the living room, so that the girl and the servants won't hear. He thanks him again for taking the trouble to come in person instead of calling him. The senator speaks in a rush, feeling his heart coming out with each word. Was he able to talk to the Chief?

"Of course, Agustín. I promised you I would, and I did. We talked about you for almost an hour. It won't be easy. But you mustn't lose hope. That's the main thing."

He wore an impeccably tailored dark suit, a white shirt with a starched collar, and a white-flecked blue tie held in place by a pearl. The top of a white silk handkerchief peeked out of the breast pocket of his jacket, and since he had raised his trousers slightly when he sat down to keep them from losing their crease, his blue hose, without a single wrinkle, was visible. His shoes gleamed.

"He's very unhappy with you, Egghead." It seemed that the wound from his surgery was bothering him, because from time to time he contorted his lips in a strange way, and Agustín Cabral could hear his dentures click. "It's not anything concrete but a number of things that have piled up over the past few months. The Chief is exceptionally perceptive. Nothing escapes him, he detects the smallest changes in people. He says that since this crisis began, since the Pastoral Letter, since the problems with the OAS unleashed by the monkey Betancourt and the rat Muñoz Marín, you've been growing cold. You haven't shown the devotion he expected."

The senator nodded: if the Chief noticed it, perhaps it was true. Nothing premeditated, of course, and certainly not due to any lessening of his admiration and loyalty. Something unconscious, fatigue, the tremendous tension of this past year, the hemispheric conspiracy against Trujillo by the Communists and Fidel Castro, the priests, Washington and the State Department, Figueres, Muñoz Marín, and Betancourt, economic sanctions, the despicable actions of the exiles. Yes, yes, it was possible that, unintentionally, his dedication to his work, the Party, the Congress, had flagged.

"The Chief doesn't accept discouragement or weakness, Agustín. He wants us all to be like him. Tireless, a rock, a man of iron. You know that."

"And he's right." Agustín Cabral banged his fist on his small desk. "Because he is the way he is, he has made this country. He is always in the saddle, Manuel, as he said in the campaign of 1940. He has a right to demand that we emulate him. I disappointed him without realizing it. Perhaps because I didn't succeed in persuading the bishops to proclaim him Benefactor of the Church? He wanted that as compensation after the villainy of the Pastoral Letter. I formed part of the commission, along with Balaguer and Paíno Pichardo. Was it that failure, do you think?"

The ambassador shook his head.

"He's very tactful. Even if he feels unhappy about that, he wouldn't have told me so. Perhaps it is one of the reasons. You have to understand him. For thirty-one years he has been betrayed by the people he helped the most. How could a man not be sensitive when his best friends stab him in the back?"

"I remember his scent," says Urania, after a pause. "Since then, and it's no lie, every time a man wearing scent happens to be near me, I see Manuel Alfonso again. And hear that gibberish he spoke on the two occasions I had the honor of enjoying his charming company."

Her right hand crumples the runner on the table. Her aunt, cousins, and niece, disoriented by her hostility and sarcasm, hesitate, feeling uncomfortable.

"If talking about this upsets you, don't do it, Urania," Manolita suggests.

"It sickens me, it makes me want to vomit," Urania replies. "It fills me with hatred and disgust. I never told anyone about this. Maybe it will do me good to finally get it off my chest. And who better than my family to listen?"

"What do you think, Manuel? Will the Chief give me another chance?"

"Why don't we have some whiskey, Egghead," the ambassador exclaims, avoiding a reply. He holds up his hands, cutting off the senator's objections. "I know I shouldn't, I'm not allowed to drink alcohol. Bah! Is it worth living if you have to deprive yourself of the good things? Great whiskey is one of those things."

"Excuse me for not asking earlier. I'll have a drink too. Let's go down to the living room. Uranita must be in bed by now."

But she still hasn't gone to her room. She has just finished supper and stands when she sees them coming down the stairs.

"You were just a little girl the last time I saw you," Manuel Alfonso compliments her, smiling. "Now you're a very beautiful young lady. You probably haven't even noticed the change, Agustín."

"See you tomorrow, Papa." Urania kisses her father. She is going to shake the visitor's hand, but he offers his cheek. She barely kisses him, and blushes: "Good night, señor."

"Call me Uncle Manuel," and he kisses her on the forehead.

Cabral tells the butler and maid that they can go to bed, and he brings in the bottle of whiskey, the glasses, the ice bucket. He pours his friend a drink and another for himself, both on the rocks.

"*Salud*, Manuel."

"*Salud*, Agustín."

The ambassador savors his drink with satisfaction, half closing his eyes. "Ah, how nice," he exclaims. But he has difficulty getting the liquor down, and his face contracts with pain.

"I've never been a drunkard, never lost control of my actions," he says. "But I've always known how to enjoy life. Even when I was wondering if I would eat the next day, I knew how to derive pleasure from small things: a good drink, a good cigar, a landscape, a well-cooked dish, a woman who bends her waist gracefully."

He laughs nostalgically, and Cabral follows suit, unwillingly. How can he get him back to the only thing that matters? To be courteous, he controls his impatience. He hasn't had a drink for days, and two or three sips go to his head. Still, after refilling Manuel Alfonso's glass, he also fills his own.

"Nobody would think you ever had money problems, Manuel." He tries to flatter him. "I always think of you as elegant, lavish, extremely generous, paying for everyone."

The former model, swirling his glass, nods, and is gratified. The light from the chandelier shines directly down on his face, and only now does Cabral notice the sinuous scar that twists around his throat. Difficult, for someone so proud of his face and body, to have been cut up like that.

"I know what it means to go hungry, Egghead. As a young man, in New York, I even slept in the streets like a tramp. There were many days when my only meal was a plate of beans or a roll. Without Trujillo, who knows what would have happened to me? I always liked women, but I never could play the gigolo, like our good Porfirio Rubirosa. I probably would have ended up as a bum on the Bowery."

He drinks what is left in his glass in one swallow. The senator fills it again.

"I owe him everything. What I have, what I became." With his head lowered, he contemplates the ice cubes. "I've rubbed elbows with ministers and presidents of the most powerful countries, I've been invited to the White House, played poker with President Truman, gone to the Rockefellers' parties. The tumor was removed at the Mayo Clinic, the best in the world, by the best surgeon in the United States. Who paid for the operation? The Chief, of course. Do you understand, Agustín? Like our country, I owe everything to Trujillo."

Agustín Cabral regretted all the times, when in the familiarity of the Country Club or Congress or an outlying estate, in a circle of intimate friends (he believed they were intimate), he had laughed at jokes about the former Colgate model who owed his high diplomatic posts, and his position as Trujillo's adviser, to the soaps, talcs, and perfumes he ordered for His Excellency and his good taste in choosing the ties, suits, shirts, pajamas, and shoes worn by the Chief.

"I also owe him everything I am and everything I've accomplished, Manuel," he declared. "I understand you very well. And that's why I'm prepared to do anything to regain his friendship."

Manuel Alfonso looked at him, his head craning forward. He did not say anything for a long time but continued to scrutinize him, as if weighing, millimeter by millimeter, the seriousness of his words.

"Then let's get to work, Egghead!"

"He was the second man, after Ramfis Trujillo, to flirt with me and pay me compliments," says Urania. "Telling me I was pretty, I looked like my mama, what nice eyes. I had already gone to parties with boys, and danced. Five or six times. But no one had ever talked to me like that. Because Ramfis's compliments were paid to a little girl. The first man who flirted with me as if I were a woman was my *uncle*, Manuel Alfonso."

She has said all this very quickly, with mute fury, and none of her relatives asks any questions. The silence in the small dining room is like the one that precedes the thunder in a violent summer storm. A distant siren cuts through the night. Samson paces nervously along his wooden bar, ruffling his feathers.

"He seemed like an old man to me, the mangled way he talked made me laugh, the scar on his neck scared me." Urania wrings her hands. "Why would he bother to flirt with me, why just then? But afterward I thought a good deal about all the compliments he paid me."

She falls silent again, exhausted. Lucinda asks a question—"You were fourteen, weren't you?"—that seems stupid to Urania. Lucinda knows they were born the same year. Fourteen, what a deceptive age. They had stopped being children but were not yet women.

"Three or four months before that, I had my first period," she whispers. "I think it made me look more mature."

"It just occurred to me, it occurred to me when I came in," says the ambassador, extending his hand and pouring himself another whiskey; he serves his host as well. "I've always been this way: the Chief comes first, then me. You're upset, Agustín. Am I wrong? I didn't say anything, forget it. I've forgotten it. *Salud*, Egghead!"

Senator Cabral takes a long drink. The whiskey burns his throat and reddens his eyes. Was that a rooster crowing at this hour?

"It's just, it's just . . . ," he repeats, not knowing what to add.

"Let's forget it. I hope you haven't taken this the wrong way, Egghead. Forget it! Let's forget it!"

Manuel Alfonso has stood up. He walks among the innocuous furnishings in the living room, neat, clean, but lacking the feminine touch an efficient housekeeper can give. Senator Cabral thinks—how many times has he thought this over the years?—that he made a mistake remaining alone after his wife's death. He should have married, had other children, then perhaps this misfortune would not have happened. Why didn't he? Was it for Uranita's sake, as he told everyone? No. It was so he could devote more time to the Chief, dedicate days and nights to him, prove to him that nothing and no one was more important in the life of Agustín Cabral.

"I didn't take it the wrong way." He makes an enormous effort to appear calm. "But I am disconcerted. It's something I wasn't expecting, Manuel."

"You think she's a little girl, you didn't realize she had become a young woman." Manuel Alfonso rattles the ice cubes in his glass. "A pretty girl. You must be proud of having a daughter like her."

"Of course." And adds, mindlessly: "She's always at the head of her class."

"Do you know something, Egghead? I wouldn't have hesitated for a second. Not to regain his confidence, not to show him that I'm capable of any sacrifice for him. Simply because nothing would give me more satisfaction, more happiness, than to have the Chief give pleasure to a daughter of mine and take his pleasure with her. I'm not exaggerating, Agustín. Trujillo is one of those anomalies in history. Charlemagne, Napoleon, Bolívar: that breed of men. Forces of Nature, instruments of God, makers of nations. He's one of them, Egghead. We've had the privilege of being at his side, watching him act, collaborating with him. That's something beyond price."

He drained his glass and Agustín Cabral raised his to his mouth but barely wet his lips. He was no longer dizzy, but now his stomach was churning. At any moment he would start to vomit.

"She's still a little girl," he stammered.

"That's even better!" exclaimed the ambassador. "The Chief will appreciate the gesture even more. He'll understand that he made a mistake, that he judged you too hastily, letting himself be guided by his own sensitivities, or listening to your enemies. Don't think only of yourself, Agustín. Don't be an egotist. Think of your daughter. What will happen to her if you lose everything and end up in jail accused of mismanagement and fraud?"

"Do you think I haven't thought about that, Manuel?"

The ambassador shrugged.

"It just occurred to me when I saw how pretty she's become," he repeated. "The Chief appreciates beauty. If I say to him: 'Egghead, to prove his affection and loyalty, wants to offer you his pretty daughter, who's still a virgin,' he won't refuse. I know him. He's a true gentleman, with a tremendous sense of honor. His heart will be touched. He'll call you. He'll return what's been taken from you. Uranita's future will be secure. Think of her, Agustín, and shake off your antiquated prejudices. Don't be an egotist."

He picked up the bottle again and splashed more whiskey into his glass and Cabral's. He used his hand to put more ice cubes in both glasses.

"It just occurred to me when I saw how attractive she's become," he intoned, for the fourth or fifth time. Did it bother him, did his throat drive him mad? He moved his head and caressed the scar with his fingertips. "If it offends you, I didn't say anything."

"You said vile and evil," Aunt Adelina suddenly explodes. "You said that about your father who's had a living death and is only waiting for the end. About my brother, the person I've loved and respected most. You won't leave this house without explaining the reason for your insults, Urania."

"I said vile and evil because there are no stronger words," Urania says very slowly. "If there were, I would have said them. He had his reasons, certainly. His extenuating circumstances, his motivations. But I haven't forgiven him and I'll never forgive him."

"Why do you help him if you hate him so much?" The old woman vibrates with indignation; she is very pale, as if she were about to faint. "Why the nurse, and the food? Why don't you let him die?"

"I want him to go on with his living death, I want him to suffer." She speaks very calmly, her eyes lowered. "That's why I help him, Aunt Adelina."

"But, but what did he do to make you hate him so much, to make you say something so horrible?" Lucindita raises her arms, incapable of believing what she has just heard. "Holy God!"

"You'll be surprised at what I'm going to tell you, Egghead," Manuel Alfonso exclaims dramatically. "When I see a beauty, a real woman, the kind that makes you turn around, I don't think of myself. I think of the Chief. Yes, of him. Would he like to hold her in his arms, make love to her? I've never told this to anyone. Not even the Chief. But he knows. Knows that for me, he always comes first, even in this. And make no mistake, I like women a lot, Agustín. Don't think I've made the sacrifice of giving him gorgeous women to flatter him, or to get favors or positions. That's what contemptible people think, what pigs think. Do you know why I do it? Out of love, compassion, pity. You can understand, Egghead. You and I know what his life has been. Working from dawn till midnight, seven days a week, twelve months a year. Never resting. Taking care of important matters and trivial ones. Constantly making decisions that determine the life and death of three million Dominicans. In order to bring us into the twentieth century. And having to be concerned about the resentful and the mediocre, the ingratitude of so many bastards. Doesn't a man like him deserve to have an occasional distraction? To enjoy a few minutes with a woman? One of the few compensations in his life, Agustín. Which is why I feel proud to be what so many vipers say I am: the Chief's procurer. I'll drink to the honor, Egghead!"

He raised the glass without whiskey to his lips and put an ice cube in his mouth. He remained silent for a long time, sucking, abstracted, exhausted by his soliloquy. Cabral observed him, saying nothing, caressing his glass full of whiskey.

"We've finished the bottle and I don't have another one," he apologized. "Take mine, I can't drink any more."

Nodding, the ambassador held out an empty glass and Senator Cabral poured in the contents of his.

"I'm moved by what you say, Manuel," he murmured. "But I'm not surprised. What you feel for him, that admiration and gratitude, is what I've always felt for the Chief. That's why I find this situation so painful."

The ambassador put his hand on his shoulder.

"It'll work out, Egghead. I'll talk to him. I know how to say things to him. I'll explain it to him. I won't say it's my idea, but yours. An initiative from Agustín Cabral. An absolutely loyal man, even in disgrace, even in humiliation. You know the Chief. He likes gestures. He may have a few years on him, a few problems with his health. But he's never refused the challenges of love. Don't worry. You'll recover your position, those who turned their backs on you will soon be lining up at your door. Now, I have to go. Thanks for the whiskey. In my house they don't let me have a drop of alcohol. How good it's been to feel that burning, bitter little tickle in my poor throat. Goodbye, Egghead. You can stop agonizing over this. Leave everything to me. Just prepare Uranita. Without going into details. It isn't necessary. The Chief will take care of that. You can't imagine the delicacy, the tenderness, the human touch he uses in cases like this. He'll make her happy, and he'll reward her, her future will be assured. He's always done that. Especially with a creature as sweet and beautiful as she is."

He staggered to the door and let it slam behind him when he left the house. From the sofa in the living room, where he still held the empty glass in his hand, Agustín Cabral heard the car pull away. He felt lassitude, an immeasurable lack of will. He would never have the strength to stand, climb the stairs, undress, go to the bathroom, brush his teeth, lie down, turn out the light.

"Are you trying to say that Manuel Alfonso proposed to your father that, that . . . ?" Aunt Adelina cannot finish, she is choked by rage, she cannot find the words that will soften, make presentable, what she wants to say. In order to conclude somehow, she shakes her fist at the parrot Samson, who has not even opened his beak: "Be still, you miserable creature!"

"I'm not trying. I'm telling you what happened," says Urania. "If you don't want to hear it, I'll stop talking and leave."

Aunt Adelina opens her mouth but cannot say anything.

For the first time in his life, the senator did not go upstairs to bed. He fell asleep in the living room, in his clothes, a glass and an empty whiskey bottle at his feet. The sight of him the next morning, when Urania came down to eat breakfast and go to school, left her shaken. Her papa wasn't a drunkard; on the contrary, he always criticized heavy drinking and dissipation. He had drunk too much because he was desperate, because he was hounded, pursued, investigated, dismissed, had his bank accounts frozen, for something he hadn't done. She sobbed and embraced her papa, who was sprawled on the armchair in the living room. When he opened his eyes and saw her next to him, weeping, he kissed her over and over again: "Don't cry, precious. We'll get out of this, you'll see, we won't let them defeat us." He stood up, straightened his clothes, sat with his daughter while she had breakfast. As he smoothed her hair and told her not to say anything about it at school, he looked at her in a strange way.

"He must have had doubts, gone back and forth," Urania imagines. "Thought about exile. But he never could have gone into an embassy. Since the sanctions, there were no more Latin American legations. And the *caliés* made the rounds, watching the entrances to the ones that were left. He must have spent a horrible day, struggling with his scruples. That afternoon, when I came home from school, he had already made his decision."

Aunt Adelina does not protest. She only looks at her from the depths of her deep-set eyes, reproach combined with horror and a disbelief that, despite all her efforts, is fading. Manolita twists and untwists a strand of hair. Lucinda and Marianita have turned into statues.

He had bathed, and was dressed with his usual propriety; there was no trace left of the bad night he had spent. But he hadn't eaten a bite of food, and his doubts and bitterness were reflected in his deathly pallor, the circles under his eyes, the glint of fear in his gaze.

"Don't you feel well, Papa? Why are you so pale?"

"We have to talk, Uranita. Come, let's go up to your room. I don't want the servants to hear us."

"They're going to arrest him," the girl thought. "He's going to tell me that I have to go live with Uncle Aníbal and Aunt Adelina."

They entered the room, Urania dropped her books on her desk and sat on the edge of the bed ("A blue spread with Walt Disney characters"), and her father leaned against the window.

"You're what I love most in the world." He smiled at her. "The best thing I have. Since your mama died, you're all I have left in this life. Do you know that, sweetheart?"

"Of course I do, Papa," she replied. "What other terrible thing has happened? Are they going to arrest you?"

"No, no," and he shook his head. "In fact, there's a chance everything will be all right."

He stopped, incapable of continuing. His lips and hands were trembling. She looked at him in surprise. But then this was a great piece of news. A chance the radio and newspapers would stop attacking him? That he'd be President of the Senate again? If that was true, why do you look like that, Papa, so discouraged and sad?

"Because I'm being asked to make a sacrifice, my dear," he murmured. "I want you to know something. I would never do anything, anything, you must understand, really understand, that wasn't for your own good. Swear to me you'll never forget what I'm saying."

Uranita begins to feel irritated. What was he talking about? Why didn't he come out and tell her what it was?

"Sure, Papa," she says finally, with a weary gesture. "But what's happened, why are you being so roundabout?"

Her father sat beside her on the bed, took her by the shoulders, pulled her to him, kissed her hair.

"There's a party and the Generalissimo has invited you." He kept his lips tight against the girl's forehead. "In the house he has in San Cristóbal, on the Fundación Ranch."

Urania slips out of his arms.

"A party? And Trujillo is inviting us? But, Papa, that means everything's all right again. Doesn't it?"

Senator Cabral shrugged.

"I don't know, Uranita. The Chief is unpredictable. His intentions aren't always easy to guess. He hasn't invited both of us. Only you."

"Me?"

"Manuel Alfonso will take you there. And he'll bring you home. I don't know why he's inviting you and not me. Certainly, it's a first gesture, a way of letting me know that everything's not lost. At least, that's what Manuel assumes."

"How bad he must have felt," says Urania, seeing that Aunt Adelina, with lowered head, no longer reproaches her with eyes from which all certainty has been erased. "He talked in circles, he contradicted himself. He was terrified I wouldn't believe his lies."

"Manuel Alfonso could have deceived him too . . . ," Aunt Adelina begins but can't continue. She makes a contrite gesture, apologizing with her hands and head.

"If you don't want to go, you won't go, Uranita." Agustín Cabral rubs his hands, as if, on that hot afternoon that is turning into night, he felt cold. "I'll call Manuel Alfonso right now and tell him you're not well, and give your regrets to the Chief. You're under no obligation, dear girl."

She doesn't know how to respond. Why did she have to make a decision like that?

"I don't know, Papa," she says, hesitant and confused. "It seems very strange. Why is he inviting just me? What am I going to do at a party with grown-ups? Or are other girls my age invited too?"

His Adam's apple moves up and down in Senator Cabral's slender throat. His eyes avoid Urania's.

"If he's invited you, there'll be other girls there too," he stammers. "It must be that he no longer considers you a little girl, but a young lady."

"But he doesn't even know me, he's only seen me at a distance, in crowds of people. How can he remember me, Papa?"

"Somebody must have told him about you, Uranita," her father says evasively. "I repeat, you're under no obligation. If you like, I'll call Manuel Alfonso and tell him you're sick."

"Well, I don't know, Papa. If you want me to, I'll go, and if not, I won't. What I want is to help you. Won't he be angry if I say no?"

"Didn't you understand anything?" Manolita dares to ask her.

Not a thing, Urania. You were still a girl, when being a girl meant being totally innocent about certain things that had to do with desire, instincts, power, and the infinite excesses and bestialities that a combination of those things could mean in a country shaped by Trujillo. She was a bright girl, and everything seemed very hasty, of course. Who ever heard of an invitation made on the day of the party, not giving the guest any time to get ready? But she was a normal, healthy girl—the last day you would be, Urania—and very inquisitive, and suddenly a party in San Cristóbal, on the Generalissimo's famous ranch, where the horses and cows that won all the prizes were raised, couldn't help but excite her, fill her with curiosity as she thought of what she would tell her friends at Santo Domingo, how jealous she would make those classmates who had made her suffer so much in recent days, telling her the awful things that were said about Senator Agustín Cabral in the newspapers and on the radio. Why would she have misgivings about something her father approved? Instead, she felt hopeful that, as the senator said, the invitation might be the first sign of making amends, a gesture to let her father know that his calvary had ended.

She suspected nothing. Like the budding young lady she was, she worried about the most trivial things. What would she wear, Papa? Which shoes? Too bad it was so late, they could have called the hairdresser who did her hair and made her up last month, when she was a lady-in-waiting to the Queen of Santo Domingo. It was her only concern from the moment when, to avoid offending the Chief, she and her father decided she would go to the party. Don Manuel Alfonso would come for her at eight. She didn't have time to do homework.

"How late did you tell Señor Alfonso I could stay?"

"Well, until people begin to leave," says Senator Cabral, squeezing his hands. "If you want to leave earlier, because you feel tired or whatever, you just tell him and Manuel Alfonso will bring you right home."

17 When Dr. Vélez Santana and Bienvenido García, General Juan Tomás Díaz's son-in-law, drove Pedro Livio Cedeño to the International Clinic, the inseparable trio—Amadito, Antonio Imbert, and Turk Estrella Sadhalá—reached a decision: it made no sense to go on waiting there until General Díaz, Luis Amiama, and Antonio de la Maza found General José René Román. What they should do is find a doctor to treat their wounds, then change their soiled clothes and look for a place to hide until things were settled. Was there a trustworthy doctor they could go to at this hour? It was close to midnight.

"My cousin Manuel," said Imbert. "Manuel Durán Barreras. He lives nearby and his office is next to his house. He can be trusted."

Tony's expression was somber, which surprised Amadito. When Salvador was driving them to Dr. Durán Barreras's house—the city was quiet and the streets were empty of traffic, the news hadn't broken yet—he asked:

"Why the long face?"

"This is all fucked up," Imbert replied quietly.

Turk and the lieutenant looked at him.

"Do you think it's normal for Pupo Román not to show up?" he added between clenched teeth. "There are only two explanations. Either they found him out and arrested him or he got scared. In either case, we're fucked."

"But we killed Trujillo, Tony!" Amadito tried to cheer him up. "Nobody's going to bring him back to life."

"Don't think I'm sorry about that," said Imbert. "The truth is, I never had much faith in the coup, the civilian-military junta, all those dreams of Antonio de la Maza. I always saw us as being on a suicide mission."

"You should have said so earlier, brother," Amadito joked. "I would have written my will."

Turk dropped them off at Dr. Durán Barreras's place and went to his own house; since the *caliés* would soon find his abandoned car on the highway, he wanted to alert his wife and children and get some clothes and money. Dr. Durán Barreras was in bed. He came out in a robe, yawning. His jaw dropped when Imbert explained why they were covered with mud and blood, and what they wanted from him. For long seconds he looked at them, astounded, his large bony face, with its full beard, contorted in bewilderment. Amadito could see the doctor's Adam's apple moving up and down. From time to time he rubbed his eyes as if he were seeing ghosts. At last he reacted:

"The first thing is to treat you. Let's go to my office."

Amadito was the most seriously hurt. A bullet had hit his ankle; you could see the entrance and exit wounds, and splinters of bone protruding from them. His foot and part of his ankle were deformed by swelling.

"I don't know how you can stand with that shattered ankle," the doctor remarked as he disinfected the wound.

"I didn't realize until now that it hurt," replied the lieutenant.

In the euphoria of what had happened, he had hardly paid attention to his foot. But now, the pain was there, along with a fiery tingling that went up to his knee. The doctor bandaged the wound, gave him an injection, and handed him a vial of pills to take every four hours.

"Do you have somewhere to go?" Imbert asked while he was being treated.

Amadito thought immediately of his Aunt Meca. She was one of his eleven great-aunts, the one who had pampered him most since he had been a little boy. The old woman lived alone, in a wooden house filled with flowerpots, on Avenida San Martín, not far from Independencia Park.

"The first place they'll look for us will be with our relatives," Tony warned. "A close friend would be better."

"All my friends are in the military, brother. Staunch Trujillistas."

He could not understand why Imbert looked so worried and pessimistic. Pupo Román would show up and they would put the Plan in effect, he was sure about that. And anyway, with the death of Trujillo, the regime would collapse like a house of cards.

"I think I can help you, son," Dr. Durán Barreras intervened. "The mechanic who fixes my station wagon has a little farm he wants to rent. Near the Ozama extension. Shall I talk to him?"

He did, and it turned out to be surprisingly easy. The mechanic was named Antonio (Toño) Sánchez, and in spite of the hour he came to the house as soon as the doctor called. They told him the truth. "Damn, tonight I'll get drunk!" he exclaimed. It was an honor to let them have his place. The lieutenant would be safe, there were no close neighbors. He would take him in his jeep and make sure he had food.

"How can I ever repay you, Doc?" Amadito asked Durán Barreras.

"By taking care of yourself, son," and the doctor shook his hand, looking at him with compassion. "I wouldn't want to be in your skin if they catch you."

"That won't happen, Doc."

He had used up his ammunition, but Imbert had a good supply and gave him a handful of bullets. The lieutenant loaded his .45 and made his farewells by stating:

"Now I feel safer."

"See you soon, Amadito." Tony embraced him. "Your friendship is one of the good things that's happened to me."

When they left for the Ozama extension in Toño Sánchez's jeep, the city had changed. They passed a couple of Beetles filled with *caliés*, and as they were crossing Radhamés Bridge they saw a truck pull up, carrying guards, who jumped out and set up a roadblock.

"They know the Goat is dead," said Amadito. "I wish I could have seen their faces when they found out they had lost their Chief."

"Nobody's going to believe it until they see and smell the body," the mechanic remarked. "Shit, this'll be a different country without Trujillo!"

The farm was a crude building in the middle of ten hectares of uncultivated land. The house was practically unfurnished: a cot with a mattress, a few broken chairs, and a demijohn of distilled water. "Tomorrow I'll bring you something to eat," Toño Sánchez promised. "Don't worry. Nobody will come here."

The house had no electricity. Amadito took off his shoes and lay down, fully dressed, on the cot. The sound of Toño Sánchez's jeep grew fainter until it disappeared. He was tired, and his heel and ankle hurt, but he felt a great serenity. With Trujillo dead, a great burden had been lifted from him. The guilt that had been gnawing at his soul ever since he was forced to kill that poor man—Luisa Gil's brother, my God!—would start to fade away now, he was sure. He would become the person he used to be, a man who could look in the mirror and not feel disgust with the face he saw reflected there. Ah, shit, if he could finish off Abbes García and Colonel Roberto Figueroa Carrión too, nothing else would matter. He would die in peace. He curled up, changed position several times, trying to get comfortable, but couldn't fall asleep. He heard noises in the dark, scurrying sounds. At dawn the excitement and pain eased, and he managed to sleep a few hours. He woke with a start. He'd had a nightmare but couldn't remember his dream.

He spent the hours of the new day peering out the windows, watching for the jeep. There was nothing to eat in the house, but he wasn't hungry. His occasional drinks of distilled water seemed to fill his stomach. But he was tormented by solitude, boredom, lack of news. If there were only a radio at least! He resisted the temptation to go out and walk to some inhabited place and find a newspaper. Control your impatience, boy, Toño Sánchez would come soon.

He didn't come until the third day. He appeared at noon on June 2, the day that Amadito, faint with hunger and desperate for news, turned thirty-two. Toño was no longer the easygoing, effusive, self-confident man who had brought him here. He was pale, devoured by anxiety, unshaven, and stammering. He handed him a thermos of hot coffee and some sausage and cheese sandwiches, which Amadito wolfed down as he heard the bad news. His picture was in all the papers and was shown frequently on television, along with those of General Juan Tomás Díaz, Antonio de la Maza, Estrella Sadhalá, Fifí Pastoriza, Pedro Livio Cedeño, Antonio Imbert, Huáscar Tejeda, and Luis Amiama. Pedro Livio Cedeño had been taken prisoner, and he had given them up. They were offering huge amounts of pesos to anyone with information about them. There was a fierce persecution of everyone suspected of being anti-Trujillista. Dr. Durán Barreras had been arrested the night before; Toño thought that if he was tortured, he'd betray them all in the end. It was extremely dangerous for Amadito to stay here.

"I wouldn't stay even if it was safe, Toño," the lieutenant said. "I'd rather be killed than have to spend another three days alone like this."

"Where will you go?"

He thought of his cousin Máximo Mieses, who had a place along the Duarte highway. But Toño discouraged him: the highways were full of patrols and they were searching every vehicle. He'd never get to his cousin's farm without being recognized.

"You have no idea what's going on." Toño Sánchez was in a rage. "Hundreds of people have been arrested. They've gone crazy, looking for all of you."

"They can go to hell," said Amadito. "Let them kill me. The Goat's gone and they can't bring him back. Don't worry, brother. You've done a lot for me. Can you get me to the highway? I'll go back to the capital on foot."

"I'm scared, but not so scared that I'd leave you out in the cold, I'm not that much of a bastard," said Toño, who had calmed down. He patted him on the shoulder. "Let's go, I'll take you. If they catch us, you put a gun to my head, okay?"

He settled Amadito in the back of the jeep, under a piece of canvas, on top of which he placed some coils of rope and gasoline cans that slammed against the hunched-over lieutenant. The position gave him cramps and made the pain in his foot worse; every pothole in the road battered his shoulders, back, and head. But he never let go of his .45; he held it in his right hand, with the safety off. Whatever happened, they wouldn't take him alive. He wasn't afraid. In fact, he didn't have much hope of getting out of this. But it didn't matter. He hadn't felt this kind of serenity since that disastrous night with Johnny Abbes.

"We're coming up on the Radhamés Bridge," he heard a terrified Toño Sánchez say. "Don't move, don't make a sound, there's a patrol."

The jeep stopped. He heard voices, footsteps, and after a pause, friendly exclamations: "Hey, it's you, Toñito." "What's up, compadre?" They authorized him to continue without searching the car. They must have been in the middle of the bridge when he heard Toño Sánchez again:

"The captain was my friend Skinny Rasputín. Shit, what a piece of luck! My balls are still up around my ears, Amadito. Where should I drop you?"

"On Avenida San Martín."

A short while later, the jeep braked to a stop.

"I don't see *caliés* anywhere, now's a good time," Toño said. "God be with you, boy."

The lieutenant lifted off the canvas and the cans and jumped to the sidewalk. A few cars were passing, but he saw no pedestrians except for a man with a stick who was walking away, his back to him.

"God bless you, Toño."

"And be with you," Toño Sánchez repeated, pulling away.

Aunt Meca's little one-story house—made of wood, with a fence, no garden, but surrounded by pots of geraniums in the windows—was about twenty meters away, which Amadito strode across, limping, not concealing his revolver. As soon as he knocked the door opened. Aunt Meca didn't have time to be astonished, because the lieutenant rushed in, moving her aside and closing the door behind him.

"I don't know what to do, where to hide, Aunt Meca. It'll be for one or two days, until I can find a safe place."

His aunt kissed and embraced him, affectionate as always. She didn't seem as frightened as Amadito had feared.

"They must have seen you, honey. How could you come in broad daylight? My neighbors are raging Trujillistas. You're covered with blood. And those bandages? Are you wounded?"

Amadito peered at the street through the curtains. There were no people on the sidewalks. Doors and windows across the street were closed.

"Ever since the news broke I've been praying to St. Peter Claver for you, Amadito, he's such a miraculous saint," his Aunt Meca said, cradling his face in her hands. "When they showed you on television and in *El Caribe*, some of my neighbors came to ask me questions, to see what they could find out. I hope they haven't seen you. You look awful, honey. Do you want anything?"

"Yes, Aunt Meca," he said with a laugh, caressing her white hair. "A shower and something to eat. I'm starving."

"And it's your birthday!" Aunt Meca recalled, and hugged him again.

She was a small, energetic old woman, with a resolute expression and deep, kind eyes. She had him take off his pants and shirt, so she could wash them, and while Amadito showered—it was a pleasure fit for the gods—she heated up all the leftovers in the kitchen. Wearing his shorts and undershirt, the lieutenant found a banquet spread on the table: fried green plantains, fried sausage, rice, deep-fried pieces of chicken. He ate with good appetite, listening to his Aunt Meca's stories. How it upset the family when they learned he was one of Trujillo's assassins. The *caliés* had come to the houses of three of her sisters in the middle of the night, asking about him. They hadn't come here yet.

"If you don't mind, I'd like to sleep for a while, Aunt Meca. I've barely closed my eyes for days. I was too bored. I'm happy to be here with you."

She led him to her bedroom and had him lie down on her bed, under an image of St. Peter Claver, her favorite saint. She closed the shutters to darken the room, and said that while he was napping, she would wash and iron his uniform. "And we'll think of a place where you can hide, Amadito." She kissed him repeatedly on his brow and head: "And I thought you were such a good Trujillista, honey." He fell asleep immediately. He dreamed that Turk Sadhalá and Antonio Imbert were calling him repeatedly: "Amadito, Amadito!" They were trying to tell him something important, but he couldn't understand their gestures or words. It seemed to him he had just closed his eyes when he felt someone shaking him. There was Aunt Meca, so pale and frightened he felt sorry for her, and guilt-ridden for having involved her in this.

"They're here, they're here," she said in a strangled voice, crossing herself. "Ten or twelve Beetles, honey, and lots of *caliés.*"

He was lucid now and knew perfectly well what to do. He made the old woman lie down on the floor, behind the bed, against the wall, at the feet of St. Peter Claver.

"Don't move, don't get up no matter what," he told her. "I love you very much, Aunt Meca."

He had the .45 in his hand. Barefoot, dressed only in his regulation khaki undershirt and shorts, he hugged the wall and crept to the front door. He peered through the curtains, staying out of sight. It was an overcast afternoon, and in the distance he could hear a bolero. Black SIM Volkswagens filled the street. At least twenty *caliés* armed with submachine guns and revolvers were surrounding the house. Three men were at the door. One of them pounded it with his fist, making the wood quiver, and shouted at the top of his voice:

"We know you're in there, García Guerrero! Come out with your hands up or you'll die like a dog!"

"Not like a dog, no," he murmured. As he opened the door with his left hand, he fired with his right. He managed to empty the clip of his pistol and saw the man who had urged him to surrender fall, bellowing, shot in the middle of the chest. But, annihilated by an untold number of bullets from submachine guns and revolvers, he did not see that in addition to killing one *calié*, he had wounded two others before dying himself. He did not see how his body was tied—the way hunters tie down deer killed in the Cordillera Central—to the roof of a Volkswagen, and how Johnny Abbes's men, who were inside the Beetle, held on to his ankles and wrists and displayed him to bystanders in Independencia Park, through which his killers drove in triumph, while other *caliés* entered the house, found Aunt Meca where he had left her, more dead than alive, and shoving and spitting at her, took her to SIM headquarters, at the same time that a greedy mob, under the mocking or impassive eyes of the police, began to loot the house, making off with everything the *caliés* hadn't stolen first, and after looting the house they destroyed it, tore down the walls, demolished the roof, and finally burned it until, at nightfall, there was nothing left but ashes and charred rubble.

18

When one of the military adjutants showed Luis Rodríguez, Manuel Alfonso's chauffeur, into the office, the Generalissimo stood to receive him, something he did not do even with the most important people.

"How is the ambassador?" he asked with concern.

"Just fair, Chief." The chauffeur put on an appropriate expression and touched his own throat. "A lot of pain, again. This morning he had me bring the doctor so he could give him an injection."

Poor Manuel. It wasn't fair, damn it. That a man who had devoted his life to caring for his body, to being handsome and elegant, to resisting the perverse law of nature that everything had to grow ugly, should be punished like this, where it would most humiliate him: in the face that had radiated life, grace, and health. He would have been better off dying on the operating table. When he saw him in Ciudad Trujillo after his operation at the Mayo Clinic, the Benefactor's eyes had filled with tears. Manuel had been ravaged. And he could hardly understand him now that they had cut out half his tongue.

"Give him my best." The Generalissimo examined Luis Rodríguez; dark suit, white shirt, blue tie, polished shoes: the best-dressed black in the Dominican Republic. "What's the news?"

"Very good, Chief." Luis Rodríguez's large eyes flashed. "I found the girl, no problem. Whenever you say."

"Are you sure it's the same one?"

The large dark face, with its scars and mustache, nodded several times.

"Absolutely sure. The one who gave you flowers on Monday, for the San Cristóbal Youth Group. Yolanda Esterel. Seventeen years old. Here's her picture."

It was a photograph from a student ID, but Trujillo recognized the languid eyes, the mouth with the plump lips, the hair hanging loose to her shoulders. The girl had led the parade of students, carrying a large photograph of the Generalissimo, past the raised platform in the main park of San Cristóbal, and then came up on the dais to present him with a bouquet of roses and hydrangeas wrapped in cellophane. He remembered her plump, rounded body, her small breasts moving suggestively inside her blouse, her flaring hips. A tingling in his testicles raised his spirits.

"Take her to Mahogany House, around ten," he said, repressing those fantasies that were wasting his time. "My best regards to Manuel. Tell him to take care of himself."

"Yes, Chief, I'll tell him. I'll bring her there a little before ten."

He left, bowing. On one of the six telephones on his lacquered desk, the Generalissimo called the guard post at Mahogany House so that Benita Sepúlveda would have the rooms perfumed with anise and filled with fresh flowers. (It was an unnecessary precaution, for the housekeeper, knowing he might appear at any moment, always kept Mahogany House shining, but he never failed to let her know ahead of time.) He ordered the military adjutants to have the Chevrolet ready and to call his chauffeur, aide-de-camp, and bodyguard, Zacarías de la Cruz, because tonight, after his walk, he was going to San Cristóbal.

He was enthusiastic at the prospect. Could she be the daughter of that school principal in San Cristóbal who recited a poem by Salomé Ureña ten years ago, during one of his political visits to his native city, and excited him so much with the shaved armpits she displayed during her performance that he left the official reception in his honor when it had just begun and took her to Mahogany House? Terencia Esterel? That was her name. He felt another gust of excitement imagining that Yolanda was the teacher's daughter or younger sister. He walked quickly, crossing the gardens between the National Palace and Radhamés Manor, and hardly listened to what one of the adjutants in his escort was telling him about repeated calls from the Minister of the Armed Forces, General Román Fernández, who was at his disposal in the event His Excellency wished to see him before his walk. Ah, the call this morning had scared him. He'd be even more scared when he rubbed his damn nose in it and showed him the puddle of filthy water.

He entered his rooms at Radhamés Manor like a whirlwind. His everyday olive-green uniform was waiting for him, laid out on the bed. Sinforoso was a mind reader. He hadn't told him he was going to San Cristóbal, but the old man had prepared the clothes he always wore to the Fundación Ranch. Why this everyday uniform for Mahogany House? He didn't know. The passion for rituals, for the repetition of gestures and actions, that he'd had since he was young. The signs were favorable: no urine stains on his underwear or trousers. His irritation with Balaguer for daring to object to the promotion of Lieutenant Victor Alicinio Peña Rivera had faded. He felt optimistic, rejuvenated by a lively tingle in his testicles and the expectation of holding in his arms the daughter or sister of that Terencia of happy memory. Was she a virgin? This time he wouldn't have the unpleasant experience he'd had with the skinny bitch.

He was glad he would spend the next hour smelling the salt air, feeling the sea breeze, watching the waves break against the Avenida. The exercise would help him wash away the bad taste most of the afternoon had left in his mouth, something that rarely happened to him: he had never been prone to depression or any of that bullshit.

As he was leaving, a maid came to tell him that Doña María wanted to give him a message from young Ramfis, who had called from Paris. "Later, later, I don't have time." A conversation with the tedious old penny-pincher would ruin his good mood.

Again he crossed the gardens of Radhamés Manor at a lively pace, impatient to get to the ocean. But first, as he did every day, he stopped at his mother's house on Avenida Máximo Gómez. At the entrance to Doña Julia's large pink residence, the twenty or so men who would accompany him were waiting, privileged persons who, because they escorted him every evening, were envied and despised by those who had not achieved that signal honor. Among the officers and civilians crowded together in the gardens of the Sublime Matriarch, who parted into two lines to let him pass, "Good afternoon, Chief," "Good afternoon, Excellency," he acknowledged Razor Espaillat, General José René Román—what concern in the poor fool's eyes!—Colonel Johnny Abbes García, Senator Henry Chirinos, his son-in-law Colonel León Estévez, his hometown friend Modesto Díaz, Senator Jeremías Quintanilla, who had just replaced Agustín Cabral as President of the Senate, Don Panchito, the editor of *El Caribe*, and, almost invisible among them, the diminutive President Balaguer. He did not shake hands with anyone. He went to the second floor, where Doña Julia usually sat in her rocker at dusk. The aged woman seemed lost in her chair. As small as a midget, she stared at the sun's fireworks display as it sank behind the horizon in an aura of red clouds. The ladies and servants surrounding his mother moved aside. He bent down, kissed the parchment cheeks of Doña Julia, and caressed her hair tenderly.

"You like the sunset a lot, don't you, Ma?"

She nodded, smiling at him with sunken but still nimble eyes, and the tiny claw that was her hand brushed his cheek. Did she recognize him? Doña Altagracia Julia Molina was ninety-six years old and her mind must be like soapy water in which memories dissolved. But instinct would tell her that the man who came punctually to visit her every afternoon was someone she loved. She had always been a very good woman, this illegitimate daughter of Haitian immigrants to San Cristóbal, whose features he and his siblings had inherited, something that never failed to mortify him despite his great love for her. Sometimes, however, at the Hipódromo, the Country Club, or Fine Arts, when he saw all the aristocratic Dominican families paying him homage, he would think mockingly: "They're licking the ground for a descendant of slaves." How was the Sublime Matriarch to blame for the black blood that ran in her veins? Doña Julia had lived only for her husband, Don José Trujillo Valdez, an easygoing drinker and womanizer, and for her children, never thinking of herself, always putting herself last in everything. He constantly marveled at this tiny woman who never asked him for money, or clothes, or trips, or property. Nothing, not ever. He had to force everything on her. Congenitally frugal, Doña Julia would have continued to live in the modest little house in San Cristóbal where the Generalissimo had been born and spent his childhood, or in one of the huts where her Haitian ancestors had died of hunger. The only thing Doña Julia ever asked of him was compassion for Petán, Blacky, Peepee, Aníbal, his slow-witted, incorrigible brothers, whenever they did something wrong, or for Angelita, Ramfis, and Radhamés, who, from the time they were children, had hidden behind their grandmother to soften their father's wrath. And Trujillo would forgive them, for Doña Julia's sake. Did she know that hundreds of streets, parks, and schools in the Republic were named Julia Molina

Widow of Trujillo? In spite of being adored and celebrated, she was still the silent, invisible woman Trujillo remembered from his childhood.

Sometimes he would spend a long time with his mother, recounting the day's events even if she couldn't understand him. Today he merely said a few tender words and returned to Máximo Gómez, impatient to breathe in the scent of the ocean.

As soon as he came out onto the broad Avenida—the cluster of civilians and officers parted again—he began to walk. He could see the Caribbean eight blocks away, aflame with the fiery gold of sunset. He felt another surge of satisfaction. He walked on the right, followed by the courtiers who fanned out behind him in groups that occupied the roadway and sidewalk. At this hour traffic was prohibited on Máximo Gómez and the Avenida, although, on his orders, Johnny Abbes had made the security on the side streets almost invisible because intersections crawling with guards and *caliés* eventually gave him claustrophobia. No one crossed the barrier of military adjutants a meter from the Chief. Everyone waited for him to indicate who could approach. After half a block, breathing in the perfume of the gardens, he turned, looked for the balding head of Modesto Díaz, and signaled to him. There was some confusion because the fleshy Senator Chirinos, who was next to Modesto Díaz, thought he was the anointed one and hurried toward the Generalissimo. He was intercepted and sent back to the crowd. For Modesto Díaz, who was very stout, keeping pace with Trujillo on these walks cost him a great effort. He was perspiring profusely. He held his handkerchief in his hand and from time to time wiped his forehead, his neck, and his fat cheeks.

"Good afternoon, Chief."

"You have to go on a diet," Trujillo advised. "Barely fifty and you're breathing hard. Learn from me, seventy years old and in great shape."

"My wife says the same thing every day, Chief. She fixes chicken broth and salads for me. But I don't feel like eating that. I can give up everything except good food."

His obese body could barely keep up with him. Modesto, like his brother, General Juan Tomás Díaz, had a broad face, flat nose, thick lips, and a complexion with unmistakable racial reminiscences, but he was more intelligent than his brother and most of the other Dominicans Trujillo knew. He had been president of the Dominican Party, a congressman, a minister; but the Generalissimo did not allow him to stay too long in the government, precisely because his mental acuity when expounding, analyzing, and solving a problem seemed dangerous, something that could puff up his pride and lead him to treason.

"What conspiracy has Juan Tomás gotten himself involved in?" He asked the question and turned to look at him. "You know what your brother and son-in-law are up to, I suppose."

Modesto smiled, as if enjoying a joke:

"Juan Tomás? Between his estates and his businesses, his whiskey and the movies he shows in his garden, I doubt he has any time left for conspiracies."

"He's conspiring with Henry Dearborn, the Yankee diplomat," Trujillo declared as if he had not heard him. "He should stop that bullshit; he went through a bad time once and he can go through another that's even worse."

"My brother isn't fool enough to conspire against you, Chief. But even so, I'll tell him."

How pleasant: the sea breeze cleared his lungs, and he could hear the crash of waves breaking against the rocks and the cement wall of the Avenida. Modesto Díaz made a move to leave, but the Benefactor stopped him:

"Wait, I haven't finished. Or can't you take it anymore?"

"For you I'd risk a heart attack."

Trujillo rewarded him with a smile. He always liked Modesto, who, in addition to being intelligent, was thoughtful, fair, affable, and unduplicitous. Still, his intelligence could not be controlled and used, like Egghead's, the Constitutional Sot's, or Balaguer's. Modesto's had an indomitable edge, an independence that could become seditious if he acquired too much power. He and Juan Tomás were also from San Cristóbal, he had known them since they were boys, and in addition to awarding him posts, he had used Modesto on countless occasions as an adviser. He had subjected him to rigorous tests, and he had always come through successfully. The first one came in the late forties, after Trujillo visited the Livestock Show for pedigree bulls and dairy cows that Modesto Díaz organized in Villa Mella. What a surprise: his farm, not very large, was as clean, modern, and prosperous as the Fundación Ranch. More than the impeccable stables and splendid cows, it was Modesto's arrogant satisfaction as he showed his breeding farm to him and the other guests that wounded the Chief's sensibilities. The following day he sent the Walking Turd, with a check for ten thousand pesos, to formalize the transfer of ownership. Without the slightest hesitation at having to sell his most prized possession at a ridiculously low price (just one of his cows cost more), Modesto signed the contract and sent a handwritten note to Trujillo expressing his gratitude that "Your Excellency considers my small cattle-breeding enterprise worthy of being developed by your experienced hand." After considering whether those lines contained some punishable irony, the Benefactor decided they did not. Five years later, Modesto Díaz had another large, beautiful ranch in a remote region of La Estrella. Did he think it was so far away it would go unnoticed? Weak with laughter, he sent Egghead Cabral with another check for ten thousand pesos, claiming he had so much confidence in his cattle-raising talents that he was buying the farm sight unseen. Modesto signed the bill of sale, pocketed the symbolic sum, and thanked the Generalissimo in another affectionate note. To reward his docility, Trujillo subsequently granted him the exclusive concession to import washing machines and electric mixers, which allowed the brother of General Juan Tomás Díaz to recoup his losses.

"The mess with those shiteating priests," Trujillo grumbled. "Does it have a solution or not?"

"Of course it does, Chief." Modesto's tongue protruded; along with his forehead and neck, his bald head dripped perspiration. "But, if you'll permit me, the problems with the Church don't matter. They'll take care of themselves if the main issue is resolved: the gringos. Everything depends on them."

"Then there is no solution. Kennedy wants my head. Since I have no intention of giving it to him, we'll be at war for a long time."

"It isn't you the gringos are afraid of, Chief, but Castro. Especially after the disaster at the Bay of Pigs. Now more than ever they're terrified that Communism will spread through Latin America. This is the moment to show them that the best defense in the region against the Reds is you, not Betancourt or Figueres."

"They've had enough time to realize that, Modesto."

"You have to open their eyes, Chief. The gringos are slow sometimes. It's not enough to attack Betancourt, Figueres, or Muñoz Marín. It would be more effective to give some very discreet help to the Venezuelan and Costa Rican Communists. And the Puerto Rican independence movement. When Kennedy sees guerrillas beginning to disrupt those countries, and compares that to the peace and quiet we have here, he'll get the idea."

"We'll talk later." The Generalissimo cut him off abruptly.

Hearing him talk about things in the past had a bad effect on him. No gloomy thoughts. He wanted to maintain the good mood he had when he started his walk. He forced himself to think about the girl with the flowers. "Dear God, do this for me. Tonight I need to fuck Yolanda Esterel right. So I can know I'm not dead. Not an old man. And can go on doing your work for you, moving this damn country of assholes forward. I don't care about the priests, the gringos, the conspirators, the exiles. I can clear away all that shit myself. But I need your help to fuck that girl. Don't be a miser, don't be stingy. Give me your help, give it to me." He sighed, with the disagreeable suspicion that the one he was pleading with, if he existed, must be observing him in amusement from the dark blue backdrop where the first stars had begun to appear.

His route along Máximo Gómez simmered with memories. The houses he was leaving behind were symbols of outstanding people and events in his thirty-one years of power. Ramfis's house, on the lot where Anselmo Paulino's had been; he had been his right hand for ten years until 1955, when he confiscated all his property, kept him in prison for a time, then sent him off to Switzerland with a check for seven million dollars for services rendered. Across from the house of Angelita and Pechito León Estévez had once stood the residence of General Ludovino Fernández, a workhorse who spilled a good deal of blood for the regime; he was obliged to kill him when he succumbed to political inconstancy. Next to Radhamés Manor were the gardens of the embassy of the United States, for more than twenty-eight years a friendly house that had turned into a nest of vipers. There was the field he had built so that Ramfis and Radhamés could have fun playing baseball. There, like twin sisters, stood Balaguer's house and the nunciature, another building that had turned irritating, ungrateful, vile. And beyond that, the imposing mansion of General Espaillat, his former head of secret services. Facing it, a little farther on, was the house of General Rodríguez Méndez, Ramfis's companion in dissipation. Then the embassies, deserted now, of Argentina and Mexico, and the house of his brother Blacky. And, finally, the residence of the Vicini family, the sugarcane millionaires, with its vast expanse of lawn and well-tended flower borders, which he was passing now.

As soon as he crossed the broad Avenida to walk along the Malecón, right next to the sea, on his way to the obelisk, he could feel the spatter of foam. He leaned against the wall, closed his eyes, and listened to the shrieking and flapping wings of flocks of seagulls. The wind filled his lungs. A purifying bath that would give him back his strength. But he mustn't be distracted; he still had work ahead of him.

"Call Johnny Abbes."

Detaching himself from the cluster of civilians and military men—the Generalissimo was walking quickly toward the cement column, a copy of the Washington Monument—the inelegant, flaccid figure of the head of the SIM took his place beside him. Despite his girth, Johnny Abbes García kept pace without difficulty.

"What's going on with Juan Tomás?" he asked, not looking at him.

"Nothing important, Excellency," the head of the SIM replied. "Today he went to his farm in Moca, with Antonio de la Maza. They brought back a bull calf. The general and his wife, Chana, quarreled because she said that cutting up and cooking a calf is a lot of work."

"Have Balaguer and Juan Tomás seen each other in the past few days?" Trujillo interrupted.

Since Abbes García did not answer immediately, he turned to look at him. The colonel shook his head.

"No, Excellency. As far as I know, they haven't seen each other for some time. Why do you ask?"

"Nothing concrete." The Generalissimo shrugged. "But just now, in his office, when I mentioned Juan Tomás's conspiracy, I noticed something strange. I *felt* something strange. I don't know what it was. Nothing in your reports to justify any suspicions of the President?"

"Nothing, Excellency. You know I have him under surveillance twenty-four hours a day. He doesn't make a move, he doesn't receive anyone, he doesn't make a phone call without our knowing about it."

Trujillo nodded. There was no reason to distrust the puppet president: his hunch could have been wrong. This plot didn't seem serious. Antonio de la Maza was one of the conspirators? Another resentful man who consoled himself for his frustrations with whiskey and huge meals. They'd be gorging on marinated unborn calf this evening. Suppose he burst into Juan Tomás's house in Gazcue? "Good evening, gentlemen. Do you mind sharing your barbecue with me? It smells so good! The aroma reached all the way to the Palace and led me here." Would their faces be filled with terror or joy? Would they think that his unexpected visit marked their rehabilitation? No, tonight he'd go to San Cristóbal, make Yolanda Esterel cry out, and feel healthy and young tomorrow.

"Why did you let Cabral's daughter leave for the United States two weeks ago?"

This time Colonel Abbes García really was surprised. He saw him run his hand over his pudgy cheeks, not knowing how to answer.

"Senator Agustín Cabral's daughter?" he mumbled, playing for time.

"Uranita Cabral, Egghead's daughter. The nuns at Santo Domingo gave her a scholarship to the United States. Why did you let her leave the country without consulting me?"

It seemed to him that the colonel was shrinking. He opened and closed his mouth, not knowing what to say.

"I'm sorry, Excellency," he exclaimed, lowering his head. "Your instructions were to follow the senator and arrest him if he tried to seek asylum. It didn't occur to me that the girl, having spent a night at Mahogany House and with an exit permit signed by President Balaguer . . . The truth is, it didn't even occur to me to mention it to you, I didn't think it was important."

"Those things should occur to you," Trujillo berated him. "I want you to investigate the personnel on my secretarial staff. Somebody hid a memo from Balaguer about that girl's trip. I want to know who it was and why he did it."

"Right away, Excellency. I apologize for this oversight. It won't happen again."

"I hope not," and Trujillo dismissed him.

The colonel gave him a military salute (it made him want to laugh) and rejoined the other courtiers. He walked a few blocks without calling anyone; he was thinking. Abbes García had only partially followed his instructions to withdraw the guards and *caliés*. At the corners he didn't see the fortified wire barricades, or the small Volkswagens, or the uniformed police with submachine guns. But from time to time, at the intersections along the Avenida, he could detect in the distance a black Beetle with the heads of *caliés* at the windows, or tough-looking civilians leaning against lampposts, pistols bulging under their armpits. Traffic had not been stopped along Avenida George Washington. People leaned out of trucks and cars and waved to him: "Long live the Chief!" Absorbed in the effort of the walk, which had made his body deliciously warm and his legs a little tired, he waved back his thanks. There were no adult pedestrians on the Avenida, only ragged children, shoeshine boys and vendors of chocolates and cigarettes, who looked at him openmouthed. As he passed, he patted their heads or tossed them some coins (he always carried change in his pockets). A short while later, he called the Walking Turd.

Senator Chirinos approached, panting like a hunting dog, and perspiring more than Modesto Díaz. The Benefactor felt encouraged. The Constitutional Sot was younger than he, and a short walk demolished him. Instead of responding to his "Good afternoon, Chief," he asked:

"Did you call Ramfis? Did he give his explanations to Lloyds of London?"

"I spoke to him twice." Senator Chirinos was dragging his feet, and the soles and tips of his misshapen shoes stumbled over paving stones raised by the roots of ancient palms and almond trees. "I explained the problem to him and repeated your orders. Well, you can imagine. But finally he accepted my reasoning. He promised to write to Lloyds, clarify the misunderstanding, and confirm that payment should be transferred to the Central Bank."

"Has he done it?" Trujillo interrupted brusquely.

"That's why I called him a second time, Chief. He wants a translator to correct his telegram. His English is imperfect and he doesn't want mistakes. He'll send it without fail. He told me he's sorry about what happened."

Did Ramfis think he was getting too old to obey him? There was a time when he wouldn't have put off following an order of his with such a trivial excuse.

"Call him again," he ordered, in a bad humor. "If he doesn't straighten out this business with Lloyds today, he'll have to deal with me."

"Right away, Chief. But don't worry, Ramfis has understood the situation."

He dismissed Chirinos and resigned himself to finishing his walk alone so as not to dash the hopes of others who yearned to exchange a few words with him. He waited for his human train and joined it, positioning himself with Virgilio Álvarez Pina and the Minister of the Interior and Religious Practice, Paíno Pichardo. The group also included Razor Espaillat, the Chief of Police, the editor of *El Caribe*, and the new President of the Senate, Jeremías (Monkey) Quintanilla, to whom he offered his congratulations and best wishes for success. The man gleamed with happiness as he poured out his thanks. At the same swift pace, still walking east on the side of the street that hugged the ocean, he asked, in a loud voice:

"Come, gentlemen, tell me the latest anti-Trujillista stories."

A wave of laughter celebrated his witticism, and a few moments later they were all chattering like parrots. Pretending to listen, he nodded and smiled. At times he caught sight of the dejected face of General José René (Pupo) Román. The Minister of the Armed Forces could not hide his anguish: what would the Chief reproach him for? You'll find out soon enough, imbecile. Moving from group to group so that no one would feel overlooked, he crossed the well-tended gardens of the Hotel Jaragua, where he heard the sounds of the orchestra that played for cocktail hour, and a block after that he passed under the balconies of the Dominican Party. Clerks and secretaries and the people who had gone there to ask for favors came out to applaud him. When he reached the obelisk, he looked at his watch: an hour and three minutes. It was growing dark. The gulls had stopped circling and had gone back to their hiding places on the beach. A handful of stars were visible, but big-bellied clouds hid the moon. At the foot of the obelisk, the new Cadillac, driven for the first time last week, was waiting for him. He said a collective goodbye ("Good evening, gentlemen, thank you for your company") while, at the same time, not looking at him, with an imperious gesture, he pointed General José René Román to the car door that the uniformed chauffeur held open:

"You, come with me."

General Román—an energetic click of his heels, a hand at the visor of his cap—quickly obeyed. He climbed into the car and sat on the edge of the seat, very erect, his hat on his knees.

"To San Isidro, the base."

As the official car drove toward the center of the city in order to cross to the eastern bank of the Ozama on the Radhamés Bridge, Trujillo contemplated the landscape, as if he were alone. General Román did not dare say a word, waiting for the storm to break. It began to loom when they had covered about three of the ten miles that separated the obelisk from the air base.

"How old are you?" he asked, without turning to look at him.

"I just turned fifty-six, Chief."

Román—everyone called him Pupo—was tall, strong, and athletic, with a very close crew cut. He played sports and maintained an excellent physique, without a trace of fat. He replied very quietly, humbly, trying to placate him.

"How many years in the Army?" Trujillo continued, looking out the window, as if he were questioning someone who wasn't there.

"Thirty-one, Chief, ever since my graduation."

He allowed a few seconds to go by without saying anything. Finally he turned toward the head of the Armed Forces, with the infinite contempt the man always inspired in him. In the shadows, which had deepened rapidly, he could not see his eyes, but he was sure that Pupo Román was blinking, or had his eyes half closed, like children when they wake at night and squint fearfully into the darkness.

"And in all those years you haven't learned that a superior answers for his subordinates? That he is responsible for their mistakes?"

"I know that very well, Chief. If you tell me what this is about, perhaps I can give you an explanation."

"You'll see what it's about," said Trujillo, with the apparent calm his collaborators feared more than his shouting. "You bathe with soap every day?"

"Of course, Chief." General Román tried to laugh, but since the Generalissimo was still very serious, he fell silent.

"I hope so, for Mireya's sake. I think it's fine that you bathe with soap every day, that your uniform is well pressed and your shoes shined. As head of the Armed Forces you're obliged to set an example of cleanliness and proper appearance for Dominican officers and soldiers. Isn't that true?"

"Of course it is, Chief." The general groveled. "I beg you to tell me how I've failed. So I can set things right and make amends. I don't want to disappoint you."

"Appearance is the mirror of the soul," Trujillo philosophized. "If somebody goes around smelling bad with snot running out of his nose, he isn't a person who can be entrusted with public hygiene. Don't you agree?"

"Of course, Chief."

"The same is true of institutions. What respect can you have for them if they don't even tend to their appearance?"

General Román chose not to speak. The Generalissimo had become more incensed and did not stop rebuking him for the fifteen minutes it took to reach San Isidro Air Base. He reminded Pupo how sorry he had been when the daughter of his sister Marina was crazy enough to marry a mediocre officer like him, which he still was despite the fact that because of his relationship by marriage to the Benefactor, he had been promoted to the very top of the hierarchy. These privileges, rather than motivating him, had led him to rest on his laurels and betray Trujillo's confidence a thousand times over. Not content with being the nonentity he was as an officer, he had taken up farming, as if you didn't need brains to raise cattle and manage lands and dairies. What was the result? He was drowning in debt and was an embarrassment to the family. Barely eighteen days ago he had personally paid with his own money the four-hundred-thousand-peso debt Román had contracted with the Agrarian Bank, so that the farm at kilometer fourteen on the Duarte Highway would not be put up for auction. And despite that, he made no effort to stop being a fool.

General José René Román Fernández remained mute and motionless as the recriminations and insults poured down on him. Trujillo did not rush; rage made him speak carefully, as if, in this way, each syllable, each letter, would strike a harder blow. The chauffeur drove at high speed, not deviating a millimeter from the center of the deserted highway.

"Stop," Trujillo ordered a little before the first sentry post along the fence that encircled the sprawling San Isidro Air Base.

He jumped out, and despite the dark, he immediately located the large puddle of pestilential water. Sewage was still pouring out of the broken pipe, and in addition to mud and filth, the air was thick with mosquitoes that rushed to the attack.

"The leading military installation in the Republic," Trujillo said slowly, barely containing a new surge of rage. "Does it seem right to you that at the entrance to the most important air base in the Caribbean, the visitor is greeted by this stinking shit pile of garbage, mud, and vermin?"

Román squatted down. He inspected, stood up, bent down again, did not hesitate to dirty his hands as he felt along the sewage pipe, looking for the break. He seemed relieved to discover the reason for the Chief's anger. Had the idiot been afraid of something more serious?

"It's a disgrace, no doubt about it." He tried to display more indignation than he felt. "I'll take all necessary steps to make certain the damage is repaired immediately, Excellency. I'll punish those responsible, from top to bottom."

"Beginning with Virgilio García Trujillo, the commander of the base," the Benefactor roared. "You're the first one responsible, and he's the second. I hope you have the courage to impose the most severe sanctions on him, even though he's my nephew and your brother-in-law. And if you don't have the courage, I'll be the one who'll impose them on both of you. Not you, not Virgilio, not any of you shitty little generals is going to destroy my work. The Armed Forces will continue to be the model institution I created, even if I have to throw you and Virgilio and all the rest of you uniformed bunglers into jail for the rest of your lives."

General Román came to attention and clicked his heels.

"Yes, Excellency. It won't happen again, I swear."

But Trujillo had already turned and was climbing into the car.

"Too bad for you if there's any trace of what I'm seeing and smelling now when I come back here. Fucking tin soldier!"

Turning to the chauffeur, he ordered: "Let's go." They pulled away, leaving the Minister of the Armed Forces in the mudhole.

As soon as he left Román behind, a pathetic figure splashing in the muck, his bad temper vanished. He gave a little laugh. He was sure about one thing: Pupo would move heaven and earth and curse out everybody necessary to make sure the pipe was repaired. If this kind of thing went on while he was alive, what would happen when he could no longer personally keep laziness, negligence, and imbecility from tearing down what it had cost him so much effort to build up? Would anarchy and misery, the backwardness and isolation of 1930, return? Ah, if only Ramfis, the son he had longed for, were capable of continuing his work. But he did not have the slightest interest in politics or the country; all he cared about was booze, polo, and women. Fuck! General Ramfis Trujillo, head of the General Staff of the Armed Forces of the Dominican Republic, playing polo and fucking the dancers at the Lido in Paris while his father did battle here alone against the Church, the United States, conspirators, and cretins like Pupo Román. He moved his head, trying to shake off those bitter thoughts. In an hour and a half he would be in San Cristóbal, in the peaceful refuge of the Fundación Ranch, surrounded by fields and gleaming stables, beautiful woods, the broad Nigua River, whose unhurried movement through the valley he would observe through the tops of mahogany trees, royal palms, and the great cashew tree by the house on the hill. It would do him good to wake there tomorrow, stroking the sweet little body of Yolanda Esterel as he contemplated the tranquil, unsullied landscape. It was the prescription of Petronius and King Solomon: a fresh little cunt to restore youth to a veteran of seventy years.

At Radhamés Manor, Zacarías de la Cruz had already taken out the light blue four-door 1957 Bel Air Chevrolet in which he always drove to San Cristóbal. A military adjutant was waiting for him with the briefcase full of documents that he would study tomorrow at Mahogany House, and 110,000 pesos in bills, for the ranch payroll, plus incidental expenses. For twenty years he had not gone anywhere, even for a few hours, without the dark brown briefcase with his engraved initials, and a few thousand dollars or pesos in cash for gifts and incidental expenses. He indicated to the adjutant that he should put the briefcase in the back seat and told Zacarías, the tall, husky black who had been with him for three decades—he had been his orderly in the Army—that he would be right down. Nine o'clock already. It was getting late.

He went up to his rooms to clean up, and as soon as he walked in the bathroom, he saw the stain. On his fly and down his leg. He felt himself trembling from head to foot: it had to happen now, damn it. He asked Sinforoso for another olive green uniform and another change of underwear. He lost fifteen minutes at the bidet and sink, soaping his testicles, his penis, his face, and his armpits, and applying creams and perfumes before he changed. His attack of bad humor, brought on by that shiteating Pupo, was to blame. Again he sank into a state of gloom. It was a bad omen for San Cristóbal. While he was dressing, Sinforoso handed him a telegram: "Lloyds matter resolved. Spoke with person in charge. Remittance directly to Central Bank. Fond regards Ramfis." His son was ashamed: that's why he sent a telegram instead of calling him.

"We're a little late, Zacarías," he said. "So step on it."

"Understood, Chief."

He leaned back against the cushioned seat and closed his eyes, prepared to rest for the hour and ten minutes the trip to San Cristóbal would take. They were driving to the southwest, toward Avenida George Washington and the highway, when he opened his eyes:

"Do you remember Moni's house, Zacarías?"

"On Wenceslao Álvarez, near where Marrero Aristy lived?"

"Let's go there."

It had been an illumination, a lightning flash. Suddenly he saw Moni's round little cinnamon-colored face, her curly mane of hair, the mischief in her star-filled almond eyes, her compact shape, high breasts, sweet ass with firm buttocks, voluptuous hips, and again he felt the delicious tingling in his testicles. The head of his penis woke up and brushed against his trousers. Moni. Why not? She was a pretty, affectionate girl who had never disappointed him, not since the time in Quinigua when her father in person brought her to the party the Americans from La Yuquera were holding for him: "Look at the surprise I have for you, Chief." The little house where she lived, in the new development at the end of Avenida México, was his present to her on the day she married a boy from a good family. When he required her, from time to time, he took her to one of the suites at El Embajador or El Jaragua that Manuel Alfonso kept ready for such occasions. The idea of fucking Moni in her own house excited him. They'd send her husband out for a beer at Rincón Pony, as Trujillo's guest—he laughed—or he could pass the time talking to Zacarías de la Cruz.

The street was dark and deserted, but a light was burning on the first floor of the house. "Call her." He saw the driver walk through the front gate and ring the bell. It took a while for anyone to answer. Finally, a maid must have come to the door, and Zacarías spoke to her in whispers. He was left at the door, waiting. Beautiful Moni! Her father had been a good leader of the Dominican Party in Cibao, and he brought her to the reception himself, a nice gesture. That was a few years ago now, and the truth was that every time he fucked this good-looking woman he felt very happy. The door opened again, and in the light coming from the house he saw Moni's silhouette. He felt another surge of excitement. After speaking for a moment with Zacarías, she walked to the car. In the darkness he couldn't see what she was wearing. He opened the door to let her in, and welcomed her with a kiss on the hand:

"You weren't expecting a visit from me, beautiful."

"Really, what an honor. How are you, Chief, how are you?"

Trujillo kept her hand between his. Feeling her so close, touching her, inhaling her scent, he felt in control of all his powers.

"I was going to San Cristóbal, but suddenly I thought of you."

"What an honor, Chief," she repeated, flustered and confused. "If I had known, I would have fixed myself up to receive you."

"You're always beautiful, fixed up or not." He pulled her to him, and as his hands caressed her breasts and legs, he kissed her. He felt the beginnings of an erection that reconciled him with the world and with life. Moni let herself be caressed, and she kissed him, with some restraint. Zacarías stood outside, a few meters from the Chevrolet, on guard as always, holding a submachine gun. What was going on? There was an edginess in Moni that was unusual.

"Is your husband home?"

"Yes," she replied, in a quiet voice. "We were about to eat."

"Have him go out for a beer," said Trujillo. "I'll go around the block. I'll be back in five minutes."

"It's just that . . . ," she stammered, and the Generalissimo felt her tensing. She hesitated, and finally she mumbled, almost inaudibly: "I have the curse, Chief."

All his excitement left him in a matter of seconds.

"Your period?" he exclaimed in disappointment.

"Please forgive me, Chief," she stammered. "The day after tomorrow I'll be fine."

He let her go and sighed deeply, repulsed.

"All right, I'll come see you soon. Goodbye." He leaned his head toward the open door through which Moni had just left. "We're leaving, Zacarías!"

A short while later he asked De la Cruz if he had ever fucked a menstruating woman.

"Never, Chief." He was shocked, and made a disgusted face. "They say it gives you syphilis."

"And worst of all, it's dirty," Trujillo lamented. What if Yolanda Esterel, by some damn coincidence, had her period today too?

They had taken the highway to San Cristóbal, and on the right he saw the lights of the Livestock Fairgrounds and the Pony, crowded with couples eating and drinking. Wasn't it strange that Moni seemed so reluctant and inhibited? She was usually so sassy, ready for anything. Did the presence of her husband make her like that? Could she have invented a period so he'd leave her alone? Vaguely he noticed that a car was blowing its horn at them. Its brights were on.

"These drunks . . . ," Zacarías de la Cruz remarked.

At that moment, it occurred to Trujillo that perhaps it wasn't a drunk, and he turned to get the revolver he carried in the back seat, but he couldn't reach it, because at that moment he heard the blast of a rifle whose bullets shattered the glass in the back window and tore off a piece of his shoulder and his left arm.

19 When General Juan Tomás Díaz, his brother Modesto, and Luis Amiama came back, and Antonio de la Maza saw their faces, he knew before they opened their mouths that the search for General Román had been futile.

"It's hard to believe," murmured Luis Amiama, biting his thin lips. "But it looks like Pupo skipped out on us. There's no sign of him."

They had gone everywhere he could have been, including the General Staff Headquarters at December 18 Fortress; but Luis Amiama and Bibín Román, Pupo's younger brother, had been thrown out in a very unpleasant way by the guards: their compadre could not or would not see them.

"My last hope is that he's putting the Plan into effect on his own," Modesto Díaz fantasized, without much conviction. "Mobilizing installations, persuading military leaders. In any event, we're in a very compromised situation right now."

They were standing in the living room of General Juan Tomás Díaz's house. Chana, his young wife, served them glasses of lemonade with ice.

"We have to hide until we know what's going on with Pupo," said General Juan Tomás Díaz.

Antonio de la Maza, who had not spoken yet, felt a wave of anger coursing through his body.

"Hide?" he exclaimed in a rage. "Cowards hide. Let's finish the job, Juan Tomás. Put on your general's uniform, give us some uniforms, and we'll go to the Palace. And that's where we'll call for a popular uprising."

"You want the four of us to take the Palace?" Luis Amiama tried to reason with him. "Have you gone crazy, Antonio?"

"Nobody's there now, just the guards," he insisted. "We have to force the hand of the Trujillistas before they can react. We'll call on the people, we can use the Palace connection to every radio station in the country. We'll tell them to take to the streets. In the end, the Army will support us."

The skeptical expressions of Juan Tomás, Amiama, and Modesto Díaz made him even angrier. They were soon joined by Salvador Estrella Sadhalá, who had just left Antonio Imbert and Amadito at the doctor's office, and Dr. Vélez Santana, who had taken Pedro Livio Cedeño to the International Clinic. They were devastated by the disappearance of Pupo Román. They agreed that Antonio's idea of infiltrating the National Palace disguised as officers was futile and rash, an act of suicide. And all of them energetically opposed Antonio's new proposal: to take the body of Trujillo to Independencia Park and hang it from the parapet so that residents of the capital could see how he had died. Rejection by his friends provoked one of those fits of uncontrolled rage De la Maza had recently been subject to. Cowards! Traitors! They weren't equal to what they had done, ridding the Nation of the Beast! When he saw Chana Díaz come into the living room, her eyes terrified by the shouting, he realized he had gone too far. He muttered apologies to his friends and fell silent. But he felt waves of nausea inside.

"We're all upset, Antonio," said Luis Amiama, patting him on the shoulder. "The important thing now is to find a safe place. Until Pupo shows up. And we see how the people react when they find out Trujillo is dead."

An ashen Antonio de la Maza nodded. Yes, after all, Amiama, who had worked so hard to bring the military and highly placed officials in the regime into the conspiracy, perhaps he was right.

Luis Amiama and Modesto Díaz decided to go their separate ways; they thought they had a better chance of avoiding detection if each was on his own. Antonio persuaded Juan Tomás and Turk Sadhalá that they should stay together. They went through possibilities—relatives, friends—and discarded them; the police would search all those houses. Vélez Santana was the one who came up with an acceptable name:

"Robert Reid Cabral. He's a friend of mine. Totally apolitical, all he cares about is medicine. He won't refuse."

He drove them in his car. General Díaz and Turk didn't know Robert personally, but Antonio de la Maza was a friend of his older brother, Donald Reid Cabral, who was working in Washington and New York in support of the conspiracy. The young doctor was dumbfounded at being awakened close to midnight. He knew nothing about the plot; he wasn't even aware that his brother Donald was collaborating with the Americans. But as soon as he regained his color and his power of speech, he hurried them into his small, Moorish-style, two-story house, which was so narrow it looked like something out of a fairy tale. He was a clean-shaven boy with kindhearted eyes who made a superhuman effort to hide his consternation. He introduced them to his wife, Ligia, who was several months pregnant. She accepted the invasion by strangers good-naturedly, without much apprehension. She showed them her two-year-old son, who slept in a corner of the dining room.

The young couple led the conspirators to a narrow little room on the top floor that was used as an attic storeroom. It had almost no ventilation, and the low ceiling made the heat intolerable. There was room for them only if they sat with their legs drawn up, and they had to crouch when they stood to avoid hitting their heads on the beams. On that first night they hardly noticed the discomfort and the heat; they spent the time whispering, trying to guess what had happened to Pupo Román: why did he drop out of sight when everything depended on him? General Díaz recalled his conversation with Pupo on May 24, Román's birthday, on his farm at kilometer fourteen. He had assured him and Luis Amiama that he was ready to mobilize the Armed Forces as soon as they showed him the body.

Marcelino Vélez Santana stayed with them, out of solidarity, for he had no reason to hide. The next morning he went out to learn the news. He returned a little before noon, highly agitated. There was no sign of a military uprising. On the contrary, one could see a frantic mobilization of SIM Beetles and jeeps and military trucks. Patrols were searching all the neighborhoods. There were rumors that hundreds of men, women, old people, and children were being dragged from their houses and taken to La Victoria, El Nueve, or La Cuarenta. In the interior as well, those suspected of anti-Trujillism were being rounded up. A colleague from La Vega told Dr. Vélez Santana that the entire De la Maza family, beginning with the father, Don Vicente, and including all of Antonio's brothers, sisters, nephews, nieces, and cousins, had been arrested in Moca. That city was now occupied by guards and *caliés*. The houses of Juan Tomás, his brother Modesto, Imbert, and Salvador were all surrounded by barbed-wire barricades and armed guards.

Antonio said nothing. He was not surprised. He always knew that if the plot did not succeed, the regime's response would be unimaginably brutal. His heart constricted as he thought of his aged father, Don Vicente, and his brothers abused and mistreated by Abbes García. At about one o'clock, two black Volkswagens filled with *caliés* appeared on the street. Ligia, Reid Cabral's wife—he had gone to his office so as not to arouse the neighbors' suspicions—came to tell them in whispers that men wearing civilian clothes and carrying submachine guns were searching a nearby house. Antonio exploded in a string of curses (though he kept his voice low):

"You should have listened to me, assholes. Wouldn't it be better to die fighting in the Palace than to be trapped here like rats?"

Throughout the day they kept arguing and reproaching one another. During one of these disputes, Vélez Santana erupted. He grabbed General Juan Tomás Díaz by the shirt and accused him of involving him for no reason in a stupid, absurd plot that hadn't even made provision for the conspirators' escape. Did he have any idea what would happen to them now? Turk Estrella Sadhalá came between them to prevent a fistfight. Antonio controlled his desire to vomit.

On the second night, they were so exhausted by arguments and insults that they slept, huddled together, using one another as pillows, dripping perspiration, almost suffocating in the burning air.

On the third day, when Dr. Vélez Santana brought a copy of *El Caribe* to their hiding place and they saw their photographs under a huge headline: "Killers Sought in Trujillo Murder," and, below that, the photograph of General Román Fernández embracing Ramfis at the Generalissimo's funeral, they knew they were lost. There would be no civilian-military junta. Ramfis and Radhamés had returned, and the entire country was mourning the dictator.

"Pupo betrayed us." General Juan Tomás Díaz seemed to be foundering. He had taken off his shoes, his feet were very swollen, and he was gasping for breath.

"We have to get out of here," said Antonio de la Maza. "We can't fuck up this family. If they find us here, they'll kill them too."

"You're right," Turk agreed. "It wouldn't be fair. We have to leave."

Where would they go? They spent all of June 2 considering possible flight plans. Shortly before noon, two Beetles carrying *caliés* pulled up to the house across the way and half a dozen armed men forced the door and went in. Alerted by Ligia, they waited, guns at the ready. But the *caliés* left after dragging out a young man in handcuffs. Of all the suggestions, Antonio's seemed the best: get hold of a car or van and try to reach Restauración, where he knew a good many people because he owned pine and coffee plantations there, and managed Trujillo's sawmill. It was so close to the border, it wouldn't be difficult to cross over into Haiti. But where would they find a car? Who would lend them one? They didn't get any sleep that night either, tormented by apprehension, fatigue, despair, and doubt. At midnight, Reid Cabral came up to their garret with tears in his eyes:

"They've searched three houses on this street," he pleaded. "Any minute now it'll be my turn. I don't care about dying. But what about my wife and little boy? And the baby she's carrying?"

They swore they'd leave the next day, no matter what. And they did, at dusk on June 4. Salvador Estrella Sadhalá decided to go alone. He didn't know where, but thought he had more chance of getting away on his own than with Juan Tomás and Antonio, whose names and faces were the ones appearing most frequently on television and in the papers. Turk was the first to leave, at ten minutes to six, when it was beginning to grow dark. Through the blinds in Reid Cabral's bedroom, Antonio de la Maza watched him walk quickly to the corner, where he raised his hand and hailed a cab. He felt very troubled: Turk had been his closest friend, and they had never completely reconciled after that damn fight. There wouldn't be another chance.

Dr. Marcelino Vélez Santana decided to stay a little while longer with his colleague and friend, Dr. Reid Cabral, who seemed overwhelmed. Antonio shaved his mustache, put on an old hat he found in the attic, and pulled it down over his ears. Juan Tomás Díaz, however, made no effort to disguise himself. They both embraced Dr. Vélez Santana.

"No hard feelings?"

"No hard feelings. Good luck."

Ligia Reid Cabral, when they thanked her for her hospitality, burst into tears and made the sign of the cross over them: "May God protect you."

They walked eight blocks along deserted streets, their hands in their pockets, clutching their revolvers, until they reached the house of Antonio de la Maza's brother-in-law, Toñito Mota. He had a Ford van; perhaps he'd lend it to them, or agree to let them steal it. But Toñito wasn't home, and the van wasn't in the garage. The servant who opened the door recognized De la Maza immediately: "Don Antonio! What are you doing here?" He had a horrified look on his face, and Antonio and the general, certain he would call the police as soon as they left, hurried away. They didn't know what the hell to do.

"Shall I tell you something, Juan Tomás?"

"What, Antonio?"

"I'm glad to be out of that rattrap. That heat, the dust that got in your nose and didn't let you breathe. The discomfort. It's good to be in the fresh air and feel your lungs clearing out."

"The only thing I need is for you to say: 'Let's go have a couple of beers and celebrate how beautiful life is.' Brother, you have a lot of balls!"

They both broke into intense, fleeting little laughs. On Avenida Pasteur they tried for a long time to hail a cab. The ones that passed had passengers.

"I'm sorry I wasn't with you on the Avenida," General Díaz said suddenly, as if remembering something important. "And didn't have the chance to shoot the Goat. Damn it to hell!"

"It's as if you had been there, Juan Tomás. Just ask Johnny Abbes, Blacky, Petán, and Ramfis, then you'll see. As far as they're concerned, you were with us on the highway pumping the Chief full of lead. Don't worry. I fired one of those shots for you."

Finally a taxi stopped. They climbed in, and when they didn't tell him right away where they wanted to go, the driver, a fat, gray-haired black in shirtsleeves, turned to look at them. Antonio de la Maza saw in his eyes that he had recognized them.

"To San Martín," he told him.

The driver nodded, not saying a word. A short while later, he murmured that he was running out of gas; he had to fill the tank. He drove along March 30, where the traffic was heavy, and stopped at a Texaco station at the corner of San Martín and Tiradentes. He got out of the car to open the gas tank. Now Antonio and Juan Tomás held the revolvers in their hands. De la Maza took off his right shoe, twisted the heel, and removed a small cellophane bag, which he put in his pocket. Juan Tomás looked at him, intrigued, and Antonio explained:

"It's strychnine. I got it in Moca; I said it was for a rabid dog."

The fat general shrugged disdainfully, and showed him his revolver:

"There's no better strychnine than this, brother. Poison is for dogs and women, don't fuck around with bullshit like that. Besides, asshole, you commit suicide with cyanide, not strychnine."

They laughed again, with the same fierce, sad little laugh.

"Did you notice the guy at the register?" Antonio de la Maza pointed at the cashier's window. "Who do you think he's calling?"

"Maybe his wife, to ask how her pussy's doing."

Antonio de la Maza laughed again, a real, long, open laugh this time.

"What the fuck are you laughing at, asshole?"

"Don't you think it's funny?" asked Antonio, who was serious again. "The two of us in this taxi. What the hell are we doing here? We don't even know where we're going."

They told the driver to go back to the colonial district. Antonio had thought of something, and once they were in the old city, they told him to turn onto Calle Espaillat from Billini. Generoso Fernández, an attorney whom they both knew, lived there. Antonio recalled hearing him say the most bitter things about Trujillo; perhaps he could get them a car. The lawyer came to the door but did not ask them in. When he recovered from the shock—he looked at them in horror, blinking—all he could do in his indignation was berate them:

"Are you crazy? How can you compromise me like this? Don't you know who went into the house across the street just a minute ago? The Constitutional Sot! Couldn't you stop and think before doing this to me? Get away, go on, I have a family. For God's sake, leave! I'm nobody, nobody."

He slammed the door in their faces. They went back to the cab. The old black was still sitting docilely at the wheel, not looking at them. After a while he mumbled:

"Where to now?"

"To Independencia Park," Antonio told him, just to say something.

Seconds after he pulled away—the streetlamps at the corners had turned on and people were coming out on the sidewalks to enjoy the cool air—the driver alerted them:

"There are Beetles behind us. I'm really sorry, gentlemen."

Antonio felt relieved. This ridiculous trip to nowhere was finally ending. Better to go out shooting than like a couple of assholes. They turned around. Two green Volkswagens were following them at a distance of about ten meters.

"I don't want to die, gentlemen," the driver pleaded, crossing himself. "By the Blessed Virgin, please!"

"Okay, get to the park however you can and drop us at the corner by the hardware store," said Antonio.

There was a good deal of traffic. The driver maneuvered his way between a truck and bus with clusters of people hanging from the doors. He braked hard a few meters from the large plate-glass windows of the Reid hardware store. When he jumped out of the cab, with his revolver in his hand, Antonio noticed that the lights in the park were coming on, as if to welcome them. There were shoeshine boys, street peddlers, cardplayers, bums and beggars leaning against the walls. It smelled of fruit and fried food. He turned around to hurry along Juan Tomás, who was fat and tired, and could not keep up with him. At that moment, shots broke out behind him. There were deafening screams all around him; people ran between cars, and automobiles drove onto the sidewalks. Antonio heard hysterical voices: "Surrender, damn it!" "You're surrounded, assholes!" When he saw that Juan Tomás was stopping, exhausted, he stopped too, beside him, and began to shoot. He fired blindly, because *caliés* and guards were hiding behind the Volkswagens that crisscrossed the road like parapets, blocking traffic. He saw Juan Tomás fall to his knees and raise the pistol to his mouth, but he couldn't fire because the impact of several shots knocked him down. By now Antonio had been hit by a number of bullets, but he wasn't dead. "I'm not dead, shit, I'm not dead." He had fired all the rounds in his clip, and as he lay on the ground, he tried to slip his hand into his pocket and swallow the strychnine. His damn fucking hand did not obey him. No need, Antonio. He could see the brilliant stars in the night that was just beginning, he could see Tavito's smiling face, and he felt young again.

20 When the Chief's limousine pulled away and left him in the stinking mudhole, General José René Román was trembling from head to toe, like the soldiers he had seen dying of malaria in Dajabón, a garrison on the Haitian-Dominican border, at the start of his military career. For many years Trujillo had been brutal with him before family and strangers, making him feel how little respect he had for him, using any excuse to call him an idiot. But he had never carried his contempt and insults to the extremes he had shown tonight.

He waited for the trembling to pass before walking to San Isidro Air Base. The guard on duty was shocked to see the head of the Armed Forces appear on foot and covered in mud, in the middle of the night. General Virgilio García Trujillo, commander of San Isidro and Román's brother-in-law—he was Mireya's twin brother—was not there, but the Minister of the Armed Forces called all the other officers together and reprimanded them: the broken pipe that had enraged His Excellency had to be repaired immediately or the punishments would be severe. The Chief would come back to check, and they all knew he was implacable with regard to cleanliness. He ordered a jeep and driver to take him home; he didn't change or clean up before he left.

In the jeep, on the way to Ciudad Trujillo, he told himself that his trembling was not really due to the Chief's insults but to the tension he had felt since the phone call letting him know the Benefactor was angry with him. Throughout the day, he told himself a thousand times over that it was impossible, absolutely impossible, that he had found out about the conspiracy plotted by his compadre Luis Amiama and his close friend General Juan Tomás Díaz. He wouldn't have phoned; he would have had him arrested and he'd be in La Cuarenta now, or El Nueve. And yet the little worm of doubt did not allow him to eat a mouthful at supper. Well, in spite of the terrible time he had been put through, it was a relief that the Chief's insults were caused by a broken sewage pipe and not a conspiracy. The mere thought of Trujillo finding out that he was one of the conspirators made his blood run cold.

He could be accused of many things, but not cowardice. From the time he was a cadet, and in all his postings, he had shown physical daring and displayed a courage in the face of danger that earned him a reputation for machismo among officers and subordinates. He was always good at boxing, with gloves or bare fists. He never allowed anyone to treat him with disrespect. But, like so many officers, so many Dominicans, before Trujillo his valor and sense of honor disappeared, and he was overcome by a paralysis of his reason and his muscles, by servile obedience and reverence. He often had asked himself why the mere presence of the Chief—his high-pitched voice and the fixity of his gaze—annihilated him morally.

Because he knew the power Trujillo had over his character, General Román's immediate response to Luis Amiama when he first spoke to him, five and a half months earlier, about a conspiracy to put an end to the regime, had been:

"Abduct him? That's bullshit! As long as he's alive nothing will change. You have to kill him."

They were on Luis Amiama's banana plantation in Guayubín, Montecristi, sitting on a sunny terrace and watching the muddy water of the Yaque River as it flowed past. His compadre explained that he and Juan Tomás were organizing this operation to keep the regime from ruining the country completely and precipitating another Cuban-style Communist revolution. It was a serious plan that had the support of the United States. Henry Dearborn, John Banfield, and Bob Owen, at the legation, had given their formal backing and made the head of the CIA in Ciudad Trujillo, Lorenzo D. Berry ("The owner of Wimpy's Supermarket?" "That's right"), responsible for supplying them with money, weapons, and explosives. The United States, uneasy about Trujillo's excesses ever since the attempt on the life of the Venezuelan President, Rómulo Betancourt, wanted to get rid of him; at the same time, they wanted to be sure he would not be replaced by a second Fidel

Castro. This was why they were backing a serious, clearly anti-Communist group that would establish a civilian-military junta and hold elections within six months. Amiama, Juan Tomás Díaz, and the gringos were in agreement: Pupo Román should preside over the junta. There was no one better to secure the cooperation of the military and an orderly transition to democracy.

"Abduct him, ask him to resign?" Pupo was appalled. "You've got the wrong country and the wrong man, compadre. Don't you know him? He'll never let you take him alive. And you'll never get him to resign. You have to kill him."

The driver of the jeep, a sergeant, was silent, and Román took deep drags from a Lucky Strike, his favorite brand of cigarettes. Why had he agreed to join the conspiracy? Unlike Juan Tomás, in disgrace and cashiered from the Army, he had everything to lose. He had reached the highest position a military man could aspire to, and though things weren't going well for him in business, his farms still belonged to him. The danger that they would be seized had disappeared with the payment of four hundred thousand pesos to the Agrarian Bank. The Chief didn't cover the debt out of respect for his person, but because of his arrogant feeling that the family must never look bad, that the image of the Trujillos and their relations must always be spotless. And it wasn't an appetite for power, the prospect of being named Provisional President of the Dominican Republic—and the possibility, which was very real, of then becoming the elected President—that led him to give his support to the conspiracy. It was rancor, the accumulated effect of the infinite offenses to which Trujillo had subjected him since his marriage to Mireya, which had made him a member of the privileged, untouchable clan. That was why the Chief had promoted him over other men, appointed him to important positions, and occasionally presented him with gifts of cash or sinecures that allowed him to enjoy a high standard of living. But he had to pay for the favors and distinctions by accepting arrogance and abuse. "And that matters more," he thought.

During these five and a half months, each time the Chief humiliated him, General Román, as he did now while the jeep was crossing Radhamés Bridge, told himself that he soon would feel like a whole man, with his own life, even though Trujillo went out of his way to make him feel absolutely worthless. Luis Amiama and Juan Tomás might not suspect it, but he was in the conspiracy to prove to the Chief that he wasn't the incompetent fool Trujillo believed him to be.

His conditions were very concrete. He would not lift a finger until he saw with his own eyes that the Chief had been executed. Only then would he proceed to mobilize troops and capture the Trujillo brothers and the officers and civilians most involved with the regime, starting with Johnny Abbes García. Luis Amiama and General Díaz must not mention to anyone—not even the head of the action group, Antonio de la Maza—that he was part of the conspiracy. There would be no written messages or telephone calls, only direct conversations. He would cautiously begin to place officers he trusted in key posts, so that when the day arrived all the installations would obey his orders.

This is what he had done, naming his classmate and close friend General César A. Oliva as the head of the Fortress of Santiago de los Caballeros, the second largest in the country. He also arranged to appoint General García Urbáez, a loyal ally, as commander of the Fourth Brigade, stationed in Dajabón. And he was counting on General Guarionex Estrella, commander of the Second Brigade, in La Vega. He wasn't very friendly with Guaro, an avid Trujillista, but he was the brother of Turk Estrella Sadhalá, who was in the action group, and it was logical to suppose he would side with his brother. He hadn't confided his secret to any of those generals; he was too clever to risk a denunciation. But he was sure that as events unfolded, they would all come over without hesitation.

When would it happen? Very soon, most likely. On his birthday, May 24, just six days earlier, Luis Amiama and Juan Tomás Díaz, whom he had invited to his country house, assured him that everything was ready. Juan Tomás was categorical: "Any day now, Pupo." They told him that President Joaquín Balaguer had probably agreed to be part of the civilian-military junta over which he would preside. He asked for details, but they couldn't give him any; the approach had been made by Dr. Rafael Batlle Viñas, married to Indiana, Antonio de la Maza's cousin, and Balaguer's principal physician. He had sounded out the puppet president, asking if, in the event Trujillo disappeared suddenly, "he would collaborate with the patriots." His reply was cryptic: "According to the Constitution, if Trujillo were to disappear, I would have to be taken into account." Was this a good piece of news? That suave, astute little man had always inspired in Pupo Román the instinctive distrust he felt for bureaucrats and intellectuals. It was impossible to know what he was thinking; behind his affable manners and eloquence lay an enigma. But, in any case, what his friends said was true: Balaguer's involvement would reassure the Yankees.

By the time he reached his house in Gazcue, it was nine-thirty. He sent the jeep back to San Isidro. Mireya and his son Álvaro, a young lieutenant in the Army who had come to visit them on his day off, were alarmed at seeing him in that condition. He explained what had happened as he removed his dirty clothes. He had Mireya telephone her brother and told General Virgilio García about the Chief's outburst:

"I'm sorry, Virgilio, but I'm obliged to reprimand you. Come to my office tomorrow, before ten o'clock."

"Shit, and all for a broken pipe," Virgilio exclaimed in amusement. "The man can't control his temper!"

He took a shower and soaped his entire body. When he came out of the tub, Mireya handed him clean pajamas and a silk bathrobe. She stayed with him while he dried himself, splashed on cologne, and dressed. Contrary to what many people believed, beginning with the Chief, he hadn't married Mireya out of self-interest. He had fallen in love with the dark, timid girl, and risked his life by courting her despite Trujillo's opposition. They were a happy couple, and in twenty years together they'd had no fights or separations. As he talked to Mireya and Álvaro at the table—he wasn't hungry, all he wanted was rum on the rocks—he wondered what his wife's reaction would be. Would she side with her husband or with the clan? His doubts mortified him. He had often seen Mireya indignant at the Chief's insulting manner; perhaps that would tip the balance in his favor. Besides, what Dominican woman wouldn't like to be the First Lady?

When supper was over, Álvaro went out to have a beer with some friends. Mireya and he went up to their bedroom and turned on the Dominican Voice. There was a program of dance music with popular singers and orchestras. Before the sanctions, the station would bring in the best Latin American performers, but due to the crisis of the past year, almost all the programs on Petán Trujillo's television station featured local artists. As they listened to the merengues and danzones of the Generalissimo Orchestra, conducted by Maestro Luis Alberti, Mireya remarked sadly that she hoped the problems with the Church would end soon. There was a bad atmosphere, and her friends, when they played canasta, talked about rumors of a revolution and Kennedy sending in the Marines. Pupo reassured her: the Chief would get his way this time too, and the country would be peaceful and prosperous again. His voice sounded so false that he stopped talking, pretending he had to cough.

A short time later, there was the screech of brakes and the frantic sound of a car's horn. The general jumped out of bed and went to the window. He made out the sharp-edged silhouette of General Arturo (Razor) Espaillat coming out of the automobile that had just pulled up. As soon as he saw his face, looking yellow in the light of the street-lamp, his heart skipped a beat: it's happened.

"What's going on, Arturo?" he asked, leaning his head out the window.

"Something very serious," said General Espaillat, coming closer. "I was at the Pony with my wife, and the Chief's Chevrolet drove past. A little while later I heard shooting. I went to see what was happening and ran into a gunfight, right in the middle of the highway."

"I'm coming down, I'm coming down," shouted Pupo Román. Mireya was putting on her robe as she crossed herself: "My God, my uncle, don't let it be true, sweet Jesus."

From that moment on, and in all the minutes and hours that followed, when his fate was decided, and the fate of his family, the conspirators, and, in the long run, the Dominican Republic, General José René Román always knew with absolute lucidity what he should do. Why did he do exactly the opposite? He would ask himself the question many times in the next few months, without finding an answer. He knew, as he went down the stairs, that under these circumstances the only sensible thing to do, if he cared anything about his life and did not want the conspiracy to fail, was to open the door for the former head of the SIM, the military man most involved in the regime's criminal operations, the one responsible for countless abductions, acts of extortion, tortures, and murders ordered by Trujillo, and empty his revolver into him. In order to avoid going to prison or being murdered, Razor's record left him no alternative but to maintain a doglike loyalty to Trujillo and the regime.

Although he knew this all too well, he opened the door and let in General Espaillat and his wife, whom he kissed on the cheek and tried to reassure, for Ligia Fernández de Espaillat had lost her self-control and was stammering incoherently. Razor gave him precise details: as his car approached, he heard deafening gunfire from revolvers, carbines, and submachine guns, and in the powder flashes he recognized the Chief's Bel Air and could see a figure on the highway, shooting, maybe it was Trujillo. He couldn't help him: he was in civilian clothes, he wasn't armed, and fearing that Ligia might be hit by a stray bullet, he had come here. It happened fifteen minutes ago, twenty at the most.

"Wait for me, I'll get dressed." Román ran up the stairs, followed by Mireya, who was waving her hands and shaking her head as if she were deranged.

"We have to let Uncle Blacky know," she exclaimed, while he was putting on his everyday uniform. He saw her run to the telephone and dial, not giving him time to open his mouth. And though he knew he ought to stop that call, he didn't. He took the receiver and, as he buttoned his shirt, he told General Héctor Bienvenido Trujillo:

"I've just been informed of a possible attempt on His Excellency's life, on the San Cristóbal highway. I'm going there now. I'll keep you apprised."

He finished dressing and went downstairs, carrying a loaded M-1 carbine. Instead of firing and finishing off Razor, he spared his life again, and nodded when Espaillat, his little rat's eyes devoured by worry, advised him to alert the General Staff and order a nationwide curfew. General Román called the December 18 Fortress and directed all the garrisons to impose a rigorous quartering of troops and to close all exits from the capital, and he told the commanders in the interior that he would shortly be in telephone or radio contact with them regarding a matter of utmost urgency. He was wasting precious time, but he had to act in this way, which, he thought, would clear away any doubts about him in Razor's mind.

"Let's go," he said to Espaillat.

"I'm going to take Ligia home," he replied. "I'll meet you on the highway. At about kilometer seven."

When General Román drove away, at the wheel of his own car, he knew he ought to go immediately to the house of General Juan Tomás Díaz, just a few meters from his own, to confirm if the assassination had been successful—he was sure it had—and start the process of the coup. There was no escape; he was an accomplice regardless of whether Trujillo was dead or wounded. But instead of going to see Juan Tomás or Amiama, he drove his car to Avenida George Washington. Near the Fairground he saw someone signaling to him from a car: it was

Colonel Marcos Antonio Jorge Moreno, head of Trujillo's personal bodyguards, accompanied by General Pou.

"We're worried," Moreno shouted, leaning his head out the window. "His Excellency hasn't arrived in San Cristóbal."

"There was an attempt on his life," Román informed them. "Follow me!"

At kilometer seven, when, in the beams from Moreno's and Pou's flashlights, he recognized the bullet-riddled Chevrolet, saw the smashed glass and bloodstains and debris on the asphalt, he knew the attempt had been successful. He had to be dead after that kind of gunfire. And therefore he ought to subdue, recruit, or kill Moreno and Pou, two self-proclaimed Trujillistas, and, before Espaillat and other military men arrived, race to the December 18 Fortress, where he would be safe. But he didn't do that either; instead, displaying the same consternation as Moreno and Pou, he searched the area with them and was glad when the colonel found a revolver in the underbrush. Moments later Razor was there, patrols and guards arrived, and he ordered them to continue the search. He would be at the headquarters of the General Staff.

While he sat in his official car and was taken by his driver, First Sergeant Morones, to the December 18 Fortress, he smoked several Lucky Strikes. Luis Amiama and Juan Tomás must be desperately looking for him, dragging the Chief's body around with them. It was his duty to send them some kind of signal. But instead of doing that, when he reached the headquarters of the General Staff he instructed the guards not to allow in any civilians, no matter who they were.

He found the Fortress in a state of bustling activity inconceivable at this hour under normal circumstances. As he hurried up the stairs to his command post and responded in kind to the officers who saluted him, he heard questions—"An attempted landing across from the Fairground, General?"—which he did not stop to answer.

He went into his office in a state of agitation, feeling his heart pound, and a simple glance at the twenty or so high-ranking officers gathered there was enough to let him know that despite the lost opportunities, he still had a chance to put the Plan into effect. The officers who, when they saw him, clicked their heels and saluted were a group representing the high command, friends, for the most part, and they were waiting for his orders. They knew or intuited that a terrifying vacuum had just been created, and, educated in the tradition of discipline and total dependence on the Chief, they expected him to assume command, with clarity of purpose. Fear and hope were on the faces of Generals Fernando A. Sánchez, Radhamés Hungría, Fausto Caamaño, and Félix Hermida, Colonels Rivera Cuesta and Cruzado Piña, Majors Wessin y Wessin, Pagán Montás, Saldaña, Sánchez Pérez, Fernández Domínguez, and Hernando Ramírez. They wanted him to rescue them from an uncertainty against which they had no defense. A speech delivered in the voice of a leader who has his balls in the right place and knows what he is doing, explaining that in this dire circumstance the disappearance or death of Trujillo, for reasons yet to be determined, provided the Republic with a providential opportunity for change. Above all, they must avoid chaos, anarchy, a Communist revolution and its corollary, occupation by the Americans. They, who were patriots by vocation and profession, had the duty to act. The country had touched bottom, placed under quarantine because of the excesses of a regime which, although in the past it had performed services that could never be repaid, had degenerated into a tyranny that provoked universal revulsion. It was necessary to move events forward, with an eye to the future. If they followed him, together they would close the abyss that had begun to open before them. As head of the Armed Forces he would preside over a civilian-military junta, composed of prominent figures and responsible for guaranteeing a transition to democracy, which would allow the lifting of sanctions imposed by the United States and elections under the supervision of the OAS. The junta had the approval of Washington, and from them, the leaders of the most prestigious institution in the country, he expected cooperation. He knew his words would have been greeted with applause, and whoever had doubts would have been won over by the conviction of the others. It would be easy then to order executive officers like Fausto Caamaño and Félix Hermida to arrest the Trujillo brothers and round up Abbes García, Colonel Figueroa Carrión, Captain Candito Torres, Clodoveo Ortiz, Américo Dante Minervino, César Rodríguez Villeta, and Alicinio Peña Rivera, thereby immobilizing the machinery of the SIM.

But, though he knew with certainty what he ought to do and say at that moment, he didn't do that either. After a few seconds of hesitant silence, he limited himself to informing the officers, in vague, broken, stammering terms, that in view of the attempt on the person of the Generalissimo, the Armed Forces must be like a fist, ready to strike. He could feel, touch the disappointment of his subordinates, whom he was infecting with his own uncertainty instead of infusing them with confidence. This was not what they were hoping for. To hide his confusion, he communicated with the garrisons in the interior. He repeated to General César A. Oliva, in Santiago, General García Urbáez, in Dajabón, and General Guarionex Estrella, in La Vega, in the same hesitant way—his tongue barely obeyed him, as if he were drunk—that due to the presumed assassination, they should confine their troops to barracks and take no action without his authorization.

After the round of phone calls, he broke out of the secret straitjacket that bound him and took a step in the right direction:

"Don't leave," he announced, getting to his feet. "I'm calling an immediate high-level meeting."

He ordered calls placed to the President of the Republic, the head of the SIM, and the former President, General Héctor Bienvenido Trujillo. He would have the three of them come here, and arrest them. If Balaguer was part of the conspiracy, he could help in the steps that followed. He saw bewilderment in the officers, glances exchanged, whispering. They passed him the telephone. They had gotten Dr. Joaquín Balaguer out of bed:

"I'm sorry to wake you, Mr. President. There has been an attempt on His Excellency, while he was driving to San Cristóbal. As Minister of the Armed Forces, I am calling an urgent meeting at the December 18 Fortress. I ask you to come here without delay."

President Balaguer did not respond for a long time, so long that Román thought they had been cut off. Was it surprise that caused his silence? Satisfaction at knowing the Plan was being put into effect? Or mistrust of this phone call in the middle of the night? At last he heard his answer, spoken without a trace of emotion:

"If something so serious has occurred, as President of the Republic my place is not in a barracks but at the National Palace. I am going there now. I suggest that the meeting be held in my office. Goodbye."

Without giving him time to reply, he hung up.

Johnny Abbes García listened to him attentively. All right, he would go to the meeting, but only after he heard the statement of Captain Zacarías de la Cruz, who was badly wounded and had just been admitted to Hospital Marión. Only Blacky Trujillo appeared to agree to his call for a meeting. "I'll be right there." He seemed unhinged by what was happening. But when he didn't show up after half an hour, General José René Román knew that his last-minute plan had no chance of being realized. Not one of the three men would fall into the trap. And he, because of his actions, had begun to sink into quicksands that it would soon be too late to escape. Unless he commandeered a military plane and had it fly to Haiti, Trinidad, Puerto Rico, the French Antilles, or Venezuela, where he would be welcomed with open arms.

From that moment on, he was in a somnambulistic state. Time was eclipsed, or, rather, instead of moving forward it spun around in a monomaniacal repetition that depressed and infuriated him. He would not leave that state again in the four and a half months of life he had remaining, if what he had deserved to be called life and not hell, nightmare. Until October 12, 1961, he did not have a clear notion of chronology but did have an idea of mysterious eternity, which had never interested him. In the sudden attacks of lucidity that reminded him he was alive, that it hadn't ended, he tortured himself with the same question: why, knowing that *this* was waiting for you, why didn't you act as you should have? The question hurt him more than the tortures he faced with great courage, perhaps to prove to himself that cowardice was not the reason he had acted so indecisively on that endless night of May 31, 1961.

Incapable of making sense of his actions, he fell into contradictions and erratic initiatives. He ordered his brother-in-law, General Virgilio García Trujillo, to dispatch four tanks and three infantry companies from San Isidro, where the armored divisions were stationed, to reinforce the December 18 Fortress. But immediately after that he decided to leave the Fortress and go to the Palace. He instructed the head of the Army General Staff, the young General Tuntin Sánchez, to keep him informed regarding the search. Before he left he called Américo Dante Minervino, at La Victoria. He categorically ordered him to immediately liquidate, with absolute secrecy, the prisoners Major Segundo Imbert Barreras and Rafael Augusto Sánchez Saulley, and to make the bodies disappear, for he feared that Antonio Imbert, a member of the action group, might have told his brother about his involvement in the conspiracy. Américo Dante Minervino, accustomed to these kinds of missions, asked no questions: "Understood, General."

He bewildered General Tuntin Sánchez by telling him to inform the SIM, Army, and Air Force patrols participating in the search that persons on the lists of "enemies" and "the disaffected," which had been distributed to them, ought to be terminated at the first sign of resisting arrest. ("We don't want prisoners who'll be used to unleash international campaigns against our country.") His subordinate made no comment. He would transmit your instructions exactly, General.

As he left the Fortress to go to the Palace, the lieutenant of the guard informed him that two civilians in a car, one of whom claimed to be his brother Ramón (Bibín), had come to the entrance demanding to see him. Following his orders, he had obliged them to leave. He nodded, not saying a word. That meant his brother was in on the plot, that Bibín too would have to pay for his doubts and evasions. Sunk in a kind of hypnosis, he thought his inaction could be due to the fact that although the body of the Chief might be dead, his soul, spirit, whatever you called it, still enslaved him.

At the National Palace he found confusion and desolation. Almost the entire Trujillo family had gathered there. Petán, in riding boots and with a submachine gun slung over his shoulder, had just arrived from his fiefdom in Bonao and was pacing back and forth like a cartoon cowboy. Héctor (Blacky), sitting on a sofa, rubbed his arms as if he were cold. Mireya, and his mother-in-law Marina, were consoling Doña María, the Chief's wife, who was as pale as a corpse and whose eyes flashed fire. The beautiful Angelita cried and wrung her hands, but her husband, Colonel José (Pechito) León Estévez, in uniform and looking glum, failed to calm her. He felt all their eyes fixed on him: any news? He embraced them, one by one: they were combing the city, house by house, street by street, and soon . . . Then he discovered that they knew more than the head of the Armed Forces. One of the conspirators, the former soldier Pedro Livio Cedeño, had been wounded and was being interrogated by Abbes García at the International Clinic. And Colonel José León Estévez had already informed Ramfis and Radhamés, who were trying to charter an Air France plane to fly them in from Paris. This was when he also learned that the power attached to his position, which he had squandered over the past few hours, was beginning to slip away; decisions no longer came from his office but from the heads of the SIM, Johnny Abbes García and Colonel Figueroa Carrión, or from Trujillo's family and relatives, like

Pechito or his brother-in-law Virgilio. An invisible force was distancing him from power. It did not surprise him that Blacky Trujillo gave him no explanation for not coming to the meeting he had asked him to attend.

He left the group, hurried to a phone booth, and called the Fortress. He ordered the head of the General Staff to send troops to surround the International Clinic, place the former officer Pedro Livio Cedeño under guard, and stop the SIM from taking him out of there, using force if necessary. The prisoner had to be transferred to the December 18 Fortress. He would come and interrogate him personally. Tuntin Sánchez, after an ominous pause, said only: "Good night, General." He told himself, in torment, that this was perhaps his worst mistake of the entire evening.

There were more people now in the reception room where the Trujillos had gathered. All of them listened, in grief-stricken silence, to Colonel Johnny Abbes García, who was standing and speaking mournfully:

"The dental plate found on the highway belongs to His Excellency. Dr. Fernando Camino has confirmed this. We must assume that if he isn't dead, his condition is grave."

"What about the assassins?" Román interrupted, in a defiant attitude. "Did the subject talk? Did he name his accomplices?"

The fat-cheeked face of the head of the SIM turned toward him. His amphibian eyes washed over him with a gaze that, in his state of extreme susceptibility, seemed mocking.

"He's given up three," Johnny Abbes said, looking at him without blinking. "Antonio Imbert, Luis Amiama, and General Juan Tomás Díaz. He's the leader, he says."

"Have they been captured?"

"My people are looking for them all over Ciudad Trujillo," Johnny Abbes García declared. "There's something else. The United States might be behind this."

He mumbled a few words of congratulation to Colonel Abbes and returned to the phone booth. He called General Tuntin Sánchez again. The patrols should immediately arrest General Juan Tomás Díaz, Luis Amiama, and Antonio Imbert, as well as their families, "alive or dead, it didn't matter, maybe dead would be better because the CIA might try to get them out of the country." When he hung up, he was certain:

the way things were going, not even exile would be possible. He'd have to shoot himself.

In the salon, Abbes García was still speaking. Not about the assassins; about the situation faced by the country.

"At a time like this, it is absolutely necessary that a member of the Trujillo family assume the Presidency of the Republic," he declared. "Dr. Balaguer should resign and hand over his office to General Héctor Bienvenido or General José Arismendi. This will let the people know that the Chief's spirit, philosophy, and policies will not be undermined and will continue to guide Dominican life."

There was an uncomfortable silence. Those present exchanged glances. The vulgar, bullying voice of Petán Trujillo dominated the room:

"Johnny's right. Balaguer should resign. Blacky or I will take over the Presidency. The people will know that Trujillo hasn't died."

Then, following the eyes of everyone in the room, General Román discovered that the puppet president, as small and discreet as ever, was listening from a chair in the corner, trying, one would say, not to be in the way. He was dressed impeccably, as usual, and displayed absolute serenity, as if this were no more than a minor formality. He gave a fleeting little smile and spoke with a tranquillity that softened the atmosphere:

"As you all know, I am President of the Republic by a decision of the Generalissimo, who always accommodated himself to constitutional procedures. I occupy this post in order to facilitate matters, not to complicate them. If my resignation will alleviate the situation, you have it. But allow me to make a suggestion. Before reaching a transcendental decision that signifies a break with legality, would it not be prudent to wait for the arrival of General Ramfis Trujillo? As the Chief's oldest son, his spiritual, military, and political heir, should he not be consulted?"

He looked at the woman who, according to the requirements of strict Trujillista protocol, was always called the Bountiful First Lady by social chroniclers. An imperious María Martínez de Trujillo reacted:

"Dr. Balaguer is right. Until Ramfis arrives, nothing should change." Her round face had regained its color.

Watching the President of the Republic shyly lower his eyes, General Román escaped for a few seconds from his gelatinous mental wandering to tell himself that, unlike him, this unarmed little man, who wrote poetry and seemed so inconsequential in a world of machos with pistols and submachine guns, knew exactly what he wanted and what he was doing, and did not lose his composure for an instant. In the course of that night, the longest in his half century of life, General Román discovered that in the vacuum and chaos created by what had happened to the Chief, this insignificant man whom everyone had always considered a mere clerk, a purely decorative figure in the regime, began to acquire surprising authority.

As if in a dream, in the hours that followed he saw this assemblage of Trujillo's family, relatives, and top leaders form cliques, dissolve them, and form them again as events began to connect like pieces filling in the gaps of a puzzle until a solid figure took shape. Before midnight they were told that the pistol discovered at the site of the attack belonged to General Juan Tomás Díaz. When Román ordered his house searched, along with the houses of all his brothers and sisters, he was informed that it was already being taken care of by patrols of the SIM under the direction of Colonel Figueroa Carrión, and that Juan Tomás's brother, Modesto Díaz, turned over to the SIM by his friend the gamecock breeder Chucho Malapunta, in whose house he had been hiding, was already in a cell at La Cuarenta. Fifteen minutes later, Pupo telephoned his son Álvaro. He asked him to bring extra ammunition for his M-1 carbine (he had not removed it from his shoulder), for he was convinced that at any moment he would have to defend his life or end it by his own hand. After conferring in his office with Abbes García and Colonel Luis José (Pechito) León Estévez regarding Bishop Reilly, he took the initiative of saying that on his authority he should be removed by force from the Santo Domingo Academy, and he supported the proposal of the head of the SIM that the bishop should be executed, for there was no doubt about the Church's complicity in the criminal plot. Angelita Trujillo's husband, touching his revolver, said it would be an honor to carry out the order. He returned in less than an hour, enraged. The operation had gone off without serious incident, except for a few punches aimed at some nuns and two Redemptorist priests, also gringos, who tried to protect the bishop. The only fatality was a German shepherd, the watchdog at the Academy, who bit a *calié* before being shot. The prelate was now in the Air Force detention center at kilometer nine on the San Isidro highway. Commander Rodríguez Méndez, head of the center, refused to execute Reilly and prevented Pechito León Estévez from doing so, claiming he had orders from the President of the Republic.

Stupefied, Román asked if he was referring to Balaguer. Angelita Trujillo's husband, no less disconcerted, nodded:

"Apparently, he seems to think he exists. What's so incredible isn't that the insolent little jerk is sticking his nose into our business, but that his orders are being obeyed. Ramfis has to put him in his place."

Pupo Román exploded in anger: "We don't have to wait for Ramfis. I'll straighten him out right now."

He strode toward the President's office but had a dizzy spell in the corridor. He managed to stagger to a chair, where he collapsed and fell asleep immediately. When he awoke a couple of hours later, he remembered a polar nightmare: trembling with cold on a snowy steppe, he watched a pack of wolves loping toward him. He jumped up and almost ran to President Balaguer's office. He found the doors wide open. He walked in, determined to make this meddling pygmy feel the weight of his authority, but, another surprise, in the office he came face to face with none other than Bishop Reilly. His eyes wide with fear, his tunic torn, his face bearing the marks of abuse, the bishop's tall figure still maintained a majestic dignity. The President of the Republic was saying goodbye to him.

"Ah, Monsignor, look who is here, the Minister of the Armed Forces, General José René Román Fernández." He introduced them. "He has come to reiterate to you the regrets of the military authorities for this lamentable misunderstanding. You have my word, and that of the head of the Army—is that not so, General Román?—that neither you, nor any prelate, nor the sisters of Santo Domingo, will be troubled again. I will personally give my apologies to Sister Wilhelmina and Sister Helen Claire. We are living through very difficult times, and you, as a man of experience, can understand that. There are subordinates who lose control and go too far, as they did tonight. It will not happen again. If you have the slightest problem, I beg you to get in touch with me personally."

Bishop Reilly, who looked at them as if he were surrounded by Martians, nodded vaguely and took his leave. Román confronted Dr. Balaguer angrily, touching his submachine gun:

"You owe me an explanation, Mr. Balaguer. Who are you to countermand an order of mine, calling a military center, a subordinate officer, passing over the chain of command? Who the hell do you think you are?"

The little man looked at him as if he were listening to the rain. After observing him for a moment, he smiled amiably. And indicating the chair in front of the desk, invited him to sit down. Pupo Román did not move. The blood was boiling in his veins, like a volcano about to erupt.

"Answer my question, damn it!" he shouted.

Dr. Balaguer did not falter this time either. With the same mildness he used when reciting or giving a speech, he counseled him paternally:

"You are confused, General, and with reason. But make an effort. We may be living through the most critical moment in the history of the Republic, and you more than anyone should set an example of calm for the country."

He withstood the general's enraged look—Pupo wanted to hit him, and, at the same time, curiosity restrained him—and after he sat down at his desk, he added, using the same intonation:

"You should thank me for having stopped you from committing a serious error, General. Killing a bishop would not have resolved your problems. It would have made them worse. For what it is worth, you should know that the President you came here to insult is prepared to help you. Although, I fear, I will not be able to do much for you."

Román detected no irony in his words. Did they hide a threat? No, judging by the benevolent manner in which Balaguer looked at him. His fury evaporated. Now, he was afraid. He envied the serenity of this honey-voiced midget.

"You should know that I've ordered the execution of Segundo Imbert and Papito Sánchez, in La Victoria," he roared at the top of his voice, not thinking about what he was saying. "They were in this conspiracy too. I'll do the same to everybody who's implicated in the assassination of the Chief."

Dr. Balaguer nodded gently, his expression not changing in the slightest.

"For great ills, great remedies," he murmured cryptically. And, standing up, he walked to the door of his office and went out without saying goodbye.

Román remained there, not knowing what to do. He chose to go to his own office. At two-thirty in the morning he drove Mireya, who had taken a tranquilizer, to the house in Gazcue. There he found his brother Bibín forcing the soldiers on guard to drink from a bottle of Carta Dorada that he brandished like a flag. Bibín, the idler, the drinker, the rake, the wastrel, good-natured Bibín could barely stand. He practically had to carry him to the upstairs bathroom on the pretext that he would help him vomit and wash his face. As soon as they were alone, Bibín burst into tears. He contemplated his brother with infinite sadness in his tear-filled eyes. A thread of spittle hung from his lips like a spiderweb. Lowering his voice, choking up, he said that he, Luis Amiama, and Juan Tomás had spent the night looking for him all over the city and became so desperate they even cursed him. What happened, Pupo? Why didn't he do anything? Why did he hide? Wasn't there a Plan? The action group did their part. They brought him the body as he had asked.

"Why didn't you do your part, Pupo?" Sighs shook his chest. "What's going to happen to us now?"

"There was a problem, Bibín. Razor Espaillat showed up, he saw everything. There was nothing I could do. Now . . ."

"Now we're fucked," Bibín said hoarsely, swallowing mucus. "Luis Amiama, Juan Tomás, Antonio de la Maza, Tony Imbert, all of us. But especially you. You, and then me, because I'm your brother. If you love me at all, shoot me right now, Pupo. Fire that submachine gun, make the most of my being drunk. Before they do it. For the sake of what you love best, Pupo."

At that moment, Álvaro knocked at the bathroom door: they had just discovered the Generalissimo's body in the trunk of a car at the house of General Juan Tomás Díaz.

He did not close his eyes that night, or the next one, or the one after that, and, probably, in four and a half months did not experience again what sleep had once been for him—resting, forgetting about himself and others, dissolving into a nonexistence from which he returned restored, his energy renewed—although he did lose consciousness often, and spent long hours, days, nights in a mindless stupor without images or ideas, with a firm desire for death to come and free him. Everything mixed up and scrambled, as if time had turned into a stew, a jumble in which before, now, and afterward had no logical sequence but were recurrent. He clearly remembered the sight, when he reached the National Palace, of Doña María Martínez de Trujillo bellowing before the corpse of the Chief: "Let the blood of his assassins run until the last drop!" And, as if it came next, but it could have happened only a day later, the svelte, uniformed, impeccable figure of Ramfis, pale and rigid, leaning without bending over the carved coffin, contemplating the painted face of the Chief, and murmuring: "I won't be as generous as you were with our enemies, Papa." It seemed to him that Ramfis was talking not to his father but to him. He gave him a hard embrace and groaned in his ear: "What an irreparable loss, Ramfis. It's good we have you."

He saw himself immediately after that, in his parade uniform, the inseparable M-1 submachine gun in his hand, in the crowded church in San Cristóbal, attending the funeral rites for the Chief. Some lines from the address by a much larger President Balaguer—"Here, ladies and gentlemen, split by a flash of treacherous lightning, lies the powerful oak that for more than thirty years defied all thunderbolts and emerged victorious from every storm"—brought tears to his eyes. He listened, sitting next to a stony Ramfis, who was surrounded by bodyguards carrying submachine guns. And he saw himself, at the same time, contemplating (one, two, three days earlier?) the line of countless thousands of Dominicans of all ages, professions, races, and social classes, waiting hours on end, under a merciless sun, to climb the stairs of the Palace and, with hysterical exclamations of grief, with fainting and screaming and offerings to the *loas* of Voodoo, to pay their final homage to the Chief, the Man, the Benefactor, the Generalissimo, the Father. And in the midst of all that, he was listening to reports from his aides regarding the capture of the engineer Huáscar Tejeda and Salvador Estrella Sadhalá, the end of Antonio de la Maza and General Juan Tomás Díaz in Independencia Park at the corner of Bolívar as they defended themselves with guns, and the almost simultaneous death, a short distance away, of Lieutenant Amador García, who also killed before he could be killed, and the mob's looting and destruction of the house where his aunt had given him refuge. And he remembered the rumors regarding the mysterious disappearance of his compadre Amiama Tió and Antonio Imbert—Ramfis was offering half a million pesos to anyone with information leading to their capture—and the fall of some two hundred Dominicans, both civilian and military, in Ciudad Trujillo, Santiago, La Vega, San Pedro de Macorís, and half a dozen other places, who had been implicated in the assassination of Trujillo.

All of that was mixed up, but at least it was intelligible. As was the final coherent memory his mind would preserve: how, when the Mass for the Generalissimo lying in state in the San Cristóbal church was over, Petán Trujillo took his arm: "Come with me in my car, Pupo." In Petán's Cadillac he knew—it was the last thing he knew with total certainty—that this was his last chance to save himself from what was coming by emptying his submachine gun into the Chief's brother and into himself, because that ride was not going to end at his house in Gazcue. It ended at San Isidro Air Base, where, Petán lied to him, not bothering to pretend, "there would be a family meeting." At the entrance to the base, two generals, his brother-in-law Virgilio García Trujillo and the head of the Army General Staff, Tuntin Sánchez, informed him that he was under arrest, accused of complicity with the assassins of the Benefactor and Father of the New Nation. Very pale, avoiding his eyes, they asked for his weapon. Obediently, he handed them the M-1 submachine gun that had not left his side for four days.

They took him to a room with a table, an old typewriter, a pile of blank sheets, and a chair. They asked him to remove his belt and shoes and hand them to a sergeant. He did so, asking no questions. They left him alone, and minutes later Ramfis's two closest friends, Colonel Luis José (Pechito) León Estévez and Pirulo Sánchez Rubirosa, came in, did not greet him, and told him to write down everything he knew about the conspiracy, giving the full names of the conspirators. General Ramfis—by supreme decree, which the Congress would confirm tonight, President Balaguer had just named him Commander-in-Chief of the Air, Sea, and Land Forces of the Republic—had full knowledge of the plot, thanks to the detainees, all of whom had denounced him.

He sat down at the typewriter and for several hours did what they had ordered. He was a terrible typist; he used only two fingers and made a good number of mistakes that he did not take the time to correct. He told everything, beginning with his first conversation with his compadre Luis Amiama six months earlier, and he named the twenty or so people he knew were implicated, but not Bibín. He explained that for him the decisive factor was the support of the United States for the conspiracy, and that he agreed to preside over the civilian-military junta only when he learned from Juan Tomás that both Consul

Henry Dearborn and Consul Jack Bennett, as well as the head of the CIA in Ciudad Trujillo, Lorenzo D. Berry (Wimpy), wanted him to head it. He told only one small lie: that in exchange for his participation, he had demanded that Generalissimo Trujillo be abducted and forced to resign, but under no circumstances was he to be killed. The other conspirators had betrayed him by not keeping this promise. He reread the pages and signed them.

He was alone for a long time, waiting, with a serenity of spirit he had not felt since the night of May 30. When they came for him, it was growing dark. It was a group of officers he did not know. They put him in handcuffs and took him out, not wearing his shoes, to the courtyard of the base, and put him in a van with tinted windows; on it he read the words "Pan-American Institute of Education." He thought they were taking him to La Cuarenta. He knew that gloomy house on Calle 40, near the Dominican Cement Factory, very well. It had belonged to General Juan Tomás Díaz, who sold it to the State so that Johnny Abbes could convert it into the setting for his elaborate methods of extracting confessions from prisoners. He had even been present, following the Castroite invasion on June 14, when one of those being interrogated, Dr. Tejeda Florentino, sitting on the grotesque Throne—a seat from a jeep, pipes, electric prods, bullwhips, a garrote with wooden ends for strangling the prisoner as he received electric shocks—was mistakenly electrocuted by a SIM technician, who released the maximum voltage. But no, instead of La Cuarenta they took him to El Nueve on the Mella Highway, a former residence of Pirulo Sánchez Rubirosa. It also housed a Throne, one that was smaller but more modern.

He was not afraid. Not now. The immense fear that since the night of Trujillo's assassination had kept him "mounted"—the term used for those who were drained of themselves and occupied by spirits in Voodoo ceremonies—had disappeared completely. In El Nueve, they stripped him and sat him on the black seat in the middle of a windowless, dimly lit room. The strong smell of excrement and urine nauseated him. The seat, misshapen and absurd with all its appendages, was bolted to the floor and had straps and rings for the ankles, wrists, chest, and head. Its arms were faced with copper sheets to facilitate the passage of the current. A bundle of wires came out of the Throne and led to a desk or counter, where the voltage was controlled. In the sickly light, as he was strapped into the chair, he recognized the bloodless face of Ramfis between Pechito León Estévez and Sánchez Rubirosa. He had shaved his mustache and was not wearing his eternal Ray-Ban sunglasses. He looked at Pupo with the lost gaze he had seen in Ramfis when he directed the torture and killing of the survivors of Constanza, Maimón, and Estero Hondo in June 1959. Ramfis continued to look at him without saying anything, while a *calié* shaved him, and another, kneeling, bound his ankles, and a third sprayed perfume around the room. General Román Fernández withstood those eyes.

"You're the worst of all, Pupo," he heard Ramfis say suddenly, his voice breaking with sorrow. "Everything you are and everything you have you owe to Papa. Why did you do it?"

"For love of my country," he heard himself saying.

There was a pause. Ramfis spoke again:

"Is Balaguer involved?"

"I don't know. Luis Amiama told me they had sounded him out, through his doctor. He didn't seem very sure. I tend to think he wasn't."

Ramfis moved his head and Pupo felt himself thrown forward with the force of a cyclone. The jolt seemed to pound all his nerves, from his head to his feet. Straps and rings cut into his muscles, he saw balls of fire, sharp needles jabbed into his pores. He endured it without screaming, he only bellowed. Although with each discharge—they came one after the other, with intervals when they threw buckets of water at him to revive him—he passed out and could not see, he then returned to consciousness. And his nostrils filled with that perfume housemaids wore. He tried to maintain a certain composure, not humiliate himself by begging for mercy. In the nightmare he would never come out of, he was sure of two things: Johnny Abbes García never appeared among his torturers, and at one point somebody—it might have been Pechito León Estévez or General Tuntin Sánchez—let him know that Bibín's reflexes were better than his because he had managed to fire a bullet into his mouth when the SIM came for him at his house on Arzobispo Nouel, corner of José Reyes. Pupo often wondered if his children, Álvaro and José René, whom he had never told about the conspiracy, had managed to kill themselves.

Between sessions in the electric chair, they dragged him, naked, to a damp cell, where buckets of pestilential water made him respond. To keep him from sleeping they taped his lids to his eyebrows with adhesive tape. When, in spite of having his eyes open, he fell into semiconsciousness, they woke him by beating him with baseball bats. At various times they stuffed inedible substances into his mouth; at times he detected excrement, and vomited. Then, in a rapid descent into subhumanity, he could keep down what they gave him. In the early sessions with electricity, Ramfis interrogated him. He repeated the same question over and over again, to see if he would contradict himself. ("Is President Balaguer implicated?") He responded, making superhuman efforts to have his tongue obey him. Until he heard laughter, and then the colorless, rather feminine voice of Ramfis: "Shut up, Pupo. You have nothing to tell me. I know everything. Now you're only paying for your betrayal of Papa." It was the same voice, with its discordant changes in pitch, that Ramfis had at the orgy of blood following June 14, when he lost his mind and the Chief had to send him to a psychiatric hospital in Belgium.

At the time of this last conversation with Ramfis, he could no longer see him. They had removed the tape, ripping off his eyebrows in the process, and a drunken, joyful voice announced: "Now you'll have some dark, so you'll sleep real good." He felt the needle piercing his eyelids. He did not move while they sewed them shut. It surprised him that sealing his eyes with thread caused him less suffering than the shocks on the Throne. By then, he had failed in his two attempts to kill himself. The first time, he banged his head with all the strength he had left against the wall in his cell. He passed out, and barely bloodied his hair. The second time, he almost succeeded. Climbing up the bars—they had removed his handcuffs in preparation for another session on the Throne—he broke the bulb that lit the cell. On all fours, he swallowed every bit of glass, hoping that an internal hemorrhage would end his life. But the SIM had two doctors on permanent call and a small first-aid station supplied with what was necessary to prevent tortured prisoners from dying by their own hand. They took him to the infirmary, made him swallow a liquid that induced vomiting, and flushed out his intestines. They saved him, so that Ramfis and his friends could go on killing him in stages.

When they castrated him, the end was near. They did not cut off his testicles with a knife but used a scissors, while he was on the Throne. He heard excited snickers and obscene remarks from individuals who were only voices and sharp odors of armpits and cheap tobacco. He did not give them the satisfaction of screaming. They stuffed his testicles into his mouth, and he swallowed them, hoping with all his might that this would hasten his death, something he never dreamed he could desire so much.

At one point he recognized the voice of Modesto Díaz, the brother of General Juan Tomás Díaz, who, people said, was as intelligent as Egghead Cabral or the Constitutional Sot. Had they put him in the same cell? Were they torturing him too? Modesto's voice was bitter and accusatory:

"We're here because of you, Pupo. Why did you betray us? Didn't you know this would happen to you? Repent for having betrayed your friends and your country."

He did not have the strength to articulate a sound or even open his mouth. Some time later—it could have been hours, days, or weeks—he heard a conversation between a SIM doctor and Ramfis Trujillo:

"Impossible to keep him alive any longer, General."

"How much time does he have?" It was Ramfis, no doubt about it.

"A few hours, perhaps a day if I double the serum. But in his condition, he won't survive another shock. It's incredible that he's lasted four months, General."

"Move away, then. I won't let him die a natural death. Stand behind me, you don't want any cartridges to hit you."

With great joy, General José René Román felt the final burst of gunfire.

21 When Dr. Marcelino Vélez Santana, who had gone out for news, came back to the airless attic of Dr. Robert Reid Cabral's little Moorish-style house, where they had already spent two days, to place a sympathetic hand on Turk's shoulder and tell him that the *caliés* had stormed his house on Mahatma Gandhi and taken away his wife and children, Salvador Estrella Sadhalá decided to turn himself in. He was sweating, gasping for breath. What else could he do? Let those savages kill his wife and children? They were certainly being tortured. He felt too much anguish to pray for his family. That was when he told his companions in the hideout what he was going to do.

"You know what that means, Turk," Antonio de la Maza argued with him. "They'll abuse and torture you in the most barbaric way before they kill you."

"And they'll go on hurting your family in front of you, to make you betray everybody," insisted General Juan Tomás Díaz.

"Nobody will make me open my mouth, even if they burn me alive," he swore with tears in his eyes. "The only one I'll name is that stinking Pupo Román."

They asked him not to leave the hiding place before they did, and Salvador agreed to stay one more night. The thought of his wife and children—fourteen-year-old Luis and Carmen Elly, who had just turned four—in the dungeons of the SIM, surrounded by sadistic thugs, kept him awake all night, gasping for breath, not praying, not thinking about anything else. Remorse gnawed at his heart: how could he have exposed his family like this? And the guilt he felt for shooting

Pedro Livio Cedeño moved to the middle distance. Poor Pedro Livio! Where was he now? What horrors had been done to him?

On the afternoon of June 4, he was the first to leave Reid Cabral's house. He hailed a cab at the corner and gave the address, on Calle Santiago, of the engineer Feliciano Sosa Mieses, his wife's cousin, with whom he had always been good friends. All he wanted was to find out if he had any news of her and the children, and the rest of the family, but that was impossible. Feliciano himself opened the door, and when he saw him, he made a gesture—*Vade retro!*—as if the devil were standing in front of him.

"What are you doing here, Turk?" he exclaimed, furious. "Don't you know I have a family? Do you want them to kill us? Get away! For the sake of everything you hold dear, get out of here!"

He closed the door with an expression of fear and revulsion that left Salvador not knowing what to do. He went back to the cab, feeling a depression that turned his bones to water. Despite the heat, he was dying of cold.

"You've recognized me, haven't you?" he asked the driver, when he was already in his seat.

The man, who wore a baseball cap pulled down to his eyebrows, did not turn around to look at him.

"I recognized you when you got in," he said very calmly. "Don't worry, you're safe with me. I'm anti-Trujillista too. If we have to run, we'll run together. Where do you want to go?"

"To a church," said Salvador. "It doesn't matter which one."

He would put himself in the hands of God and, if possible, make confession. After he had unburdened his conscience, he would ask the priest to call the guards. But after driving toward the center of town for a short time, along streets where the shadows were deepening, the driver warned him:

"That guy turned you in, señor. There are the *caliés*."

"Stop," Salvador ordered. "Before they kill you too."

He crossed himself and got out of the cab, holding up his hands to indicate to the men with submachine guns and pistols in the Volkswagens that he would offer no resistance. They put him in handcuffs that bit into his wrists and pushed him into the back seat of one of the Beetles; the two *caliés* who were half sitting on him gave off a stink of sweat and feet. The car pulled away. Since they were on the road to San

Pedro de Macorís, he assumed they were taking him to El Nueve. He made the trip in silence, trying to pray, saddened because he could not. His head was a seething, noisy, chaotic place where nothing was still, not a thought, not an image: everything was popping, like soap bubbles.

There was the famous house, at kilometer nine, encircled by a high concrete wall. They crossed a garden and he saw a comfortable country estate, with an old chalet surrounded by trees and flanked by rustic buildings. They shoved him out of the Beetle. He walked down a darkened hall lined with cells that held clusters of naked men, and they made him go down a long staircase. An acrid, sharp odor of excrement, vomit, and burned flesh made him feel faint. He thought of hell. There was hardly any light at the bottom of the stairs, but in the semidarkness he could see a line of cells with iron doors and little barred windows, crowded with heads struggling to see out. At the end of the cellar they tore off his trousers, shirt, underwear, shoes, and socks. He was naked, and still wearing handcuffs. The soles of his feet felt wet with a sticky substance that covered the rough flagstone floor. They kept shoving him and forced him into another room that was almost completely dark. They sat him down and fastened him into a shapeless chair lined with metal plates—he shuddered—that had straps and metal rings for his hands and feet.

For a long time nothing happened. He tried to pray. One of the men in shorts who had tied him down—his eyes were becoming used to the darkness—began to spray the air, and he recognized the cheap perfume called Nice that was advertised on the radio. He felt the cold of the metal plates against his thighs, buttocks, back, and at the same time he was sweating, almost suffocating in the sultry atmosphere. By now he could make out the faces of the people crowded around him; their silhouettes, their odors, some facial features. He recognized the flabby face with the double chin, the deformed body with its prominent belly. He was sitting very close to him, on a bench between two other people.

"It's shameful, damn it! A son of General Piro Estrella involved in this shit," said Johnny Abbes. "There's no gratitude in your fucking blood."

He was about to say that his family had nothing to do with what he had done, that his father, his brothers, his wife, certainly not Luisito and little Carmen Elly, none of them knew anything about this, when the electrical current picked him up and flattened him against the straps and rings that held him down. He felt needles in his pores, his head exploded into little fireballs, and he pissed, shat, and vomited everything he had inside. A bucket of water revived him. He immediately recognized the other figure to the right of Abbes García: Ramfis Trujillo. He wanted to insult him and at the same time plead with him to release his wife and Luisito and Carmen, but his throat produced no sound.

"Is it true that Pupo Román is part of the plot?" asked Ramfis's discordant voice.

Another bucket of water returned his powers of speech.

"Yes, yes," he said, not recognizing his own voice. "That coward, that traitor, yes. He lied to us. Kill me, General Trujillo, but let my wife and children go. They're innocent."

"It won't be that easy, asshole," Ramfis replied. "Before you go to hell, you have to pass through purgatory. You son of a bitch!"

A second electrical discharge catapulted him against his bonds—he felt his eyes popping out of their sockets, like a frog's—and he lost consciousness. When he came to, he was on the floor of a cell, naked and handcuffed, in the middle of a slimy puddle. His bones and muscles ached, and he felt an unbearable burning in his testicles and anus, as if they had been flayed. But the thirst was even more agonizing: his throat, tongue, and palate were like fiery sandpaper. He closed his eyes and prayed. He could, with intervals when his mind went blank; then, for a few seconds, he was able to concentrate again on the words. He prayed to Our Lady of Mercy, reminding her of the devotion with which he had made the pilgrimage, as a young man, to Jarabacoa, and climbed to Santo Cerro to kneel at her feet in the Sanctuary devoted to her memory. Humbly he implored her to protect his wife, and Luisito, and Carmen Elly from the cruelty of the Beast. In the midst of the horror, he felt grateful. He could pray again.

When he opened his eyes, he recognized his brother Guarionex lying beside him, his body naked and battered, covered with wounds and bruises. My God, they had left poor Guaro in a terrible state! The general's eyes were open, looking at him in the dim light that a bulb in the hallway allowed to filter through the little barred window. Did he recognize him?

"I'm Turk, your brother, I'm Salvador," he said, dragging himself over to him. "Can you hear me? Can you see me, Guaro?"

He spent an infinite time trying to communicate with his brother but did not succeed. Guaro was alive; he moved, moaned, opened and closed his eyes. At times he made bizarre remarks and gave orders to his subordinates: "Move that mule, Sergeant!" And they had kept the Plan secret from General Guarionex Estrella Sadhalá because they considered him too much of a Trujillista. What a surprise for poor Guaro: to be arrested, tortured, and interrogated because of something he knew nothing about. He tried to explain this to Ramfis and Johnny Abbes the next time he was taken to the torture chamber and seated on the Throne, and he repeated it and swore it over and over again, between fainting spells brought on by the electrical currents, and while they flogged him with those whips, the "bull's balls," that tore off pieces of skin. They did not seem interested in knowing the truth. He swore in God's name that Guarionex, his other brothers, certainly not his father, none of them had been part of the conspiracy, and he shouted that what they had done to General Estrella Sadhalá was a monstrous injustice that they would have to answer for in the next life. They did not listen, they were more interested in torturing him than in interrogating him. Only after an interminable period of time—had hours, days, weeks passed since his capture?—did he realize that with a certain regularity they were giving him a bowl of soup with pieces of yuca, a slice of bread, and jugs of water into which the jailers spat as they passed them to him. By now nothing mattered. He could pray. He prayed in all his free and lucid moments, and sometimes even when he was asleep or unconscious. But not when they were torturing him. On the Throne, pain and fear paralyzed him. From time to time a SIM doctor would come to listen to his heart and give him an injection that revived him.

One day, or night, for in the jail it was impossible to know the time, they took him out of the cell, naked and handcuffed, made him climb the stairs, and pushed him into a small, sunlit room. The white light blinded him. At last he recognized the pale, elegant face of Ramfis Trujillo, and at his side, erect as always despite his years, his father, General Piro Estrella. When he recognized the old man, Salvador's eyes filled with tears.

But instead of being moved at seeing the desolate creature his son had become, the general roared in indignation:

"I don't know you! You're not my son! Assassin! Traitor!" He gesticulated, choking with rage. "Don't you know what I, you, all of us owe to Trujillo? He's the man you murdered? Repent, you miserable wretch!"

He had to lean against a table because he began to reel. He lowered his eyes. Was the old man pretending? Was he hoping to win over Ramfis and then beg him to spare his life? Or was his father's Trujillista fervor stronger than his feelings for his son? That doubt tore at him constantly, except during the torture sessions. These came every day, every two days, and now they were accompanied by long, maddening interrogations in which they repeated, a thousand and one times, the same questions, demanded the same details, and tried to make him denounce other conspirators. They never believed he did not know anyone other than those they already knew about, or that no one in his family had been involved, least of all Guarionex. Johnny Abbes and Ramfis did not appear at those sessions; they were conducted by subordinates who became familiar to him: Lieutenant Clodoveo Ortiz, the lawyer Eladio Ramírez Suero, Colonel Rafael Trujillo Reynoso, First Lieutenant Pérez Mercado of the police. Some seemed to enjoy passing electric prods along his body, or beating him on the head and back with blackjacks covered in rubber, or burning him with cigarettes; others seemed disgusted or bored. Always, at the beginning of each session, one of the half-naked bailiffs responsible for administering the electric shocks would spray the air with Nice to hide the stink of his defecations and charred flesh.

One day—what day could it be?—they put in his cell Fifí Pastoriza, Huáscar Tejeda, Modesto Díaz, Pedro Livio Cedeño, and Tunti Cáceres, Antonio de la Maza's young nephew, who, in the original Plan, was going to drive the car that Antonio Imbert eventually drove. They were naked and handcuffed, like him. They had been in El Nueve the whole time, in other cells, and received the same treatment of electric shocks, whippings, burnings, and needles in the ears and under the nails. And they had been subjected to endless interrogations.

From them he learned that Imbert and Luis Amiama had disappeared, and that in his desperation to find them, Ramfis was now offering half a million pesos to anyone facilitating their capture. From them he also learned that Antonio de la Maza, General Juan Tomás Díaz, and Amadito had died fighting. He had been kept in isolation, but they had been able to talk with their jailers and learn what was happening on the outside. Huáscar Tejeda had heard from one of his torturers, with whom he had become friendly, about the conversation between Ramfis Trujillo and Antonio de la Maza's father. The son of the Generalissimo came to inform Don Vicente de la Maza, in prison, that his son had died. The old caudillo of Moca asked, without a tremor in his voice: "Did he die fighting?" Ramfis nodded. Don Vicente de la Maza crossed himself: "Thank you, Lord!"

It did him good to see that Pedro Livio Cedeño had recovered from his wounds. Nigger felt absolutely no rancor toward Turk for shooting him in the confusion of that night. "What I can't forgive any of you for is not killing me," he joked. "What did you save my life for? For this? Assholes!" The resentment all of them felt toward Pupo Román was very deep, but nobody was happy when Modesto Díaz said that from his cell on a higher floor, he had seen Pupo naked, handcuffed, his eyelids sewn shut, being dragged by four bailiffs to the torture chamber. Modesto Díaz was not even the shadow of the elegant, intelligent politician he had been all his life; he had lost many kilos, had wounds over his entire body, and wore an expression of infinite despair. "That's what I must look like," thought Salvador. He had not looked in a mirror since his arrest.

He often asked his interrogators to allow him a confessor. At last, the jailer who brought their meals asked who wanted a priest. They all raised their hands. He had them put on trousers and brought them up the steep staircase to the room where Turk had been insulted by his father. To see the sun and feel its warm touch on his skin renewed his spirit. Even more so when he confessed and took communion, something he thought he would never do again. When the military chaplain, Father Rodríguez Canela, asked them to join him in a prayer in memory of Trujillo, only Salvador kneeled down and prayed with him. His companions, disconcerted, remained standing.

From Father Rodríguez Canela he learned the date: August 30, 1961. Only three months had gone by! To him it seemed as if this nightmare had lasted for centuries. Depressed, debilitated, demoralized, they spoke little among themselves, and conversations always revolved around what they had seen, heard, and experienced in El Nueve. Of all the statements his cellmates made, the one indelibly etched into Salvador's brain was the story told by a sobbing Modesto Díaz. For the first few weeks he had been in a cell with Miguel Ángel

Báez Díaz. Turk remembered his surprise on May 30 when this individual appeared in his Volkswagen on the San Cristóbal highway to assure them that Trujillo, with whom he had walked along the Avenida, would come, which was how Salvador learned that this powerful man among the Trujillista faithful was also part of the conspiracy. Abbes García and Ramfis, infuriated with him because he had been so close to Trujillo, were present for all the sessions of electric shocks, beatings, and burnings inflicted on him, and ordered the SIM doctors to revive him so the torture could continue. After two or three weeks, instead of the usual plate of foul-smelling corn mush, a pot with pieces of meat was brought to them in their cell. Miguel Ángel Báez and Modesto gulped it down, choking, eating with both hands until they were full. A short time later the jailer came in. He confronted Báez Díaz: General Ramfis Trujillo wanted to know if eating his own son didn't make him sick. From the floor, Miguel Ángel insulted him: "You can tell that filthy son of a bitch for me that I hope he swallows his tongue and poisons himself." The jailer started to laugh. He left and came back, and from the door he showed them the head of a boy, holding it up by the hair. Miguel Ángel Báez Díaz died a few hours later, in Modesto's arms, of a heart attack.

The image of Miguel Ángel recognizing the head of Miguelito, his oldest son, obsessed Salvador; he had nightmares in which he saw Luisito and Carmen Elly decapitated. He would scream in his sleep, annoying his cellmates.

Unlike his friends, several of whom had tried to end their lives, Salvador was determined to resist until the end. He had reconciled himself with God—he prayed day and night—and the Church forbade suicide. Besides, it wasn't easy to kill oneself. Huáscar Tejeda made the attempt with a tie he stole from one of the jailers (who kept it folded in his back pocket). He tried to hang himself but failed, and because he tried, his punishment intensified. Pedro Livio Cedeño tried to get himself killed by provoking Ramfis in the torture chamber: "son of a bitch," "bastard," "motherfucker," "your slut of a mother La Españolita worked in a whorehouse before she was Trujillo's girlfriend," and he even spat on him. Ramfis did not fire the shots he longed for: "Not yet, not so fast. That'll come at the end. You have to keep paying first."

The second time Salvador Estrella Sadhalá learned the date, it was October 9, 1961. They had him put on trousers, and again he climbed the stairs to the room where the sunlight hurt his eyes and brought joy to his skin. Ramfis was there, pale and impeccable in his uniform of a four-star general, with that day's *El Caribe* in his hand: October 9, 1961. Salvador read the large headline: "Letter from General Pedro A. Estrella to General Ramfis, son of Rafael Leonidas Trujillo."

"Read this letter your father sent me." Ramfis handed him the paper. "He talks about you."

Salvador, his wrists cut by handcuffs, grasped *El Caribe*. He felt vertigo and an indefinable mixture of revulsion and sadness, but he read the entire letter. General Piro Estrella called the Goat "the greatest of all Dominicans," boasted of having been his friend, bodyguard, and protégé, and alluded to Salvador with vile epithets; he spoke of "the felony of a son gone astray" and of "my son's treason when he betrayed his protector" and his own family. Worse than the insults was the final paragraph: his father thanked Ramfis, with bombastic servility, for giving him money to help him survive the confiscation of the family's property because of his son's participation in the assassination.

He returned to his cell sick with disgust and shame. He did not hold up his head again, although he attempted to hide his demoralization from his companions. "It isn't Ramfis, it's my father who has killed me," he thought. And he envied Antonio de la Maza. What luck to be the son of a man like Don Vicente!

A few days after that cruel October 9, when he and his five cellmates were moved to La Victoria—they were hosed down and the clothes they were wearing when they were arrested were returned to them—Turk was a walking corpse. Not even the possibility of having visitors—half an hour, on Thursdays—and hugging and kissing his wife, Luisito, and Carmen Elly, could melt the ice that had formed around his heart after he read General Piro Estrella's public letter to Ramfis Trujillo.

In La Victoria the torture and interrogations stopped. They still slept on the floor but were no longer naked: they wore clothes sent to them from home. The handcuffs were removed. Their families could send food, soft drinks, and some money, with which they bribed their jailers to sell them newspapers, give them information about other prisoners, or carry messages to the outside. President Balaguer's speech at the United Nations, condemning the Trujillo dictatorship and promising democratization "while maintaining order," brought a rebirth of hope in the prison. It seemed incredible, but there was a burgeoning political opposition, with the Civic Union and June 14 operating in the light of day. Above all, his friends were encouraged to learn that in the United States, Venezuela, and elsewhere, committees had been formed to demand that they be tried in a civil court, with international observers. Salvador made an effort to share the optimism of the others. In his prayers, he asked God to give him back his hope. Because he had none. He had seen the implacable expression on Ramfis's face. Would he let them go free? Never. He would carry his revenge through to the end.

There was an explosion of rejoicing in La Victoria when it was learned that Petán and Blacky Trujillo had left the country. Now Ramfis would go too. Balaguer would have no recourse but to declare an amnesty. Modesto Díaz, however, with his powerful logic and cold analytical method, convinced them that their families and attorneys had to mobilize in their defense, now more than ever. Ramfis would not leave before he had exterminated his papa's executioners. As he listened, Salvador observed the ruin that Modesto had become: he was still losing weight and he had the face of a wrinkled old man. How many kilos had he shed? The trousers and shirts his wife brought swam on him, and every week he had to make new holes in his belt.

Salvador was always sad but spoke to no one about his father's public letter, which he carried with him like a knife in the back. Even though their plans did not work out as they had hoped, and there had been so much death and so much suffering, their action had helped to change things. The news filtering into the cells of La Victoria told of meetings, of young people decapitating statues of Trujillo and tearing down plaques with his name and the names of his family, of some exiles returning. Wasn't this the beginning of the end of the Trujillo Era? None of it could have happened if they hadn't killed the Beast.

The return of the Trujillo brothers was an ice-cold shower for the prisoners in La Victoria. Making no effort to hide his joy, on November 17 Major Américo Dante Minervino, the prison warden, told Salvador, Modesto Díaz, Huáscar Tejeda, Pedro Livio, Fifí Pastoriza, and the young Tunti Cáceres that at nightfall they would be transferred to the cells in the Palace of Justice because the next day there would be another reconstruction of the crime on the Avenida. They pooled all their money and, through one of the jailers, sent urgent messages to their families, telling them that something suspicious was going on; there was no doubt the reconstruction was a farce and Ramfis had decided to kill them.

At dusk the six men were handcuffed and taken away, with an escort of three armed guards, in the kind of black van with tinted windows that people in Santo Domingo called the Dogcatcher. Salvador closed his eyes and begged God to take care of his wife and children. Contrary to their worst fears, they were not taken to the cliffs, the regime's favorite spot for secret executions, but to the center of town and the Palace of Justice at the Fairgrounds. They spent most of the night standing, since the cell was so narrow they could not all sit down at the same time. They took turns sitting, two by two. Pedro Livio and Fifí Pastoriza were in good spirits; if they had been brought here, the story about the reconstruction was true. Their optimism infected Tunti Cáceres and Huáscar Tejeda. Yes, yes, why not? They'd be turned over to the Judicial Branch to be tried by civilian judges. Salvador and Modesto Díaz remained silent, concealing their skepticism.

In a very quiet voice, Turk whispered in his friend's ear: "This is the end, isn't it, Modesto?" The lawyer nodded, not saying anything, squeezing his arm.

Before the sun came up they were taken out of the prison and put into the Dogcatcher again. There was an impressive military deployment around the Palace of Justice, and Salvador, in the uncertain light, saw that all the soldiers wore Air Force insignia. They were from San Isidro Air Base, the fiefdom of Ramfis and Virgilio García Trujillo. He said nothing, not wanting to alarm his companions. In the cramped van he tried to talk to God, as he had for part of the night, asking that He help him die with dignity, that he not dishonor himself with any show of cowardice, but he could not concentrate now. His failure caused him great anguish.

After a short drive, the van came to a stop. They were on the San Cristóbal highway. This had to be the site of the assassination. The sun gilded the sky, the coconut palms along the road, the ocean that murmured as it broke against the rocks. There were a great many guards. They had cordoned off the highway and blocked traffic in both directions.

"As far as this circus is concerned, the boy turned out to be as much of a clown as his papa," he heard Modesto Díaz say.

"Why should it be a circus?" Fifí Pastoriza protested. "Don't be such a pessimist. It's a reconstruction. Even the judges are here. Don't you see?"

"The same kind of joke his papa liked," Modesto insisted, shaking his head in disgust.

Farce or not, it went on for many hours, until the sun was in the middle of the sky and began to drill into their skulls. One by one, they were made to pass in front of a campaign table set up outdoors, where two men in civilian clothing asked the same questions that had been asked in El Nueve and La Victoria. Typists recorded their answers. Only low-ranking officers were present. None of the top brass—Ramfis, Abbes García, Pechito León Estévez, Pirulo Sánchez Rubirosa—were visible during the tedious ceremony. They were not given anything to eat, only some glasses of soda at noon. It was early afternoon when the rotund warden of La Victoria, Major Américo Dante Minervino, put in an appearance. He was chewing nervously on his mustache and his face looked more sinister than usual. He was accompanied by a corpulent black with the flattened nose of a boxer, a submachine gun on his shoulder and a pistol tucked into his belt. They were returned to the Dogcatcher.

"Where are we going?" Pedro Livio asked Minervino.

"Back to La Victoria," he said. "I came to take you back myself so you won't get lost."

"What an honor," replied Pedro Livio.

The major was behind the wheel and the black with the boxer's face sat beside him. The three guards escorting them in the rear of the Dogcatcher were so young they looked like new recruits. They seemed tense, overwhelmed by the responsibility of guarding such important prisoners. In addition to handcuffs, their ankles were tied rather loosely, allowing them to take short steps.

"What the hell do these ropes mean?" Tunti Cáceres protested.

One of the guards pointed at the major and lifted a finger to his mouth: "Quiet."

During the long ride, Salvador realized they were not going back to La Victoria, and judging by the faces of his companions, they had guessed the same thing. They were silent, some with their eyes closed and others with their eyes opened wide, and blazing, as if trying to see through the metal sides of the vehicle to find out where they were. He did not try to pray. His anxiety was so great, it would have been use-less. God would understand.

When the van stopped, they heard the ocean crashing at the foot of a high cliff. The guards opened the door. They were at a deserted spot with reddish earth and sparse trees, on what seemed to be a promon-tory. The sun was still shining, but it had already begun its descending arc. Salvador told himself that dying would be a way to rest. What he felt now was immense weariness.

Dante Minervino and the powerful black with the face of a boxer had the three adolescent guards climb out of the van, but when the six prisoners tried to follow, they stopped them: "Stay where you are." Im-mediately after that, they began to fire. Not at them, at the young soldiers. The three boys fell, riddled with bullets, without time to be surprised, to understand, to scream.

"What are you doing, what are you doing, you criminals!" Salvador bellowed. "Why kill those poor guards? Murderers!"

"We're not killing them, you are," Major Dante Minervino replied, very seriously, as he reloaded his submachine gun; the black with the flattened face rewarded him with a giggle. "And now you can get out."

Stunned, stupid with surprise, the six men were taken down, and, stumbling—the ropes obliged them to move in ridiculous little jumps—over the corpses of the three guards, they were taken to an-other, identical van parked a few meters away. One man in civilian clothes was guarding it. After locking them into the back of the van, the three men squeezed into the front seat. Once again, Dante Mi-nervino was at the wheel.

And now Salvador could pray. He heard one of his companions sobbing, but this did not distract him. He prayed with no difficulty, as he had in better times, for himself, his family, the three guards who had just been murdered, his five companions in the van, one of whom, in an attack of nerves, was cursing and banging his head against the metal plate that separated them from the driver.

He did not know how long this trip lasted, because he did not stop praying for an instant. He felt peace and an immense tenderness think-ing of his wife and children. When they pulled to a stop and opened the door, he saw the sea, the dusk, the sun sinking in an inky blue sky.

The men pulled them out. They were in the courtyard-garden of a large house, next to a pool. There were a handful of silver palms with lofty crowns, and, about twenty meters away, a terrace with figures of men holding glasses. He recognized Ramfis, Pechito León Estévez, Pechito's brother Alfonso, Pirulo Sánchez Rubirosa, and two or three others he did not know. Alfonso León Estévez ran over to them, still holding his glass of whiskey. He helped Américo Dante Minervino and the black boxer shove them toward the coconut palms.

"One at a time, Alfonso!" Ramfis ordered. "He's drunk," Salvador thought. The son of the Goat had to get drunk to give his last party.

The first one they shot was Pedro Livio, who collapsed instantly under the barrage of revolver and submachine-gun fire that cut him down. Next, they pulled Tunti Cáceres over to the palms, and before he fell he insulted Ramfis: "Degenerate, coward, faggot!" And then, Modesto Díaz, who shouted: "Long live the Republic!" and lay writhing on the ground before he died.

Then it was his turn. They did not have to shove or drag him. Taking the short little steps allowed by the ropes around his ankles, he walked by himself to the palm trees where his friends were lying, thanking God that he had been permitted to be with Him in his final moments, and telling himself, with a certain melancholy, that he would never see Basquinta, the Lebanese village left behind by the Sadhalás to preserve their faith and seek their fortune in this land of our Lord.

22 When he heard the telephone ring, President Joaquín Balaguer, still not fully awake, had a presentiment of something very serious. He picked up the receiver at the same time that he rubbed his eyes with his free hand. He heard General José René Román summon him to a high-level meeting at the Army General Staff. "They've killed him," he thought. The conspiracy had been successful. He was completely awake now. He could not waste time indulging in pity or anger; for the moment, the problem was the head of the Armed Forces. He cleared his throat and said, slowly: "If something so serious has occurred, as President of the Republic my place is not in a barracks but at the National Palace. I am going there now. I suggest that the meeting be held in my office. Goodbye." He hung up before the Minister of the Armed Forces had time to answer.

He got up and dressed, not making any noise so as not to awaken his sisters. They had killed Trujillo, no doubt about it. And a coup was under way, led by Román. Why would he call him to the December 18 Fortress? To force him to resign, or arrest him, or demand that he support the uprising. It seemed crude, badly planned. Instead of telephoning, he should have sent a patrol for him. Román, though he might command the Armed Forces, lacked the prestige to impose his will on the garrisons. It was going to fail.

He went out, and at the sentry box he asked the guard to wake his driver. As the chauffeur drove him to the National Palace along a dark, deserted Avenida Máximo Gómez, he foresaw the next few hours: confrontations between rebellious and loyal garrisons, and possible military intervention by the United States. Washington would require some constitutional pretense to take that action, and at this moment, the President of the Republic represented legality. True, his post was purely decorative. But with Trujillo dead, it was taking on reality. The transformation from mere figurehead to the authentic Head of State of the Dominican Republic depended on his conduct. Perhaps without knowing it, he had been waiting for this moment since his birth in 1906. Once again he repeated to himself the motto of his life: never, for any reason, lose your composure.

This determination was reinforced as soon as he entered the National Palace and saw the reigning confusion. The guards had been doubled, and armed soldiers wandered corridors and stairways, looking for someone to shoot. Some officials saw him walking calmly toward his office, and seemed relieved; perhaps he would know what to do. He never reached his office. In the reception room adjoining the Generalissimo's office, he saw the Trujillo family: wife, daughter, brothers and sisters, nephews and nieces. He went to them, wearing the grave expression the moment demanded. Angelita's eyes were filled with tears, and she was pale; but on the heavy, avaricious face of Doña María there was rage, immeasurable rage.

"What's going to happen to us, Dr. Balaguer?" Angelita stammered, seizing his arm.

"Nothing, nothing is going to happen to you," he consoled her. He also embraced the Bountiful First Lady: "The important thing is to remain calm. To arm ourselves with courage. God will not permit His Excellency's death."

A simple glance was enough to let him know that this tribe of poor devils had lost its compass. Petán, waving a submachine gun, walked in circles like a dog trying to bite its own tail, sweating and shouting nonsense about the mountain fire beetles, his own private army, while Héctor Bienvenido (Blacky), the former President, seemed the victim of catatonic idiocy: he stared at nothing, his mouth full of saliva, as if trying to remember who and where he was. And even the most unfortunate of the Chief's brothers, Amable Romeo (Peepee), was there, dressed like a beggar, cowering in a chair, his mouth hanging open. Sitting in armchairs, Trujillo's sisters—Nieves Luisa, Marina, Julieta, Ofelia Japonesa—wiped their eyes or looked at him, pleading for help. He murmured words of encouragement to all of them. There was a vacuum, and it had to be filled as soon as possible.

He went to his office and called General Santos Mélido Marte, the

Inspector General of the Armed Forces, the officer in the top military hierarchy with whom he had the longest relationship. He had heard nothing and was so stunned by the news that for half a minute the only thing he could say was "My God, oh my God." Balaguer asked him to call all the commanding generals and heads of garrisons in the Republic, assure them that the probable assassination had not altered the constitutional order and that they had the confidence of the Head of State, who was reconfirming their appointments. "I'll get on it right away, Mr. President," the general said, and hung up.

He was told that the apostolic nuncio, the American consul, and the chargé d'affaires of the United Kingdom were at the entrance to the Palace, held there by guards. He had them come in. What had brought them was not the assassination but the violent capture of Monsignor Reilly by armed men, who had broken down the doors of the Santo Domingo Academy and forced their way in. They fired their guns into the air, beat the nuns and the Redemptorist priests from San Juan de la Maguana who accompanied the bishop, killed a watchdog, and dragged the prelate away.

"Mr. President, I am holding you responsible for the life of Monsignor Reilly," the nuncio warned.

"My government will not tolerate any attempt against his life," threatened the representative of the United States. "I don't need to remind you of Washington's interest in Reilly, who is an American citizen."

"Have a seat, please," he said, indicating the chairs that surrounded his desk. He picked up the telephone and asked to speak to General Virgilio García Trujillo, head of San Isidro Air Base. He turned to the diplomats: "Believe me, I regret this more than you do. I will spare no effort to remedy this act of barbarism."

A short while later, he heard the voice of the Generalissimo's nephew. Without moving his eyes away from the trio of visitors, he said, slowly and deliberately:

"I am speaking to you as President of the Republic, General. I am addressing you as the head of San Isidro and also His Excellency's favorite nephew. I will spare you the preliminaries in view of the gravity of the situation. In an act of enormous irresponsibility, some subordinate, perhaps Colonel Abbes García, has arrested Bishop Reilly after taking him by force from the Santo Domingo Academy. Sitting here now are representatives of the United States, Great Britain, and the Vatican. If anything happens to Monsignor Reilly, who is an American citizen, it can be catastrophic for the country. There may even be a landing of Marines. I do not need to tell you what that would mean for our nation. In the name of the Generalissimo, your uncle, I urge you to avoid a historical calamity."

He waited for General Virgilio García Trujillo's reaction. That nervous panting betrayed his indecision.

"It wasn't my idea, Dr. Balaguer," he heard him murmur at last. "I wasn't even informed about this."

"I know that very well, General Trujillo," Balaguer helped him along. "You are a sensible, responsible officer. You would never commit such an outrage. Is Monsignor Reilly at San Isidro? Or have they taken him to La Cuarenta?"

There was a long, barbed silence. He feared the worst.

"Is Monsignor Reilly alive?" Balaguer persisted.

"He's being held at an outpost of the base about two kilometers from here, Dr. Balaguer. The commander of the detention center, Rodríguez Méndez, did not allow him to be killed. I was just told."

The President sweetened his voice:

"I implore you to go there in person, as my emissary, to rescue the monsignor. And to ask his forgiveness, in the name of the government, for the error. And then bring the bishop to my office. Safe and sound. This is a request to a friend, and also an order from the President of the Republic. I have full confidence in you."

The three visitors looked at him in confusion. He stood and walked over to them. He accompanied them to the door. As he shook their hands, he murmured:

"I am not certain of being obeyed, gentlemen. But, as you can see, I am doing everything in my power to restore rationality."

"What's going to happen, Mr. President?" the consul asked. "Will the Trujillistas accept your authority?"

"A good deal will depend on the United States, my friend. Frankly, I do not know. And now, if you will excuse me, gentlemen."

He returned to the room where the Trujillo family waited. More people had arrived. Colonel Abbes García was explaining that one of the assassins, held prisoner at the International Clinic, had given the names of three accomplices: the retired general Juan Tomás Díaz, Antonio Imbert, and Luis Amiama. No doubt there were many others. Among those assembled, he saw General Román; his khaki shirt was soaked, his face covered in perspiration, and he held his submachine gun in both hands. His eyes boiled with the frenzy of an animal that knows it is lost. Clearly, things had not gone well for him. In his thin, tuneless voice, the corpulent head of the SIM asserted that according to the former soldier, Pedro Livio Cedeño, the conspiracy had no ramifications inside the Armed Forces. As he listened, he told himself that the moment had arrived to confront Abbes García, who detested him. He merely had contempt for the head of the SIM. At times like this, unfortunately, pistols, not ideas, tended to prevail. He asked God, in whom he sometimes believed, to be on his side.

Colonel Abbes García launched the first attack. Given the vacuum left by the assassination, Balaguer ought to resign so that someone in the family could occupy the Presidency. With his intemperate vulgarity, Petán supported him: "Yes, let him resign." He listened, silently, his hands folded across his stomach, like a mild-mannered parish priest. When their eyes all turned to him, he nodded timidly, as if apologizing for finding himself obliged to intervene. Modestly, he reminded them that he held the Presidency by a decision of the Generalissimo. He would resign immediately if that would serve the nation, of course. But he would permit himself to suggest that before disrupting constitutional order, they wait for the arrival of General Ramfis. Could the Chief's firstborn be excluded from so serious a matter? The Bountiful First Lady immediately agreed: she would accept no decision without her oldest son being present. According to Colonel Luis José (Pechito) León Estévez, Ramfis and Radhamés were already making preparations in Paris to charter an Air France plane. The question was tabled.

As he returned to his office, he told himself that the real battle should be waged not against Trujillo's brothers, that pack of idiotic thugs, but against Abbes García. He might be a demented sadist, but he had the intelligence of Lucifer. Abbes had just made a mistake, forgetting about Ramfis. María Martínez had become Balaguer's ally. He knew how to seal the alliance: the Bountiful First Lady's avarice would be useful in the present circumstance. But the most urgent matter was to prevent an uprising. When it was the usual time for him to be at his desk, the call came from General Mélido Marte. He had spoken with all the military regions, and the commanders had assured him of their loyalty to the constituted government. Still, General César A. Oliva in Santiago de los Caballeros, General García Urbáez in Dajabón, and General Guarionex Estrella in La Vega were disturbed by contradictory communications from the Minister of the Armed Forces. Did the President know anything about that?

"Nothing concrete, but I imagine the same thing you do, my friend," Balaguer said to General Mélido Marte. "I will telephone those commanders and attempt to reassure them. Ramfis Trujillo is on his way home to guarantee leadership of the country's military."

Without wasting any time, he called the three generals and reiterated that they enjoyed his full confidence. He asked them to assume all administrative and political powers and guarantee order in their regions, and, until General Ramfis arrived, to speak only to him. As he was saying goodbye to General Guarionex Estrella Sadhalá, his aides informed him that General Virgilio García Trujillo was in the anteroom with Bishop Reilly. He had Trujillo's nephew come in alone.

"You have saved the Republic," he said, embracing him, something he never did. "If Abbes García's orders had been carried out and the irreparable had happened, the Marines would be landing in Ciudad Trujillo."

"They weren't only Abbes García's orders," the head of San Isidro Air Base replied. He seemed confused. "The one who ordered Commander Rodríguez Méndez, at the Air Force detention center, to shoot the bishop was Pechito León Estévez. He said it was my brother-in-law's decision. Yes, Pupo. I don't understand. Nobody even consulted me. It was a miracle that Rodríguez Méndez refused to act until he talked to me."

General García Trujillo cared for his appearance and dress—a thin Mexican-style mustache, brilliantined hair, a well-cut, pressed uniform, as if he were about to go on parade, and the inevitable Ray-Ban sunglasses in his pocket—as coquettishly as his cousin Ramfis, whose intimate friend he was. But now his shirt was not tucked all the way in, and his hair was disheveled; suspicion and doubt were in his eyes.

"I don't understand why Pupo and Pechito made a decision like that without talking to me first. They wanted to compromise the Air Force, Dr. Balaguer."

"General Román must be so affected by what happened to the Generalissimo that he has lost control of his nerves." The President made excuses for him. "Fortunately, Ramfis is already on the way. His presence is absolutely necessary. It falls to him, as a four-star general and the son of the Chief, to assure the continuity of the Benefactor's policies."

"But Ramfis isn't a politician, he hates politics; you know that, Dr. Balaguer."

"Ramfis is a very intelligent man, and he adored his father. He cannot refuse to assume the role that the Nation expects of him. We will persuade him."

General García Trujillo looked at him warmly.

"You can count on me to do what is needed, Mr. President."

"Dominicans will know that you saved the Republic tonight," Balaguer repeated as he accompanied him to the door. "You have a great responsibility, General. San Isidro is the most important base in the country, and for that reason, maintaining order depends on you. If anything happens, call me; I have ordered priority status for your calls."

Bishop Reilly must have spent terrifying hours in the hands of the *caliés*. His habit was torn and muddied, and deep furrows lined his pale, thin face that still bore the imprint of a grimace of horror. He was erect and silent. He listened with dignity to the excuses and explanations of the President of the Republic, and even made an effort to smile as he thanked him for the steps he had taken to free him: "Forgive them, Mr. President, for they know not what they do." At that point, the door opened, and, submachine gun in hand, drenched in sweat, eyes brutalized by fear and rage, General Román burst into the office. A moment was all the President needed to know that if he did not take the initiative, this ape would start to fire. "Ah, Monsignor, look who is here." Effusively, he thanked the Minister of the Armed Forces for coming to apologize, in the name of the military, to His Grace the Bishop of San Juan de la Maguana for the misunderstanding of which he had been the victim. General Román, turned to stone in the middle of the office, blinked with a stupid expression on his face. He had crusts in his eyes, as if he had just awakened. Without saying a word, after hesitating for a few seconds, he extended his hand to the bishop, who was as disconcerted as the general by what was happening. The President said goodbye to Monsignor Reilly at the door.

When he returned to his desk, Pupo Román shouted: "You owe me an explanation. Who the hell do you think you are, Balaguer?" and waved his submachine gun in his face. The President remained imperturbable, looking him in the eye. He felt invisible rain on his face, the general's spittle. This lunatic would not dare to fire now. After a stream of insults and curses and incoherent phrases, Román fell silent. He was still in the same spot, panting. In a soft, deferential voice, the President advised him to make an effort to control himself. At a time like this, the head of the Armed Forces should set an example of equilibrium. Despite his insults and threats, he was prepared to help him, if he needed him. General Román exploded once again into a semidelirious monologue during which he let him know, for no good reason, that he had given the order to execute Major Segundo Imbert and Papito Sánchez, imprisoned in La Victoria, for complicity in the assassination of the Chief. He did not want to go on listening to such dangerous confidences. Without saying a word, he left the office. There could be no doubt: Román was involved in the death of the Generalissimo. His irrational behavior could not be explained in any other way.

He returned to the reception room. They had discovered the body of Trujillo in the trunk of a car, in the garage of General Juan Tomás Díaz. In all the long years of his life, Dr. Balaguer would never forget the contorted faces, the weeping eyes, the expressions of abandonment, loss, despair, among civilians and military men, when the bloody, bullet-ridden corpse, its face destroyed by the bullet that had shattered the chin, was laid out on the bare table in the dining room of the Palace (where, a few hours earlier, Simon and Dorothy Gittleman had been regaled at a luncheon) and stripped and washed so that a team of doctors could examine the remains and prepare the body for the wake. The reaction of the widow made more of an impression on him than anyone else's response. Doña María Martínez stared at the victim as if she were hypnotized, standing very straight in the high-platform shoes on which she always seemed to be perched. Her eyes were dilated and red, but she was not crying. She gesticulated suddenly and roared: "Vengeance! Vengeance! They all have to be killed!" Dr. Balaguer hurried to her and placed an arm around her shoulders. She did not move away. He could hear her deep, heavy breathing. She was trembling convulsively. "They will have to pay, they will have to pay," she repeated. "We will move heaven and earth to make it so, Doña María," he whispered in her ear. At that instant he had a presentiment:

now, at this moment, he had to drive home what he had achieved with the Bountiful First Lady; afterward it would be too late.

Pressing her arm tenderly, as if to move her away from the sight that caused her suffering, he led Doña María Martínez to one of the small rooms adjoining the dining room. As soon as he was certain that they were alone, he closed the door.

"Doña María, you are an exceptionally strong woman," he said fondly. "That is why I presume, at such a sorrowful time, to disturb your grief with a matter that may seem inopportune. But it is not. My actions are guided by admiration and affection. Please, sit down."

The round face of the Bountiful First Lady looked at him with distrust. He smiled at her sadly. It was undoubtedly impertinent to pester her with practical matters when her spirit had to absorb a terrible blow. But what about the future? Doña María had a long life ahead of her, did she not? Who could tell what might happen after this cataclysm? It was imperative that she take certain precautions, thinking always of the future. The ingratitude of nations was a proven fact, ever since Judas' betrayal of Christ. The country might cry for Trujillo today, and raise its voice against the assassins. But would it remain loyal tomorrow to the memory of the Chief? Suppose resentment, that national disease, triumphed? He did not want to waste her time. And therefore he would come straight to the point. Doña María had to protect herself, had to secure against all eventualities the legitimate property acquired through the efforts of the Trujillo family, which had, moreover, provided so many benefits to the Dominican people. And do it before subsequent political readjustments became an obstacle. Dr. Balaguer suggested she discuss this with Senator Henry Chirinos, who was entrusted with the management of the family businesses, and determine what portion of the patrimony could be transferred overseas immediately, without incurring too much of a loss. It was something that still could be done with absolute discretion. The President of the Republic had the power to authorize operations of this kind—the conversion of Dominican pesos into foreign currency by the Central Bank, for example—but there was no way to know if it would still be possible later on. The Generalissimo was always reluctant to make these transfers because of his high moral scruples. Maintaining this policy under current circumstances would be, if she would forgive the expression, sheer stupidity. It was a piece of friendly advice, inspired by devotion and friendship.

The Bountiful First Lady listened in silence, looking into his eyes. Finally she nodded appreciatively:

"I knew you were a loyal friend, Dr. Balaguer," she said, very sure of herself.

"I hope to prove it to you, Doña María. I trust you have not been offended by my counsel."

"It's good advice. In this country you never know what can happen," she grumbled. "I'll talk to Dr. Chirinos tomorrow. Everything will be done with the greatest discretion?"

"On my honor, Doña María," the President declared, touching his chest.

He saw a doubt altering the expression of the Generalissimo's widow. And he guessed what she was going to say to him:

"I ask that you don't even speak to my children about this little matter," she said, very quietly, as if she were afraid they might hear her. "For reasons it would take too long to explain."

"Not to anyone, not even to them, Doña María," the President reassured her. "Of course. Allow me to reiterate how much I admire your character, Doña María. Without you, the Benefactor could never have accomplished all that he did."

He had won another point in his strategic war with Johnny Abbes García. Doña María's response had been predictable: her greed was stronger than any other passion. And, in fact, the Bountiful First Lady inspired a certain respect in Dr. Balaguer. In order to keep herself at Trujillo's side for so many years, first as mistress, then as wife, La Española had been obliged to strip away all sensitivity, all sentiment— especially pity—and take refuge in calculation, cold calculation, and, perhaps, hatred as well.

The reaction of Ramfis, on the other hand, disconcerted him. Within two hours of his arrival with Radhamés, Porfirio Rubirosa, and a group of friends at San Isidro Air Base, on a chartered Air France plane—Balaguer was the first to embrace him at the bottom of the steps—and freshly shaved and dressed in his uniform of a four-star general, he came to the National Palace to pay his respects to his father. He did not cry, he did not say a word. His grief-stricken, handsome face was ashen and wore a strange expression of surprise, befuddlement, denial, as if that recumbent figure in evening clothes, the chest covered with medals, lying in the sumptuous casket surrounded by candelabra, in a room filled with funeral wreaths, could not and should not be there, as if the fact that it was there revealed a failure in the order of the universe. He spent a long time looking at his father's corpse, his face twisting into grimaces he could not control; it seemed as if his facial muscles were trying to shake off a spiderweb sticking to his skin. "I won't be as generous as you were with your enemies," he heard him say at last. Then Dr. Balaguer, who was at his side, dressed in strict mourning, whispered in his ear: "It is indispensable that we speak for a few minutes, General. I know this is a very difficult moment for you. But there are matters that cannot be put off." Ramfis nodded, regaining his self-control. They went, alone, to the President's office. On the way, they could see through the windows the huge, growing crowd, swelling with the arrival of groups of men and women from the outskirts of Ciudad Trujillo and nearby towns. The line, in rows of four or five, was several kilometers long, and the armed guards could scarcely control it. They had been waiting for hours. There were heartrending scenes, outbursts of weeping, hysterical displays among those who had already reached the steps of the Palace and felt themselves close to the Generalissimo's funeral chamber.

Dr. Joaquín Balaguer always knew that his future, and the future of the Dominican Republic, depended on this conversation. As a consequence, he decided on something that he did only in extreme cases, since it went against his cautious nature: he would gamble everything on a single play. Holding off until Trujillo's oldest son was sitting on a chair that faced his desk—through the windows, moving like a turbulent sea, the immense, eddying crowd waited to reach the body of the Benefactor—and not wavering from his tranquil manner, not betraying the slightest uneasiness, he said the words he had carefully prepared:

"It depends on you, and only on you, whether some, a good deal, or nothing at all of Trujillo's work endures. If his legacy disappears, the Dominican Republic will sink back into barbarism. We will compete again with Haiti, as we did before 1930, for the privilege of being the poorest, most violent nation in the Western Hemisphere."

He spoke at length, but Ramfis did not interrupt once. Was he listening? He did not nod or shake his head; his eyes, fixed on him for part of the time, wandered periodically, and Dr. Balaguer told himself that this kind of look probably indicated the onset of the crises of withdrawal and acute depression for which he had been committed to psychiatric hospitals in France and Belgium. But, if he was listening, Ramfis would weigh what he was saying. For although he was a drinker, a womanizer with no political vocation or civic concerns, a man whose sensibilities seemed limited to the feelings aroused in him by women, horses, planes, and liquor, and one who could be as cruel as his father, he clearly was intelligent. Probably the only one in the family with the brains to see past his nose, his belly, his phallus. He had a quick, sharp mind that, if cultivated, might have borne excellent fruit. He directed his recklessly frank exposition to that intelligence. He was convinced this was his last card if he did not want to be swept away like wastepaper by the gentlemen with guns.

When he stopped speaking, General Ramfis was even paler than when he had been looking at his father's body.

"You could lose your life for half of the things you've said to me, Dr. Balaguer."

"I know, General. The situation left me no choice but to speak to you frankly. I have laid out for you the only policy I believe possible. If you see any other, so much the better. I have my resignation here in this drawer. Shall I submit it to Congress?"

Ramfis shook his head no. He took a breath, and after a moment, in his melodious, radio actor's voice, he said:

"A long time ago I reached a similar conclusion, by a different route." He moved his shoulders in resignation. "It's true, I don't believe there is another policy. To save ourselves from the Marines and the Communists, and to have the OAS and Washington lift the sanctions. I accept your plan. You'll have to consult with me and wait for my okay before each step, each measure, each agreement. I insist on that. Command of the military, questions of security, are my affair. I will tolerate no interference, not from you or civilian bureaucrats, and not from the Yankees. No one who has been involved, directly or indirectly, in Papa's assassination will go unpunished."

Dr. Balaguer rose to his feet.

"I know you adored him," he said solemnly. "It speaks well of your filial sentiments that you want to avenge this horrendous crime. No one, least of all me, will stand in the way of your determination to see justice done. That, too, is my most fervent desire."

When he had said goodbye to Trujillo's son, he sipped a glass of water. His heart was recovering its natural rhythm. He had staked his life and won the bet. Now, to put into effect what they had agreed on.

He began at the Benefactor's funeral in the church in San Cristóbal. His eulogy, filled with moving tributes to the Generalissimo yet attenuated by sibylline critical allusions, made some uninformed courtiers shed tears, disconcerted others, raised the eyebrows of still others, and left many confused, but it earned the congratulations of the diplomatic corps. "Things are beginning to change, Mr. President," the new American consul, recently arrived on the island, said approvingly. The next day, Dr. Balaguer urgently summoned Colonel Abbes García. The moment he saw him, his bloated face consumed with annoyance—he was wiping away perspiration with his inevitable red handkerchief—he told himself that the head of the SIM knew perfectly well why he was here.

"Did you call me to let me know I've been dismissed?" he asked, without greeting him. He was in uniform, his trousers slipping down and his cap comically to one side; in addition to the pistol at his waist, a submachine gun hung from his shoulder. Behind him Balaguer saw the thuggish faces of four or five bodyguards, who did not come into the office.

"To ask you to accept a diplomatic post," the President said amiably. His tiny hand indicated a chair. "A patriot with talent can serve the nation in many different areas."

"Where is this golden exile?" Abbes García did not attempt to hide his frustration or his anger.

"In Japan," said the President. "I have just signed your appointment as consul. Your salary and expenses will be those of an ambassador."

"Couldn't you send me any farther away?"

"There is no other place," Dr. Balaguer apologized, without irony. "The only country more distant is New Zealand, but we do not have diplomatic relations with them."

The rotund figure shifted in his seat, snorting. A yellow line of infinite dislike surrounded the irises of his bulging eyes. He held the red handkerchief to his lips for a moment, as if he were going to spit in it.

"You believe you've won, Dr. Balaguer," he said in an abusive tone. "You're wrong. You are as closely identified with this regime as I am. As dirty as I am. Nobody will swallow the Machiavellian ploy of you leading the transition to democracy."

"It is possible I will fail," Balaguer admitted, with no hostility. "But I must try. And to that end, some people have to be sacrificed. I am sorry you are the first, but it cannot be avoided: you represent the worst face of the regime. A necessary, heroic, tragic face, I know. The Generalissimo himself, sitting in the same chair you occupy now, pointed that out to me. But for that very reason, it is impossible to save you at a time like this. You are an intelligent man, I do not need to explain it to you. Do not create needless complications for the government. Go abroad and be discreet. It is to your benefit to leave, to make yourself invisible until people forget you. You have many enemies. And any number of countries that would like to get their hands on you. The United States, Venezuela, Interpol, the FBI, Mexico, all of Central America. You know this better than I. Japan is a safe haven, even more so with diplomatic immunity. I understand you have always been interested in spiritualism. The Rosicrucian doctrine, I believe? Use the opportunity to deepen your studies. Finally, if you wish to settle someplace else, please do not tell me where; you will continue to receive your salary. I have signed a special order for your traveling and moving expenses. Two hundred thousand pesos, which you can draw on the Treasury. Good luck."

He did not extend his hand, because he supposed the former soldier (the night before, he had signed the decree separating him from the Army) would not shake it. For a long time Abbes García sat motionless, observing him with bloodshot eyes. But the President knew he was a pragmatic man, who, instead of reacting with some stupid piece of bravado, would accept the lesser evil. He saw him stand and leave, without saying goodbye. He personally dictated to a secretary the communiqué stating that *former* Colonel Abbes García had resigned from the Intelligence Service to accept a diplomatic post overseas. Two days later, among five columns announcing the deaths and arrests of the Generalissimo's killers, *El Caribe* published a photograph in which Dr. Balaguer could see Abbes García, wearing a braid-trimmed coat and the bowler hat of a character out of Dickens, walking up the steps to an airplane.

By this time, the President had decided that the new parliamentary leader, whose mission would be to discreetly turn the Congress toward positions more acceptable to the United States and the West, would be not Agustín Cabral but Senator Henry Chirinos. He would have preferred Egghead, whose sober habits coincided with his own way of life, while he found the alcoholism of the Constitutional Sot repugnant. But he chose him because the sudden rehabilitation of a man who had fallen into disgrace through a recent decision of His Excellency could anger the hard-core Trujillistas, whom he still needed. He must not provoke them too much, not yet. Chirinos was physically and morally repulsive, but his talent for intrigue and legalistic scheming was infinite. Nobody knew parliamentary tricks better than he. They had never been friends—because of alcohol, which disgusted Balaguer—but as soon as he was called to the Palace and the President let him know what he expected of him, the senator exulted, just as he did when Balaguer asked him to facilitate, in the speediest and most invisible way possible, the transfer of the Bountiful First Lady's funds overseas. ("A noble concern of yours, Mr. President: to assure the future of an illustrious matron in her misfortune.") On that occasion, Senator Chirinos, still in the dark regarding what was being planned, admitted that he had been honored to inform the SIM that Antonio de la Maza and General Juan Tomás Díaz were wandering around the old colonial city (he had spotted them in a car parked in front of the house of a friend, on Calle Espaillat) and requested the President's good offices in claiming the reward Ramfis was offering for any information leading to the capture of his father's assassins. Dr. Balaguer advised him to forgo the money and not publicize his patriotic denunciation: it could prejudice his political future in an irremediable way. The man whom Trujillo called the Walking Turd to his intimates, understood immediately:

"Allow me to congratulate you, Mr. President," he exclaimed, gesturing as if he were on a speaker's platform. "I have always believed that the regime ought to open up to modern times. With the Chief gone, no one better than you to weather the storm and steer the Dominican ship of state into the port of democracy. You can count on me as your most loyal and dedicated collaborator."

And, in fact, he was. In the Congress he introduced the motion granting General Ramfis Trujillo supreme power in the military hierarchy and maximum authority in all military and police matters in the Republic, and he instructed the deputies and senators regarding the new policy proposed by the President, intended not to negate the past or reject the Trujillo Era but to go beyond it dialectically, adapting it to different times so that as the Republic—with no steps backward—was perfecting her democracy, she would be welcomed again by her sister nations of the Americas into the OAS and, once sanctions were lifted, reintegrated into the international community. In one of his frequent working meetings with President Balaguer, Senator Chirinos asked, not without a certain uneasiness, about His Excellency's plans with respect to former senator Agustín Cabral.

"I have ordered his bank accounts unfrozen and his services to the State acknowledged so that he can receive a pension," Balaguer informed him. "For the moment, his return to political life does not seem opportune."

"We are in full agreement," the senator said approvingly. "Egghead, with whom I have a long-standing relationship, is a conflictive man who creates enemies."

"The State can make use of his talent as long as he is not too prominent," the chief executive added. "I have proposed to him that he serve as a legal adviser in the administration."

"A wise decision." Again Chirinos approved. "Agustín always had an excellent juridical mind."

Barely five weeks had passed since the death of the Generalissimo, and the changes were considerable. Joaquín Balaguer could not complain: in that brief time, he had transformed himself from a puppet president, a nonentity, into an authentic Head of State, an office recognized by all factions, and, in particular, by the United States. They had been hesitant at first, but after he explained his plans to the new consul, they now took more seriously his promise to move the country gradually toward full democracy while maintaining order and not allowing any advantage to the Communists. Every two or three days he had meetings with the efficient John Calvin Hill—a diplomat with the body of a cowboy, who spoke plainly and to the point—whom he had just convinced that, at this stage, it was necessary to have Ramfis as an ally. The general had accepted his plan of gradual opening. He had control of the military, and consequently those thuggish brutes Petán and Héctor, as well as the more primitive adherents of Trujillo in the Armed Forces, were kept in check. Otherwise, they would already have deposed the President. Perhaps Ramfis believed that with the concessions he granted Balaguer—the return of certain exiles, the appearance of timid criticism of the Trujillo regime on the radio and in the papers (the most belligerent, *La Unión Cívica*, was published for the first time in August), increasingly visible public meetings of opposition forces, the rightist National Civic Union of Viriato Fiallo and Ángel Severo

Cabral, and the leftist June 14 Revolutionary Movement—he could have a political future. As if anyone named Trujillo could ever figure again in the public life of this nation! For the moment, best not to disabuse him of his error. Ramfis controlled the weapons and had the support of the military; shaking up the Armed Forces until Trujillism had been eradicated would take time. Relations between the government and the Church were excellent again; he sometimes had tea with the apostolic nuncio and Archbishop Pittini.

The problem that could not be resolved in a manner acceptable to international opinion was the question of "human rights." There were daily protests on behalf of political prisoners, victims of torture, the disappeared, the murdered, at La Victoria, El Nueve, La Cuarenta, and prisons and garrisons in the interior. His office was inundated with manifestos, letters, telegrams, reports, diplomatic communications. He could not do much. Or, rather, anything, except make vague promises and look away. He kept his part of the bargain to give Ramfis a free hand. Even if he had wanted to, he could not have broken his word. The Generalissimo's son had sent Doña María and Angelita to Europe, and tirelessly continued the search for accomplices, as if multitudes had taken part in the conspiracy to kill Trujillo. One day, the young general asked him point-blank:

"Do you know that Pedro Livio Cedeño tried to implicate you in the plot to kill Papa?"

"I am not surprised," the impassive President said with a smile. "The best defense the assassins have is to compromise everyone. Especially those who were close to the Benefactor. The French call it 'intoxication.' "

"If only one other assassin had corroborated it, you'd have suffered the same fate as Pupo Román." Ramfis seemed sober despite the smell of alcohol on his breath. "Right now he's cursing the day he was born."

"I do not want to know about it, General," Balaguer interrupted, holding up a tiny hand. "You have the moral right to avenge the crime. But do not give me any details, I beg you. It is easier to deal with the criticisms I receive from all around the world if I am not aware that the excesses they denounce are true."

"All right. I'll only inform you of the capture of Antonio Imbert and Luis Amiama, if we do capture them." Balaguer saw his handsome actor's face contort, as it always did whenever he mentioned the only two participants in the plot who were not imprisoned or dead. "Do you think they're still in the country?"

"In my judgment, yes," Balaguer declared. "If they had gone abroad, they would have held press conferences, received prizes, appeared on television. They would be enjoying their status as so-called heroes. They are in hiding here, no doubt about it."

"Then sooner or later we'll get them," Ramfis murmured. "I have thousands of men searching, house by house, hideout by hideout. If they're still in the Dominican Republic, we'll get them. And if not, there's no place in the world where they can escape paying for Papa's death. Even if I spend my last cent finding them."

"I hope your wish comes true, General," said an understanding Balaguer. "Allow me one request. Be sure to follow correct form. The delicate operation of proving to the world that the country is opening to democracy will be frustrated if there is a scandal. Another Galíndez, let us say, or another Betancourt."

Only with regard to the conspirators was the Generalissimo's son intractable. Balaguer did not waste time interceding for their freedom; the fate of those arrested was sealed, as Imbert's and Amiama's would be if they were captured, and, moreover, he was not sure doing so would further his plans. True, times were changing, but the sentiments of the masses were fickle. The Dominican people, Trujillista to the death until May 30, 1961, would have torn out the eyes and hearts of Juan Tomás Díaz, Antonio de la Maza, Salvador Estrella Sadhalá, Luis Amiama, Huáscar Tejeda, Pedro Livio Cedeño, Fifí Pastoriza, Antonio Imbert, and their associates, if they had laid hands on them. But the mystical consubstantiation with the Chief, in which Dominicans had lived for thirty-one years, was disappearing. Street meetings called by students, the Civic Union, or June 14, sparsely attended at first by a few fearful people, had grown after a month, two months, three months. Not only in Santo Domingo (President Balaguer had prepared the motion to change back its name from Ciudad Trujillo, which Senator Chirinos would have the Congress approve by acclamation at the proper moment), where they sometimes filled Independencia Park, but also in Santiago, La Romana, San Francisco de Macorís, and other cities. Fear was dissipating and the rejection of Trujillo was increasing. His fine historical nose told Dr. Balaguer that the new feeling would grow, irresistibly. And in a climate of popular anti-Trujillism, the assassins would become powerful political figures. That was to no one's advantage. Which is why he struck down a timid attempt by the Walking Turd when, as parliamentary leader of the new Balaguerista movement, he came to ask him if he believed that an agreement by Congress to grant amnesty to the May 30 conspirators would persuade the OAS and the United States to lift the sanctions.

"The intention is good, Senator. But what about the consequences? Amnesty would wound the sensibilities of Ramfis, who would immediately order the murder of everyone who had been pardoned. Our efforts could crumble away."

"The astuteness of your perceptions will never fail to amaze me," exclaimed Senator Chirinos, practically applauding.

Except in this area, Ramfis Trujillo—whose life was devoted to daily bouts of drunkenness at the San Isidro Air Base and in his house on the beach at Boca Chica, where he had installed, along with her mother, his latest girlfriend, a dancer at the Lido in Paris, leaving his pregnant wife, the young actress Lita Milán, in the French capital—had displayed a more willing disposition than Balaguer could have hoped. He had resigned himself to changing Ciudad Trujillo back to Santo Domingo and renaming all the cities, localities, streets, squares, accidents of geography, and bridges called Generalissimo, Ramfis, Angelita, Radhamés, Doña Julia, or Doña María, and he was not insisting on harsh punishments for the students, subversives, and idlers who destroyed the statues, plaques, busts, photos, and posters of Trujillo and family on streets and avenues, in parks, and along highways. He accepted without argument Dr. Balaguer's suggestion that "in an act of patriotic altruism" he cede to the State—that is, the people—the lands, farms, and agricultural enterprises that had belonged to the Generalissimo and his children. Ramfis did so in a public letter. In this way, the State became owner of forty percent of all arable land, making it the government which controlled more enterprises than any other in the hemisphere, except Cuba. And General Ramfis pacified the souls of those degenerate brutes, the Chief's brothers, who were perplexed by the systematic disappearance of the trappings and symbols of Trujillism.

One night, after eating his usual austere supper, with his sisters, of chicken broth, white rice, salad, and milk pudding, the President fainted when he stood to go up to bed. He lost consciousness for only a few seconds, but Dr. Félix Goico warned him: if he continued working at this pace, before the end of the year his heart or his brain would explode like a grenade. He had to rest more—since the death of Trujillo he had slept no more than three or four hours a night—exercise, and relax on weekends. He forced himself to spend five hours a night in bed, and after lunch he would walk, though far from Avenida George Washington, to avoid compromising associations; he would go to the former Ramfis Park, renamed for Eugenio María de Hostos. And to ease his spirit, for several hours on Sundays following Mass he would read romantic or Modernist poems, or the Castilian classics of the Golden Age. On occasion some irate citizen would insult him on the street—"Balaguer, the paper doll!"—but most of the time people offered a greeting: "Good afternoon, Mr. President." He would thank them ceremoniously, tipping his hat, which he was in the habit of wearing pulled down all the way to his ears so the wind would not blow it off.

On October 2, 1961, when he announced in the General Assembly of the United Nations, in New York, that "in the Dominican Republic an authentic democracy and a new set of circumstances are being born," he acknowledged, before approximately one hundred delegates, that the Trujillo dictatorship had been an anachronism that had savagely infringed rights and freedoms. And he asked the free nations to help him restore law and liberty to the Dominicans. A few days later, he received a bitter letter from Doña María Martínez, in Paris. The Bountiful First Lady complained that the President had drawn an "unjust" picture of the Trujillo Era, omitting "all the good things my husband also did, and that you yourself praised so highly over the course of thirty-one years." But it wasn't María Martínez who troubled the President; it was Trujillo's brothers. He learned that Petán and Blacky had held a stormy meeting with Ramfis, demanding to know whether he was going to allow that little weakling to go to the UN and insult his father. The time had come to get him out of the National Palace and put the Trujillo family back in power, which is what the people were demanding! Ramfis replied that if he led a coup, an invasion by the Marines would be inevitable: John Calvin Hill had told him so personally. The only chance for holding on to anything was to close ranks behind the fragile legality of the President. Balaguer was skillfully maneuvering to get the OAS and the State Department to lift sanctions.

And to achieve this he was obliged to give speeches like the one at the UN, which were contrary to his convictions.

But at the meeting he had with the chief executive shortly after Balaguer returned from New York, Trujillo's son displayed much less tolerance. His animosity was so intense that a rupture seemed inevitable.

"Are you going to keep attacking Papa the way you did in the General Assembly?" Sitting on the chair that the Chief had occupied during their last interview, only hours before he was killed, Ramfis spoke without looking at him, his eyes fixed on the sea.

"I have no alternative, General," the President said mournfully. "If I want them to believe that everything is changing, that the country is opening to democracy, I must make a self-critical examination of the past. It is painful for you, I know. It is no less painful for me. At times politics demands this kind of anguish."

For a long time, Ramfis did not reply. Was he drunk? On drugs? Was it one of those mental crises that brought him to the brink of madness? With large bluish shadows around his blazing, restless eyes, he was grimacing in a strange way.

"I explained to you what I would do," Balaguer added. "I have strictly abided by our agreement. You approved my project. But, of course, what I told you then still stands. If you prefer to take the reins, you do not need to bring in tanks from San Isidro. I will give you my resignation right now."

Ramfis gave him a long look filled with ennui.

"Everybody's asking me to do it," he murmured without enthusiasm. "My uncles, the regional commanders, the military, my cousins, Papa's friends. But I don't want to sit where you're sitting. I don't want the job, Dr. Balaguer. Why would I? So they can repay me the way they did him?"

He fell silent, profoundly dejected.

"So then, General, if you do not want power, help me to exercise it."

"More than I already have?" Ramfis asked mockingly. "If it weren't for me, my uncles would have taken you out and shot you a long time ago."

"It is not enough," Balaguer said. "You see the turmoil in the streets. The meetings of the Civic Union and June 14 grow more violent every day. This will get worse if we do not gain the upper hand."

The color returned to the face of the Generalissimo's son. He waited, his head craned forward, as if wondering whether the President would dare to request the thing he suspected he wanted.

"Your uncles have to leave," Dr. Balaguer said softly. "As long as they are here, neither the international community nor public opinion will have faith in the change. Only you can convince them."

Was he going to insult him? Ramfis looked at him in astonishment, as if he could not believe what he had heard. There was another long pause.

"Are you going to ask me to leave too, leave this country that Papa made, so that people will swallow all the bullshit about a new era?"

Balaguer waited several seconds.

"Yes, you too," he murmured, his heart in his mouth. "You too. Not yet. After you arrange for your uncles to leave. After you help me consolidate the government and make the Armed Forces understand that Trujillo is no longer here. This is not news to you, General. You always knew. Knew that the best thing for you, your family, and your friends, is for this project to move forward. With the Civic Union or June 14 in power, it would be worse."

He did not pull out his revolver, he did not spit at him. He turned pale again and made that lunatic face. He lit a cigarette and exhaled several times, watching the smoke disappear.

"I would have left a long time ago, left this country of assholes and ingrates," he muttered. "If I had found Amiama and Imbert, I wouldn't be here. They're the only ones missing. Once I keep the promise I made to Papa, I'll go."

The President informed him that he had authorized the return from exile of Juan Bosch and his colleagues from the Dominican Revolutionary Party, the PRD. It seemed to him that the general did not listen to his argument that Bosch and the PRD would become involved in a fierce struggle with the Civic Union and June 14 for leadership of the anti-Trujillista movement. And would, in this way, perform a service for the government. Because the real danger lay in the gentlemen of the Civic Union, people of wealth, conservatives with influence in the United States, such as Severo Cabral; Juan Bosch knew this, and would do everything reasonable—and perhaps some unreasonable things too—to block access to the government of so powerful a rival.

There were some two hundred real or supposed accomplices to the conspiracy remaining in La Victoria, and once the Trujillos had gone, it would be a good idea to grant them amnesty. But Balaguer knew that Trujillo's son would never allow the executioners who were still alive to go free. He would vent his rage on them, as he had with General Román, whom he tortured for four months before announcing that the prisoner had killed himself out of remorse for his betrayal (the body was never found), and with Modesto Díaz (if he was still alive, Ramfis must still be abusing him). The problem was that the prisoners—the opposition called them executioners—were a blemish on the new face he wanted to give to the regime. Missions, delegations, politicians, and journalists were constantly arriving to express their interest in them, and the President had to do some deft juggling to explain why they had not yet been sentenced, and swear that their lives would be respected and their absolutely scrupulous trial would be attended by international observers. Why hadn't Ramfis finished them off, as he had with almost all of Antonio de la Maza's brothers—Mario, Bolívar, Ernesto, Pirolo—and many cousins, nephews, and uncles, who were shot or beaten to death on the very day of his arrest, instead of keeping them in jail as a fermenting agent for the opposition? Balaguer knew that the blood of the executioners would spatter onto him: this was the charging bull he still had to face.

A few days after this conversation, a telephone call from Ramfis brought him excellent news: he had persuaded his uncles, Petán and Blacky, to go on long vacations. On October 25, Héctor Bienvenido flew with his American wife to Jamaica. And Petán sailed on the frigate *Presidente Trujillo* for a supposed cruise around the Caribbean. Consul John Calvin Hill confessed to Balaguer that now the possibility of sanctions being lifted was growing stronger.

"I hope it does not take too long, Consul Hill," urged the President. "Every day the stranglehold on our country grows tighter."

Industrial enterprises were almost paralyzed because of political uncertainty and limitations on imports; shops were empty because of the drop in income. Ramfis was selling firms not registered in the name of the Trujillos, and bearer shares, at a loss, and the Central Bank had to transfer those sums, converted into foreign currency at the unrealistic official exchange rate of one peso to a dollar, to banks in Canada and Europe. The family had not transferred as much foreign currency overseas as the President feared: Doña María, twelve million dollars; Angelita, thirteen; Radhamés, seventeen; and Ramfis, about twenty-two so far, which added up to sixty-four million dollars. It could have been worse. But the reserves would soon be wiped out, and soldiers, teachers, and public employees would not be paid.

On November 15, he received a call from a terrified Minister of the Interior: Generals Petán and Héctor Trujillo had unexpectedly returned. He implored the President to seek asylum; at any moment there would be a military coup. The bulk of the Army supported them. Balaguer had an urgent meeting with Consul John Calvin Hill. He explained the situation to him. Unless Ramfis stopped it, many garrisons would back Petán and Blacky in their attempt at insurrection. There would be a civil war whose outcome was uncertain, and a widespread massacre of anti-Trujillistas. The consul knew everything. In turn, he informed him that President Kennedy himself had just ordered a war fleet sent in. The aircraft carrier *Valley Forge*, the cruiser *Little Rock*, flagship of the Second Fleet, and the destroyers *Hyman*, *Bristol*, and *Beatty* had left Puerto Rico and were sailing toward the Dominican coast. Some two thousand Marines would land if there was a coup.

In a brief telephone conversation with Ramfis—he spent four hours trying to reach him—he heard ominous news. He'd had a violent argument with his uncles. They wouldn't leave the country. Ramfis had warned them he would go if they didn't.

"What will happen now, General?"

"It means that from this moment on, you're alone in the cage with the wild animals, Mr. President." Ramfis laughed. "Good luck."

Dr. Balaguer closed his eyes. The next few hours and days would be crucial. What did Trujillo's son plan to do? Leave the country? Shoot himself? He would go to Paris to rejoin his wife, his mother, and his brothers and sisters, console himself with parties, polo games, and women in the beautiful house he had bought in Neuilly. He had already taken out all the money he could, leaving some real estate that sooner or later would be confiscated. In short, that was not a problem. But the wild animals were. The Generalissimo's brothers would begin shooting soon, the only thing they did with any skill. Balaguer's name was first on all the lists of enemies to be liquidated, which, according to rumor, had been drawn up by Petán. And so, as one of his favorite proverbs said, he would have to "ford this river nice and slow, and keep to the rocks." He was not afraid, he was only saddened that the exquisite piece of work he had undertaken would be ruined by a hoodlum's bullet.

At dawn the next day he was awakened by his Minister of the Interior, who informed him that a group of military men had removed Trujillo's body from its crypt in the church in San Cristóbal and taken it to Boca Chica, where the yacht *Angelita* was anchored at General Ramfis's private dock.

"I have not heard anything, Minister," Balaguer cut him off. "And you have told me nothing. I advise you to rest for a few hours. We have a long day ahead of us."

Contrary to the advice he gave the minister, he did not go back to sleep. Ramfis would not leave without wiping out his father's assassins, a killing that could demolish his laborious efforts of the past few months to convince the world that with him as President the Republic was becoming a democracy without the civil war or chaos feared by the United States and the Dominican ruling classes. But what could he do? Any order of his regarding the prisoners that contradicted those issued by Ramfis would be disobeyed, testifying to his absolute lack of authority with the Armed Forces.

And yet, mysteriously, except for the proliferation of rumors regarding imminent armed uprisings and massacres of civilians, nothing happened on November 16 or 17. He continued to take care of ordinary matters, as if the country were enjoying complete tranquillity. At dusk on November 17 he was informed that Ramfis had abandoned his beach house. A short while later, he was seen getting out of a car, inebriated, and hurling curses and a grenade—which did not explode—at the facade of the Hotel El Embajador. After that, no one knew his whereabouts. The following morning, a delegation from the National Civic Union, led by Ángel Severo Cabral, asked to meet immediately with the President: it was a matter of life and death. He received them. Severo Cabral was beside himself. He brandished a sheet of paper scrawled by Huáscar Tejeda to his wife, Lindín, and smuggled out of La Victoria, which revealed that the six men accused of killing Trujillo (including Modesto Díaz and Tunti Cáceres) had been separated from the rest of the political prisoners and were to be transferred to another prison. "They're going to kill us, my love," the letter ended. The leader of the Civic Union demanded that the prisoners be placed in the hands of the Judicial Branch, or freed by presidential decree. The wives of the prisoners were demonstrating, with their lawyers, at the doors of the Palace. The international press had been alerted, as well as the State Department and the Western embassies.

An alarmed Dr. Balaguer assured them that he would intervene personally in the matter. He would not allow a crime to be committed. According to reports he had received, the transfer of the six conspirators had as its object an acceleration of the investigation. It was merely a step in the reconstruction of the crime, after which the trial would begin without delay. And, of course, with observers from the World Court at The Hague, whom he would personally invite to the country.

As soon as the leaders of the Civic Union had gone, he called the Solicitor General of the Republic, Dr. José Manuel Machado. Did he know why the head of the National Police, Marcos A. Jorge Moreno, had ordered the transfer of Salvador Estrella Sadhalá, Huáscar Tejeda, Fifí Pastoriza, Pedro Livio Cedeño, Tunti Cáceres, and Modesto Díaz to the cells of the Palace of Justice? The Solicitor General of the Republic knew nothing. He reacted with indignation: someone was misusing the name of the Judicial Branch, no judge had ordered a new reconstruction of the crime. Appearing to be very troubled, the President declared that it was intolerable. He would immediately order the Minister of Justice to carry out a thorough investigation, determine those responsible, and bring charges against them. In order to leave written proof that he had done so, he dictated a memorandum to his secretary and told him it was urgent that it be delivered right away to the Ministry of Justice. Then he called the minister on the phone. He found him in a state of agitation:

"I don't know what to do, Mr. President. I have the prisoners' wives at the door. I'm being pressured on all sides to make a statement, and I don't know anything. Do you know why they've been transferred to the cells of the Judicial Branch? Nobody can explain it to me. They're taking them to the highway for a new reconstruction of the crime, which no one has ordered. And no one can get near them because soldiers from the San Isidro Air Base have cordoned off the area. What should I do?"

"Go there personally and demand an explanation," the President told him. "It is absolutely imperative that there be witnesses to the fact that the government has done all it can to stop the breaking of the law. Go there with the representatives of the United States and Great Britain."

Dr. Balaguer personally called John Calvin Hill and begged him to support this step by the Minister of Justice. At the same time, he informed him that if, as it seemed, General Ramfis was preparing to leave the country, Trujillo's brothers would move into action.

He continued attending to affairs, apparently absorbed by the critical financial situation. He did not move from his office at lunchtime, and, working with the Minister of Finance and the director of the Central Bank, refused to receive calls or visits. At dusk, his secretary handed him a note from the Minister of Justice, informing him that he and the American consul had been prevented from approaching the scene of the reconstruction of the crime by armed members of the Air Force. He confirmed that no one in the ministry, the prosecutor's office, or the courts had requested or been informed of such an inquiry; it was an exclusively military decision. When he arrived home, at eight-thirty in the evening, he received a call from Colonel Marcos A. Jorge Moreno. The van with three armed guards that was to return the prisoners to La Victoria after completion of the judicial inquiry had disappeared.

"Spare no effort to find them, Colonel. Mobilize all the forces you need," ordered the President. "Call me no matter the time."

He told his sisters, disturbed by rumors that the Trujillos had killed the men who assassinated the Generalissimo, that he knew nothing. The stories were probably inventions of extremists intended to worsen the climate of agitation and uncertainty. As he reassured them with lies, he speculated: Ramfis would leave tonight, if he had not done so already. That meant the confrontation with the Trujillo brothers would take place at dawn. Would he order them arrested? Would he have them killed? Their minuscule brains were capable of believing that if they eliminated him, they could halt a historical process that would soon erase them from Dominican politics. He did not feel apprehensive, only curious.

As he was putting on his pajamas, Colonel Jorge Moreno called again. The van had been found: the six prisoners had fled after murdering the three guards.

"Move heaven and earth until you find the fugitives," he intoned, with no change in his voice. "You will answer to me for the lives of those prisoners, Colonel. They must appear in court to be tried according to law for this new crime."

Before he fell asleep, he felt a sudden surge of pity. Not for the prisoners, undoubtedly slaughtered this afternoon by Ramfis in person, but for the three young soldiers whom Trujillo's son also had murdered in order to give an appearance of truth to the farce of the flight. Three poor guards killed in cold blood, to give the veneer of reality to a ridiculous sham no one would ever believe. What useless bloodshed!

The next day, on his way to the Palace, he read on the inside pages of *El Caribe* about the flight of "Trujillo's assassins, after treacherously taking the lives of the three guards who were escorting them back to La Victoria." Still, the scandal he feared did not occur; it was dimmed by other events. At ten in the morning, the door of his office was kicked open. Submachine gun in hand, and with clusters of grenades and revolvers at his waist, General Petán Trujillo burst into the room, followed by his brother Héctor, also dressed as a general, and twenty-seven armed men from his personal guard, whose faces looked not only thuggish but drunk. The revulsion this ill-mannered mob produced in him was stronger than his fear.

"I cannot offer you seats, I do not have that many chairs, forgive me," the small President apologized, sitting very straight. He seemed composed, and there was an urbane smile on his round little face.

"The moment of truth has arrived, Balaguer," roared the savage Petán, spraying saliva. He flourished his submachine gun in a menacing way, and waved it in the President's face. He did not draw back. "Enough bullshit and hypocrisy. Just like Ramfis finished off those sons of bitches yesterday, we're going to finish off the ones still walking around free. Beginning with the Judases, you treacherous dwarf!"

This vulgar imbecile was also drunk. Balaguer hid his indignation and apprehension with complete self-control. Calmly, he indicated the window:

"I ask you to accompany me, General Petán." Then he spoke to Héctor. "You too, please."

He walked to the window and pointed at the ocean. It was a brilliant morning. Facing the coastline one could see very clearly, gleaming in the sun, the silhouettes of three American warships. Their names were not visible, but one certainly could admire the long cannons on the *Little Rock*, a cruiser equipped with missiles, and on the aircraft carriers *Valley Forge* and *Franklin D. Roosevelt*, all aimed at the city.

"They are waiting for you to take power to begin firing," said the

President, very slowly. "They are waiting for you to give them an excuse to invade us again. Do you want to go down in history as the Dominicans who allowed a second Yankee occupation of the Republic? If that is what you want, shoot and make me a hero. My successor will not sit in this chair for even an hour."

Since they had permitted him to say what he had said, he told himself, it was unlikely they would kill him. Petán and Blacky were whispering, talking at the same time and not understanding a word. The thugs and bodyguards looked at one another in confusion. Finally, Petán ordered his men to leave. When he found himself alone in the office with the two brothers, he concluded he had won the game. They sat down in front of him. Poor devils! How uncomfortable they looked! They did not know where to begin. He had to make the task easier for them.

"The country is waiting for a gesture from you," he said amiably. "Hoping you will act with the generosity and patriotism of General Ramfis. Your nephew has left the country in the interest of peace."

Petán, ill-humored and direct, interrupted him:

"It's very easy to be a patriot when you have millions overseas and the properties Ramfis owns. But me and Blacky don't have houses outside the country, or stocks, or bank accounts. All we own is here, in this country. We were the only assholes who obeyed the Chief when he prohibited taking money overseas. Is that fair? We're not idiots, Mr. Balaguer. All the lands and goods we have here they're going to confiscate."

He felt relieved.

"That can be remedied, gentlemen," he reassured them. "Of course it can. A magnanimous gesture such as the one the Nation asks of you must be compensated."

From this moment on, it was nothing but a tedious financial negotiation, which confirmed for the President the contempt he felt toward those who were greedy for money. It was something he had never coveted. He finally settled on amounts he considered reasonable, given the peace and security the Republic would gain in return. He ordered the Central Bank to pay two million dollars to each of the brothers, and to convert into foreign currency the eleven million pesos they already had, some of it in shoeboxes and the rest on deposit in banks in the capital. To be certain the agreement would be respected, Petán and

Héctor demanded that it be countersigned by the American consul. John Calvin Hill agreed immediately, delighted that matters would be settled with goodwill and no bloodshed. He congratulated the President and declared: "It is in a crisis that you know a true statesman." Lowering his eyes modestly, Dr. Balaguer told himself that, with the departure of the Trujillos, there would be such an explosion of exultation and joy—and some chaos too—that few people would remember the murder of the six prisoners, whose bodies—how could there be any doubt?—would never be found. The episode would not do him too much damage.

In the Council of Ministers he asked for unanimous agreement from the cabinet for a general political amnesty, which would empty the prisons and nullify all judicial proceedings against subversion, and he ordered the Dominican Party dissolved. The ministers rose to their feet and applauded. Then, with somewhat flushed cheeks, his Minister of Health, Dr. Tabaré Álvarez Pereyra, informed him that for the past six months he had hidden in his house—most of the time confined in a narrow closet with robes and pajamas—the fugitive Luis Amiama Tió.

Dr. Balaguer praised his humanitarian spirit and asked him to accompany Dr. Amiama to the National Palace, when both he and Don Antonio Imbert, who would undoubtedly reappear at any moment, would be received in person by the President of the Republic with the respect and gratitude they deserved for the great services they had rendered the Nation.

23 After Amadito left, Antonio Imbert remained a while longer in the house of his cousin, Dr. Manuel Durán Barreras. He had no hope that Juan Tomás Díaz and Antonio de la Maza would find General Román. Perhaps the political-military Plan had been discovered and Pupo was dead or in prison; perhaps he had lost his courage and stepped back. He had no alternative but to go into hiding. He and his cousin Manuel reviewed his options before deciding on a distant relative, Dr. Gladys de los Santos, Durán's sister-in-law. She lived nearby.

In the small hours of the morning, when it was still dark, Manuel Durán and Imbert walked the six blocks at a rapid pace without seeing any vehicles or pedestrians. Dr. De los Santos took some time to open the door. She was in her bathrobe, and rubbed her eyes vigorously as they explained the situation. She was not particularly frightened. She reacted with a strange equanimity. A stout but agile woman in her forties, she displayed enormous self-assurance and regarded the world with dispassion.

"I'll put you up the best I can," she told Imbert. "But this isn't a safe hiding place. I was arrested once, and the SIM has me in its files."

To keep the maid from finding him, she put him in a windowless storeroom next to the garage, and placed a folding mattress on the floor. It was a tiny, unventilated space. Antonio could not close his eyes for the rest of the night. He kept the Colt .45 beside him, on a shelf filled with canned goods; he was tense, his ears alert to any suspicious sound. He thought about his brother Segundo, and his skin crawled: they must be torturing him in La Victoria, or had already killed him.

Dr. De los Santos, who had locked the storeroom with a key, came to let him out at nine in the morning.

"I gave the maid the day off so she could visit her family in Jarabacoa." She tried to cheer him. "You can move anywhere you want in the house. But don't let the neighbors see you. What a night you must have spent in that cave."

While they ate breakfast in the kitchen—mangú, fried cheese, and coffee—they listened to the news. There was no mention of the assassination on the radio. Dr. De los Santos left for work a short while later. Imbert took a shower and went down to the living room, where, sprawled in an armchair, he fell asleep, the Colt .45 on his lap. He gave a great start and groaned when somebody shook him awake.

"The *caliés* took away Manuel this morning, not long after you left his house," said an extremely agitated Gladys de los Santos. "Sooner or later they'll get it out of him that you're here. You have to go, right away."

Yes, but where? Gladys had passed by the Imberts' house, and the street was crawling with guards and *caliés*; no doubt about it, they had arrested his wife and daughter. It seemed as if invisible hands were beginning to tighten around his throat. He hid his anguish so as not to increase the terror of Dr. De los Santos, who was a changed woman, so perturbed she could not stop blinking her eyes.

"There are *caliés* in Beetles and trucks full of guards everywhere," she said. "They're searching cars, asking everybody for papers, going into houses."

Nothing had been reported yet on television or radio, or in the papers, but rumors were flying. The human tom-tom was sending the news all over the city that Trujillo had been killed. People were frightened and confused about what might happen. For close to an hour he racked his brain: where could he go? He had to leave now. He thanked Dr. De los Santos for her help and went out, his hand on the pistol in his right trouser pocket. He walked for some time, in no particular direction, until he thought of his dentist, Dr. Camilo Suero, who lived near the Military Hospital. Camilo and his wife, Alfonsina, let him in. They could not hide him, but did help him go over other possibilities. And then the image came into his mind of Francisco Rainieri, an old friend, the son of an Italian, and an ambassador of the Order of Malta; Francisco's wife, Venecia, and his wife, Guarina, had tea together and played canasta. Perhaps the diplomat could help him seek asylum in one of the legations. Taking every precaution, he called the Rainieris' residence and passed the receiver to Alfonsina, who pretended to be Guarina Tessón, the maiden name of Imbert's wife. She asked to speak to Queco. He came to the phone immediately, and she was startled by his extremely cordial greeting:

"How are you, my dear Guarina? I'm delighted to hear from you. You're calling about tonight, aren't you? Don't worry. I'll send the car for you. At seven sharp, if that's all right. Just give me your address again, all right?"

"Either he's a mind reader or he's gone crazy or I don't know what," said Alfonsina when she hung up the receiver.

"And now, what do we do until seven o'clock, Alfonsina?"

"Pray to Our Lady of Altagracia," she said, and crossed herself. "If the *caliés* come, just use your gun."

At exactly seven a shiny blue Buick, with diplomatic plates, stopped at the door. Francisco Rainieri was at the wheel. He pulled away as soon as Antonio Imbert sat down beside him.

"I knew the message was from you because Guarina and your daughter are at my house," said Rainieri by way of greeting. "There aren't two women named Guarina Tessón in Ciudad Trujillo, it could only have been you."

He was very calm, even cheerful, wearing a freshly ironed guayabera and smelling of lavender water. He drove Imbert to a distant house, along remote streets, taking a huge detour because there were roadblocks along the main streets where vehicles were stopped and searched. Less than an hour had passed since the official announcement of Trujillo's death. The atmosphere was heavy with apprehension, as if everyone were expecting an explosion. Elegant as always, the ambassador did not ask a single question regarding Trujillo's assassination or the other conspirators. Very casually, as if he were talking about the next tennis championship at the Country Club, he remarked:

"With things the way they are, it's unthinkable that any embassy would give you asylum. And it wouldn't do much good. The government, if there is still a government, wouldn't respect it. They'd drag you out no matter where you were. The only thing you can do, for the moment, is hide. At the Italian consulate, where I have friends, there are too many employees and visitors going back and forth. But I found someone, and he's totally reliable. He did this once before, when they were hunting down Yuyo d'Alessandro. He has only one condition. Nobody can know, not even Guarina. For her own safety, more than anything else."

"Of course," Tony Imbert murmured, astounded that on his own initiative this man who was no more than a casual friend would risk so much to save his life. He was so disconcerted by Queco's daring generosity that he did not even manage to thank him.

At Rainieri's house he embraced his wife and daughter. Considering the circumstances, they were remarkably calm. But when he held her in his arms, he could feel Leslie's body trembling. He stayed with them and the Rainieris for approximately two hours. His wife had brought an overnight bag for him, with clean clothes and his shaving kit. They did not mention Trujillo. Guarina told him what she had learned from neighbors. Their house had been stormed at dawn by uniformed and plainclothes police; they had emptied it, breaking and smashing what they did not take away in two vans.

When it was time, the diplomat made a small gesture, pointing at his watch. Antonio Imbert embraced and kissed Guarina and Leslie, and followed Francisco Rainieri through the service entrance onto the street. Seconds later, a small vehicle with headlights dimmed pulled to a stop in front of them.

"Goodbye, and good luck," said Rainieri, shaking his hand. "Don't worry about your family. They won't want for anything."

Imbert got into the car and sat down next to the driver. He was a young man, wearing a shirt and tie, but no jacket. In impeccable Spanish, though with an Italian lilt, he introduced himself:

"My name is Cavaglieri and I'm an official at the Italian embassy. My wife and I will do everything possible to make your stay at our apartment pleasant. Don't worry, in my house there are no prying eyes. We live alone. We don't have a cook or servants. My wife loves keeping house. And we both like to cook."

He laughed, and Antonio Imbert imagined that courtesy required him to attempt a laugh as well. The couple lived on the top floor of a new building, not far from Calle Mahatma Gandhi and Salvador Estrella Sadhalá's house. Señora Cavaglieri was even younger than her husband—a slender girl with almond-shaped eyes and black hair—and she welcomed him with lively, smiling courtesy, as if he were an old family friend coming to spend the weekend. She did not display the slightest misgiving at having a stranger in her house, the assassin of the country's supreme ruler, the man whom thousands of hate-filled guards and police were avidly hunting down. During the six months and three days he lived with them, never, not once, did either one make him feel—despite his extreme sensitivity and a situation that predisposed him to seeing phantoms—that his presence was in any way an inconvenience. Did they know they were risking their lives? Of course. They heard and saw detailed reports on television of the panic those nefarious assassins had provoked in Dominicans, many of whom, not satisfied with denying them refuge, rushed to inform on them. The first one they saw fall was the engineer Huáscar Tejeda, shamefully forced out of the church of Santo Cura de Ars by the terrified priest, and into the arms of the SIM. They followed every detail of the odyssey of General Juan Tomás Díaz and Antonio de la Maza as they drove through the streets of Ciudad Trujillo in a taxi and were denounced by the people they turned to for help. And they saw how the *caliés* killed Amadito García Guerrero and then dragged away the poor old woman who had given him shelter, and how the mob dismantled and destroyed her house. But these scenes and reports did not intimidate the Cavaglieris or lessen their cordial treatment of him.

After Ramfis's return, Imbert and his hosts knew that his confinement would be a long one. The public embraces of Trujillo's son and General José René Román were eloquent: Pupo had betrayed them, and there would be no military uprising. From his small universe in the Cavaglieris' penthouse, he saw the crowds standing in line, hour after hour, to pay homage to Trujillo, and he saw himself on the television screen, pictured beside Luis Amiama (whom he did not know), under captions that offered first a hundred thousand, then two hundred thousand, and finally half a million pesos to anyone reporting his whereabouts.

"Hmm, with the devaluation of the Dominican peso, it's not an interesting deal anymore," Cavaglieri remarked.

His life quickly fell into a strict routine. He had a small room to himself, with a bed, a night table, and a lamp. He got up early and did push-ups and sit-ups, and ran in place, for about an hour. He had breakfast with the Cavaglieris. After long discussions, he convinced them to let him help with the cleaning. Sweeping, running the vacuum, passing the feather duster over objects and articles of furniture, became both a diversion and an obligation, something he did conscientiously, with total concentration and a certain joy. But Señora Cavaglieri never allowed him into the kitchen. She cooked very well, especially pasta, which she served twice a day. He had liked pasta since he was a boy. But after six months of confinement, he would never again eat tagliarini, tagliatelle, ravioli, or any other variant of that popular Italian specialty.

When his domestic chores were concluded, he read for many hours. He had never been a great reader, but in those six months he discovered the pleasure of books and magazines, which were his best defense against the periodic depression brought on by confinement, routine, and uncertainty.

When it was announced on television that a commission from the OAS had come to interview political prisoners, he learned that Guarina, along with the wives of all his friends in the conspiracy, had been in prison for several weeks. The Cavaglieris had kept Guarina's arrest from him. But a few weeks later, they were overjoyed to give him the good news that she had been released.

Never, not even when he was mopping, sweeping, or running the vacuum, did he fail to keep the loaded Colt .45 with him. His decision was unshakable. He would do the same as Amadito, Juan Tomás Díaz, and Antonio de la Maza. He would not be taken alive, he would die shooting. It was more honorable to die that way than to be subjected to abuses and tortures devised by the twisted minds of Ramfis and his cronies.

In the afternoon and at night he read the papers his hosts brought him and watched television newscasts with them. Without believing much of what he saw and read, he followed the confused dualism of the path the regime had embarked upon: a civilian government led by Balaguer, who made reassuring gestures and statements asserting that the country was democratizing, and a military and police power, headed by Ramfis, that continued to kill, torture, and disappear people with the same impunity as when the Chief was alive. Yet he could not help feeling encouraged by the return of the exiles, the appearance of small opposition papers—published by the Civic Union and June 14— and student demonstrations against the government, which were sometimes reported in the official media, though only to accuse the protesters of being Communists.

Joaquín Balaguer's speech at the United Nations, criticizing the

Trujillo dictatorship and pledging to democratize the country, left him dumbfounded. Was this the same little man who for thirty-one years had been the most faithful and constant servant of the Father of the New Nation? In their long conversations at the table, when the Cavaglieris had supper at home—on many evenings they went out to eat, but then Señora Cavaglieri would prepare the inevitable pasta for him—they filled in the gaps in his information with the gossip that was churning through the city, soon rebaptized with its old name, Santo Domingo de Guzmán. Though everyone worried about a coup by the Trujillo brothers that would restore the cruel, harsh dictatorship, people clearly were losing their fear, or, rather, breaking the spell that had kept so many Dominicans devoted, body and soul, to Trujillo. A growing number of anti-Trujillista voices, declarations, and attitudes gradually appeared, as well as more support for the Civic Union, June 14, or the Dominican Revolutionary Party, whose leaders had just returned to the country and opened an office in the center of the city.

The saddest day of his odyssey was also the happiest. On November 18, as the departure of Ramfis was being announced, it was reported on television that the six assassins of the Chief (four killers and two accomplices) had fled after murdering the three soldiers escorting them back to La Victoria prison following a reconstruction of the crime. Sitting in front of the television screen, he lost control and burst into tears. So, then, his friends—Turk, his dearest friend—had been killed, along with three poor guards who provided the alibi for the farce. Of course, the bodies would never be found. Señor Cavaglieri handed him a glass of cognac:

"Take heart, Señor Imbert. Just think, soon you'll see your wife and daughter. This is coming to an end."

A short while later, there was an announcement of the imminent departure of the Trujillo brothers and their families. This really was the end of his confinement. For the moment at least, he had survived the hunt in which, with the exception of Luis Amiama—he soon learned that he had spent six months hiding in a closet for many hours a day—practically all of the principal conspirators, along with hundreds of innocents, among them his brother Segundo, had been killed or tortured, or still languished in prison.

The day after the Trujillo brothers left the country, a political amnesty was declared. The jails began to open. Balaguer announced a commission to investigate what had happened to the "executioners of the tyrant." From that day on, radio, television, and the newspapers stopped calling them assassins; executioners, their new designation, would soon become heroes, and not long after that, streets, squares, and avenues all over the country would begin to be renamed for them.

On the third day, very discreetly—the Cavaglieris would not even allow him to take the time to thank them for what they had done, and all they asked was that he not reveal their identity to anyone, so as not to compromise their diplomatic status—he left his confinement at dusk and appeared, alone, at his house. For a long time he, Guarina, and Leslie embraced, unable to speak. They examined one another and found that while Guarina and Leslie had lost weight, he had gained five kilos. He explained that in the house where he had been hiding—he could not tell them where—they ate a lot of spaghetti.

They could not speak for too long. The ruined house of the Imberts began to fill up with bouquets of flowers and relatives, friends, and strangers, who came to embrace him, congratulate him, and—sometimes, trembling with emotion, their eyes brimming with tears—to call him a hero and thank him for what he had done. Suddenly, a military man appeared among the visitors. He was an aide-de-camp to the President of the Republic. After the obligatory greetings, Major Teofronio Cáceda told him that he and Don Luis Amiama—who had also just emerged from his hiding place, incredibly enough, the house of the current Minister of Health—were invited to the National Palace at noon tomorrow to be received by the Head of State. And, with a complicitous little laugh, he informed him that Senator Henry Chirinos had just introduced in Congress ("Yes, sir, the same Trujillo Congress") a law naming Antonio Imbert and Luis Amiama three-star generals in the Dominican Army for extraordinary services to the Nation.

The next morning, accompanied by Guarina and Leslie—the three of them in their best clothes, though Antonio's were too tight—he kept his appointment at the Palace. A swarm of photographers greeted them, and a military guard in dress uniforms presented arms. In the waiting room he met Luis Amiama, a very slim, somber man with an almost lipless mouth who would be his inseparable friend from that time on. They shook hands and agreed to meet, after their audience with the President, to visit the wives (the widows) of all the conspirators who had died or disappeared, and to tell each other their own adventures. At that point, the door to the office of the Head of State opened.

Smiling, wearing an expression of deep joy, as the photographers' cameras flashed, Dr. Joaquín Balaguer walked toward them, arms opened wide.

24 "Manuel Alfonso came for me right on time," says Urania, staring at nothing. "The cuckoo clock in the living room was sounding eight o'clock when he rang." Her Aunt Adelina, her cousins Lucinda and Manolita, her niece Marianita, avoid one another's eyes so as not to increase the tension; breathless and frightened, they look only at her. Samson is dozing, his curved beak buried in his green feathers.

"Papa hurried to his room, on the pretext of going to the bathroom," Urania continues coldly, almost legalistically. " 'Bye-bye, sweetheart, have a good time.' He didn't have the courage to say goodbye while he was looking me in the eye."

"You remember all those details?" Aunt Adelina moves her small, wrinkled fist, without energy or authority now.

"I forget a good number of things," Urania replies briskly. "But I remember everything about that night. You'll see."

She remembers, for example, that Manuel Alfonso was dressed in sports clothes—sports clothes for a party given by the Generalissimo?—a blue shirt with an open collar, a light cream-colored jacket, loafers, and a silk scarf hiding his scar. In his peculiar voice he said that her pink organdy dress was beautiful, that her high-heeled shoes made her look older. He kissed her on the cheek: "Let's hurry, it's getting late, beautiful." He opened the car door for her, had her go in first, sat down beside her, and the chauffeur in uniform and cap—she remembered his name: Luis Rodríguez—pulled away.

"Instead of going down Avenida George Washington, the car took an absurd route. It went up Independencia and drove across the old city, taking its time. Not true that it was getting late; it was still too early to go to San Cristóbal."

Manolita extends her hands, leans her plump body forward.

"But if you thought it was strange, didn't you say anything to Manuel Alfonso about it? Nothing at all?"

Not at first: nothing at all. It was very strange, of course, that they were driving through the old city, just as it was strange that Manuel Alfonso had dressed for the Generalissimo's party as if he were going to the Hipódromo or the Country Club, but Urania didn't ask the ambassador anything. Was she beginning to suspect that he and Agustín Cabral had told her a lie? She remained silent, half listening to the awful, ruined speech of Manuel Alfonso, who was telling her about parties long ago for the coronation of Queen Elizabeth II, in London, where he and Angelita Trujillo ("She was a young girl at the time, as beautiful as you are") represented the Benefactor of the Nation. She was concentrating instead on the ancient houses that stood wide open, displaying their interiors, their families out on the streets—old men and women, young people, children, dogs, cats, even parrots and canaries—to enjoy the cool evening after the burning heat of the day, chatting from rockers, chairs, or stools, or sitting in the doorways or on the curbs of the high sidewalks, turning the old streets of the capital into an immense popular get-together, club, or festival, to which the groups of two or four domino players—always men, always mature— sitting around tables lit by candles or lanterns, remained totally indifferent. It was a show, like the scenes of small, cheerful grocery stores with counters and shelves of white-painted wood, overflowing with cans, bottles of Carta Dorada, Jacas, and Bermúdez cider, and brightly colored boxes, where people were always buying things; Urania preserved a very vivid memory of this spectacle that had perhaps disappeared or was dying out in modern Santo Domingo, or perhaps existed only in the rectangle of streets where centuries earlier a group of adventurers came from Europe, established the first Christian city in the New World, and gave it the melodious name of Santo Domingo de Guzmán. The last night you would see that show, Urania.

"As soon as we were on the highway, perhaps when the car was passing by the place where they killed Trujillo two weeks later, Manuel Alfonso began . . ." A sound of disgust interrupts Urania's story.

"What do you mean?" asks Lucindita after a silence. "Began to what?"

"To prepare me." Urania's voice is firm again. "To soften me up, frighten me, charm me. Like the brides of Moloch, pampered and dressed up like princesses before they were thrown in the fire, into the mouth of the monster."

"So you've never met Trujillo, you've never talked to him," Manuel Alfonso exclaims with delight. "It will be the experience of a lifetime, my girl!"

Yes, it would. The car moved toward San Cristóbal under a star-filled sky, surrounded by coconut palms and silver palms, along the shores of the Caribbean Sea crashing noisily against the reefs.

"But what did he say to you?" urges Manolita, because Urania has stopped speaking.

He described what a perfect gentleman the Generalissimo was in his treatment of ladies. He, who was so severe in military and governmental matters, had made the old proverb his philosophy: "With a woman, use a rose petal." That's how he always treated beautiful girls.

"How lucky you are, dear girl." He was trying to infect her with his enthusiasm, an emotional excitement that distorted his speech even further. "To have Trujillo invite you personally to his Mahogany House. What a privilege! You can count on your fingers the girls who have deserved something like this. I'm telling you, girl, believe me."

And then Urania asked him the first and last question of the night:

"Who else has been invited to this party?" She looks at her Aunt Adelina, at Lucindita and Manolita: "Just to see what he would say. By now I knew we weren't going to any party."

The self-assured male figure turned toward her, and Urania could see the gleam in the ambassador's eyes.

"No one else. It's a party for you. Just for you! Can you imagine? Do you realize what it means? Didn't I tell you it was something unique? Trujillo is giving you a party. That's like winning the lottery, Uranita."

"And you? What about you?" her niece Marianita exclaims in her barely audible voice. "What were you thinking, Aunt Urania?"

"I was thinking about the chauffeur, about Luis Rodríguez. Just about him."

How embarrassed you were for that chauffeur in his cap, a witness to the ambassador's hypocritical talk. He had turned on the car radio, and two popular Italian songs—"Volare" and "Ciao, Ciao, Bambina"— were playing, but she was sure he didn't miss a word of the ploys

Manuel Alfonso was using to cajole her into feeling happy and fortunate. A party that Trujillo was giving just for her!

"Did you think about your papa?" Manolita blurts out. "Did you think my Uncle Agustín had, that he . . . ?"

She stops, not knowing how to finish. Aunt Adelina's eyes reproach her. The old woman's face has collapsed, and her expression reveals profound despair.

"Manuel Alfonso was the one who thought about Papa," says Urania. "Was I a good daughter? Did I want to help Senator Agustín Cabral?"

He did it with the subtlety acquired in his years as a diplomat responsible for difficult missions. And wasn't this an extraordinary opportunity for Urania to help his friend Egghead climb out of the trap set for him by perpetually envious men? The Generalissimo might be hard and implacable when it came to the country's interests. But at heart he was a romantic; with a charming girl his hardness melted like an ice cube in the sun. If she, being the intelligent girl she was, wanted the Generalissimo to extend a hand to Agustín, to return his position, his prestige, his power, his posts, she could achieve it. All she had to do was touch Trujillo's heart, a heart that could not deny the appeals of beauty.

"He also gave me some advice," says Urania. "What things I shouldn't do because they annoyed the Chief. It made him happy when girls were tender, but not when they exaggerated their admiration, their love. I asked myself: 'Is he really saying these things to me?' "

They had entered San Cristóbal, a city made famous because the Chief had been born there, in a modest little house next to the great church that Trujillo had constructed, and to which Senator Cabral had taken Uranita on a visit, explaining the biblical frescoes painted on the walls by Vela Zaneti, an exiled Spanish artist to whom the magnanimous Chief had opened the doors of the Dominican Republic. On that trip to San Cristóbal, Senator Cabral also showed her the bottle factory and the weapons factory and the entire valley watered by the Nigua. And now her father was sending her to San Cristóbal to beg the Chief to forgive him, to unfreeze his accounts, to make him President of the Senate again.

"From Mahogany House there is a marvelous view of the valley, the Nigua River, the horses and cattle on the Fundación Ranch," Manuel Alfonso explained in detail.

The car, after passing the first guard post, began to ascend the hill; at the top, using the precious wood of the mahogany trees that were beginning to disappear from the island, the house had been erected to which the Generalissimo withdrew two or three days a week to have his secret assignations, do his dirty work, and negotiate risky business deals with complete discretion.

"For a long time the only thing I remembered about Mahogany House was the rug. It covered the entire room and had a gigantic national seal, in full color, embroidered on it. Later, I remembered other things. In the bedroom, a glass-doored closet filled with uniforms of every style, and above them, a row of military hats and caps. Even a Napoleonic two-cornered hat."

She does not laugh. She looks somber, with something cavernous in her eyes and voice. Her Aunt Adelina does not laugh, and neither does Manolita, or Lucinda, or Marianita, who has just come back from the bathroom, where she went to vomit. (She heard her retching.) The parrot is still sleeping. Silence has fallen on Santo Domingo: no car horns or engines, no radios, no drunken laughter, no barking of stray dogs.

"My name is Benita Sepúlveda, come in," the woman said to her at the foot of the wooden staircase. Advanced in years, indifferent, and yet with something maternal in her gestures and expression, she wore a uniform, and a scarf around her head. "Come this way."

"She was the housekeeper," Urania says, "the one responsible for placing fresh flowers in all the rooms, every day. Manuel Alfonso stayed behind, talking to the officer at the door. I never saw him again."

Benita Sepúlveda, pointing with a plump little hand at the darkness beyond the windows protected by metal grillwork, said "that" was a grove of oaks, and in the orchard there were plenty of mangoes and cedars; but the most beautiful things on the place were the almond and mahogany trees that grew around the house and whose perfumed branches were in every corner. Did she smell them? Did she? She'd have a chance to see the countryside—the river, the valley, the sugar mill, the stables on the Fundación Ranch—early in the morning, when the sun came up. Would she have a Dominican breakfast, with mashed plantains, fried eggs, sausage or smoked meat, and fruit juice? Or just coffee, like the Generalissimo?

"It was from Benita Sepúlveda that I learned I was going to spend the night there, that I would sleep with His Excellency. What a great honor!"

The housekeeper, with the assurance that comes from long practice, had her stop on the first landing and go into a spacious, dimly lit room. It was a bar. It had wooden seating all around it, the backrests against the wall, leaving ample room for dancing in the center; an enormous jukebox; and shelves behind the bar crowded with bottles and different kinds of glasses. But Urania had eyes only for the immense gray rug, with the Dominican seal, that stretched from one end of the huge space to the other. She barely noticed the portraits and pictures of the Generalissimo—on foot and on horseback, in military uniform or dressed as a farmer, sitting at a desk or standing behind a lectern and wearing the presidential sash—that hung on the walls, or the silver trophies and framed certificates won by the dairy cows and thoroughbred horses of the Fundación Ranch, intermingled with plastic ashtrays and cheap decorations, still bearing the label of Macy's in New York, that adorned the tables, sideboards, and shelves of the monument to kitsch where Benita Sepúlveda left her after asking if she really didn't want a nice glass of liqueur.

"I don't think the word 'kitsch' existed yet," she explains, as if her aunt or cousins had made some observation. "Years later, whenever I heard it or read it, and knew what extremes of bad taste and pretension it expressed, Mahogany House always came to mind. A kitsch monument."

And she herself was part of the kitsch, on that hot May night, with her debutante's pink organdy party dress, the silver chain with the emerald and the gold-washed earrings that had belonged to her mama and that Papa allowed her to wear on the special occasion of Trujillo's party. Her disbelief made what was happening unreal. It seemed to her she wasn't really that girl standing on a branch of the national seal, in that extravagant room. Senator Agustín Cabral had sent her, a living offering, to the Benefactor and Father of the New Nation? Yes, she had no doubt at all, her father had arranged this with Manuel Alfonso. And yet, she still wanted to doubt.

"Somewhere, not in the bar, somebody put on a Lucho Gatica

record. 'Bésame, bésame mucho, como si fuera esta noche la última vez.' "

"I remember." Manolita, embarrassed at interrupting, apologizes with a grimace: "They played 'Bésame Mucho' all day, on the radio, at parties."

Standing next to a window that let in a warm breeze and a dense aroma of fields, grass, trees, she heard voices. The damaged one of Manuel Alfonso. The other, high-pitched, rising and falling, could only be Trujillo's. She felt a prickle at the back of her neck and on her wrists, where the doctor took her pulse, an itch that always came when she had exams, and even now, in New York, before she made important decisions.

"I thought about throwing myself out the window. I thought about getting down on my knees, begging, crying. I thought I had to clench my teeth and let him do whatever he wanted, so I could go on living and take my revenge on Papa one day. I thought a thousand things while they were talking down below."

In her rocking chair, Aunt Adelina gives a start, opens her mouth. But says nothing. She is as white as a sheet, her deep-set eyes filled with tears.

The voices stopped. There was a parenthesis of silence; then, footsteps climbing the stairs. Had her heart stopped beating? In the dim light of the bar, the silhouette of Trujillo appeared, in an olive-green uniform, without a jacket or tie. He held a glass of cognac in his hand. He walked toward her, smiling.

"Good evening, beautiful," he whispered, bowing. And he extended his free hand, but when Urania, in an automatic movement, put forward her own, instead of shaking it Trujillo raised it to his lips and kissed it: "Welcome to Mahogany House, beautiful."

"The story about his eyes, about Trujillo's gaze, I had heard it often. From Papa, from Papa's friends. At that moment, I knew it was true. A gaze that dug deep, all the way down to the bottom. He smiled, he was very gallant, but that gaze emptied me, left me a hollow skin. I was no longer myself."

"Benita hasn't offered you anything?" Not letting go of her hand, Trujillo led her to the best-lit part of the bar, where a fluorescent tube cast a bluish light. He offered her a seat on a two-person sofa. He examined her, moving his eyes slowly up and down, from her head to her feet, openly, as he would examine new bovine and equine acquisitions for the Fundación Ranch. In his gray, fixed, inquisitive eyes she perceived no desire, no excitement, but only an inventory, a gauging of her body.

"He was disappointed. Now I know why, but that night I didn't. I was slender, very thin, and he liked full-bodied women with prominent breasts and hips. Voluptuous women. A typically tropical taste. He even must have thought about sending this skeleton back to Ciudad Trujillo. Do you know why he didn't? Because the idea of breaking a virgin's cherry excites men."

Aunt Adelina moans. Her wrinkled fist raised, her mouth half opened in an expression of horror and censure, she implores her, grimacing, but does not manage to say a word.

"Forgive my frankness, Aunt Adelina. It's something he said, later. I'm quoting him exactly, I swear: 'Breaking a virgin's cherry excites men. Petán, that animal Petán, gets more excited breaking them with his finger.' "

He would say it afterward, when he had lost control and his mouth was vomiting disjointed phrases, sighs, curses, discharges of excrement to ease his bitterness. Now, he still behaved with studied correctness. He did not offer her what he was drinking, Carlos I might burn the insides of a girl so young. He would give her a glass of sweet sherry. He served her himself and made a toast, clinking glasses. Though she barely wet her lips, Urania felt something flame in her throat. Did she try to smile? Did she remain serious, showing her panic?

"I don't know," she says, shrugging. "We were close together on that sofa. The glass of sherry was trembling in my hand."

"I don't eat little girls," Trujillo said with a smile, taking her glass and placing it on a table. "Are you always so quiet or is it only now, beautiful?"

"He called me beautiful, something that Manuel Alfonso had called me too. Not Urania, Uranita, girl. Beautiful. It was a game the two of them were playing."

"Do you like to dance? Sure you do, like all the girls your age," said Trujillo. "I like to, a lot. I'm a good dancer, though I don't have time to go to dances. Come on, let's dance."

He stood up and Urania did too. She felt his strong body, his somewhat protruding belly rubbing against her stomach, his cognac breath, the warm hand holding her waist. She thought she was going to faint. Lucho Gatica wasn't singing "Bésame Mucho" now, but "Alma Mía."

"He really did dance very well. He had a good ear, and he moved like a young man. I was the one who lost the beat. We danced two boleros, and a guaracha by Toña la Negra. Merengues too. He said they danced the merengue in clubs and decent homes now thanks to him. Before, there had been prejudices, and respectable people said it was music for blacks and Indians. I don't know who was changing the records. When the last merengue ended, he kissed me on the neck. A light kiss that gave me gooseflesh."

Holding her by the hand, their fingers intertwined, he walked her back to the sofa and sat down very close to her. He examined her, amused, as he breathed in and drank his cognac. He seemed serene and content.

"Are you always a sphinx? No, no. It must be that you have too much respect for me." Trujillo smiled. "I like beautiful girls who are discreet, who let themselves be admired. Indifferent goddesses. I'm going to recite a poem, it was written for you."

"He recited a poem by Pablo Neruda. Into my ear, brushing my ear, my hair, with his lips and his little mustache: 'I like it when you're quiet, it's as if you weren't here; as if your eyes had flown away, as if a kiss had closed your mouth.' When he came to 'mouth,' his hand moved to my face and he kissed me on the lips. That night I did so many things for the first time: I drank sherry, wore Mama's jewelry, danced with an old man of seventy, and received my first kiss on the mouth."

She had gone to parties with boys and danced, but a boy had kissed her only once, on the cheek, at a birthday party in the mansion of the Vicini family, at the intersection of Máximo Gómez and Avenida George Washington. His name was Casimiro Sáenz, the son of a diplomat. He asked her to dance, and when they had finished she felt his lips on her face. She blushed to the roots of her hair, and at Friday confession with the school chaplain, when she mentioned the sin, her voice broke with embarrassment. But that kiss was nothing like this one: the little brush mustache of His Excellency scratched her nose, and now, his tongue, its tip hot and sticky, was trying to force open her mouth. She resisted and then parted her lips and teeth: a wet, fiery viper pushed into her mouth in a frenzy, moving greedily. She felt herself choking.

"You don't know how to kiss, beautiful." Trujillo smiled at her, kissing her again on the hand, agreeably surprised. "You're a little virgin, aren't you?"

"He had become aroused," says Urania, staring at nothing. "He had an erection."

Manolita gives a short, hysterical laugh, but her mother, her sister, her niece don't follow suit. Her cousin lowers her eyes in confusion.

"I'm sorry, I have to talk about erections," says Urania. "If the male becomes aroused, his sex stiffens and grows larger. When he put his tongue in my mouth, His Excellency became aroused."

"Let's go up, beautiful," he said, his voice somewhat thickened. "We'll be more comfortable. You're going to discover something wonderful. Love. Pleasure. You'll like it. I'll teach you. Don't be afraid of me. I'm not an animal like Petán, I don't enjoy being brutal to girls. I like them to enjoy it too. I'll make you happy, beautiful."

"He was seventy and I was fourteen," Urania specifies for the fifth or tenth time. "We were a mismatched couple, climbing that staircase with the metal railing and heavy wooden bars. Holding hands, like sweethearts. The grandfather and his granddaughter on their way to the bridal chamber."

The lamp on the night table was lit, and Urania saw the square wrought-iron bed, the mosquito netting raised, and she heard the blades of the fan turning slowly on the ceiling. A white embroidered spread covered the bed, and a number of pillows and cushions were piled against the headboard. It smelled of fresh flowers and grass.

"Don't undress yet, beautiful," Trujillo murmured. "I'll help you. Wait, I'll be right back."

"Do you remember how nervous we were when we talked about losing our virginity, Manolita?" Urania turns toward her cousin. "I never imagined I'd lose it in Mahogany House with the Generalissimo. I thought: 'If I jump off the balcony, Papa will really be sorry.' "

He soon returned, naked under a blue silk robe with white flecks and wearing garnet-colored slippers. He took a drink of cognac, left his glass on a dresser among photographs of himself surrounded by his grandchildren, and, grasping Urania by the waist, sat her down on the edge of the bed, on the space left open by the mosquito netting, two great butterfly wings crossed over their heads. He began to undress her, slowly. He unbuttoned the back of her dress, one button after another, and removed her belt. Before taking off her dress, he kneeled, and with some difficulty leaned forward and bared her feet. Carefully, as if a sudden movement of his fingers could shatter the girl, he pulled off her nylon stockings, caressing her legs as he did so.

"Your feet are cold, beautiful," he murmured tenderly. "Are you cold? Come here, let me warm them for you."

Still kneeling, he rubbed her feet with both hands. From time to time he lifted them to his mouth and kissed them, beginning at the instep, going down to her toes and around to her heels, asking with a sly little laugh if he was tickling her, as if he were the one feeling a joyful itch.

"He spent a long time like that, holding my feet. In case you're interested, I didn't feel the least excitement, not for a second."

"You must have been so scared," Lucindita says encouragingly.

"Not then, not yet. Later on, I was terrified."

With difficulty His Excellency stood, and sat down again on the edge of the bed. He took off her dress, the pink bra that held her budding little breasts, the triangle of her panties. She allowed him to do it, not offering any resistance, her body limp. When Trujillo slid the pink panties down her legs, she noticed that His Excellency's fingers were hurrying; they were sweaty, burning the skin where they touched her. He made her lie down. He stood, took off his robe, and lay down beside her, naked. Carefully, he moved his fingers through the girl's sparse pubic hair.

"He was still very excited, I think. When he began to touch and caress me. And kiss me, his mouth always forcing my mouth open. Kissing my breasts, my neck, my back, my legs."

She did not resist; she allowed herself to be touched, caressed, kissed, and her body obeyed with the movements and postures that His Excellency's hands indicated for her. But she did not return the caresses, and when her eyes were not closed, she kept them glued on the slow blades of the fan. Then she heard him say to himself: "Breaking a virgin's cherry always excites men."

"The first dirty word, the first vulgarity of the night," Urania declares. "Later, he would say much worse. That was when I realized that something was happening to him. He began to get angry. Because I was still, limp, because I didn't kiss him back?"

That wasn't it: she understood that now. Whether or not she participated in her own deflowering wasn't anything His Excellency cared about. To feel satisfied, it was enough for her to have an intact cherry that he could break, making her moan—howl, scream—in pain, with his battering ram of a prick inside her, squeezed tight by the walls of that newly violated intimate place. It wasn't love, not even pleasure, that he expected of Urania. He had agreed to the young daughter of Senator Agustín Cabral coming to Mahogany House only to prove that Rafael Leonidas Trujillo Molina, despite his seventy years, despite his prostate problems, despite his headaches with priests, Yankees, Venezuelans, conspirators, was still a real man, a stud with a prick that could still get hard and break all the virgin cherries that came his way.

"I had no experience, but I knew." Her aunt, cousins, and niece lean their heads forward to hear her whisper. "Something was happening to him, I mean down below. He couldn't. He was about to go wild and forget all his good manners."

"That's enough playing dead, beautiful," she heard him order, a changed man. "On your knees. Between my legs. That's it. Take it in your hands and mouth. And suck it, the way I sucked your cunt. Until it wakes up. Too bad for you if it doesn't, beautiful."

"I tried, I tried. In spite of my terror, my disgust. I did everything. I squatted on my haunches, I put it in my mouth, I kissed it, I sucked it until my gorge rose. Soft, soft. I prayed to God it would stop."

"That's enough, Urania, that's enough!" Aunt Adelina isn't crying. She looks at her in horror, without compassion. Her eyes roll back in her head, the whites bulging, sclerotic; she is shocked, violently agitated. "What are you telling us for, Urania? My God, that's enough!"

"But I failed," Urania insists. "He covered his eyes with his arm. He didn't say anything. When he moved his arm away, he hated me."

His eyes were red and his pupils burned with a yellowish, feverish light of rage and shame. He looked at her without a hint of courtesy, with belligerent hostility, as if she had done him irreparable harm.

"You're wrong if you think you're leaving here a virgin so you can laugh at me with your father," he spelled out, with mute fury, spitting as he spoke.

He seized her by the arm and threw her down beside him. Assisted by movements of his legs and waist, he mounted her. That mass of flesh crushed her, pushed her down into the mattress; the smell of cognac and rage on his breath made her dizzy. She felt her muscles and bones crumbling, ground to dust. She was suffocating, but that did not prevent her from feeling the roughness of that hand, those fingers, exploring, digging, forcing their way into her. She felt herself pierced, stabbed with a knife; a lightning bolt ran from her head down to her feet. She cried out, feeling as if she were dying.

"Go on and screech, you little bitch, see if you learn your lesson," the wounding, offended voice of His Excellency spat at her. "Now open up. Let me see if it's really broken or if you're faking it."

"It really was. I had blood on my legs; it stained him, and the spread, and the bed."

"That's enough, that's enough! Why tell us more, Urania?" her aunt shouts. "Come, let's make the sign of the cross and pray. For the sake of what you hold most dear, Urania. Do you believe in God? In Our Lady of Altagracia, patron saint of Dominicans? Your mother was so devoted to her, Uranita. I remember her getting ready every January 21 for the pilgrimage to the Basilica of Higüey. You're full of rancor and hate. That's not good. No matter what happened to you. Let's pray, Urania."

"And then," says Urania, ignoring her, "His Excellency lay on his back again and covered his eyes. He was still, very still. He wasn't sleeping. He let out a sob. He began to cry."

"To cry?" Lucindita exclaims.

Her reply is a sudden jabbering. The five women turn their heads: Samson is awake and announces it by chattering.

"Not for me," declares Urania. "For his enlarged prostate, his dead prick, for having to fuck virgins with his fingers, the way Petán liked to do."

"My God, Urania, for the sake of what you hold most dear," her Aunt Adelina implores, crossing herself. "No more."

Urania caresses the old woman's wrinkled, spotted hand.

"They're horrible words, I know, things that shouldn't be said, Aunt Adelina." Her voice sweetens. "I never use them, I swear. Didn't you want to know why I said those things about Papa? Why, when I went to Adrian, I didn't want anything to do with the family? Now you know why."

From time to time he sobs, and his sighs make his chest rise and fall. A few white hairs grow between his nipples and around his dark navel. He keeps his eyes hidden under his arm. Has he forgotten about her? Has she been erased by his overpowering bitterness and suffering? She is more frightened than before, when he was caressing her or violating her. She forgets about the burning, the wound between her legs, her fear of the bloodstains on her thighs and the bedspread. She does not move. Be invisible, cease to exist. If the weeping man with hairless legs sees her, he won't forgive her, he'll turn the rage of his impotence, the shame of his weeping, on her and annihilate her.

"He said there was no justice in this world. Why was this happening to him after he had fought so hard for this ungrateful country, these people without honor? He was talking to God. The saints. Our Lady. Or maybe the devil. He shouted and begged. Why was he given so many trials? The cross of his sons that he had to bear, the plots to kill him, to destroy the work of a lifetime. But he wasn't complaining about that. He knew how to beat flesh-and-blood enemies. He had done that since he was young. What he couldn't tolerate was the low blow, not having a chance to defend himself. He seemed half crazed with despair. Now I know why. Because the prick that had broken so many cherries wouldn't stand up anymore. That's what made the titan cry. Laughable, isn't it?"

But Urania wasn't laughing. She listened, not moving, scarcely daring to breathe, hoping he wouldn't remember she was there. His soliloquy was discontinuous, fragmented, incoherent, interrupted by long silences; he raised his voice and shouted, or lowered it until it was almost inaudible. A pitiful noise. Urania was fascinated by that chest rising and falling. She tried not to look at his body, but sometimes her eyes moved along his soft belly, white pubis, small, dead sex, hairless legs. This was the Generalissimo, the Benefactor of the Nation, the Father of the New Nation, the Restorer of Financial Independence. The Chief whom Papa had served for thirty years with devotion and loyalty, and presented with a most delicate gift: his fourteen-year-old daughter. But things didn't happen as the senator hoped. And that meant—Urania's heart filled with joy—he wouldn't rehabilitate Papa; maybe he'd put him in prison, maybe he'd have him killed.

"Suddenly, he lifted his arm and looked at me with red, swollen eyes. I'm forty-nine years old, and I'm trembling again. I've been trembling for thirty-five years, ever since that moment."

She holds out her hands and her aunt, cousins, and niece see it is true: she is trembling.

He looked at her with surprise and hatred, as if she were a malevolent apparition. Red, fiery, fixed, his eyes froze her. She couldn't move. Trujillo's eyes ran over her, moved down to her thighs, darted to the bloodstained spread, and glared at her again. Choking with revulsion, he ordered:

"Go on, get washed, see what you've done to the bed? Get out of here!"

"A miracle that he let me go," Urania reflects. "After I saw him desperate, crying, moaning, feeling sorry for himself. A miracle from our patron saint, Aunt Adelina."

She sat up, jumped out of bed, picked up the clothes scattered on the floor, and, stumbling against a chest of drawers, took refuge in the bathroom. There was a white porcelain tub stocked with sponges and soaps, and a penetrating perfume that made her dizzy. With hands that barely responded she cleaned her legs, used a washcloth to stanch the bleeding, got dressed. It was difficult to button her dress, buckle her belt. She didn't put on her stockings, only her shoes, and when she looked at herself in one of the mirrors, she saw her face smeared with lipstick and mascara. She didn't take the time to wash it off; he might change his mind. Run, get out of Mahogany House, escape. When she returned to the bedroom, Trujillo was no longer naked. He had covered himself with his blue silk robe and held the glass of cognac in his hand. He pointed to the stairs:

"Get out, get out," he said in a strangled voice. "Tell Benita to bring fresh sheets and a spread and clean up this mess."

"On the first step I tripped and broke the heel of my shoe and almost fell down three flights of stairs. My ankle swelled up afterward. Benita Sepúlveda was on the ground floor. Very calm, smiling at me. I tried to say what he had told me to. Not a word came out. I could only point upstairs. She took my arm and walked me to the guards at the entrance. She showed me a recess with a seat: 'Here's where they polish the Chief's boots.' Manuel Alfonso and his car weren't there. Benita Sepúlveda had me sit on the shoeshine stand, surrounded by guards. She left, and when she came back, she led me by the arm to a jeep. The driver was a soldier. He brought me to Ciudad Trujillo. When he asked: 'Where's your house?' I said: 'I'm going to Santo Domingo Academy. I live there.' It was still dark. Three o'clock. Four, maybe. It took them a long time to open the gate. I still couldn't talk when the caretaker finally appeared. I could only talk to Sister Mary, the nun who loved me so much. She took me to the refectory, she gave me water, she put wet cloths on my forehead."

Samson, who has been quiet for a while, displays his pleasure or displeasure again by puffing out his feathers and shrieking. No one says anything. Urania picks up her glass, but it is empty. Marianita fills it; she is nervous and knocks over the pitcher. Urania takes a few sips of cool water.

"I hope it's done me good, telling you this cruel story. Now forget it. It's over. It happened and there's nothing anyone can do about it. Maybe another woman might have gotten over it. I wouldn't and couldn't."

"Uranita, my dear cousin, what are you saying?" Manolita protests. "What do you mean? Look what you've done. What you have. A life every Dominican woman would envy."

She stands and walks over to Urania. She embraces her, kisses her cheeks.

"You've really battered me, Uranita," Lucinda scolds her affectionately. "But how can you complain? You have no right. In your case it's really true that some good always comes out of the bad. You studied at the best university, you've had a successful career. You have a man who makes you happy and doesn't interfere with your work . . ."

Urania pats her arm and shakes her head. The parrot is quiet and listens.

"I lied to you, Lucinda, I don't have a lover." She smiles vaguely, her voice still breaking. "I've never had one, I never will. Do you want to know everything, Lucindita? No man has ever laid a hand on me again since that time. My only man was Trujillo. It's true. Whenever one gets close and looks at me as a woman, I feel sick. Horrified. I want him to die, I want to kill him. It's hard to explain. I've studied, I work, I earn a good living. But I'm empty and still full of fear. Like those old people in New York who spend the whole day in the park, staring at nothing. It's work, work, work until I'm exhausted. You have no reason to envy me, I assure you. I envy all of you. Yes, yes, I know, you have problems, hard times, disappointments. But you also have families, husbands, children, relatives, a country. Those things fill your life. But Papa and His Excellency turned me into a desert."

Samson has begun to move nervously around the bars of his cage; he sways back and forth, stops, sharpens his beak on his claws.

"Those were different times, dear Uranita," stammers Aunt Adelina, swallowing her tears. "You have to forgive him. He has suffered, he is suffering. It was terrible, darling. But those were different times. Agustín was desperate. He could have gone to prison, they could have killed him. He didn't want to hurt you. Perhaps he thought it was the only way to save you. Those things happened, even though nobody can understand it now. That's how life was here. Agustín loved you more than anyone else in the world, Uranita."

The old woman wrings her hands, distraught, and moves in her rocking chair, overcome with emotion. Lucinda goes to her, smooths her hair, gives her a few drops of valerian: "Calm down, Mama; don't upset yourself."

Through the window that looks out on the garden, the stars twinkle in the peaceful Dominican night. Were they different times? Gusts of warm wind blow into the dining room from time to time, fluttering the curtains and the flowers in a pot that stands among statues of saints and family photographs. "They were and they weren't," thinks Urania. "Something from those times is still in the air."

"It was terrible, but it let me learn about the generosity, the delicacy, the humanity of Sister Mary," she says, sighing. "Without her I'd be crazy or dead."

Sister Mary found solutions for everything, and was a model of discretion. From her first aid in the school infirmary to stop the bleeding and ease the pain, to her calling on the Superior of the Dominican Sisters, in less than three days, and convincing her to cut through red tape and grant Urania Cabral, an exemplary student whose life was in danger, a scholarship to Siena Heights in Adrian, Michigan. Sister Mary spoke to Senator Agustín Cabral (reassuring him? frightening him?) in the office of the director, the three of them alone, urging him to allow his daughter to travel to the United States. And persuading him as well not to see her again because of how disturbed she was after what happened in San Cristóbal. Urania has often wondered what face Agustín Cabral wore for the nun: hypocritical surprise? discomfort? confusion? remorse? shame? She never asked, and Sister Mary never told her. The sisters went to the American consulate to obtain her visa and requested an audience with President Balaguer, asking him to expedite the authorization that Dominicans needed to apply for in order to leave the country, a process that took weeks. The school paid her fare, since Senator Cabral was now insolvent. Sister Mary and Sister Helen Claire accompanied her to the airport. When the plane took off, what pleased Urania most was that they had kept their promise not to let Papa see her again, not even from a distance. Now, she was also grateful to them for saving her from the belated rage of Trujillo, who could have kept her confined on this island or fed her to the sharks.

"It's very late," she says, looking at her watch. "Almost two in the morning. I haven't even packed yet and I have an early plane."

"You're going back to New York tomorrow?" Lucinda asks sadly. "I thought you'd stay a few days."

"I have to work," says Urania. "A pile of papers is waiting for me at the office, high enough to give you vertigo."

"It won't be like before, will it, Uranita?" Manolita embraces her. "We'll write, you'll answer our letters. Once in a while you'll come for a vacation, visit your family. Won't you, Urania?"

"Absolutely," Urania agrees, embracing her in turn. But she isn't sure. Perhaps, once she's left this house, this country, she'll prefer to forget this family again, these people, her past; she'll regret coming here and talking the way she did tonight. Or maybe not. Maybe she'll want to rebuild somehow the connection with these remnants of her family. "Can I call a cab at this hour?"

"We'll drive you." Lucindita stands up.

When Urania leans over to embrace her Aunt Adelina, the old woman clutches at her, digging her sharp fingers, curved like talons, into her. She seemed to have regained her composure but now she is agitated again, with an anguished look of astonishment in her sunken eyes, surrounded by wrinkles.

"Perhaps Agustín didn't know," she stammers with difficulty, as if her dentures were loose. "Manuel Alfonso could have deceived my brother, he was basically very naive. Don't be so angry with him, Urania. He's had a lonely life, he's suffered a lot. God teaches us to forgive. For the sake of your mother, she was such a good Catholic."

Urania tries to calm her: "Yes, yes, Aunt Adelina, whatever you say, don't be upset, I beg you." Her two daughters stand by the old woman, trying to soothe her. Finally she grows calmer and shrinks into her chair, her face contorted.

"Forgive me for telling you these things." Urania kisses her on the forehead. "It was stupid. But it's been burning in me for so many years."

"She'll be all right now," says Manolita. "I'll stay with her. You did the right thing by telling us. Please write, and call us once in a while. Let's not lose touch again, Urania."

"I promise," says Urania.

She walks with her to the door and says goodbye as they stand beside Lucinda's old car, a secondhand Toyota parked at the entrance. When she embraces her again, Manolita's eyes are filled with tears.

In the car, on the way to the Hotel Jaragua, as they drive along the deserted streets of Gazcue, Urania is tormented. Why did you do it? Are you going to feel different, free of all the incubi that have sucked out your soul? Of course not. It was a weakness, a fall into the kind of sentimentality and self-pity you've always hated in other people. Were you hoping they'd feel sorry for you, pity you? Is that the satisfaction you wanted?

And then—sometimes it's a cure for depression—she finally thinks of Johnny Abbes García. She heard the story years ago, from Esperancita Bourricaud, a colleague of hers at the World Bank who had been assigned to Port-au-Prince, where the former head of the SIM had settled after traveling through Canada, France, and Switzerland— he never set foot in Japan—in the golden exile imposed on him by Balaguer. Esperancita and the Abbes Garcías were neighbors. He went to Haiti as an adviser to President Duvalier. But, after a time, he began to plot against his new chief, supporting the subversive plans of Colonel Dominique, the Haitian dictator's son-in-law. Papa Doc resolved the problem in ten minutes. In the middle of the morning, Esperancita saw about twenty Tonton Macoutes climb out of two vans and storm her neighbors' house, guns blazing. Ten minutes, that's all. They killed Johnny Abbes, they killed Johnny Abbes's wife, they killed Johnny Abbes's two young children, they killed Johnny Abbes's two servants, and they also killed Johnny Abbes's chickens, rabbits, and dogs. Then they set fire to the house and left. Esperancita Bourricaud needed psychiatric help when she returned to Washington. Is that the death you would have wanted for Papa? Are you filled with rancor and hatred, as Aunt Adelina said? She feels empty—again.

"I'm very sorry about that scene, all the melodrama, Lucindita," she says at the door of the Jaragua. She has to speak loudly because the music playing in the casino on the ground floor drowns out her voice. "I've made the night a very bitter one for Aunt Adelina."

"What are you talking about, girl? Now I understand what happened, the reason for the silence that made us all so sad. Please, Urania, come back and see us. We're your family, this is your country."

When Urania says goodbye to Marianita, the girl embraces her as if she wanted to weld herself to her, bury herself in her. The girl's slender body trembles as if it were a sheet of paper.

"I'm going to love you very much, Aunt Urania," she whispers in her ear, and Urania feels paralyzed by sadness. "I'm going to write every month. It doesn't matter if you answer or not."

She kisses her several times on the cheek, her thin lips like the peck of a little bird. Before she goes into the hotel, Urania waits until her cousin's old car is lost from view on Avenida George Washington, with its backdrop of noisy white waves. She walks into the Jaragua, and on her left the casino and adjoining nightclub are bright and noisy: rhythms, voices, music, slot machines, exclamations of the players at the roulette wheel.

As she heads for the elevators, a male figure cuts her off. He is a tourist in his forties, a redhead in a checked shirt, jeans, and loafers, slightly drunk:

"May I buy you a drink, dear lady?" he says in English, making a courtly bow.

"Get out of my way, you dirty drunk," Urania replies, not stopping but seeing the bewildered, astonished expression on the face of this incautious man.

In her room she begins to pack, but in a little while she goes to sit by the window and look at the twinkling stars and foaming waves. She knows she won't sleep and has all the time in the world to finish packing her suitcase.

"If Marianita writes to me, I'll answer all her letters," she decides.